Veronica Henry is a scriptwriter who has written for *The Archers*, *Heartbeat* and most recently *Holby City*. She lives in North Devon with her husband and three sons. Visit her website at www.veronicahenry.co.uk.

By Veronica Henry

An Eligible Bachelor
Love on the Rocks

THE HONEYCOTE NOVELS

Honeycote
Making Hay
Wild Oats
Just a Family Affair
Marriage and Other Games

Marriage and Other Games

Veronica Henry

An Orion paperback

First published in Great Britain in 2009
by Orion
This paperback edition published in 2009
By Orion Books Ltd,
Orion House, 5 Upper St Martin's Lane,
London WC2H 9EA

An Hachette UK company

1 3 5 7 9 10 8 6 4 2

A CIP catalogue record for this book is
available from the British Library.

ISBN 978-0-7528-8984-9

Typeset at the Spartan Press Ltd,
Lymington, Hants

Printed and bound in Germany by
GGP Media GmbH, Pößneck

The Orion Publishing Group's policy is to use papers that
are natural, renewable and recyclable products and
made from wood grown in sustainable forests. The logging
and manufacturing processes are expected to conform to
the environmental regulations of the country of origin.

www.orionbooks.co.uk

For Peter, who ran away with me.

One

Sebastian Turner sprawled like a starfish in his favourite armchair, a bottle of Grey Goose swinging from the paint-smothered fingers of one hand, a roll-up in the other. He narrowed his eyes through the smoke, gazing around the walls at his companions. He'd spent the last six months with them, and it was nearly time to say goodbye. There was Madonna, slumped in front of *EastEnders* stuffing in a Big Mac; Katie Price in a pair of horn-rimmed glasses, engrossed in Dostoevsky's *Crime and Punishment*; Pete Doherty in the middle of a flower-bed, deadheading some roses.

Alter Egos.

It had seemed like such a great idea at the time, to do an entire exhibition based on the infamous painting that had got him all the publicity in the first place: a portrait of the Queen, slobbing out in her dressing gown and a pair of leopard-skin mules, smoking a fag and watching the Channel 4 racing. Sebastian wasn't fooled by anyone's public image. There was always an alter ego just below the surface. And he didn't believe that Madonna was virtuous all the time, or Pete Doherty a villain. Just as he wasn't always a temperamental, highly strung artist. He had days when he was perfectly down-to-earth and balanced.

Only today wasn't one of them.

This latest exhibition was bound to be a success, not because it was controversial, but because here was art that people – the public – could actually understand. The paintings were visual puns, easy to grasp; not intellectual conundrums like pickled sharks or unmade beds that would have the Arts sections of the broadsheets locked in debate. And they were stunning. The subjects were instantly recognisable, almost photographic. Hyper-realism, if the man on the street did but know it. Which he probably wouldn't.

Sebastian Turner loathed every last one of them. As he scrutinised his work, he could feel the bitter bile of self-loathing in his mouth. What a cop-out. What a waste of time. How could he have deluded himself that this was worth doing? It was a cynical, money-making exercise, a joke at other people's expense. Admittedly, they were all people who could afford to have jokes made about them, and to be included in the exhibition would bring a certain kudos, affording them notoriety and guaranteed column inches. They would all be there at the preview – their publicists would make sure of that, because Sebastian Turner was, along with Damien Hirst and Tracy Emin, one of the few living artists that your average punter could actually name.

The son of boho-aristo parents, he had been expelled from three major public schools before finally settling down at a 'progressive' school in Devon which succeeded where everyone else had failed by tapping into his artistic talent and sending him on to art college, where he flourished. He first became known for his nudes. Exquisite and mouth-wateringly erotic, the skin of his subjects glowed with a shimmering luminosity that it didn't seem possible to create with mere oil paint. In their eyes, he captured a look of unrequited lust or total satiation that earned his work the description of 'posh porn'. Celebrities queued up to be painted by him. No one knew the identity of his client list, although Victoria Beckham was rumoured to have sat for him recently – a birthday present for David. But if he didn't fall in love with his subject, he refused to let them sit for him. In his own words, his brush 'couldn't get it up for just anyone'.

When *Saturday Afternoon at Buck House* had first appeared, the painting had been decreed positively treasonous but had tripled the already considerable price of his work overnight, as well as catapulting Sebastian into the public awareness. Critics had been shocked and delighted in equal measure; the tabloids had been scandalised. Brian Sewell had declared him a genius; the *Sun* had demanded his head on a plate. The painting had gone to a mysterious private buyer who had reputedly paid over two million for the privilege. The Palace had refused to comment.

Job done. Sebastian Turner didn't need to pick up a paintbrush for another year if he didn't feel like it. And in the meantime, he had become an overnight celebrity. He was ravishing, of course, which always helped, with his tortured lettuce-green eyes and his overgrown pageboy, skeletally thin because of his decadent lifestyle. And he was difficult. Even Parkinson had struggled with his fiercely intense aggression. He was capriciously snarling and uncooperative. Spoiled and world-weary. Some said entirely charmless. Yet the public was fascinated, because underneath there was a little boy lost. And a genius. England was always

3

proud of her geniuses, even if they were tricky. In a world where the chat-show sofa was increasingly filled with the anodyne, guests with attitude were like gold-dust. He sparked debate: you either loved him or hated him.

Infamy breeds success and success breeds more success. Sebastian was now a commodity and there was immense pressure on him to produce, from dealers, agents, collectors, the media. Four white walls in a prestigious gallery were waiting to be filled. Hence these Alter Egos. He lifted the bottle of vodka and took another swig, wincing at the flaccid warmth of the fluid – it had lost the crisp icy edge it had had when he'd pulled it from the freezer an hour ago. But he was grateful to it nevertheless. Its purity and clarity had made him see his work for what it was. There was nothing for it. He dropped the now empty bottle carelessly to the floor, where it bounced, then rolled under his chair.

Then he picked up the Holland and Holland shot-gun that had been resting across his lap. He ran his hand along the barrel, looking at his father's initials engraved in gold underneath the family crest.

He looked around his studio with a smile.

'Adios, amigos,' he murmured as he cocked the gun.

Some hours later, Catkin Turner came in search of her husband.

When Sebastian's parents decided to move to Barbados two years ago, they had given Sebastian and Catkin first refusal on their home on the wilds of Exmoor. She had leaped at the chance. It gave them space and tranquillity, and kept Sebastian away from the hard core of rather dissolute and decadent art college friends who were hanging on his coat-tails and leading him into bad ways: all-night parties and drinking binges that Sebastian ended up subsidising. And Withybrook was the perfect environment in which to create. For it was vital for him to create. If he didn't, he plunged back into the black abyss that had threatened to swallow him up in the past. It was Catkin who had to force him to the easel. She was the only one he listened to. And she was quite happy to play bad cop and wield the stick. She understood him.

At least, she thought she did.

She picked through the detritus in the studio fastidiously, her long legs bare. She was wearing a gold sequinned tunic, beaten-up plimsolls and a felt fedora: a hybrid outfit that was a result of having to run to the train from the television studio earlier that afternoon. The room was in chaos. Empty mugs and glasses and bottles littered every surface. Every possible receptacle was utilised as an ashtray. The air was thick with stale smoke, turpentine, spilled wine, linseed, old coffee. And . . .

Cordite?

Sharp panic pierced her gut. Marriage to Sebastian meant Catkin was always ready for a shock, a disaster, a crisis. But gun smoke? Then she saw him, slumped in his chair, the gun crooked over his arm, the tell-tale empty bottle under his feet. Her heart leaped into her mouth. She shut her eyes, then opened them again, surveying the scene more carefully. There was no sign of any blood. And she could just detect the rise and fall of his chest. She waited for her racing pulse to drop back to normal and the adrenalin to subside. As she took in deep calming breaths, she looked around for further evidence of foul play.

Then she saw what he'd done, and instead of panic she felt nausea. His marksmanship was surprisingly accurate, given that he must be completely plastered. He'd managed to hit every single bloody work of art; every last one of the paintings he'd been working on for the past six months. She'd been so proud of his dedication, his conscientiousness, the fact that he had seemed focused and absorbed and happy with his work for the first time in his life. He hadn't thrown his toys out of his pram once. The calm before the storm, it seemed.

For a moment, her composure slipped. Why did he have to do it to her every time? It was exhausting, living with someone so hell-bent on destruction. Maybe she should just give in. Give Sebastian the satisfaction of knowing he had annihilated everything. It must be what he wanted, because he kept on doing it, again and again.

She sighed wearily, knowing she had no intention of capitulating. It wasn't in her nature. That was why she was the nation's favourite agony aunt, a sexy, modern-day Claire Rayner dispensing relationship advice on daytime television: because she had an optimism that was infectious, an objectivity that dispelled the knottiest of problems; and all delivered with a mischievous wink that stopped her from being sanctimonious.

Oh, the irony . . .

Here she was again, little Polly Positive, having to take her own advice.

*

Sebastian could hear a voice calling him from far, far away. He stirred, looked up, and saw his wife gazing down at him. She smiled, and it lit up her face. Why was she looking so excited?

'Darling, you're a genius,' she was saying. 'They're going to love this!'

'What?' Sebastian sat up, wondering how something so pure could give him such a blinding headache. He kicked the bottle of vodka out of the way in a temper.

Catkin waved her hand around the room.

'It's such a fantastic statement: the artist destroying his own work so nobody else can. They're going to be queuing up.'

She looked round at the desecrated paintings in awe.

Sebastian scowled. She was so much cleverer than him. She always had been. It was typical of her, to sweep in and diminish his gesture, turn it into something it wasn't. She was refusing to recognise his mental anguish. She was supposed to be horrified by what he had done. She was supposed to rush to his side, console and reassure him. But here she was, jumping up and down with glee and declaring his act of defiance, his attempt to destroy six months' labour, as an artistic triumph.

Of course, Catkin never had a bad day, or even a moment's doubt, about her ability. That's why her star was in the ascendant; a meteoric rise that had, as yet, showed no sign of reaching its zenith. Sebastian knew he had been perched on his for some time, and it was a long way down from where he was sitting, which was why he was transfixed with fear, dissatisfied, filled with self-loathing and lacking in confidence. And why it was easier for him to destroy his work than let it be judged.

7

Catkin, however, was clearly not going to allow him the luxury of wallowing in his perceived imminent failure.

'The process of wilful self-destruction,' she proclaimed from the centre of the room. 'The ultimate artistic statement – nihilistic, perhaps, yet undeniably profitable.'

'Where do you get all this shit from?' Sebastian slurred.

'You, darling.' She beamed triumphantly. 'And it's all bollocks. We know that. Which is why this is going to be your most successful exhibition yet.'

'But they're ruined. I can't sell this lot.'

He'd shot more than a dozen paintings from his chair. Some of them had gaping holes. Others were merely sprinkled with shot. Madonna's Big Mac had been blown to buggery, while Jordan had escaped with a gentle peppering. The studio hadn't got away so lightly. Chunks of plaster had come off the wall and a Velux window had been blown out.

Catkin took off her hat and twirled it on her finger. The sharp edges of her signature Sassoon bob barely moved as she shook her head.

'In the words of Andy Warhol,' she said, 'art is whatever you can get away with.'

She was quite right. Three weeks later, Sebastian's exhibition opened. Every painting was sold before the rapturous reviews could even be read in the papers. And for those who couldn't afford the real thing, there was a fake rifle range, where punters could line up and take pot-shots at limited-edition prints, then take them home. Interactive art; DIY destruction.

It was a triumph.

Sebastian came back to Withybrook Hall considerably richer, then sank into an even deeper depression.

Two

The girl sat on the edge of the bed and stared at the dress hanging in front of her. Slippery black silk trimmed with lace and jet beads, it had puffed sleeves, a high neck and a trailing fishtail skirt. Although it was designed to reveal no flesh whatsoever, it was nevertheless dramatic; a frock not to be ignored. And as she contemplated the outfit, a strange feeling came over her. A feeling she remembered from a long, long time ago.

It was excitement. Excitement at the prospect of getting dressed up and going out for the night. She'd thought she'd felt the sensation earlier in the hairdresser's, when Yves had teased her unruly blonde curls into an elaborate and uncharacteristically elegant chignon. She hadn't felt like herself at all, but Yves had told her she looked sensational and he never lied. She'd trusted him for years. Besides, as he pointed out, as hostess of the ball, she had to look the part. Nevertheless, she hoped no one thought she was taking this new look seriously; that she was taking herself seriously. She didn't do serious. She was bubbly, vivacious, as fizzy as a bottle of champagne that has been rolling around in the boot of a car before being opened.

On the surface, anyway.

She stood up and walked towards the mirror. Her strapless bra and tiny pants shimmered silver under the lights. She ran her hands down her body and felt an unfamiliar flicker deep inside. She frowned, puzzled, then smiled. Her reflection responded by smiling back at her with dancing eyes and a mouth as pink and soft and sweet as Turkish delight.

'Charlotte Briggs!' she exclaimed in delighted recognition. 'Long time no see. And welcome back!'

It was as if someone had flicked a switch and brought her back to life after she'd been cryogenically frozen. For the first time in ages, she felt like herself. How long had it been? Two years? At least, she calculated rapidly.

She and Ed had resolved on New Year's Day to give the treatment a rest. It had been such a hideous ordeal. The blood tests. The probes. The injections. The nasal sprays. The scans. Nausea. Headaches. Weight gain. Mood swings. Hot flushes. Swollen breasts. And all the time pretending to the world at large that everything was fine, because it was so much easier than people asking you (or very obviously not asking you, which was worse) if you'd had any luck yet.

They hadn't had any luck. Twelve thousand pounds later – though it wasn't about the money; of course, it wasn't about the money – and her womb was as empty as it ever had been, a cold desolate space deep inside her that was destined never to incubate. And they hadn't even had the benefit of an explanation. That would have made it so much easier to bear – a trump card to produce when asked why you had no children at the age of thirty-three when you had been trying since your honeymoon night. Which people knew only too well, because she had always proclaimed that she wanted shitloads of babies. At least three. If not five.

Unexplained infertility. What a cruel diagnosis. It provided no comfort whatsoever. Because it didn't actually give you a cut-off point, a reason to give up. It didn't let you draw a line, so it was entirely up to you to take a deep breath and say 'enough' when you couldn't take it any more: the relentless cycle of hope, expectation and disappointment.

No wonder that among it all, Charlotte Briggs had got lost. The sweet-faced sparkly eyed girl who found it easy to make friends, and keep them, had slipped away quietly somewhere. Oh, she'd been able to pretend. Charlotte could chat incessantly when called upon, she could get any party started, she made strangers feel at ease, but her heart wasn't in it. It was a carefully calculated cover-up designed to deflect suspicion. She didn't want questions or pity, so she'd kept the mask in place. Underneath, she'd been desperate and distraught, engulfed by a terrible sense of claustrophobia as each month slipped by and she realised that her dream was never going to come true.

She had thrown herself into her work, to give her life momentum and meaning. The consultant had told her to ease up, even take some time off, but the prospect of doing nothing had appalled her. How was sitting staring at the walls supposed to help? Instead, she had doubled her workload, thereby minimising the amount of time free to spend bemoaning her lot. She fell into bed each night exhausted, and slept too deeply to dream of tiny fingers and the sweet, shallow breath of the infant she was yet to conceive. Weekends were spent socialising, preparing for and recovering from cocktail parties, brunches, nights at the opera, days at the races. Corporate freebies, which both she and Ed enjoyed as part of their work, he as a consultant in the incomprehensible but profitable world of spread-betting, she as an interior designer to the filthy rich. Not the merely wealthy footballers and pop-stars and supermodels who peppered the pages of the tabloids, but the silently, stealthily super-rich who had been quietly invading London courtesy of the tax breaks and wanted no publicity, just total discretion.

Now it was June, six months after they'd decided to stop the IVF, and it must have taken all that time for the hormones and drugs finally to leave her body, for tonight, as she stood in front of the mirror, she caught a glimpse of her true self again. There was a gleam in her eye and a radiance to her skin. Her hair was glossy. She felt . . .

Happy?

Perhaps that was too strong a description. But somehow, in the past few weeks, she had moved on. She had come to terms with the fact that she and Ed would probably be childless. She wasn't ready to consider other options yet. The prospect of adoption brought with it a whole new set of dilemmas and ordeals. If she needed anything it was a break, a chance to enjoy herself again. And that's what she was going to do. She was tired of putting everything on hold, tired of her mood being dictated by circumstances beyond her control. She was going to grab her life back with both hands.

In that one moment, she felt as if she could cope again.

*

She and Ed met six years previously. One of the senior partners in the firm he worked for was moving his wife and family from New York to London, and wanted the Chelsea town-house they had bought decorated from top to bottom. Ed had been charged with overseeing the project, rather inexplicably as he was the first to admit he didn't have a clue about 'housey stuff' – as long as he had a comfy sofa to stretch out on and a big telly to watch the rugby and reruns of *Buffy the Vampire Slayer*, he was happy. But for some reason the partner seemed to trust his judgement, and so Ed had dutifully gone to Breathtaking Designs, the company Charlotte worked for, to see if they could help. Charlotte's boss, a garrulous Dubliner called Connor, had assigned the project to her.

She went to Ed's office in the City to give him their pitch. As soon as she saw him, she knew it was going to be an uphill struggle to win him over. In his blue and white striped shirt and gold cufflinks, jumpy with endless cups of Americano, he was offhand and fidgety, his eyes constantly flicking over to his computer. He could not be less interested in what she had to say. He only had eyes for the figures on the screen as he assessed, presumably, his profit and loss. Charlotte didn't have a clue about spread-betting, but it clearly engrossed Ed.

'I'm sorry,' she said eventually, in as firm a voice as she could manage, 'if I'm wasting your time, perhaps I could leave the designs here for you to look at when you're under less pressure?'

He looked at her, startled, obviously not realising how rude he had been.

'Shit, I'm terribly sorry. This isn't my field, that's all.

And we've got deals going down all over the shop. Please – accept my apologies.' He put a freckled hand over his silver mouse, clicked, then gave her a disarming smile. 'The computer's off. I'm all yours. Really.'

She took a deep breath and started again. This time, he really did seem to be paying attention. Soon, she had scattered his desk with a bewildering array of swatches and paint charts. He listened, fascinated, as she described the thinking behind what she called the storyboard. He scarcely understood a word she said, yet he was completely captivated by her passion as she spoke of fabrics – georgette and moiré and chenille – that he had never encountered, in colours that seemed to come out of a fairy story. All the time her fingers were fluttering over the samples she had brought, stroking the material, urging him to feel them so he could appreciate their softness, their weight, their luxurious finish. He obeyed, just to please her, but he took in none of the detail.

All he knew was that his senses had suddenly been hijacked by this creature in the pea-green corduroy jacket with the diamanté swan brooch on the lapel, and the almost-but-not-quite transparent chiffon skirt, and the lilac suede ballet shoes. It was her he wanted to touch, so he could feel the warmth of her skin through the fabric, hold her close and breathe in deeply whatever it was she smelled of. Violets, he thought; something sweet and flowery and old-fashioned but unbelievably haunting. He tried to hold the scent in his head, so he could recall it later. Her voice washed over him: slightly breathless and slightly clipped, it was from another age.

Jenny Agutter in *The Railway Children*. No one spoke like that any more, surely?

He was spellbound. He was used to women in immaculately cut suits and sheer tights and court shoes who never showed a chink of femininity, let alone vulnerability – tough ball-breaking risk-takers whom he admittedly admired, but who considered sex a competitive sport and who never showed a softer side. He'd slept with his fair share, but had never taken a relationship to the next level. He couldn't imagine being married to any of those women. Why would you marry one of them? Not for their home-making skills, or their maternal instincts, certainly. Not that he was sexist, but what would be the point?

This girl was different. He could imagine waking up next to her and wanting to explore everything life had to offer.

She was outlining the designs for the master en-suite when he found he could bear it no longer. She was holding up a glass tile she had described as absinthe, but which he would have called green. Tendrils of blonde hair had escaped from her plait. All he could think about was undoing the whole thing, running his fingers through her hair, pulling that heart-shaped face to him and tasting those lips – he imagined they'd taste like the sugar mouse he'd had in his stocking when he was small . . .

'. . . Here, we've created a sexy and stimulating environment with dual functions. There are facilities for two people to get ready at speed in the morning, then relax and enjoy some spa-style leisure time together in the evening. The double shower introduces the twin elements of convenience and decadence—'

Ed put a large hand over the CAD drawing on the desk in front of them and looked into her eyes.

'Stop.'

She frowned at him anxiously. 'You don't like it? We can go for something more traditional. A roll-top—'

'For Christ's sake,' he rolled his eyes. 'It's a fucking bathroom. You've got the job, OK? Let's go out for lunch.'

For a second, Charlotte was tempted to take umbrage. No one had ever interrupted a pitch before. She stared at Ed. He was ignorant. Impatient. And rude, she decided. But there was something else about him. Something . . . quixotic? Impulsive, at the very least. And Charlotte loved people who acted on impulse. Not for her the careful, measured, cautious type. She was intrigued. He was looking at her, his eyes bright and urgent with challenge. He made her feel, in that moment, as if the end of the world was nigh and this was their last chance of happiness.

Thus she had found herself following him to a table for two in Quaglino's, where he had ordered a bottle of Billecart-Salmon and a plateau de fruits de mer. He barely spoke during the meal, just gazed at her as she devoured her way salaciously through the lobster and langoustines, aware that she was re-enacting every literary and filmic cliché as she licked the juices from her fingers. She was behaving both in and out of character – it was in Charlotte's make-up to enjoy herself, but she never usually let the barriers down while she was working. Within half an hour, and definitely once the champagne had kicked in, she felt as if she had stepped over a line with Ed. She felt as if she could be herself. As if, in fact, they had been together for ever.

The seafood devoured, they shared a chocolate fondue. He fed her strawberries and kiwi and bananas and marshmallows dipped in Valrhona chocolate. When she could eat no more, she sat back, glazed and sated and smiling.

'It's wonderful to sit with a girl who enjoys her food,' he noted.

'It's one of life's pleasures,' replied Charlotte, wiping the last trace of chocolate from the corner of her mouth. Ed gazed at her, thinking of another of life's pleasures. She crumpled her napkin and smiled at him sweetly. She had a strong suspicion what was coming next. There was no denying the current between them.

To her astonishment, he didn't hit on her, but found her a taxi and put her inside, waving his arm in farewell as it drove away from the kerb, then turning on his heel and walking away in the other direction. She craned her neck to watch him disappear out of sight. Her tummy felt funny, probably not surprising after seafood and champagne and melted chocolate. She felt rather deflated, then wondered if, when, he would phone. She dived in her bag and checked that her mobile was on, that there was a signal. She'd never done that before. She sat back in her seat, her mind whirring. No one had ever had this effect on her. For two pins she would have asked the taxi driver to turn round and find him, but her instincts told her to play it cool. He would be in touch. And anyway, she had the perfect excuse to call him, to follow up on her pitch. At which point she realised she had left her portfolio in his office – all the sketches, the samples and the costings. She chewed on her thumbnail and wondered whether to go back and fetch it in person, then decided she would send a bike. He'd probably just been bored, and had decided that going out for lunch was more interesting than listening to her twittering on about recessed lighting. Any illusions she had had about mutual attraction must have been courtesy of the champagne. By the time she got back to her office, she felt filled with gloom, telling Connor that the pitch had gone as well as could be expected then hiding herself away for the rest of the day.

Weeks later, Ed admitted to her that he had been terrified, at a loss for the first time in his life as to how to deal with a woman, petrified that by moving in too quickly he would lose her. He had waited three agonising days before caving in and sending her a hand-tied bunch of peonies, sweet peas and freesias. She was charmed. She would have had him down as a fifty red roses merchant – extravagant but tasteless.

Two days later he called and asked her on a picnic. Again, she was enchanted when he turned up with a proper basket filled with things he had assembled himself. She would have expected him to cart along a showy Fortnum's hamper, but he had brought a French stick, some rough terrine, a punnet of ripe nectarines and a bag of sugary doughnuts. They went to Hampton Court, where they had wandered through the maze for nearly an hour, talking and laughing, then shared their meal on the lawn. Yet again she was filled with chagrin when he drove her back into town and dropped her at the most convenient tube station: he had a long-standing work engagement that evening. She spent the night tossing and turning, wondering why she was falling for what she and her friends had always called a 'wanker banker'. Ed was definitely ruthless and hard-edged, and thrived in the high-risk business he worked in. Yet there was another side to him. He seemed awkward and unsure at times, which surprised her. She sensed he was usually of the 'wham bam thank you ma'am' school of seduction. But he seemed to be holding back, treating her like the most precious bone china – with care, courtesy and awe. She had no idea that it had been all he could do not to kiss the doughnut sugar off her lips as she lay on the picnic rug.

He continued to be a perfect gentleman, merely bestowing a solicitous kiss on each cheek as he yet again put her into a taxi after each date, and she sensed he was going against type. She wished he wouldn't.

In the end, Charlotte couldn't bear it any longer, sliding her arms round his neck as yet another cab door opened.

'For heaven's sake,' she whispered in his ear, nearly swooning at the scent of Amalfi Fig that engulfed her. 'Come home with me.'

She had practically dragged him inside the cab. Happy that he wasn't forcing her into doing something she didn't want to do, he had followed. On the back seat, she had unleashed her passion, devouring him with as much pleasure as she had devoured every meal they had shared so far. He felt giddy with the intensity of it all and, he realised as they pulled up outside her mansion block, they had still only kissed.

Half an hour later, as they lay naked on the floor of her living room gazing at each other in wonder, he asked her to marry him and she said yes. The triumph in his eyes and his jubilant grin made her realise that the chivalry had been an act. A trap that she had fallen into head first. But by then she didn't care. She was passionately in love.

When they declared their engagement to the world at large, Charlotte found herself warned off Ed in no uncertain terms by everyone who knew him. He was, in no particular order, a womaniser, a drinker – though not a drunk – a spendthrift with no inhibitions who enjoyed fast cars and faster women. His work was high-octane, anti-social, performance-related, relentless. No one with any sense saw Ed as husband material. But Charlotte somehow tamed him, without emasculating him. Seemingly overnight he had come to heel, become a one-woman man. He still lived life at a million miles an hour, because in the industry he worked in you had to be one step ahead and take risks, and he was constantly pushing the boundaries in the hopes of achieving success. But that he worshipped her was clear to anyone who met them. He was devoted, solicitous and only had eyes for Charlotte. His friends were delighted, for *their* wives and girl-friends had always been wary of Ed, convinced that he was a bad influence, even though Ed never made anyone do anything they didn't want to. If people followed in his footsteps, it was because he made it look like fun, not because he had talked them into it. Now, however, with Charlotte by his side, he was considered safe.

He wasn't conventionally good-looking, with his strawberry-blonde crop and the broad, broken nose courtesy of a rugby injury, but he had a presence. His skin was freckled, but tanned underneath to a light gold as he frequently took off on foreign jaunts at the drop of a hat. He was tall, six foot three, and would have been lanky if it wasn't for his dedication to the cross-trainer and dumb-bells. His resulting six-pack and biceps made him one of those lucky men who look even more masculine in a floral shirt. Charlotte loved the feel of his iron-hard muscles through Liberty lawn. The dichotomy made her shiver.

They had the definitive London wedding. Charlotte's parents were divorced; Ed's father was dead, so they felt as if it was theirs to arrange. They had it just as they wanted: a small civil ceremony then everyone they knew for a slap-up feast at Quaglino's in memory of their first meal together. They sold each of their flats and bought a sweet three-bedroom terraced house in Parsons Green, which Charlotte slowly and thoughtfully transformed from a Sloaney chintz nightmare to a light, airy, but most of all comfortable home. Ed was slightly alarmed that everything was white, from the high-gloss kitchen to the modular sofa in the living room, but it seemed to stay clean by some miracle. Moreover, everything worked and everything had its place: she got a carpenter to build in shoe-racks and bookcases and window seats with storage underneath wherever there was an awkward space. It was slick without being showy. Soft-close drawers in the kitchen, power showers that practically concussed you, the softest carpet with under-floor heating that was incredibly cosy in winter, doors that folded right back to reveal the tiny garden in the summer – she had thought of every eventuality, exploited the house's strong points and turned its weaknesses into strengths. A poky space in the attic was transformed into a mini gym with a rowing machine. And to stop it looking too sterile there were intermittent splashes of intense colour – a lime-green Murano vase, blood-red lacquered bowls, crazy cushions embroidered with sequinned bulldogs and crowns and Union Jacks.

Ed was awkward at first. It was a million miles from his shabby, lived-in bachelor pad. But he soon became used to it. And his mates could still come round to watch the rugby. In fact, they liked going there best, as the fridge was always filled with Budweiser, and Charlotte made them nachos covered in salsa and melted cheese with fiery jalapeños followed by hot dogs slathered in ketchup, which they were allowed to eat in front of the telly. It was generally agreed that Charlotte was the perfect wife. Their own wives looked as if they had been sucking lemons when the rugby came on and refused to do any catering whatsoever.

The day the house was officially finished, Charlotte and Ed had decided to start trying for a baby properly. The third bedroom could, after all, be rapidly transformed from an office into a nursery.

Five years later, the office was still intact.

But today, Charlotte was determined not to dwell on their misfortune any longer. As Ed came into the bedroom half-dressed, still fresh from his shower, she moved towards him, running her hands under the tails of his dress shirt, feeling for the smooth micro-fibre of his black Boss briefs. She slid the tips of her fingers under the waistband and pulled him towards her.

'Well, hello.' His eyes widened in surprise. It had been a very long time since she had initiated recreational sex.

They looked at each other for a full ten seconds,

both unable to hide their smiles, hers slightly mischievous, his lopsided and accompanied by a raised eyebrow. Anticipation throbbed in the air between them. Wordlessly, he pushed her onto the edge of the bed, standing between her legs, then placed a pillow beneath her so she was at just the right height. He slid into her and she gasped, feeling consumed, relishing his length, his thickness, hooking her legs around his waist and pulling him more deeply inside her. She came before he did, with a sigh of unadulterated pleasure, and as he felt her pulsate around him he realised that it was a long time since she had done that. Attempts at reproduction for her had not involved orgasm, while Ed had never had any problem reaching climax when he made love to Charlotte, no matter what the circumstances.

Then it was his turn, and he shut his eyes with the intensity, and fell onto her. He buried his face in her hair, kissing her, revelling in the Charlotte that had come back, the Charlotte he had feared had gone for good. She felt his tears on her neck. She sat up in alarm. Ed didn't cry. She had wept enough for both of them.

'I'd do anything to make you happy, you know that?' His voice was hoarse.

She sat up, sliding her arms around his waist and kissing his chest. She could still feel his heartbeat against her lips. She knew how much it had torn him apart every time the news had been bad. Not so much for himself, but for her. She could feel him desperately trying to control his rage every time the scan came up blank. She could sense him wanting to pick up the monitor and throw it across the room, fighting back the temptation to punch the sonographer. She did tears, while he did anger, but never directed at her.

'I am happy,' she told him, but he looked agonised.

'Anything,' he repeated, his eyes stormy.

She pressed her forehead against his.

'There's nothing you can do,' she told him. 'It's just you and me, and I'm happy with that. I love you, Ed . . .'

He pulled away from her and stood up.

'We better get going,' he said curtly, as if he was embarrassed that, after all this time, he had actually shown his vulnerability and that it still mattered.

Just when she had decided that it didn't.

She looked at the clock on the wall. Six thirty-five. Their car was collecting them just before seven.

'Oh my God, look at me. I'm going to have to do my make-up all over again. And my hair—'

She scrambled to her feet. Ed put his hands on her waist and looked down at her.

'Don't you dare change a thing. You look stunning.'

She glanced in the mirror. She did. Her pupils were huge and dark; her hair was tousled; her skin glowed where the blood had risen to the surface.

'I can't turn up looking like this!' Charlotte grabbed her comb and tried to smooth her once immaculate chignon back into place.

Ten minutes later, Ed zipped her into her dress. They stood in front of the mirror, him behind her, his hands on her shoulder. The perfect couple.

The doorbell rang. Ed dropped a kiss on her neck and went to answer it.

Charlotte stared at herself for a few more moments. She felt different, somehow. Ripe. Womanly. Was it just the sex? Or was it something more . . . ? What if a miracle had happened in that second? What if, because she had been relaxed and hadn't been giving it a second thought, the right conditions had presented themselves for once? What if one, just one, of Ed's sperm had inveigled its way into the wall of a waiting egg? What if the cells were reproducing now, this second, multiplying into a little person—

'Chaz!' Ed's voice came up the stairs.

Charlotte snatched up her evening bag, scooping her lipstick and mobile into its satin depths, furious with herself. She mustn't think like that. She wasn't supposed to torture herself any longer, or allow herself to fantasise. After all, she'd got over it, hadn't she?

The Black Ball was being held at the sumptuous and newly revamped Askew Hotel. Breathtaking Designs had masterminded the interior, and so Charlotte had been able to negotiate the use of its splendid new ballroom for next to nothing, especially as it was in a good cause.

Ed had a schoolfriend, Simon, whose young son had tragically died of a rare form of leukaemia at the age of six. When Simon expressed a desire to raise money to build a new unit for the hospice where the boy had spent his final days, Ed had taken up the challenge on his behalf. The target to be raised was a hundred thousand pounds – a daunting sum for just one night, but Ed and Charlotte and a team of supporters had been working tirelessly on the project for over a year. At a hundred and fifty pounds a head, it necessarily attracted a certain calibre of guest, but nevertheless they had sold five hundred tickets by ruthless networking and the promise of a glamorous evening out. This in turn enabled them to attract high-profile advertisements in the programme and elicit luxury prizes for the auction, ranging from a week in a five-star hotel in Koh Samui down to an organic food hamper.

They had chosen the theme because it was simple. People's attitudes to fancy dress ranged from enthusiastic to horrified, but even the biggest party pooper could manage black. At one point Charlotte had worried that the overall effect might be a little funereal and sombre, but she worked hard with the hotel and the florist to soften the impact. They kept the table-cloths, napkins and crockery white. On each table was a black glass candelabra stuffed with fat, mellow beeswax candles, and a bowl of deep, dark velvety Bacarra roses intertwined with green ivy. Elegantly beaded table mats and napkin rings glittered in the candlelight. By the time they had finished, the ballroom looked chicly monochromatic rather than starkly Gothic.

Now, as they pulled up outside the hotel, Charlotte felt nervous. If the evening was a flop there was no one but themselves to blame. Everything had been checked and double-checked. She had spoken to the band and the DJ and the magician earlier that day, none of whom had so far been struck down with laryngitis or food poisoning or stage fright. Nevertheless, she clutched her leather-bound notebook to her: it held lists, telephone numbers, contingency plans, timetables.

Ed leaned across and squeezed her shoulder.

'Hey,' he said softly. 'It's going to be fine, Chaz.

Nothing can go wrong now. And in an hour's time, everyone will be too drunk to notice.'

Charlotte tried to smile. She always panicked at the eleventh hour. She was like this when she showed clients the finished results of her work, terrified that they were going to throw up their hands in horror and demand a refund as well as compensation. Of course, that had never happened. They were always delighted, and the ensuing elation was always worth the agony. Deep down, she knew in four hours' time she would be able to bask in the glory of success, but in the meantime the responsibility lay heavy upon her and she felt the tight knot of uncertainty expand and contract in her stomach.

The taxi drew up and she shot through the entrance of the hotel like a rabbit out of a trap and into the kitchen, where the chef reassured her that everything was on target. The two of them had spent hours debating the menu, black not being the most inviting of food colours, but with some careful research and a bit of artistic licence they had settled upon caviar with Melba toast to start, then chicken with black Périgord truffles, finishing with individual Black Forest gateaux, the gleaming cherries drenched in kirsch and wrapped in a feather-light chocolate roulade. And judging by the wonderful smells wafting from the ovens and the pots, it was going to be delicious. Charlotte sampled a dollop of salty sevruga, savouring the sensation of the tiny pearls on her tongue, took a sip of the rich but subtle truffle sauce, and finished with a spoon of boozy cherries.

'Wonderful!' she told the chef, who beamed with delight.

The heat of the kitchen was making her feel quite faint, so she hurried into the ballroom, keenly aware that in fifteen minutes the first of the guests would start trickling in. Straight away, she spotted Ed's personal assistant, Melanie, who'd been helping them with the administration.

Charlotte narrowed her eyes, not quite able to believe what she saw. For Melanie was in white. Bright, white, skin-tight satin. In a nod to the theme, she had stuffed her fat little arms into elbow-length black gloves. Charlotte marched over, anger bubbling up inside. Melanie had always reminded her of a lap dog: small, self-important, with bright, slightly bulging eyes that didn't miss a trick. In her opinion, Melanie was over-confident for her age and position, with a tendency to be outspoken and opinionated. This was yet another example of her not quite knowing her place. A little voice inside her told her not to make a scene, as Melanie had only flouted the dress code in order to get attention, so she paused for a moment to compose herself.

'Which bit of "black" didn't you understand?' she finally asked, as sweetly as she could manage.

'I can't believe it!' said Melanie, looking at her with her round pug eyes. 'I tried on my dress last week and it fitted perfectly, but I couldn't get into it today. I am *such* a yoyo. I *knew* I shouldn't have had that Indian on Thursday. Honestly, Charlotte – I'm so sorry. This was the only smart dress I had in my wardrobe. I am *so* embarrassed.'

The dress in question looked brand new. In fact, Charlotte wouldn't be surprised if the price tag was still swinging off the label. Melanie was the type to buy a dress and return it the next day pretending it had never been worn. Charlotte could just imagine her hustling for her money back. But she gritted her teeth, and told herself not to rise to the bait.

'Could you do the seating plan for the top table?' she asked, handing Melanie her diagram and carefully written name cards. 'Then make sure all the auction prizes are laid out properly so people can have a look before they start bidding. And check all the goody bags; make sure no one's nicked anything.'

Melanie flashed her a glance. For a moment she thought she was going to tell her to stuff it; that she was Ed's assistant, not Charlotte's. But something made her think better of it.

'Of course,' she replied, oozing saccharine. 'And by the way, you look stunning.'

Charlotte felt suitably chastened. She shouldn't over-react. She supposed she was just nervous about the evening ahead. Across the room, she could see the chief executive of the hospice arrive with his wife, and Ed walk over to greet them. He looked knee-tremblingly handsome in his dinner jacket, as if he should be striding across the moonlit terrace of a Monte Carlo casino. Charlotte swallowed down a lump that had appeared mysteriously in her throat. The evening probably mattered even more to him than it did to her, yet he was managing to stay calm.

'Thank you.' She smiled, touching Melanie lightly on the shoulder in a gesture of forgiveness. She shouldn't be such a bitch. Melanie was harmless enough.

Less than an hour later, the room was heaving as guests knocked back Black Russian cocktails. A magician moved stealthily among them, performing card tricks and sleights of hand. Everyone had pulled out the stops to look gorgeous: bare backs and décolletages that were usually hidden revealed themselves buffed and golden, hair was glossy and flowing, wrists and necks throbbed with exotic scents. Jewels had been extricated from velvet-lined boxes; unfamiliar high heels made the journey across the room treacherous but exciting. The walls resounded with chatter, gossip, greetings, kisses, laughter. Cheeks met, lips puckered, warm hands were placed on upper arms, shoulders, waists . . .

Charlotte allowed herself a moment to take it all in. This was her world: a *mélange* of influential, wealthy, attractive people who had come together for a good cause. Yet suddenly she felt a flash of doubt. The cost of it all didn't sit easily with her. The flower bill alone would go a long way towards equipping the new unit. And the guests weren't really here for the chance to change lives. Wasn't this just an opportunity for them all to show off their money, taste, good looks and dress sense? Would they have responded so enthusiastically to a simple request for a donation, without the chance to spend the evening guzzling, drinking, dancing – and, no doubt by the end of it, flirting and groping?

She told herself to stop being so prim. This was how the world worked. If thousands of pounds had to be spent in order to lure people into parting with more, then so be it. And why shouldn't they have fun in the meantime? No one was being exploited. The chief exec of the hospice looked quite happy with the deal. Besides, who was she to question the morality of it all? She wasn't exactly grubbing about saving lives in a war-torn sub-continent for a living. She peddled dreams; convinced people they needed things they absolutely didn't, seducing them into wanton spending in order to create luxurious, opulent and utterly profligate surroundings, some of which bordered on the indecent.

Charlotte swiped a cocktail from the tray of a passing waiter, took a hefty slug and decided to stop being such a bloody hypocrite.

After dinner, Ed stood up and tinged the side of his glass to call the room to attention. Cupping his brandy in one hand, he smiled round at the guests, thanking them for their attendance, and also name-checking all the people who had given their time to make the evening a success. But it soon became clear he had lulled them into a false sense of security and that he had another agenda.

On the wall behind him flashed up a photograph of Simon's son, the pitifully brief dates of his life in white underneath. Ed proceeded to outline the role that the hospice had taken in the boy's last few weeks, and described the strength and hope it had given his loved ones, making his eventual death a positive and uplifting experience – as far as it was possible, anyway – and how his family wanted to be able to replicate that experience for more people by expanding the accommodation the hospice offered. It wasn't a mawkish speech, but there were few guests who didn't have a tear in their eye by the end of it. By tugging on their heart strings, he was also tugging at their purse strings, for the auction was about to start.

As Ed came back to the table Charlotte gave his hand a heartfelt squeeze, feeling immensely proud.

'That was brilliant,' she whispered.

'Should get them to dig deeper into their pockets,' Ed responded with a nonchalant shrug, but she knew he was just pretending to be hard-bitten and cynical. She knew how moved he had been by his friend's predicament; how he had taken Simon out on several occasions both before and after his son's death, and had provided both a shoulder for him to cry on and a temporary escape from the horror of it all. She had seen how angry he was after the little boy's funeral; that same pent-up fury that she had witnessed time and again at the consultant's. She'd heard him take it out on the punch bag in the spare room.

In some ways, organising the ball had given both of them something to focus on. The auction began. Bidding was spirited right from the outset, as wives urged their husbands into über-generosity, Ed's words fresh in their minds. Lot after lot went for ridiculous prices: haircuts and spa days; an evening at the races; an animal portrait. Ed milked the guests for all they were worth, goading them on, winningly inciting them into higher and higher bids until it was a veritable frenzy. The star lot went for over six thousand pounds, to a burst of rapturous applause and a standing ovation. Everyone hit the dance floor with elation, the knowledge that they had all done a little good clearly a mood enhancer.

Then it was all nearly over. How could something that had taken almost a year to organise be over before you had time to blink? Even their own wedding hadn't involved as much preparation, reflected Charlotte, as the DJ announced the last song. Couples conjoined on the dance floor as the familiar strains of 'Everything I Do' struck up. Charlotte snuggled herself into Ed's embrace, her cheek resting against his shoulder. They barely moved on the dance floor, just an infinitesimal sway, gentle, soothing. Charlotte shut her eyes. She felt so safe, wrapped up in his arms, the smell of him, the sound of the music . . .

They had each other. That was all that mattered. They would have each other for the rest of their lives. They could do all those things and go to all those places that their friends with children constantly moaned they couldn't. Thailand, the Maldives, skiing, New York for the weekend, Florence. And they each had godchildren they could spoil and take for treats – the pantomime, football matches, maybe take them for a weekend's proper camping in Cornwall to give their parents a break. Being childless didn't mean their lives were empty and meaningless. Surely the most important thing in life was finding the person you wanted to spend it with? After that, everything was a bonus. Well, she had found Ed, and she wasn't going to let him go. She tightened her grip around his neck. His lips brushed her collarbone and she shivered. They could go back to love-making without the pressure of baby-making. They could live again. Their lives had been on hold, but now they were free.

Gradually, the guests departed, most of them notably more dishevelled than when they'd arrived: lipstick had faded, hairdos collapsed, ties were undone, some women carried their shoes. Drunken promises were made to meet again soon; overenthusiastic kisses were bestowed. A flotilla of taxis waited outside the hotel to take the guests home, as few had had the willpower to abstain from drinking.

The lights in the ballroom came on, illuminating the carnage of a well-spent evening: pools of spilled wine, crumpled napkins, crumbs, upturned chairs, party poppers. Charlotte made her way to the cloak-room to retrieve her coat. She was surprised to see Ed and Melanie in a darkened doorway, locked in an intense debate. Melanie was trying to hammer some-thing home to Ed, who looked unhappy, shaking his head in a manner that Charlotte knew definitely meant no negotiation. What on earth could they be dis-cussing? Should she interrupt? Melanie was glaring up at him, shaking her finger. The top of her head barely reached his chest, but judging by the way he was recoiling she was nevertheless a daunting adver-sary. Charlotte decided Melanie was taking the title of personal assistant too literally and needed taking down a peg or two.

Melanie looked up and saw her as she approached. She stepped neatly away from Ed and turned to Charlotte with a luminous smile.

'Charlotte! I was just telling Ed that Mr Thompson has made a donation of ten thousand pounds. Isn't that fantastic?'

Ed's head snapped round and as he saw his wife his scowl disappeared to be replaced by a rather strained smile. Charlotte felt fairly certain they hadn't been discussing Mr Thompson's generosity at all, but before she could confront them, Melanie had melted away into the shadows while Ed seamlessly took her coat and held it out for her. As she slid her arms somewhat reluctantly into the sleeves, he pulled her to him, wrapping her into his embrace.

'I'm so proud of you,' he murmured. 'Tonight was wonderful. We raised a fortune. I don't know the exact total yet, but we couldn't have done it without you. Simon will be thrilled.'

Charlotte managed a smile in response, still mulling over what she had seen. Ed put his arm round her and steered her out of the hotel to the last waiting taxi.

'By the way, I'm sorry about Melanie,' he added as they settled into the back seat. 'I pulled her up for wearing white. She shouldn't be allowed to get away with it. I didn't want to do it at the beginning of the evening, obviously. But you know what she's like. She got a bit stroppy.'

Charlotte let her head fall onto his shoulder. She was unbelievably tired, but she still felt a small wave of relief wash over her. That explained the intensity of their little tête-á-tête. But good for Ed for not being afraid to tear Melanie off a strip. So many men let their PAs take advantage of them, letting them rule rather than run their lives.

It was nearly three by the time they fell into bed. And even though they were both exhausted, they turned to each other and made love. It was even better than earlier. Charlotte felt a delicious warmth seep through her like spilled treacle.

'It's going to be OK. I'm going to make it OK,' whispered Ed, as they lay in each other's arms drifting off to sleep.

'It already is OK,' Charlotte whispered back. 'I'm happy, Ed, truly happy.'

But he had already fallen asleep. Charlotte lay awake

for a few minutes longer, wallowing in the sleepy satisfaction of knowing that the evening had been a success, but also relishing the blissful state of relaxation that only perfect and uncomplicated sex can bring. Then she flung her arm over Ed's inert form, breathed in the very smell of him, and fell asleep too.

Three

In the days following the ball, Ed was unusually tense. He seemed to be keeping a deliberate distance from Charlotte, who was bewildered by his hostility. As soon as he got home from work, he went up to his office, only coming out to pick disinterestedly at his supper before disappearing again. She didn't interrogate him. She knew he had constant targets to hit, that it was a competitive world and if he didn't keep one step ahead he could easily be replaced. He was best left to wrestle with his problems alone. He'd plough his way through it eventually, and emerge smiling. He always managed to find a tactic that brought him out on top. He thrived on the pressure, and Charlotte had got used to the highs and lows, the stress that preceded the elation of success. Only this time, the tension seemed to be going on longer than usual.

By the time the weekend came around he was still on edge, and Charlotte decided he needed a break. He'd been up till three; had finally fallen into bed next to her, and she'd smelled whisky on his breath. He needed to relax and take his mind off whatever was bothering him. She tried to suggest several distractions, but Ed wasn't interested.

'Just leave me alone, will you? I don't want to go to

the fucking cinema, or out for lunch. I just want some peace and quiet.'

Charlotte's lip trembled and her eyes filled with tears. Ed had never made her cry before. Of course, she had shed tears in front of him, but not because of an argument. She couldn't understand what was making him so vicious, but something told her not to probe. She'd got the message. He wanted to be on his own.

'OK. I'm going to go . . .' She didn't have a clue where. She shrugged. 'Shopping,' she finished lamely.

'Good.' He fixed her with a belligerent glare. He didn't seem to care that she was upset.

Charlotte drove off, her hands shaking and her stomach churning. She had no intention of going shopping; she just drove blindly through the streets. Eventually she found a parking space by the Thames and got out to walk along the riverbank. The sun was shining brightly on the water; there were people out walking their dogs, kids rollerblading, couples strolling arm in arm. It was one of those days when London was at its best; everyone seemed to be in a good mood and not in a tearing hurry. She should be here with Ed, tucked under his arm, the two of them making plans, on their way to a lovely lunch somewhere. But he had made it quite clear he didn't want to come out with her. Or indeed be with her at all.

She didn't have a clue what was the matter with him. She knew his work was difficult, but he usually thrived on it – he loved the uncertainty, the risks, the peaks and troughs. Something was getting to him; something serious, she could feel it in her gut. Just when she thought she'd turned the corner, just when she'd got it together and worked out how she was going to get through the rest of her life, Ed had changed beyond recognition.

Perhaps it was simply the anticlimax after the ball? It had been a huge undertaking, and it could have been a total failure instead of a resounding success – they had cleared their target of over a hundred thousand pounds. It had taken up such a lot of their time and mental energy over the past few months that maybe now, in the vacuum, Ed was dwelling on their own predicament. Perhaps he hadn't come to terms with it like she had?

Or perhaps . . . oh God. Her hand flew to her mouth as she choked back a gasp of dismay. Perhaps he had decided that he didn't want to be with her any more? That if she couldn't bear him any children, then he wanted the chance to try with someone else? Perhaps he even had someone in mind? And how could she deny him that chance? She couldn't sentence him to a life without kids. Charlotte stopped in her tracks on the riverbank, looking across the water, her eyes blinking at the harsh reflection of the sun. She had been so wrapped up in herself, so smug and self-congratulatory, that she hadn't thought about where Ed was. It was his future as much as hers. Just because she felt resigned to her fate didn't necessarily mean he was happy with his.

And thinking back on it, if she was honest, it was always Ed who had put the pressure on to have one more try. She knew he was desperate. She'd watched him with the children of their friends, whenever they'd gone round for a barbecue or Sunday lunch. He threw himself into their little worlds, making paper aeroplanes and rabbits out of handkerchiefs, while Charlotte had deliberately held back. Not because she didn't want close contact with children, but because she didn't want whoever it was out there that decided these things to think she was too desperate. And there was an element of self-preservation in it too. Downy heads and pudgy knees and starfish hands were a one-way ticket to the ultimate heartbreak. But Ed had never been ashamed to admit that he was as broody as hell. He embraced other people's kids in the optimistic assumption that he would one day have his own.

But Charlotte couldn't provide him with hope any more. She knew she had reached the end of the line. That she was resigned to childlessness. That she couldn't bear to try one more time, because that meant there would probably be another, and another. It was up to her to say stop. And if Ed didn't want to stop . . .

Charlotte sat down on a bench, her heart so heavy she could barely stand. She would have to drive home and tell him that if he wanted his freedom, then she wasn't going to stand in his way and that he could go with her blessing. All she would ask is that they share one last holiday together: a fortnight in some tropical paradise where they could bask in the sun and swim in the sea and sleep naked, entwined under an Egyptian cotton sheet, so she could take away one pure memory of him. Then she would go without protest.

Her heart was hammering as she drove up to the house. There was a police car parked in her usual space, and she tutted: on a Saturday afternoon it was a nightmare getting a place. She could be driving round

42

for hours. She hit lucky in the next road, grabbed her handbag and got out of the car. She had to do this straight away, without thinking about it.

She was about to put her key into the lock when the door opened. She stepped back in alarm when she looked up into the grim gaze of a policeman.

'Mrs Briggs?'

Her first thought was that Ed had done something terrible. Surely he wouldn't be the type to kill himself? Yet he had dark moments, especially when he'd been drinking – she remembered now the smell of whisky when he came to bed, and the empty bottle in the recycling bin as she left the house. Where was he? Panicking, she went to rush in.

'Ed . . . ?'

The policeman put out a hand to stop her.

'Mrs Briggs – I'm afraid your husband's under arrest.'

Twenty minutes later, Charlotte sat bolt upright on the sofa, her hands pressed in between her clenched knees, her teeth biting down on her bottom lip to stop her from crying.

Ed had taken the ball money. He had taken all the profits raised from the tickets, the raffle, the auction, and the donations and bought a tranche of shares on a tip-off from a friend in the City. A small but dynamic software firm was about to be taken over by a larger company. It was a given that the shares would quadruple overnight. Obviously Ed's plan had been to sell the shares on straight away, put the money back into the ball account ready to be handed over ceremoniously to the hospice, and keep the substantial difference.

But by a million to one chance, the deal hadn't come off. The dynamic managing director, the brains and therefore the intrinsic value of the company, had died in a helicopter crash on the way to signing the buy-out. Without him the company was worthless. The buy-out was pointless; the share prices crashed to zero. The money was wiped out. Ed was left with nothing.

Or rather, the charity was left with nothing.

It hadn't taken long for his misdemeanour to be detected. He had forged the signature on the cheque in the hopes that the money would be back in the account before the other committee members noticed it was missing. But of course they were all clamouring to organise the presentation to the hospice, all relishing the prospect of a ceremony and a photo-shoot. Ed had had little choice but to put his hands up and turn himself in. It was either that or flee the country. No wonder he had been tense all week. He must have been waiting for the hammer to fall from the minute he had heard about the helicopter crash. And praying for some miracle. Praying that the original deal would be salvaged, though God knows how. And now, the police were preparing to take Ed down to the station for further questioning. They'd wondered at first if Charlotte was involved, but he'd made it clear she had nothing to do with it.

He'd gone to fetch his jacket. He came back into the room looking dreadful, his skin pale, blue rings under his eyes.

Charlotte looked at him, bewildered.

'Why, Ed . . . ?'

'I did it for us,' he said in a choked voice. 'I thought . . . if we could get out of London, get a house in the country, take the pressure off . . . I thought if you could stop work, then maybe . . . We didn't have time to wait for me to be able to afford it. I was trying to speed things up.'

Charlotte felt a surge of fury.

'Is that what it was about?' she demanded. 'The bloody baby thing? You took that risk, took someone else's money, just for another shot at it?'

'I wanted things to be different! I thought maybe it was London stopping you . . . us . . .'

'But I told you I couldn't go through it again!'

Ed looked distraught. 'I can't take no for an answer, Charlotte. I love you. I want us to have children. More than anything.'

Charlotte felt tears spring into her eyes – tears of frustration that Ed couldn't seem to grasp the simple truth.

'You're insane! I don't know how you could have thought it would work, even for a moment.'

'I spoke to the consultant. He suggested a change of scene, a change of lifestyle.'

'He was clutching at straws, Ed. Just like you. And now where has it got us?'

She stood up, trembling. She thought she was going to be sick. She felt cold and clammy and nauseous. 'Well, thank God I *didn't* have your children.'

It was the harshest thing she could think of to say.

Ed recoiled as if he had been slapped. The policeman stepped forward.

'Mr Briggs? If you're ready to come to the station now?'

45

Charlotte sank back down onto the sofa as Ed was escorted from the room. She couldn't look at him. She pressed her face into her palms, shutting out the world. Moments later the room was still, empty, and she felt very small inside it. There was nothing to do but wait.

When Ed came back later that night, Charlotte was scrunched up in a ball on the bed, shivering like a kitten that had been left out in a thunderstorm. She had been beside herself all afternoon, but she hadn't been able to think of a single soul she could call on for sympathy or advice. How on earth could she admit to any of her friends and family what Ed had done – though they would find out soon enough? So she had wandered the house in turmoil, her emotions veering from rage to despair to total bewilderment. She'd necked down half a bottle of red wine, in the hope that it might calm her down, but it only made her feel worse and made her already throbbing head pound. In the end, she threw herself on the bed and sobbed herself to sleep.

Ed stood awkwardly in the doorway.

'They've let me out on bail. But I've been charged with obtaining money by deception. God knows when the trial will be.'

There was silence.

'Charlotte?'

She sat up suddenly.

'Why didn't you just take out a loan? Or extend the mortgage?' she demanded. 'Surely it would have been better to risk our own money? Better than stealing somebody else's, at any rate.'

Ed darted a nervous look at her. Charlotte swallowed.

'Ed . . . ?'

'I did. As well. I needed another fifty grand to make it worthwhile.'

'What?'

'We'd have walked away with half a million . . .'

'You extended our mortgage?'

'Yes.'

'Shouldn't I have signed the paperwork?'

'You did.'

'I'd remember borrowing that kind of money . . .' She trailed off, remembering Ed coming in with some forms from the building society one Sunday morning when she was still sleeping off last night's party. He'd said something about moving mortgages because they'd come to the end of their tie-in period. Something about getting a better deal. Of course she'd signed it. He dealt with all that sort of thing. And of course she hadn't looked at the small print. She wouldn't have suspected her own husband of trying to pull a fast one.

She buried her head in the pillow. He sat on the bed next to her and put a hand on her back, stroking her gently.

'I did it for you,' he was saying, his voice soft and urgent. 'I can't bear it, watching you run yourself ragged. You throw yourself into your work to forget your unhappiness. And then you exhaust yourself. And then of course you don't get . . .'

He couldn't even bring himself to say the word.

'Pregnant!' Charlotte looked up and shouted it at him. 'No, I bloody don't. And thank goodness. Lucky

47

escape. God must have been on my side all this time. I don't want a psycho-fraudster fathering my child.'

'I wanted a big house in the country,' he went on, ignoring her outburst. 'Trees, and a pond, and a big kitchen, and a huge attic room to put train sets in. And a chocolate Labrador.'

'I hate the countryside!'

'You wouldn't.' Ed shook his head. 'You'd love it once we were there.'

Charlotte sat up wearily.

'So,' she said, 'this was all about *your* dream. Your fantasy. You've ruined our lives because of what you wanted.'

'I wanted it for both of us.'

He reached out to stroke her hair. She ducked away.

'Don't touch me,' she snarled.

'Charlotte—' His voice cracked. Etched on his face was utter misery and despair. But Charlotte didn't feel as much as a flicker of sympathy.

'We're going to lose our house because of this. You'll go to prison. You'll be out of a job. How can you expect me to understand? We've lost everything, because all you can think about is yourself!'

'I was thinking about us.'

'No. You were thinking about Ed Briggs, and the fact that you want hundreds of your offspring running about the place. What about what I want?'

'I know deep down that's what you want too.'

'I don't! I've tried to tell you often enough, but you can't take it in, can you? I've had enough of it all. I can't go through it any more. I've come to terms with the fact that I won't ever have children. It's just a pity you can't deal with the fact.'

She fell back on the bed and looked up at the ceiling.

'Fine,' Ed replied flatly. 'If you don't understand that I wasn't prepared to accept defeat, that I wanted to fight—'

'So you stole over a hundred grand? From a charity? From your best friend's dead son, effectively?'

'It wasn't supposed to go wrong.'

'Wrong?' Charlotte knew she was shouting now, but she was so filled with fury that she couldn't help herself. 'Wrong is the whole point. Even if it had gone right it would have been wrong. I don't want a baby on those terms!'

'You'd never have known.'

'So what would you have told me?'

'I don't know. That I'd won the lottery?'

He was shouting back now, equally frustrated that she couldn't – wouldn't – ever understand his motives. It was the first proper row they'd ever had. They had minor squabbles, of course, and the occasional difference of opinion, but it never became heated.

'I'm sorry, Ed.' Charlotte scrambled off the bed in an effort to put some distance between them. 'There's nothing you can say that will make me change my mind. What you did was evil. Selfish. Foolhardy. Irresponsible . . .'

She was running out of adjectives.

'Well, I'm sorry.' Ed spoke softly. 'But I did it because I love you.'

Charlotte regarded him coldly.

'Don't you ever, ever dare use me as an excuse.'

She turned on her heel and walked out of the room.

She walked around the streets for hours, knowing there was no one she could go to. Besides, she didn't want to be influenced. She wanted to make up her mind about what she was going to do without the world and his wife giving her their opinions, although it was unlikely that anyone would consider Ed's crime anything other than heinous.

She knew Ed had dreams, delusions of grandeur, almost, about a big country pile to bring up their putative children in. A lot of people he worked with came from that sort of background: they did their stint in a flat in the City, but when they started families they shot off to the country, no doubt with substantial financial help from their parents. But neither Ed nor Charlotte came from wealthy families; their respective parents were comfortable, but not sufficiently well endowed to be able to hand out lump sums to put down on a dear little rectory. And while between them they earned a good six-figure sum, it really wasn't enough to sustain a mortgage on the type of home Ed had in mind.

Yet he was always ploughing through copies of *Country Life*, sighing with longing, and sending off to posh estate agents with triple-barrelled names for details. Charlotte found the glossy brochures strewn all over the living room and in the downstairs loo, with Ed's mathematical calculations scrawled over the envelopes. His vision was to find something that needed doing up, and for Charlotte to be able to leave her job and work her way through it until they had the home of their dreams. But the maths never worked. Anything with potential was always snapped up by builders; anything with a remotely affordable price tag always had something badly wrong, like a motorway on the doorstep or a mobile phone mast in the apple orchard.

Charlotte had never really played along, because she never believed it would come to anything. She was practical and down-to-earth, knowing that with the best will in the world they could probably afford a substantial but dull modern-ish house on a pleasant-ish housing estate somewhere semi-rural but commutable, and she was happy to accept that. But Ed was perfectly entitled to dream.

But that dream had obviously become an obsession. It was the world they moved in that was to blame. Some of their colleagues and most of their clients had luxurious homes and fabulous cars and glamorous lifestyles. She had underestimated just how badly Ed wanted that too, not realising he was so consumed by his desire, or that he would go to such drastic lengths to achieve what he felt he was entitled to.

She turned down yet another street, realising she hadn't a clue where she was. The terraced houses were smaller and shabbier than the area they lived in, with peeling paintwork and rusty gates hanging off their hinges, the hedges unkempt. She wondered how many criminals were harboured behind the doors, and what they had done. TV licence evasion, benefit fraud, possession of an offensive weapon, drug dealing, driving a car without insurance – she would bet that any number of crimes were going on inches from her nose. But none of them would be as despicable as what Ed had done. A young man on a good salary who just got greedy.

Her cheeks burned with the shame. She cringed inside as she recollected his rousing speech at the charity ball, the way he had urged the crowd on into competitive bidding. And all along he had known the more they bid the bigger his pot would be.

How long had he been planning it? More to the point, would people think she was in on it? Would they imagine that she had spent the best part of a year deciding themes, choosing menus, booking entertainers, all as part of an elaborate scam to get rich quick? Charlotte, who was generally good-natured and didn't hate anyone, felt a sudden surge of pure loathing for her husband. How could he profess love for her and compromise her like that? Never mind his reputation; what about hers? No one was going to believe she was innocent. Even if he said she was, they would have their doubts.

She shivered. The night air was damp, and she only had on a thin cardigan. Short of checking into a hotel there was nowhere else she could go, and actually she was buggered if she was going to be shut out of her own home. She'd have to go back and face him. Anyway, there were questions to be answered. She tried to get her bearings, heading for what looked like a main road at the end of the street, searching in vain for the lights of a taxi.

It was just before dawn before she got in. Ed was passed out on top of the bed. She felt too exhausted for confrontation, so she slipped fully clothed under the duvet, trying to get warm, her eyelids burning from lack of sleep. Outside the dawn chorus started, and Charlotte knew there was no way she was going to be able to get to sleep. She felt as if there was a heavy stone in place of her heart, and a nest of writhing adders in her stomach. She hadn't been able to face food. She'd managed half a piece of toast earlier, which had gone straight through her, and the half bottle of wine she'd resorted to felt like hydrochloric acid swirling round in her gut.

How did life manage to do this? Trip you up when you least expected it? When as far as you knew you hadn't done anything to deserve it? In the blink of an eye, all her security had gone. She had made a grave error of judgement about the man she was supposed to be spending the rest of her life with; the man whose babies she had been trying to have. Yet again she thanked goodness she wasn't pregnant. How would she have coped with that? Homeless, with a jailbird for a father? In the meantime, how were they supposed to manage? How long before your house was actually repossessed? Would they take her stuff as well as his? Was her name going to be dragged through the mud?

She rolled over, pressing her face into the pillow, longing for sleep but knowing that it wouldn't come. Next to her, she heard Ed's breathing become deeper, and she felt filled with rage. How could he sleep, knowing what he had done, while she was wide awake with worry?

She sat up and grabbed him by the front of his T-shirt.

'You bastard!'

'Jesus!'

He started awake and sat up in alarm.

'What is it?'

She was sobbing violently, totally out of control. He put his arms around her, and she longed to be able to sink into them, longed to hear his reassurance. That was what husbands were for, wasn't it? They were supposed to be your rock. They were supposed to make you feel safe. Not terrified. Petrified of the next day and what it might bring.

'Hey,' he said. 'Hey, it's OK.'

'How can you say that?' she demanded.

She pushed his arms away and jumped out of the bed. She couldn't bear to be near him a moment longer. She wanted to get as far away from him as possible. Outside the spare room she stopped. It was four o'clock in the morning. Where else was she going to go?

Ed stood in the doorway of their bedroom behind her.

'Charlotte. Sweetheart. Come back to bed.'

'Leave me alone,' she snarled. 'And I'm not your sweetheart.'

For a moment she thought he was going to protest, then he sighed and slipped back into their room.

She pushed open the door of the spare room and clambered into the spare bed, grateful that she always kept it made up with fresh linen in case one of Ed's mates stayed over after a boozy evening. She was also glad that she kept the room well equipped, second-guessing every guest's need: she found a pair of ear plugs in the chest of drawers, along with pillow mist, condoms and a box of Alka Seltzer. Satisfied that they would shut out the almost deafening dawn chorus, she curled up and eventually fell asleep.

She woke at half eleven the next morning, confused for a moment as to why she was in the spare room. And then she remembered. She pulled the duvet over her head, trying to take refuge from the painful truth, but it wouldn't go away. She was going to have to face the day, the consequences, Ed . . .

Feeling sick at heart she pushed back the covers and climbed wearily out of bed. She was still dressed from the night before; she felt grubby, worn at the edges, exhausted from the shock. Her limbs ached, her head throbbed, her eyes were gritty with unshed tears. She decided to have a shower, put on some fresh clothes and go to get some food. She hadn't eaten properly since breakfast the day before, and although she didn't feel like eating, she knew she would feel better if she did.

There was no sign of Ed as she crept into the bathroom and stood under a red-hot shower for ten minutes, allowing the powerful jets to pummel some life back into her. She pulled a pair of tracksuit trousers and a sweatshirt from the airing cupboard on the landing, picked up her shoes and went downstairs, stopping to rummage in her handbag on the newel post for her purse.

Then she opened the front door.

No sooner had she set her foot on the top step than a bevy of photographers rushed forwards, light bulbs popping. She froze in fear, wondering what on earth they were doing there, then realised they had probably been banging on the door since daybreak. With her ear plugs in, she wouldn't have heard a thing.

Of course word would have got out. If the papers hadn't got the sordid details from the police, then someone else would have been all too quick to inform them. Someone on the hospice committee, perhaps, hoping they could sweep up public sympathy and some nationwide exposure in the light of the scandal.

She was tempted for a moment to flee back inside. But she couldn't stay locked in for ever. She needed to eat. And, she reminded herself, she wasn't actually guilty of anything. Hiding from the press would make them even hungrier for dirt. So she held her head up high and descended the last of the steps, not looking straight at any of the cameras or the reporters who were jostling for her attention, firing questions at her. 'Where are you off to, Charlotte? It is Charlotte, isn't it?' 'Where's Ed? Is he in there?' 'How do you feel about what your husband did?'

She put her head down and ran blindly to the car, her hands shaking as she put the key in the ignition. As the engine started up she pulled into the road, scattering photographers in her wake. They were wasting their time. She didn't have anything to say. Yes, she could sit down and tell them how she really felt. Eviscerated. As if the last six years had been snuffed out like a candle. Hopeless. Bewildered. Betrayed. What would she get for selling her story? Not enough. Besides, she might no longer have her dignity, but she was going to hold on to her pride if it killed her.

She made it to the shop, and kept her head down in the queue. She bought a bag of Danish pastries and some doughnuts, and made her escape before she saw anyone she knew. Sunday morning here was usually a social whirl, as people compared hangovers and dithered over which overweight newspaper to take home. Thankfully she was spared the embarrassment of having to pretend to be polite, despite harbouring a ghastly secret that everyone would be privy to soon enough.

By the time she got home, Ed was sitting at the kitchen table. She dumped the pastries in front of him wordlessly, and went to get plates.

'Do you want a coffee?' he managed to ask.

Charlotte gripped the sides of the china she was carrying. How dare he try to pretend things were normal? She felt an overwhelming urge to throw the plates at his head, even though she wasn't normally a violent creature.

'No,' she managed in a strangled voice. 'I just want someone to tell me that this has all been a silly mistake. But that's not going to happen, is it?'

Ed looked down at the table, spreading his hands out on it, taking in slow, deep breaths.

'No, it's not,' he agreed eventually. 'Charlotte . . . let's try to get through this. Without—'

'Without what?' she demanded.

'Without . . . doing any damage to us. I mean, that's all that matters, isn't it? You and me?'

She stared at him in disbelief. 'Are you saying you want me to pretend it doesn't matter? That it's just a little hiccup?'

'I screwed up. I know I screwed up.'

'This isn't something I can condone, or excuse, or rationalise. This puts a whole new light on the person you are, Ed.'

'I was under stress. I wasn't thinking straight. It's been a tough few years. Even you've got to admit that.'

'But this wasn't something you did on the spur of the moment. You must have been planning it for months.'

'No! Not until I heard about the buy-out. It just seemed like . . . such a great opportunity. We could change our lives in the blink of an eye without doing anyone any harm. It was a million to one that it went wrong. I guess I got unlucky.'

He looked up at her, his expression so bleak that for a moment her heart went out to him. Then she realised the truth: he just didn't get it.

'The problem is,' she explained as patiently as she could, 'that what you are blaming yourself for is the fact the deal went wrong. You can't seem to see that the whole scam was inherently immoral. If you could have got away with it, you would. Even now. And that's what I can't handle.'

Ed's face was expressionless.

'Are you saying it's over?' he asked flatly.

'I don't know.' This was the truth. Charlotte had no idea at all how she was going to deal with what had happened. She couldn't bring herself to be supportive to Ed, to console him at all, to show him even a modicum of sympathy. But to walk out after six years of marriage, when until the night before she had loved him with every bone in her body, was anathema.

She looked at him. She could hardly believe that just over a week ago she had clung to him, trying to absorb his very skin into hers in her desire to be close to him. Now the man in front of her seemed a stranger. She didn't want to touch him; the very thought of close contact made her recoil.

Would that repulsion fade over time? Did she want it to? Did she want to be able to forgive him for what he had done? Or would she live the rest of her life wondering what else he was capable of? She had misread him so severely; to have overlooked the fact that he had such a calculating streak showed she was an appalling judge of character.

'I need time to think,' she said softly. 'I'm not going to walk out, or kick you out. That's not going to change anything, or help our situation. But at the moment, I can't forgive you. Or see how we've got a future together.'

He nodded in understanding, then managed a smile.

'At the moment?' He was repeating her words back to her. In a flash she understood him completely. He was a gambler, a risk-taker. He always had hope, which was why he would never come to terms with their childlessness. That was the difference between them. And that was, in the end, what would drive them apart.

The following week was a nightmare. Ed's misdemeanour was all over the papers on Monday, with varying degrees of disparaging editorial comment. Ed was put on immediate gardening leave pending an investigation into what he had done. As Charlotte was essentially self-employed, she negotiated a few days off work, shuffling her diary around to give herself some breathing space. It wasn't that she wanted to be at home for Ed; it was more that she couldn't face the people she worked with, or her clients.

They barely spoke. Charlotte threw herself into

spring-cleaning: a mindless task, but vaguely thera-peutic, and as they would no doubt have to sell up, her time wasn't wasted. Everything was filed, or folded, or shredded, or thrown away. She dusted, polished and buffed until everything shone. There wasn't a misshapen pair of pants or an out-of-date magazine or a worn towel left. She defrosted the freezer, chucking out anything that couldn't be identified.

She didn't know what Ed did, apart from go run-ning along the riverbank, and then shut himself in the office. She cooked enough supper for two, but didn't set the table as usual; just helped herself to what she wanted and went and sat in front of the television. For once she was grateful for the inanity of reality shows and soap operas. They helped avoid the need for conversation, and filled in the hours before bedtime. When Charlotte found herself actually looking forward to the next episode of *EastEnders*, she wondered in how many marriages it helped to paper over the cracks.

Not a single friend had phoned to commiserate, or see how they were. This wasn't surprising, as many of their friends worked in finance or in the City, and to be associated with a high-profile fraud like this, even though it involved relatively small amounts of money compared to the sums they were used to dealing with, was professional suicide. Throughout the course of the week Charlotte picked up several voice-mail messages cancelling social engagements they had been invited to.

'I'm afraid we're cancelling our drinks party on the twenty-third, as my mother is coming to stay . . .'

'Can't do dinner on the twelfth after all. The au pair's going back to Romania for the holidays . . .'

One was refreshingly blunt: 'Won't be coming to the races with you, under the circs. Will give you a bell when it all dies down.'

That said it all, really.

They were social lepers.

She had taken the precaution of phoning each of her parents before the news hit the papers, in order to prepare them for the worst. Her father was sweet. Gruff but sanguine, he had told her she could come and stay until the furore was over, but she couldn't imagine going to live in a three-bed semi in Potters Bar with his second wife and her two stroppy teenager daughters. Her father, she suspected, was under enough stress.

Her mother was icily disapproving.

'You'll have to come home to me. You can't stay there with him.'

Charlotte wanted to retort that her mother was making Ed sound like a criminal, then realised that of course he was.

'I can't just leave him. He is my husband.'

'By staying with him you're condoning what he's done.'

'I am not.' Charlotte was defiant. It had taken her till she was thirty to be able to stand up to her mother, and she still resented having to defend her decisions. 'And he knows that perfectly well.'

'What about other people?'

'They can think what they like.'

'You're being very foolish.'

Charlotte didn't give her the benefit of a reply.

Nothing would change her mother's opinion, and the only way to stop the debate was not to retaliate. Her mother rang off in a huff.

The only person who hadn't treated her like a leper was Gussie, her dearest and oldest friend. Gussie had been the witness at her wedding; Charlotte was godmother to Gussie's oldest son Pip. Gussie was a brick, reminiscent of a *Famous Five* farmer's wife, capable, comfortable. But Charlotte knew that if she went to see Gussie she would fall apart, would fall into her arms sobbing, and lose all her resilience. And so she kept away, but appreciated Gussie's regular texts and phone calls.

In the meantime, life had to go on. On Wednesday morning Charlotte dragged herself out of bed and headed for Sainsbury's. They had to eat, even though she didn't feel like it. As she rounded the pasta aisle, she spotted Davina Cumiskey loading linguine and papardelle into her trolley. Davina and her husband Dom had been for supper on countless occasions, and they'd been to theirs, usually for drunken Sunday lunches. But as Davina looked up and spotted Charlotte approaching, she turned on her heel, pulled her trolley round and marched smartly off down the aisle and round the corner, her retreating back stating very clearly that she did not want to be followed.

Charlotte stood by the rice, shaking. She felt utterly humiliated. Davina wasn't Charlotte's best friend, but she was certainly more than an acquaintance. Her cheeks burning, Charlotte carried on with her shopping. By the time she got to the freezer section, her eyes were filled with tears and she couldn't find what she was looking for. Unable to face finishing her shop, she purchased the few items she already had and fled to the car park.

She sat at the wheel of her car for a few moments, taking deep breaths to calm herself down. Was she a total pariah? Was she going to be blanked for the rest of her life, even though she was guilty of nothing? Was that how shallow everybody she knew really was? Backing away from her as if they might be able to catch something nasty? As if fraudulent tendencies were transmitted like germs through the air?

As she started up the ignition and drove out, she saw Davina wheeling her shopping towards her car. Charlotte quailed for a moment, feeling the urge to duck down behind the steering wheel so she wouldn't be noticed, unable to face the ignominy of being blanked again. Then she gave herself a talking-to. She wasn't going to be a victim of this hideous situation.

She wound down the window and stuck out her head, waving madly, determined to confront Davina, determined that she should be recognised.

'Yoo hoo!'

Davina looked up, startled, then stood petrified in the middle of the car park, clearly searching her mental guide to etiquette for the appropriate greeting.

'Hello!' she responded eventually, her voice an octave higher than usual, her face fixed in a false grin. 'Must dash – my frozen goods are melting.'

She shot between two cars, even though there was barely enough room for the trolley to pass between them. Charlotte left her engine idling for a moment, knowing that Davina was trapped, that she couldn't come out until she was sure Charlotte had gone. But eventually someone gave an impatient pip behind her and so she drove off.

When she got back home, Ed was ashen.

'I called Simon,' he told her. 'I called him to apologise. And to try to explain.'

Charlotte started unpacking food from the plastic bags. Ed raked his fingers through his crop. His voice was shaking.

'He told me that using my wife's infertility to justify my crime was lower than low. That he would have preferred it if I had just admitted to wanting to make a fast buck, as that would have made me more of a man.'

Charlotte looked at a pot of Greek yoghurt with honey, as if it might have some sort of answer written on the label.

'Stop looking for absolution, Ed,' she said. 'There is no justification for what you did.'

She slammed the pot down on the island and it promptly burst open. Yoghurt shot everywhere. Over the work surface. Over the shopping. Over Ed.

'Jesus Christ!' he swore violently. 'Jesus! What did you do that for?'

Charlotte looked at him coldly.

'It was an *accident*. I didn't do it on *purpose*. It wasn't *pre-meditated* . . .'

She couldn't believe she was so bitter; that the words falling from her mouth were so unreservedly acerbic.

Ed stood there, splattered in white, as if someone had flicked a paintbrush full of emulsion over him, and seemed to deflate before her very eyes.

'Why doesn't anybody understand?' he asked. 'The

only person who seems to get what I did is my mother.'

'That's what mothers are for, isn't it? Unconditional love?' She spat this back at him, and he sank onto a stool, his head in his hands.

'I had no idea you could be so cruel.'

'We're learning a lot about each other, aren't we?' retorted Charlotte, opening the fridge and feeling an overwhelming urge to climb in and shut the door, then curl up inside its cool white walls to become gradually, comfortably numb.

It was over. She knew she would never be able to trust him again. Or respect him. She felt sure she could feel her heart break in two as she made the decision; there was a physical pain deep inside her chest that wouldn't go away.

Things went from bad to worse.

On Friday, on page five of one of the red-tops, there was a picture of Charlotte parked in front of the Gucci flagship store on Bond Street, climbing out of Ed's Porsche, which she had borrowed the day before to go to drop off some samples to a client who had been badgering her.

With her sleek groomed mane, her designer clothes and her fifty-thousand-pound Porsche, Charlotte Briggs carries on with life quite oblivious to the fact that her husband has deprived any number of terminally ill children of a comfortable place to die. Never mind – she's got her Gucci!

'It's not fair!' Charlotte stormed to Gussie on the

phone. 'They must have tailed me for days before they got me parked outside there. I wasn't going to Gucci! I was going to a client, for heaven's sake, not bloody shopping. And I have to look the part. I can't turn up in dungarees and a headscarf. I'm selling a lifestyle.'

'In two weeks' time they'll have forgotten all about it,' soothed Gussie.

'But it's so unfair. I knew nothing about it.'

'You're not the first, and you won't be the last, to be made guilty by association.'

'Fucking Ed.'

'Forget it. Chuck it in the bin. No one who knows you will believe it. And it doesn't matter what anyone else thinks.'

But it did. That afternoon, Charlotte had a call from Connor.

'I'm sorry,' he said, sounding quite genuine. 'I can't let you work on any of my projects for the time being. My clients are very high profile. They won't want to be associated with a scandal like this.'

'But it wasn't anything to do with me!'

'Darling, I know that. But that's not how it works.'

'So, I'm sacked?'

'Not sacked, because I don't actually employ you. I'll honour your most recent contract, but that's it.'

'Thanks for nothing, Connor.'

'It's business, sweetie.'

'Well, I hope I can return the favour one day,' snapped Charlotte and hung up with trembling hands. She thought of all the times she had worked into the small hours to help him meet a deadline, the work she had put his way, the trade secrets she had shared with him. And this was how he repaid her loyalty.

Her palms were sweating. Her chest felt tight. The edges of her vision went blurry. She thought she might be having a panic attack. She sat down and took several slow deep breaths to calm herself. She had to pull herself together. She'd already lost her husband, her job, and her home. She didn't want to lose her mind.

On Saturday, another of the tabloids ran a heart-wrenching story about a little girl who had been waiting for a place at the hospice. Next to her photograph were juxtaposed pictures of Charlotte and Ed holidaying and partying – pictures that could only have come from friends. Charlotte wondered just how much money they had got for their betrayal. Probably not even enough to cover a decent meal out, but they obviously hadn't been able to resist. Did it make them feel better about themselves in some way? She couldn't imagine wanting to put someone else through the degradation she was now going through.

As she came out of the newsagent's she bumped into a thickset middle-aged man with a plethora of tattoos.

'I'm so sorry,' she apologised automatically, then frowned as he folded his arms and looked into her eyes. She could feel the hostility radiating from him, and her stomach twitched with fear. She hadn't meant to bump into him—

Then she understood. He knew who she was. And what she was supposed to have done. He turned his head and spat on the pavement next to her, a magnificent quivering blob of spittle that said everything.

She drew herself up with as much dignity as she could muster.

'For your information,' she informed him, 'it was nothing to do with me.'

'Yeah, right,' he sneered, pushing past her.

Charlotte stood in the centre of the pavement with her eyes shut. She wanted the ground to swallow her up. She felt as if everyone's gaze was upon her, as if every last whispered word was directed at her, as if people were crossing the street to avoid her. A double-decker bus drew up next to her, and without thinking she jumped on it, ran upstairs and hid herself away in the furthest corner, away from any other passengers. She sat on it for miles, with no idea where it was heading, until she alighted in some far-off corner of south-west London – a dreary high street with rows of dull, utilitarian shops selling cheap jewellery, kebabs, insurance, pet food. It smelled of petrol fumes and frying onions. It was a million miles from the bijou parade of shops she frequented near home, with its fishmonger boasting monkfish and red snapper, the bakery crammed with *pains au chocolat* and cupcakes.

Get used to it, she told herself grimly as she jumped off the bus.

She chose the least salubrious hairdresser she could find, not least because she couldn't afford the usual hundred pounds it cost her to have her tresses tended to. She walked in with trepidation and asked for an appointment. She got one straight away. There was a three-month waiting list at her salon.

She showed the stylist a picture of a Kiera Knightley crop in a magazine.

'You won't end up looking like her,' the stylist said, not unkindly.

'I know,' replied Charlotte with a sigh. 'But I want a change.'

'If you're sure.' The girl picked up her scissors, clearly unconvinced. 'Some people think they can just walk in with a picture and walk out looking like a film star.'

Charlotte didn't answer. She just wanted to look as unlike herself as possible, but she didn't want to explain.

Ten minutes later she looked at the mirror in horror. She'd imagined that she might look chic and gamine. Instead, a twelve-year-old boy stared back at her. The shortness meant her usual blonde looked mousy. It was as severe and unflattering as a haircut could get.

She blinked back the tears, cursing Ed for the trillionth time.

'What you need,' said the girl helpfully, 'is some false eyelashes. To give you some definition. It takes a bit of getting used to, a crop.'

Charlotte managed a smile of thanks, handed over twenty pounds then fled the salon. She looked back and saw the junior sweeping her golden locks into a dustpan. She went back to the bus-stop and tried to work out how on earth she was going to get back to civilisation. She decided to give in and go to see Gussie. She needed her friend's sympathy almost as much as she needed one of her industrial-strength gin and tonics.

She gazed at her reflection in the window, as-tonished at how unlike herself she felt, unable to believe how she seemed to have been stripped of all her femininity with a mere snip of the scissors. In any other circumstances she might have broken down and wept, but at this point in time she was just grateful that it was unlikely that anyone on the planet would be able to recognise her.

It took Gussie a good ten seconds to clock who it was on her doorstep.

'Crikey!' Gussie wasn't the type to give false reassurance. 'Sinead O'Connor, eat your heart out.'

'Is it that bad?'

'It's pretty drastic.'

Charlotte put her hand up to her shorn scalp.

'It'll grow.' Then she sighed. 'Someone spat at me in the street.'

Gussie was her dearest friend. Forthright, no non-sense and fourteen stone, she dispensed advice and Pinot Grigio from her kitchen while a stream of children came and went demanding Pritt sticks, Pringles and reassurance, all of which she produced without turning a hair.

'You'd better come in.' Gussie opened the door wider, and Charlotte picked her way carefully through an assault course of rugby boots and dismembered Barbies into the heart of the house.

Once Gussie had unscrewed the lid on a bottle of Tanqueray and poured them each a sharpener, Charlotte felt a little calmer. She filled her friend in on the hopelessness of her predicament: the fact that Ed was undoubtedly going to do time, that they would have to sell their house, that she was out of a job. Gussie listened carefully, non-judgemental, and then replenished their glasses.

'Right,' she said, fixing Charlotte with a look that meant she knew she wouldn't like what she was about to say, but she was going to say it anyway. 'I've got a proposition. You know the Millstone?'

Charlotte nodded. Eighteen months before, Gussie's Great-aunt Flo had left Gussie and her two brothers a decrepit cottage in Withybrook, a remote village on Exmoor. It had stood empty for all that time, as they didn't have a clue what to do with it. It was too small for any of their families to holiday in, too shabby to let out, and none of them wanted to sell for sentimental reasons. So it was fondly referred to as the Millstone, as they still had to insure it and pay council tax.

'We've decided to bite the bullet and sell,' Gussie informed her with a sigh. 'We'll all come out of it with a good whack towards the school fees for the next ten years. There's no point in hanging on to it.'

'It makes sense,' agreed Charlotte. 'It's just sitting there empty.'

She knew very well that Gussie and her husband could do with the money. They never had any spare cash. Charlotte couldn't remember the last time Gussie had bought a new outfit. Not that she was a vain creature; she was quite happy to live in jeans and rugby shirts. But sometimes she saw the strain of it all on Gussie's face. She wanted to go back to work, but the children were her priority. If selling the cottage meant that Gussie could have a bit of fun, then Charlotte was all for it.

But she wasn't sure where she came in as part of the plan.

'The thing is,' Gussie went on, 'the place is a total wreck at the moment. We know it's structurally sound – Flo had a new roof put on about eight years ago, and it's been rewired. But we think we'd get a much better price if we did it up. Gave it some kerb appeal. Slapped a bit of white paint around.'

'Ah . . .' Charlotte could see where she was heading.

'Why don't you do it for us?' Gussie pulled out a sheaf of photos and spread them out on the kitchen table. 'You'd have a roof over your head. And a project. And a chance to think things over. You need some space, Charlotte.'

Charlotte chewed her lip and looked at the pictures. The cottage was sweet – made of stone, double-fronted, a typical *Play School* house with four windows and a door. But judging by the interior shots it hadn't been touched since the fifties at least. It was stuck in a time warp, and not in a good way.

'So – what's my budget?'

There was a small pause.

'Well, we've scraped around between us and we reckon we can raise five grand each . . .' Gussie gave a small gulp.

Charlotte stared at her in disbelief. Gussie had two brothers. She did the maths. A complete refurb for fifteen thousand? That was less than she usually spent on lighting. As she looked at the photos of the gloomy interior, with the nasty bricked-up fireplaces and Formica worktops and hideous wallpaper, her heart sank.

'Fifteen thousand? To do it up completely? New kitchen, new bathroom, new flooring . . . ?'

'I know, I know. But we'll give you a cut of the profit when we sell. We'll split it four ways. I know it won't be a fortune, but . . .' Gussie looked anguished, knowing what she was offering was pitiful in comparison to Charlotte's usual fee. 'It's the only way I can help you, Chaz.'

Charlotte looked at her friend and realised that Gussie couldn't even afford this lifeline. The money she was investing in the project wouldn't have been readily available; she and Will would have probably had to borrow it, no doubt from one of the other brothers who would get the interest on it ultimately. She couldn't throw this offer back in her face. And actually, what choice did she have?

But how on earth was she going to survive, stuck in the wilds of Exmoor? It was remote even for Gussie, who was a country girl at heart. But Charlotte wasn't a country mouse at all. The closest she came to the countryside was the evening race meeting at Windsor. Horses made her nervous, dogs made her cringe, mud made her recoil, grass made her sneeze. She didn't even own a pair of wellies. She was a city chick through and through.

A project like this was going to take three months at least. How would she manage? What would she do in her spare time?

But what was the alternative? She wasn't going to go back to either of her parents. Her father had enough on his plate, and her mother would go on and on until Charlotte would want to throttle her with her bare hands.

Oh God. Life was so complicated. What wouldn't she give to be Gussie? With a house that was a home,

73

not a showcase? With a divinely cuddly husband who was kind and responsible, and a raft of spirited, happy children? Who really cared about Eames chairs and Roche-Bobois modular seating and Corbusier lighting? Were you really happier if you parked your arse on a thousand pounds' worth of chrome and leather, instead of a scuffed old kitchen chair?

She put the photos down with a sigh.

'It's not as savage as you might think,' Gussie reassured her anxiously. 'It's becoming very fashionable. Lots of celebs have bolt-holes down there. Sebastian Turner's got a big pile down the road. You don't get more A-list than that.'

'The artist?' Charlotte raised an eyebrow. She'd seen a few of his paintings in some of the houses she'd been allowed in over the past few years.

'It was his parents' house. He's got a studio down there.'

Gussie was obviously eager to impart gossip, but Charlotte wasn't that interested. As far as she was concerned, the quieter it was in Withybrook the better. The likes of Sebastian Turner round the corner might mean press intrusion. Not that she was on his scale.

She fingered the photographs thoughtfully. At least Gussie's offer gave her a roof over her head. It might mean temporary exile, but by the time she finished the mud-slinging might have abated and she could venture back out in public. Who knows, Connor might even have her back.

She looked at the interior shots of the cottage and thought about possibilities. Something very washed-out that took advantage of the natural light; lots of pale grey, perhaps . . . She certainly had enough stuff stored up from over the years to dress it. Remnants of fabric and wallpaper; ornaments and pictures. She was going to have to get rid of it all otherwise; at least this way she could hang on to it for a bit longer.

She took in a shaky breath.

'Ok,' she said. 'I'll do it.'

Four

'Please, Daddy. Pleeease.'

Jade was always the spokeswoman. Amber stood behind her, eyes wide. They both looked similar, with their long brown plaits and their skinny legs stuck into lurid pink Crocs smothered in badges, but their personalities were poles apart. Jade was the negotiator, the manipulator, despite being the younger by eighteen months. Amber bobbed along in her sister's wake, more cautious, but it was the look in her eyes that made Fitch capitulate. He was putty in their hands. He always gave in eventually, which Jade knew perfectly well and exploited mercilessly.

'OK,' he relented, and he smiled as the two girls grinned at each other triumphantly and rushed off to the DVD player. He prided himself on not having to resort to television when they were with him, but they were shattered and starting to whine because they sensed that Hayley's non-appearance was making their father not so much annoyed as worried.

Once Fitch knew that she was all right, *then* he would be annoyed, because it would inevitably be lack of consideration that was delaying Hayley, not one of the hideous eventualities he was imagining as he took the lunch things out of the dishwasher and put them away. Fitch hadn't always been house proud, but now he was on his own again he was determined not to become a slob. It would be so easy not to bother and live in fetid bachelordom, with washing-up, take-away cartons and empty bottles piling up. Every time she came round, he could see Hayley mocking the fact that the house was spotless, the eyes that had once laughed with him now laughing at him as they swept their gaze over the gleaming surfaces and the neatly folded pile of tea towels. OK, so when they'd been together there had been better things to do than housework. Now, each evening stretched interminably, the hours between six and half eleven, when he usually went to bed, seeming to take up as much time as his nine-hour working day. Half an hour's cleaning and tidying each night urged the hands of the clock forward more quickly, and that, it seemed, was all it needed to make the house ready for the approval of the most pernickety household inspector.

She was supposed to be back by three. It was written in stone. It wasn't that he minded looking after his daughters – he never resented a moment with them – but the agreement was Hayley would take them back to her parents' farm, where the three of them were living, early on a Sunday afternoon so the girls had plenty of time to sort out their things for the week, wash and condition their long, brown curls, have their nails cut, check through their homework, sort out their ballet things, their gym kit, their reading bags. All the things Fitch had helped with until eight months ago. Without complaining. His speciality had been nits. He was so much more patient with the nit-comb. Hayley went at their hair like a bull at a gate, while Fitch was gentle. He didn't mind how long it took. He told them funny stories while he did it.

Sometimes, he wondered how on earth he had got here. Fitch, the Jack the Lad, the rough diamond, with his devil-may-care attitude, had found himself a family man and was surprised to find it was a role he relished.

Until it all went pear-shaped . . .

Fitch had always been a square peg in a round hole. As a child, he had suffered the ignominy of an itinerant lifestyle without the glamour of actually being a gypsy. His father was a glorified farmhand, and they went wherever the work was – fruit and vegetable picking, mostly – peas, plums, strawberries, mangles, sugarbeet. In the winter they picked holly and made wreaths to sell in the market. They lived in whatever accommodation was on offer; more often than not a ramshackle mobile home or a tumbledown cottage adjoining whichever farm they were working on. Fitch knew his father had other ways of procuring money, and that he had light fingers, which was why they were so often moved on. When he was fourteen, it seemed as if they might have settled at last when they got a council house outside Pershore, and his dad took to driving an unlicensed taxi.

Fitch didn't remember his mother ever lifting a finger to help the situation. Once a ravishing beauty, the drink had raddled her completely by the time she was forty. Her skin was a map of red broken veins, her teeth were rotting, her eyes bloodshot; but she still laboured under the delusion that she was magnetically attractive to men, because she still had her figure despite her alcohol consumption: slender legs, a trim waist and an impressive embonpoint, which she flashed to great effect in all the local pubs. She was a laughing stock, but that didn't stop the more unscrupulous taking advantage of her need to be the centre of attention.

Ironically and miraculously, Fitch was bright, very bright, at school but he did disastrously, because teachers rarely bothered to engage with him, or encourage him, largely because he didn't make it easy. He had an impregnable defence mechanism that made it difficult to communicate with him. He constantly skived and wagged off, undermining the teaching staff (whom he was often cleverer than), and narrowly escaped expulsion. All the time he was looking for a way out, but there weren't many opportunities in this rural ghetto if you had no qualifications.

At sixteen, when he was legally entitled to escape, he read and reread the local college prospectus looking for inspiration, but would have needed a gun at his head to do any of the courses on offer. Something inside told him he needed to get away: from Pershore, from his parents, from the drinking and the disappointment. He was convinced there was more to life; that one didn't have to be downtrodden and eke out a mean existence while playing the system. He had no respect for his parents. He had never received any encouragement or guidance from either of them. They'd given him no ambition, no sense that he could in any way better himself. They were happy to accept their lot, were resigned to packing up their things every three, six, nine months and moving on. They never seemed to learn by their mistakes, just repeated the pattern.

Fitch was determined to make it on his own. And as

luck would have it, he fell into a trade that suited him down to the ground. He got a job helping out a local stonemason, initially just as an extra pair of hands, but found he had stumbled upon a world he felt he belonged in. He fell in love with stone – smooth, white marble; harsh, black granite; soft, crumbling limestone – and threw himself into learning everything he could about the craft. It was hard, unforgiving work, arduous and at the mercy of the elements, as he shivered in the icy workshop or fixed headstones into the frost-hard ground in the local cemeteries. But eventually his boss saw his potential, and he was weaned off the donkey work and taught the skill. Soon, with a simple chisel he could carve the most exquisite and intricate patterns into the stone. He rented a small flat from his boss in the stonemason's yard. He didn't miss his parents, and he was pretty sure they didn't miss him, except possibly for his erstwhile financial contributions. For the first time in his life he was if not ecstatically happy, then at least content.

After three years' hard graft, he had enough money saved to put a deposit down on a tiny one-bedroom cottage in the picturesque village of Chipping Campden. He loved having his own roof over his head, four solid walls around him that no one could take away. He worked hard and he partied hard. He bought himself a hatchback Subaru, a wolf in sheep's clothing that went like shit off a shovel. He instinctively went for good-time girls and made it clear that all he wanted was no-strings sex. He appreciated beautiful women, but there wasn't room in his life for anything serious. His rugged, dark features, his impressive physique and his bad-boy aura made him an attractive proposition and he had no shortage of admirers. But no one cracked the façade, or found their way to the real Fitch. How could they, when he wasn't sure who he was himself?

Eventually, he realised that he had gone as far as he could for the firm he was with, and that there was nothing his boss could do that he couldn't. It was time for him to strike out on his own. He sold his house and gave his boss two weeks' notice. He'd searched the West Country for the right premises, and eventually bought an old bakery with an adjoining workshop in the Exmoor village of Withybrook. Then he set up in business, putting an advert in the church magazine and leaving flyers in builders' merchants.

The bread and butter of his work was headstones and memorials, but he could also turn his hand to restoration work, fireplaces and kitchen tops. He repaired façades, cornices, canopies, mullion windows, chimneys, staircases, fire surrounds, balustrading and pillars. He could produce garden ornaments, plaques, sculptures and sundials. There were often pretty women to be found in his yard, after bird baths and house signs and pastry boards. They loved to watch him work, painstakingly carving an elaborate Celtic knot with the edge of his chisel, slicing away the stone like butter. He had been pleasantly surprised to find himself inundated with work. There were, it seemed, a lot of restoration projects in the area.

His workshop was freezing, but Fitch didn't mind the cold. Besides, he worked so hard he didn't notice it. He was often seen manhandling lumps of stone off the back of his truck, with a carelessness that would make any health and safety inspector shudder. He was always covered in a layer of fine stone dust.

He quickly earned the respect of the locals, because he worked with his hands. He wasn't a typical incomer. He hadn't come down with a dream of getting away from it all, to set up some airy-fairy internet business, pushing up the local house prices. He spent all of his money locally; didn't dash off to London at the drop of a hat for social engagements or business meetings. He soon had a network of local builders and craftsmen who put work his way, and vice versa.

All in all, Fitch felt comfortable in Withybrook. It was down-to-earth, unpretentious, unspoiled, with stunning scenery and a pub that sold decent beer. He knew he would always be an outsider, but Fitch was used to not quite fitting in, not belonging. It didn't bother him in the least. He found it liberating, not having to put on a false front and pretend to be pleased to see people. He ticked over quite nicely all by himself for the first six months, grafting, doing up his house, and training Dido, the Border terrier puppy he'd been seduced into buying from a local farmer in the pub. The little dog dozed with him by the wood-burning stove he kept in his workshop, jumped in his pick-up whenever he went out on a job, then slept on his feet at night, and Fitch had to admit that it was nice to have the company, to have something else to worry about so he didn't become too introspective. Not that he was desperate for company. He felt confident that the right girl would appear eventually.

Which she did.

And now he could hear her key in the lock. He took a gulp of wine, tensed for the confrontation that was so sadly inevitable. Maybe this time it would be different . . .

But no. He could feel his hackles rise as she strode into the kitchen in her four-inch ankle boots, her white jeans impossibly tight, the leather and diamanté belt digging into her flesh. She smelled toxic, of booze and fags and hairspray and too much perfume.

'Traffic was a nightmare,' she offered by way of a perfunctory explanation, shoving her handbag on the island. 'Got stuck outside Bristol.'

She shouldn't have elaborated. It proved she was lying. Fitch had checked the traffic on the internet and there had been no problems at all on the M5.

'God, I'm knackered.' She perched on a stool and propped her head in her hands. 'Are the girls ready to go?'

Fitch peered at her. She looked appalling. He wouldn't be surprised if she was still drunk.

'You shouldn't drive back in that state,' he told her. 'Are you still over the limit?'

'You wouldn't want them for another night, would you?' she snarled back. 'You wouldn't be able to get them to school. You have to be at work by half seven. Remember?'

She didn't forgive or forget easily. Fitch always liked to start work early, to get a couple of hours in before the phone started ringing. Somehow she had misconstrued that as him not wanting to be part of the family, seemingly forgetting that he was the breadwinner.

He sighed. 'I'd have them with pleasure if it stopped you having an accident.'

She looked at him, over-plucked eyebrows archly raised.

'I thought you'd be glad if I ended up under an articulated lorry.'

'God, no!' Fitch was horrified she should think that.

'You hate me, don't you?'

He shook his head sadly. 'No, I don't hate you. If anything, I feel sorry for you.'

She laughed at that. 'You don't need to feel sorry for me,' she crowed. 'I've been treated like a princess all weekend. Anyway,' she went on, 'Kirk gave me something to keep me awake.'

Fitch frowned. 'What?'

She didn't look him in the eye. He grabbed her arm urgently.

'What's he given you?'

She gazed back at him, all innocence.

'Just a couple of cans of Red Bull.'

He didn't believe her. Not for a moment.

'If I find out you've been taking class-A drugs . . .'

She did a cruel imitation of him.

'*Class-A drugs* . . . You are such a square, Fitch.'

Fitch looked at her witheringly. He was hardly a square. He'd dabbled often enough in his youth.

'The Social Services wouldn't look very kindly on it.'

She stared at him hard. 'Is that some sort of a threat?'

'If I catch you with coke, or speed, that's the last you'll see of Jade or Amber. I promise you.'

He let go of her arm. They glared at each other. He could see that he had frightened her, as she fell quiet for a moment. He felt sick. How had it come to this?

He loathed the antagonism and the bitterness that hung heavy between them. He couldn't wait for her to go. The very scent of her was turning his stomach.

'Where are the girls?' Hayley asked eventually.

'Watching a DVD.'

'Oh dear. Standards slipping?'

Why did she have to mock him? Just because he'd told her he thought the girls watched too much television, and that he didn't approve of them watching *Hollyoaks* and *EastEnders* at their age.

'I think it's fine, when they've been outside most of the day—'

'When it suits you, you mean.'

Fitch pressed his lips together, not trusting himself to speak, and turned to put the kettle on. Hayley tossed back her hair, got up and went through into the sitting room to chivvy Jade and Amber along. Moments later they came into the kitchen in a flurry of pink, picking up their pencil cases and hairbrushes and girly stuff.

'Bye, Daddy.' Jade threw her arms round his neck and squeezed hard.

Amber followed suit, not quite so demonstrative, but she held on to him longer.

'See you both for swimming,' he told them, ruffling their hair, which they pretended to hate.

Then they were gone, and a hostile silence fell.

He stared gloomily out of the window. Where had she gone, that girl he had fallen in love with? Would she ever come back? Somehow, he didn't think so.

It was a bright, crisp November morning when he first saw her, so sharply cold it hurt your lungs. The hunt was meeting outside the Speckled Trout. Fitch wandered out of his workshop and along the road to view the spectacle. The horses gathered in the car park, prancing impatiently on the tarmac, the air rich with the scent of dung and diesel. The hounds were beetling around busily as the hunt members greeted each other and gossiped, slurping on their steaming stirrup cup. The barmaid was handing round sausage rolls. Fitch bit into one. It was proper homemade flaky pastry and it melted on his tongue.

He noticed her immediately. She was astride a seventeen-hand chestnut, her cheeks rosy, her lips red, her hair pulled back in a net. Her breeches clung to her thighs, her boots shone as bright as her eyes. Her black jacket accentuated her large breasts and her tiny waist. Fitch put out a hand to stroke the horse's neck, caressing the velvety warmth.

'She's beautiful.'

'You don't fancy riding out with us, then?'

Fitch shrugged. 'I don't have a horse. And anyway, I can't ride.'

She touched his shoulder with her crop, teasingly.

'I could sort you out a horse, if you wanted. And there're no jumps in our country. You'd just have to hold tight. I'd look out for you.'

'Thanks, but I need to stay able-bodied.'

She looked him up and down and he felt a little shiver run down his spine.

'You look that all right,' she said softly.

The horns tooted, the dogs bayed. The hunt was off. Her horse danced impatiently in front of him. She wheeled it round to follow, then called back over her

87

shoulder. 'I'll be in the Trout later. Mine's a brandy and ginger ale.'

He watched as her horse did a collected canter along the village street, and felt a quickening of his heart he hadn't experienced for a long time. It didn't take him long to find out who she was. A brief description to Norman behind the bar did the trick. Norman was the fount of all local knowledge, and she was quickly identified as Hayley Poltimore.

'She's been working for her uncle over at Tiverton,' explained Norman. 'But they fell out. So she's come back home.'

He gave Fitch a potted history. The Poltimores were one of the oldest families in Withybrook, and owned swathes of surrounding land. They had a decrepit farm at the end of the village: a thatched Devon longhouse that would once have been picturesque but had long fallen into disrepair, like a dissipated supermodel. The thatch was balding, the windows were never opened as they would fall apart at the touch, and the render was falling off in chunks, leaving the façade pockmarked. The yard was covered in cracked concrete, reigned over by a huge silage clamp smothered in car tyres and filled with wrecked cars jacked up on breeze blocks that the various Poltimore boys did up and raced around the adjoining fields, much to the despair of their long-suffering mother. Barbara Poltimore was the backbone of the village; chairwoman of the WI, clerk to the PCC, stalwart of the Neighbourhood Watch, hunt secretary and keen campanologist. She looked permanently washed out and harassed; it was rumoured that her family treated her like a slave. Her husband was a bearded monosyllabic bigot. There were four Poltimore boys and two girls. Hayley was the youngest.

'Spoiled,' warned Norman. 'Apple of her father's eye. The older sister's a lezzer and has gone off to live in Bamford. They won't have anything to do with her.'

Fitch imagined that coming out in Withybrook would be tricky.

'Hayley's not, though?' he ventured to guess.

'Hayley a lezzer?' Norman laughed darkly. 'Oh no, definitely not. Though . . .' He hesitated, obviously thinking better of what he was about to say.

'Though what?' prompted Fitch.

'Though there's not much she won't do when she's had a few.'

Norman busied himself clearing away glasses, leaving Fitch with food for thought.

Four hours later, when Hayley came in to the pub, rosy-cheeked and mud-spattered from the afternoon's sport, he pushed a glass of Remy topped up with Canada Dry along the bar top to her. He was intrigued, by her curves courtesy of the creamy milk from her parents' dairy farm, by her preposterously luscious mouth and by her merry eyes that seemed to dance a jig. She was Mariette Larkin; Bathsheba Everdene; a fulsome bucolic heroine, plump with promise. She shook her hair free from its net, and he felt lust like a lightning flash zip through his veins as her curls snaked down her white neck. He watched as she put her lips to the glass and drank thirstily. He could smell perspiration on her, mixed with a musky perfume. It was hard to tell where one began and the other finished. It made his head swim.

She set her empty glass back on the bar and smiled at him.

'So. You're the stonemason.'

He nodded in reply.

'You're from upcountry?'

Fitch had noticed that everyone referred to anything north of Tiverton as 'upcountry', as if it was another planet.

'Gloucestershire. Chipping Campden.'

Hayley shook her head. 'Never heard of it,' she pronounced, as if that meant it couldn't possibly exist. 'But welcome to Withybrook. Have you been initiated yet?'

Her eyes were laughing.

'Not as far as I know,' he replied mildly. She leaned into him.

'Oh, you'd know all right,' she breathed in his ear, and he shivered. Then she sat back and stretched her arms high in the air, yawning. 'Well, thanks for the drink. I'm going to go home now. I need a hot bath full of Radox and a change of clothes.'

Fitch felt a prickle of disappointment. He'd been enjoying her company. Then she put a hand on his arm, and he felt a tingle run right through him.

'Don't you move an inch,' she instructed. 'I'll be back as soon as I've cleaned myself up.'

He watched her move through the pub, talking and laughing with people, carelessly accepting and bestowing kisses, sliding her arm snake-like around people's necks, ignoring the inevitable pats on the bum that her skin-tight breeches invited. She had the confident nonchalance of the indigenous. This was her village, her territory and no mistake. She was probably related to half of the pub.

He sat at the bar for the next hour, hating himself for the fact that every time the door opened he glanced over to see if it was her. She reappeared at last, wearing jeans, no make-up and a tight red T-shirt that read 'I like boys but I like shopping better'. Her hair was still damp from the shower. He couldn't imagine any other woman he knew appearing in public like that and looking so completely edible. He couldn't take his eyes off her.

'What I need now,' she purred, and as she leaned in he was engulfed in the scent of Radox fumes from her bath. 'Is a Sloegasm. Have you ever had one?'

Fitch considered his reply carefully. 'No,' he ventured eventually.

'Two Sloegasms, please,' said Hayley to Norman, who proceeded to pour an inch of unctuous, incarnadine liquid into two flutes and top them up with Moët.

'Sloe gin and champagne. It's the drink of choice round here,' Hayley told Fitch, passing him a glass. 'It warms you up after a day's hunting or shooting. Gets you in the mood.'

After one sip, Fitch could quite see how it would. The liqueur gave him a boot to his stomach and the bubbles went straight to his head, resulting in a very pleasant glow and a certain amount of oblivion. After three, all he could concentrate on were Hayley's mouth and cleavage, both equally inviting.

He learned that she'd lived in the village all her life, she'd never been to London – unless you counted Heathrow, because she'd been to the Maldives and the Dominican Republic – and that she'd spent the last six months doing secretarial work for her uncle who had an egg-packing factory over Tiverton way, but she'd walked out when he became over-friendly.

'Just because he's loaded, and he's given me a job, doesn't give him the right to help himself.'

'Never mind the fact that he's your uncle.'

She laughed. 'Don't worry; he's not my blood uncle. He's married to my mum's sister. So it makes him a dirty old man, not incestuous.'

By eleven o'clock, the pub was heaving and Norman was preparing for one of his notorious lock-ins. Fitch could feel the chemistry between the two of them; the sly glances, the banter, the laughs, and, most tellingly of all, the silences all pointed in the direction of bed. But if that was where they were heading, Fitch wanted to do it on his terms, and not in public. He didn't want to be the source of speculation for the next few days. He hated gossip, particularly when he was the target. So he waited until she had gone to the loo, then slipped out into the cold night and strode up the road to his house, knowing full well that if she was interested that wouldn't be the last he saw of her . . .

In the early hours of the morning, his phone rang, starting him out of his sleep. He picked up the receiver with a smile.

'Where did you bugger off to, then?' came an indignant voice.

'Have you only just noticed?'

'I thought we were getting on well. I didn't know I was boring you.'

'You weren't boring me at all. I had to let the dog out.'

'You could have brought me with you.'

'I could.' He wondered where she was. Not still in the pub. There was no background chatter. 'So where are you now?'

'Look outside your window.'

He walked over and hooked back his curtain cautiously. The night outside was smoky-grey velvet, softly wrapping itself around the rooftops.

'I'm in the phone box.'

He looked up the street towards the post office. Sure enough, he could see the shadowy outline of a figure. It waved up to him.

'And?' he demanded, bemused.

'Come and see,' she commanded.

Fitch stood at the window for a moment, not sure what to do. He had a gut instinct that this was one of those moments where his decision would dictate his future. He let his eyes wander back to the phone box. His curiosity was going to get the better of him. He was only human, for heaven's sake.

'Give me two minutes.' His voice was husky with desire as he spoke the words, then hung up and pulled on his jeans.

She was wearing a floor-length mink coat, hold-up stockings and four-inch stilettos. He opened the door, expecting to be hit with the traditional phone-box aroma of urine and stale fags, but all he could smell was her.

She pulled him inside. He ran his hands over the soft fur.

'Not very politically correct,' he murmured.

She shrugged. 'It's not as if I went out and bought

93

it,' she replied. 'It was my grandmother's. Not wearing it isn't going to bring them back to life.'

She put her arms around his neck and pulled her to him. The warmth of her skin, the softness of the fur, the sweetness of her mouth, the dizzying scent, the claustrophobic confines of the phone box: add to all of these the fact that he hadn't had sex for nearly a year and he wasn't going to last a minute.

Hold on a minute. Sex in a phone box?

'Everyone will see,' he objected.

'Well, you'll have to be quick, then.'

She wrapped the capacious coat around the two of them and he sank into its warmth. Her warmth. It was, quite simply, bliss.

Six months later they got married. It was a proper country wedding, in the church in Withybrook, then back to the Poltimores' farm where the brood had made an enormous effort to clean the place up – the scrapped cars had vanished, every square inch of concrete was jet-washed, the fences were repaired, and although it would never merit a spread in *Country Living* it looked a thousand times more presentable. The barn was filled with hay bales and trestle tables and everyone ate pork pie and coleslaw and got totally smashed on pints of Exmoor ale and scrumpy. Fitch remembered thinking it was positively Hardy-esque: flushed wenches in low-cut frocks dancing with young men awkward in their best suits and dusty work boots. And he adored his beautiful bride, who danced with every man at the wedding but who only had eyes for him.

Less than a year later, Amber was born, followed almost indecently quickly by Jade. Fitch thought he was the happiest he'd ever been. He was delighted with his new little family, his dark-haired, round-eyed baby girls. The house became a home. He worked hard, but at the end of the day he looked forward to finishing and coming home. Marrying Hayley gave him automatic acceptance by the locals. He went out to the pub with the lads on a Thursday night, though he didn't take the piss and stay out till gone midnight like some of them. At last he had found somewhere he belonged. He knew that technically he would always be an outsider, but at least he had a place in Withybrook. He knew where he was in the pecking order. Marrying a Poltimore meant he was higher up than some people who had been born and bred in the village. He enjoyed his status, his work, and being a husband and father. He figured he'd worked out the equation at long last. It was as if his past had never happened. He blotted it out of his memory. He was living for the present.

But his contentment was to be short-lived. It soon became apparent that motherhood didn't suit Hayley one bit. She put on weight, lost her spark, became sulky and resentful and found even the most menial of tasks beyond her capabilities. She'd stopped hunting after her mare had been put down two years ago. She could barely be bothered to cook, just chucked unidentifiable frozen food into the deep-fat fryer every evening. Fitch found himself taking over the catering, getting up extra early to put a casserole into the slow cooker before he left. He didn't want to argue with her, or put his foot down, or make unreasonably sexist demands. It was easier to do it himself. Meanwhile, Hayley plummeted further into a deep fug of sluttishness, chain-smoking John Player Specials which one of her brothers got off the back of a lorry and watching endless daytime telly. Fitch hit the roof when he got the phone bill and realised she had been calling prime-time competition numbers.

'It's the only chance I've got,' she shouted, 'of anything exciting happening to me.'

As he looked at her, her hair now lank, her skin lacklustre, her eyes bloodshot, the realisation came to him. She'd seen him as a way out. Whereas he'd seen her as a way in. And the fact that he seemed to so enjoy the way of life in Withybrook that she was hoping to escape seemed to enrage her.

'I'm trapped!' she screamed at him one night. 'Fuck-ing trapped in this God-forsaken place.'

'You've got no idea how lucky you are,' Fitch fired back, but he knew he couldn't convince her.

He thought she'd turned the corner when she decided to go beating with the local shoot. It was the beaters' job to stride through the rough flushing the birds out for the guns to take aim. Fitch was pleased. Beating was tough work but good fun and would get Hayley out of the house; get her some fresh air, as well as giving her a social life. It would give her something to think about.

Perhaps too much to think about. The strenuous exercise meant the weight fell off her, and she enjoyed the social side of it so much that she frequently didn't come back till gone midnight, having followed the other beaters and loaders back to the Speckled Trout for liquid sustenance. And then one day she met Kirk Lambert, who belonged to the shooting syndicate and had caught sight of her inviting cleavage during lunch.

With his shaved head and his thick neck and his

dark glasses, his top-of-the-range Range Rover and shiny, shiny new shotguns, Kirk represented everything Fitch loathed. Conspicuous consumption, status symbols, disregard for everyone who didn't treat him as if he was the dog's bollocks. Kirk was an ex-boxer who now had a string of what he called 'elf' clubs. Fitch had a mental image of a gym full of pixies and leprechauns. Hayley told him he shouldn't laugh, because Kirk was loaded. Beyond loaded.

He could see she was hooked. The weeks Kirk came shooting, she became effervescent, spending hours on her appearance before venturing out in her tightest jeans underneath the wax jacket and Dubarry boots that were prescribed beating gear. And although the shoot was incredibly feudal, and the guns didn't really mix with the beaters, it didn't seem to bother Kirk. Fitch reasoned he was the type who didn't care who he got his leg over; he was the sort who would happily fork out for a private dance in a lap-dancing club and would think it a fair transaction. But Hayley, poor, naïve Hayley, who was clearly on a quest for something that was never going to make her any happier, couldn't see that Kirk was morally bankrupt. His actual bank balance blinded her to the fact.

Fitch felt sad. Incredibly sad. He knew he was going to lose her. He tried his best to stop it happening, but he knew that, at this point in her life, he wasn't what she wanted. After all, he'd seen it before with his mother. His feckless, dissatisfied, slattern of a mother, who blamed everyone else for her unhappiness, who had slept with every other Sunday fisherman on the banks of the river Severn in the hope of finding escape. She'd trawled the riverbanks in her too-short denim skirt, her tanned freckled breasts bursting out of skimpy tops she might as well not bother with. Fitch's father had known what she got up to only too well, but had tolerated her behaviour with a lugubrious passivity because it had been his own fault, for being a loser, for not earning enough for them to buy their own house, for not having a flash enough car.

Fitch knew all about unsatisfied women, and how they nearly always came to a sticky end.

'Hayley,' he pleaded, 'I'm begging you not to go near him. Not because of me, but because he'll hurt you.'

She just rolled her eyes and gave him a look that said it all. The next time she went beating, she didn't come home, and didn't even attempt to apologise for the fact that she had spent the night in Kirk's hotel room when she eventually turned up.

Fitch didn't put up a fuss. He figured it was best for her to get it out of her system. He was confident that Kirk would show his true colours before long. All that concerned him was that Jade and Amber were looked after and kept happy and secure and had no inkling of the hideous cracks in their marriage. So he didn't rock the boat. He felt sure it was a phase.

It wasn't. Hayley professed herself in love with Kirk, declared their marriage over and insisted on moving out of the house and back to her parents' farm. Fitch was accepting, until he realised that she intended to take Jade and Amber with her. She broke his heart the day they all left, but somehow she managed to make him feel that it was his fault. That he had in some way neglected her. Fitch was bewildered. How had he become the enemy, when he had done nothing but support her? It didn't occur to him that perhaps she didn't like herself very much, that she knew her behaviour was appalling, and that Fitch's tolerance only made her feel more unworthy, and that was why she was leaving.

Every weekend she dropped the children off with him after school so she could drive full-pelt up to Kirk's place. During the weeks she didn't bother with her appearance, but she clearly spent all day Friday on it. On Sunday nights she returned, her skin pasty, her eyes swollen and her breath smelling of stale booze and cigarettes. They had got used to the routine. To her credit, she wasn't usually late, which was why he had been so concerned when she hadn't turned up on time.

Fitch sighed and looked at the kitchen clock. Another two hours till opening time. He'd go down to the Trout, have a couple of beers and maybe a game of darts. He slumped onto the sofa and put his head back on a cushion. He'd shut his eyes for ten minutes. He always felt exhausted after a confrontation with Hayley. Dido jumped on his lap and he scratched between her ears. He should have stuck to being a loner with just his dog for company, he thought ruefully. But then, he wouldn't have had his girls, his beautiful girls. Frankly, they were all he lived for these days.

Five

Charlotte prayed that her truck didn't give up the ghost while she was crossing the moor. She had no idea where she was, or how far away Withybrook might be. The last sign had clearly stated three miles, yet she was sure she must have driven at least six since then. She'd passed nothing that might give her a clue as to her whereabouts. Just miles and miles of bleak, scrubby, dun-coloured moorland that stretched as far as the eye could see. It was, allegedly, an area of outstanding natural beauty, but Charlotte shuddered as she took in its relentless emptiness. Dramatic, maybe, but beautiful? She was yet to be convinced, although to be fair she wasn't in the most forgiving of moods and the sulky grey sky wasn't doing the landscape any favours.

There had been times in the last few months when Charlotte had thought she was going to go under, and if it hadn't been for the stalwart Gussie, bolstering her up, then she might well have lost the will to carry on. The stress had been huge. She'd blanked most of it out of her mind, but it had been a living nightmare. The house had been sold, to pay back the charity – at least Ed had been gentleman enough to insist on that straight away. But there had been nothing left, once they had paid the debt, and the mortgage, and the legal fees. All their years of hard work, evaporated into nothing. Then there was the trial. Charlotte had stayed away. She'd had no desire to see Ed in the dock, or listen to him being sentenced, or to have her photo taken as she left. Two years, he'd got, though he'd probably be out in six months.

In the meantime, Charlotte had hidden in Gussie's attic, virtually a recluse, although Gussie had tried to drag her to the cinema, to the gym. Finally, she had felt strong enough to take on Gussie's project. She needed a clean slate, to start again. After all, she had her entire self to rebuild. There was nothing left of her former life or identity. She was just an empty shell.

And so here she was. The journey had taken her twice as long as she expected, as she had barely been able to urge the truck past sixty on the motorway. She'd bought the tired old pick-up for two hundred quid off the car dealer down the road. It had six months' tax and MOT left, but after that it would be ready for the dump. At that price she could afford to run it into the ground and then chuck it away, but in the meantime it would be perfect for trips to the builders' merchants. If there were builders' merchants on Exmoor. She hadn't seen a shop of any description for the past thirty miles.

Or a garage. She eyed the petrol gauge warily. It was hovering just below a quarter. She prayed it didn't suddenly plummet and show empty. She hadn't brought a petrol can. You didn't bother with petrol cans when you lived in London, not when there was a garage on every other street corner. But now she wished she'd put her Girl Guide head on, and packed a blanket and a Thermos and a packet of chocolate biscuits into the bargain. If she ran out of fuel and was stranded here, it could be weeks before she was found. She imagined herself being discovered by a passing sheep farmer, stiff at the wheel.

Finally she saw a sign that told her Withybrook was only half a mile, and she felt suffused with relief. She was desperate for a wee, a cup of tea, and to stretch her legs. The truck rumbled over a cattle grid that signalled they were leaving the national park, and Charlotte felt comforted by the sight of ranks of trees assembling at the side of the road. Civilisation, she felt sure, was nigh.

As if to welcome her, a watery sun began to push its way through the cloud cover, which wearily stepped to one side as if it had become too weak to resist. She passed an isolated farmhouse, and imagined a weather-beaten shepherd and his red-cheeked wife taking tea by an inglenook fireplace. As she rounded a corner, the misty horizon boasted a line of ancient pollarded oaks crowning the heathland. The sun finally burst through the remaining clouds, lighting up the land-scape. The colours were extraordinary: donkey brown, khaki and burned orange – a palette that no interior designer worth his or her salt would propose, but that worked to dramatic effect when set against the bruised pinks and purples of the late-afternoon sky. As the road dipped down she was overjoyed to see a sign proclaiming Withybrook. She went over a medieval stone bridge, holding her breath as she negotiated its narrowness, not yet used to the pick-up's width. A shallow river burbled away underneath, the water rushing over the fat stones in a hurry to get some-where.

Just past the bridge was the village cricket pitch, then the line of houses that made up Withybrook began, grey stone edifices squaring up to their opposite neighbours, some standing upright, square and tall, some slumped as if the effort was too much, their rooflines sagging dispiritedly. Her expert eye could tell the houses that had been purchased by out-of-towners, their front doors sporting National Trust estate paint in muted tones of grey, green and cream. Others had committed the cardinal sin of succumbing to double-glazing salesmen, their windows ripped out and re-placed with UPVC. No doubt the owners gave thanks repeatedly for the warmth and protection they gave from the bitter moorland winds, not caring that they had ripped the heart and soul out of their homes.

As she carefully negotiated a sharp bend, a car came flying round the corner. Charlotte had to slam on the brakes and swerve to the left to avoid a collision. The other driver wound her window down. A girl with a pale face and a mane of dark, straightened hair glared out. Two small children peered over her shoulder from the back seat.

'Look where you're fucking going!'

Charlotte opened her mouth to defend herself, but the girl threw her car into first gear and raced off. Shaking, she put her hand on the ignition key to restart the car, which had stalled. She was only two inches away from the wall of the house she had been passing. Did people always drive like that round here? she wondered She'd have to be more careful in future.

The engine didn't respond to her coaxing. The truck seemed to have died completely. She tried again and again, feeling more and more desperate. She jumped as someone tapped sharply on the window.

'You're flooding it.' A pair of rheumy, bloodshot eyes gazed at her from an unshaven face. It was an old man dressed entirely in sludge green from head to toe; a jaunty piece of baler twine around his waist. 'You sit and wait there while I let the cows go past. It'll be all right in a minute.'

Charlotte smiled her thanks and sat in the truck nervously. A moment later she was surrounded by a sea of black and white as a herd of dairy cows swarmed round her and made their way majestically up the little high street, hips swaying, udders swinging like chandeliers. They walked obediently to the top and disappeared through a gate, followed by their master. Moments later it was as if they'd never been there.

Tentatively, Charlotte switched on the engine, and it sprang into life. Relieved, she made her way slowly along the street, her eyes peering in the half-light as she tried to find Myrtle Cottage.

There it was. Halfway along, tucked a little way back off the main drag like a shy wallflower. It looked tired and weary, but its proportions were pleasing, it was in keeping with its neighbours, and best of all it had the benefit of a cobbled area in front where Charlotte could park her truck. She got out just as the sun retreated bashfully back behind the clouds, its duty as official greeter now over, and the rain began to fall.

The air smelled of wood-smoke, and the sweet scent of dairy cattle, and wet tarmac. The wind buffeted her and teased her hair. The rain lashed sideways. Charlotte felt in her pocket for the big key that Gussie had given her. Her fingers closed around the cold iron as she looked up and down the high street. It was still and silent, no sign of life, and she wondered if she had imagined the cows. Only the evidence of several gently steaming khaki pats convinced her she hadn't been hallucinating.

She pushed back the hair from her eyes, shivering. It had been sweatshirt weather when she left this morning; now she needed her thermal underwear and duck-down anorak, which were packed away in the back of the truck somewhere. Gussie had warned her Withy-brook would probably be a few degrees colder, but she hadn't mentioned icy blasts from the tundra.

It wasn't too late to turn round and drive back to London. If it wasn't for the fact that she wasn't sure she had enough petrol to get to the nearest garage, she would have leaped into the driver's seat and driven hell for leather out of Withybrook, across the moor and back to the bright lights.

Catkin pulled back the curtain and peered out of the drawing-room window. She was relieved to see head-lights making their way up the drive. Tommy Yeo was bang on time, and so he should be. It wasn't often that a taxi driver had a new car bought for him. Sebastian and Catkin were his best clients, but she couldn't bear the stifling squalor of his ancient Renault Scenic any longer, so she'd subsidised his purchase of a smart Chrysler Grand Voyager with leather seats and blacked-out windows. In return, he ferried Catkin back and forth from the station in Tiverton, as well as the Turners' many guests when they came to stay for the weekend. There were things Tommy had seen in the back of the car that you wouldn't believe, but he kept his mouth shut. Until he'd worked for the Turners, the mainstay of his work had been taking old ladies to the supermarket and the odd airport run. He knew which side his bread was buttered all right.

Tommy jumped out of the car to open the door for Catkin, taking her cases off the step and loading them into the back. She smiled gratefully and slid into the back seat.

'Thanks, Tommy,' she breathed as she sank into the soft leather, then leaned forward to wave at Sebastian who'd appeared at the front door.

Catkin hated Sunday nights. Leaving Sebastian made her nervous, but she had little option since the show she worked for had upped her appearance from twice a week to every day. She couldn't afford not to do it. Correction, they couldn't afford for her not to do it. The truth, which Catkin knew only too well and Sebastian chose to ignore, was that they were struggling financially. Despite her career and Sebastian's success, it didn't take long to blast through the money they had. Keeping a flat in London was bleeding them dry. The travelling up and down was exorbitant, and was at her own expense, because it was her choice to go back to Devon every weekend and she had to travel first class. Then there was her wardrobe, the hair, the beauty treatments. Sebastian's studio had cost an arm and a leg, because Catkin had spared no expense in the hope of creating an environment where he could be productive, and everything had to be just so. He had protested that he would be just as happy in the old barn as it had been, but Catkin had got the bit between her teeth. Quarter of a million pounds later he had forty by thirty foot of bright light, with a state-of-the-art sound system on which he could play Iggy Pop or Rachmaninov, a kitchen and a wet room. There were racks and racks of gleaming tubes of paint flown in from New York, sable brushes as fine as an eyelash and as thick as a fox's tail; banks of blank canvasses. She was furious that he absolutely refused to allow any magazines or newspapers to come and do a feature on it, but if Sebastian prized anything it was his privacy. Then there had been last year's tax bill, which neither of them had anticipated being so large.

So there had been no question of her turning down her contract with *Hello, England*. And now her shooting schedule had become so hectic that they had no hope of seeing each other during the week. She hated leaving Sebastian to his own devices, but there was little harm he could come to in Withybrook. In London, he would find a million and one distractions – a poker school, a billiard hall, a bar, a club, a party. And besides, Catkin paid Stacey, their housekeeper, good money to look after him and keep an eye out. Stacey was under strict instructions to phone Catkin if she felt there was anything amiss.

She didn't like controlling Sebastian like this, but he didn't seem to have any self-discipline. She suspected it was the way he had been brought up. His parents had been loving, but over-indulgent. Not like Catkin's mother and father, who had been dry, dusty academics. Her mother had left the marital home when Catkin was just thirteen. Not for another man, but for a prestigious job in an American university. Catkin had fended for herself and her distant father; had left school as soon as she could and had steadfastly refused to have anything to do with further education as a rebellion against her parents' obsession with academia. And she thought she'd done pretty well for herself, all things considered. She wasn't quite a household name, but she had begun to be recognised wherever she went.

She flipped open the lid of her laptop and started reading through the script the producer had sent her for the next day. It was dreadful – verbose and patronising. She started going through her lines, rewriting them in her own style, adding in a few humorous observations so that she didn't seem too intense and worthy. After all, she was supposed to come across as a big sister, not a social worker.

By the time they reached the motorway, Catkin was totally absorbed in her work and had forgotten Sebastian altogether.

Charlotte stood on the doorstep of Myrtle Cottage and gave herself a severe talking to. She'd been given a way out of her sticky situation and she wasn't to wimp out at the first opportunity. She slid the key into the lock and turned it, praying that the wood of the door wouldn't have warped. But it opened easily, and she stepped inside.

The smell hit her immediately: a combination of damp, cat pee and the stale, lingering scent of . . . death? Something sickly sweet and cloying. Charlotte hastily put out her hand to flick on the light switch.

Nothing.

Shit. Gussie had assured her that the electricity was still connected, but she had warned her that Withybrook was prone to impromptu power cuts, particularly in inclement weather. So no doubt the house was fused. Charlotte tried to remember from the floor plans she'd been given where the fuse box was. In the kitchen, which was at the back of the house. She peered down the gloomy hall, disconcerted to find she was too scared to go any further. She wasn't usually highly strung, but the house had been empty for some time, she was on her own and as far as she could make out there was no one around she could call on for help except the ancient farmer. What if there was a squatter, or a corpse?

There was nothing for it but to go back out to the car and find her torch. Luckily she'd packed it near the top. Feeling slightly more secure with its powerful beam, she swallowed her fear and inched down the corridor until she found the kitchen. A quick inspection revealed the fuse box, and she heaved the heavy black switch back up. There was an encouraging clunk and the light came on, a weedy twenty-watt glow that made the house even more tenebrous. The first thing she would do, she decided, was change all the light bulbs.

She thought she would give Gussie a ring and tell her she had arrived safely. She was the only person who would care, and Charlotte wanted to hear a friendly voice. She looked at her mobile. No signal. Not even one tiny bar. With a heavy heart, she turned to head back out to the car and get her luggage, then stopped in her tracks. Right in the middle of the kitchen, scrutinising her with its beady eyes, was an enormous black rat.

She didn't even stop to shut the front door. She ran down the high street as fast as her feet would carry her, imagining the rat following, teeth bared, eyes gleaming.

She flung herself against the double doors of the pub, pushing at the handle desperately, but it was locked. She stood back, choking a stifled sob, and realised there was someone standing behind her.

It was a tall man, six foot three at least. His hair was long and dark, and reached to his broad shoulders. He was wearing a padded blue lumberjack shirt and combat trousers. He gave her a disconcerted smile.

'Let me,' he said, and she felt his deep voice rumble through her.

He put his hand out to the other handle, and the door opened easily. She'd been pushing at the wrong one.

'Are you all right?' He looked at her, concerned.

'There was a rat,' she stammered. 'In the kitchen. I can't go back in. Do you know if they do bed and breakfast here?'

'Not as far as I know.' He looked her up and down. 'You're shaking.'

Charlotte took in a deep breath to calm herself down. She knew she was on the verge of tears.

'Sorry.' She managed a smile. 'I must look a total idiot. I've only just got here. And the first thing I see . . .'

'Not the greatest of welcomes. I can understand that.' He put a hand in the small of her back and guided her into the pub. 'Let me get you a drink. For the shock.'

He settled her at the bar and bought her a large gin and tonic.

'Now wait there,' he commanded. 'I won't be long.'

Charlotte finished her drink in half a dozen gulps as she took in her surroundings. The pub was warm and cosy, with a flagstone floor and dark red walls sporting landscapes by local artists and photos of the regulars embroiled in jolly japes. All around the bar were the decapitated heads of some malevolent-looking furry creatures with sharp teeth and bright eyes. Otters? Could they be otters? People didn't decapitate otters, did they? She shuddered slightly, then noticed one of them was sporting a beret and a pair of sunglasses, which made her smile and made the whole thing less sinister.

The chalked-up menu looked enticing: steak and mushroom pie, lamb shanks, baked trout. She thought she might come back later and have supper here. She'd packed a few things from Waitrose, but she wanted something hot and nourishing that someone else had cooked.

There was a large framed Ordnance Survey map on the wall near the bar, and she wandered over to take a look. The glass was smeary with fingerprints; it had obviously been put up for the benefit of walkers rather than locals. She found Withybrook quickly, and the large scale of the map allowed her to get the lie of the land more than the cursory glance she had given it on her atlas. The rocky North Devon coast was about two miles away; the small town of Comberton about four, and Bamford, which according to Gussie boasted a railway station, a cinema *and* a Marks and Spencer, was about ten miles inland. Between Withybrook and supposed civilisation were acres and acres of the sludge green that represented Exmoor, peppered with the occasional hamlet. Charlotte quailed at this evidence of just how remote she was.

She turned to find her rescuer standing behind her with a tiny, wire-haired dog under his arm.

'This is Dido,' he said, which made Charlotte realise she hadn't introduced herself properly. She reached out to give Dido a scratch between the ears.

'I'm Charlotte, by the way,' she offered. 'Charlotte Dixon.'

She used her maiden name, her professional name. She had already decided that she couldn't risk calling herself Charlotte Briggs. Too many people might have read the articles.

'Fitch.' He smiled and held out his hand to formalise their introduction.

'Fitch?' She frowned. Was that his first name or his last?

He nodded. 'Just plain Fitch.'

She took his hand, and her paw felt very tiny in his grasp.

'Come on, then,' he said. 'Show me the offending rodent.'

Slightly anaesthetised by her gin and tonic, she led him up the street to Myrtle Cottage and showed him in, following behind with trepidation. For twenty minutes, Charlotte stood shivering in the hall, while behind the kitchen door she could hear Fitch's murmurs of encouragement and Dido's excited yaps. Eventually they emerged looking triumphant.

'They've been nesting in your larder, getting in through the airbrick,' he explained. 'I've blocked it up, so they won't be able to get back in.'

'Have they all gone?'

'Oh yes,' Fitch assured her, pointing to Dido, who was happily lying on her back in the hall waving her legs in the air. 'She wouldn't be doing that if there were any still around.'

Charlotte looked at the heavy weight in the bottom of Fitch's sack, and imagined the oily grey corpses.

'What will you do with them?' she asked, swallowing down her disgust.

'Burn 'em,' he said matter-of-factly.

'I don't know how to thank you.'

'You're all right,' he said. 'Beats watching *Heartbeat*.'

He smiled, and immediately his rather stern features softened.

'You bought this place then?' he asked. 'Didn't know it was on the market.'

'I'm doing it up for a friend,' Charlotte explained. 'She wants to sell it. I'm an interior designer.'

He raised one of his thick, dark eyebrows.

'Shouldn't go too mad,' he said. 'They won't appreciate it down here.'

'Are you . . . not from round here then?'

'My wife is, born and bred. But I'm from *away*.' He gave the word a heavy irony. 'Only Gloucestershire, but it might as well be Timbuktu.'

'Oh. Are they that bad about outsiders, then?'

'No, no, no – they're fine, as long as you don't try to rock the boat, or change anything. Or start any anti-bloodsports campaigns. And I wouldn't recommend marrying in.'

'Don't worry,' said Charlotte hastily. 'I'm not here to look for a husband.'

Fitch looked at her, rather puzzled, and she felt perhaps she had loaded her comment rather too much. Her voice went up an octave, as it always did when she was nervous. She smiled at him, eyes wide with innocence.

'I'm young, free and single, and I intend to stay that way.'

'Fair enough,' he said, and she felt embarrassed. She'd have to learn to play it cool if she wasn't going to blow her cover.

'Thank you so much for helping me,' she went on. 'I don't know what I'd have done if you hadn't.'

'No problem.' He clicked his fingers to attract Dido's attention. 'Just give me a shout if you have any more unwanted visitors.'

He let himself out, and the two of them melted away into the shadows.

Charlotte stood in the doorway for a moment, watching them go. She felt the urge to call him back. She didn't want to face the cold emptiness of the house. She was going to be incarcerated here for the next few months, and she knew already that she had made a dreadful mistake. But where else could she go?

She took in a deep breath to steel herself. She'd confront her fear, find the heating and put it on, get her things in from the car, then go back down to the pub for a meal and a large glass of red wine.

An hour and a half later she was feeling a little better about things. Once she'd turned the central heating on, the house heated up quickly. Gussie and her brothers had cleared out most of the old lady's detritus, but had left behind the better furniture, so there were tables and chairs, a sofa and a bed, which Charlotte made up with her best linen sheets and goose-down duvet. She unpacked her clothes and put them in the wardrobe, put the food she had brought into the fridge, and decided to leave everything else in the back of the truck for tomorrow. She put her digital radio in the kitchen, and once she'd found a decent jazz station and the syncopated notes poured out into the emptiness, the house felt less threatening. She decided to leave a full inspection until the morning. Everything would look better in the light of day.

At seven o'clock she decided to venture back down to the Speckled Trout in search of sustenance. She kept her jeans on, but put on her favourite cable-knit cashmere sweater, knotted a Georgina von Etzdorf scarf round her throat, and put on some pale pink lipgloss. She didn't want to look overdressed, like some fancy out-of-towner, but making an effort to look nice was part of her default.

The pub was virtually empty when she went in. Apart from the barman, there was just one lone figure sitting at the bar: a boy, with a mop of dishevelled dirty blonde hair, wearing skinny jeans, Converse trainers, and a V-neck jumper that looked as if it had shrunk in the wash. From a distance, he looked like a fourteen-year-old in need of a good meal. But as he looked up at her and met her eyes, Charlotte saw a bleakness that no fourteen-year-old could summon up. He gave her a wintry smile and looked back down into his glass.

Feeling slightly self-conscious, she ordered some food and went to sit down at a small table for two near the huge inglenook fireplace. There was a merry blaze, and soon she felt the warmth defrosting her bones. While she waited, several people came in and ordered drinks, and went to sit on their own. Sunday night, it seemed, was a time of solitary contemplation: the time when all the fun of the weekend was over but the hurly-burly of the week hadn't yet started. A time of reflection and resolution.

Her steak and mushroom pie duly arrived. It had a thyme pastry topping, and came with buttery carrots and new potatoes and crunchy mange touts. She felt strengthened by the fare, and went back up to the bar to order another glass of wine and a pudding.

'Lemon sponge, please,' she told the barman. 'And another glass of red wine.'

The boy at the bar slid his own glass across the counter.

'And another in there, when you're ready, Norman.'

He ran his hands through his hair in what was obviously a nervous habit. His knuckles were raw, the nails ragged and bitten, and the skin looked chapped and angry. He turned to look at Charlotte, scrutinising her warily.

'You're not from round 'ere, are you?' he asked Charlotte in a cod West Country accent.

'Is it that obvious?'

'You're not in the obligatory fleece. And you're wearing lipstick.' He leaned into her confidentially. 'The sheep are more enticing than most of the women in Withybrook.'

Charlotte wasn't sure how to respond.

'Are you?' she managed eventually. 'From round here, I mean?'

He picked up his replenished glass.

'My parents bought a place here in the sixties. I went to the village school till I was eight. And the locals still view me with suspicion.'

Charlotte took a gulp of her wine. She felt unnerved, as if she was about to receive some portentous warning not to stray off the path.

'Oh,' was all she could think of in reply.

'Sorry.' He gave her a rueful smile. 'I'm not trying to put you off. I've had too much too drink. As usual. Call it the Sunday-night blues. My wife's gone back up to London and I'm faced with the prospect of a week in my own company.'

He mimed putting a gun into his mouth and pulling the trigger.

Now she was up close, Charlotte could see fine lines at the corners of his eyes. He was much older than she'd first thought. Definitely over thirty. Not a boy, at any rate.

'What does your wife do, then?'

'She's an agony sister. Like an agony aunt, only younger and hipper. Talks about clitoral piercing and Facebook stalkers. It's just a pity she doesn't know how to repair the cracks in her own marriage,' he added bitterly.

'Too much information!' Norman the barman intervened. 'I'm sure the young lady doesn't want to know all this.'

For reply, Charlotte's new acquaintance slid his glass back for another refill. Norman looked at it askance, but picked it up nevertheless.

'So. What brings you to sunny Withybrook?'

'I'm doing up a house.'

He nodded knowingly. 'Pushing up the prices so the locals can't afford to buy?'

Charlotte was starting to get annoyed. 'No. Just hoping to get a fair price for my clients.'

'You'll be lucky.'

Charlotte turned away, wishing that Norman would hurry up with her lemon pudding. This bloke was obnoxious, bordering on unbearable. And he didn't need any more to drink – he was already swaying slightly on his bar stool. And he had that disrespect for personal space that only comes from a surfeit of alcohol. He was leaning into her again . . .

'What's your name, then?' he asked.

'Charlotte,' she told him slightly reluctantly, not sure if she wanted to venture any further on this relationship.

'Charlotte.' He savoured her name appreciatively, then held out his hand. 'Sebastian. Turner.'

'Hello.' Of course. Now she twigged. Gussie had mentioned that he lived down here, and on closer inspection Charlotte recognised him from photographs and chat shows. And that explained his raw, chapped hands – oil paint and turpentine. And his wife was Catkin Turner. Charlotte had seen her on morning television occasionally, when she'd been at home nursing a cold.

'Welcome to Withybrook,' he carried on. 'I'm sure you'll be very happy here. As long as you fit into one of the categories.'

'Which are?'

Sebastian counted carefully on his fingers. 'There're four, roughly. Category One is the landowners and farmers. Mingy bastards for the most part. Tight as a mouse's ear. And they don't like change. Spend their lives killing things and counting their money. Category Two is the posh, potty brigade who flutter round the vicar and organise coffee mornings and open their gardens to the public once a year. Then Three is the incomers, who've bought down here cheaply in the hope of living the dream, but who are rapidly getting pissed off and now can't get out. Finally, Category Four is the great indigenous unwashed with their delinquent youths, who go round joyriding and sniffing glue and dropping illegitimate babies.'

Charlotte raised her eyebrows. 'You don't paint a pretty picture.'

Sebastian narrowed his eyes. 'No. Well, behind all the scenery, it's not awfully pretty. Despite what the Sunday papers might tell you.'

Charlotte considered his reply. 'So which category are you?'

'We don't fit in. We're the token bit of local colour. Minor celebs, eccentric, more money than sense. Dabble in lots of wife-swapping and drug-taking.'

'You're winding me up,' said Charlotte.

'I'm just repeating what the locals say. It's a bloody hard reputation to live up to, I'm telling you.'

'I can imagine,' replied Charlotte drily.

'What about you? Nice-looking bit of posh totty moves down here on her own? There's got to be history.'

Charlotte felt panic rise in her throat. This was the first time she had been challenged about her reasons for being here. And she sensed Sebastian wasn't the type to be fobbed off. She could feel him observing her, with his painter's eye, looking for clues, for details.

'I needed a change. And a challenge. And some time out.'

'So. You've come here to find yourself?'

Charlotte considered his interpretation. 'Maybe.'

Her voice must have sounded very small, because Sebastian suddenly looked guilt-stricken.

'Hey. Listen. Tell me to fuck off and shut up. I just live in the perpetual hope that someone is having a harder time than I am.'

'Are you having a hard time, then?'

'On paper, I'm the luckiest man alive. I've got the Midas touch, a stunning successful wife, a house most people would kill for . . .'

'But?'

'Living everyone else's dream is a bloody nightmare,' Sebastian admitted gloomily.

Norman came over and wiped the counter with a cloth.

'Sebastian isn't happy unless he's suicidal,' he informed Charlotte, with the air of someone who had listened to this diatribe every Sunday night for years.

'Nobody understands how difficult it is.'

'Being the tortured artist?' ventured Charlotte. 'I should think it's hell.'

'Really?' said Sebastian, looking at her with renewed interest. 'You're about the only person who does, then. Everyone else thinks it's a doddle, slapping a bit of paint around.'

'A blank canvas? All that expectation? Knowing you're only as good as your last piece of work and that your next one's got to be better?' Charlotte shook her head in disagreement.

Sebastian narrowed his eyes. 'Are you taking the piss?'

'No, I'm not,' she retorted stoutly. 'You must be under terrible pressure. And I know exactly how you feel. Everyone thinks all I do is faff about with paint samples and curtain swatches.' Oh God. She was saying too much. She'd drunk far more than she was used to. She better be careful or she'd start spilling her life story. But she was into her stride. 'Someone once said to me I was just good at choosing!' she went on indignantly. 'Nobody understands that you're trying to recreate somebody's dream *and* bring it in on budget. It's not easy.' She put a hand on Sebastian's arm. 'So I totally sympathise. They haven't got a clue.'

Norman shot her a warning glance. 'Don't pander to him. You'll only make him worse.'

But it was too late. Sebastian was already hanging on her every word.

Fitch had slung the sack of dead rats into his workshop, ready to burn the next morning, then went inside to make a beef sandwich out of the remains of Sunday's roast.

He knew the whole village would already be speculating about his mercy mission. They would feign disinterest in front of Charlotte, of course. But behind the kitchen curtains they would be chewing over every little morsel of detail. You could bet by now her registration would already be being checked on the police computer by someone's cousin who worked at the station in Bamford.

Fitch had felt it his duty to come to her rescue. There was no way of knowing which way the inhabitants of Withybrook would jump, whether they would choose to co-operate or simply stand back and watch her suffer. He could see she was terrified, and he didn't want to watch her being toyed with by the locals. They had known better than to mess him about when he arrived, but a naïve city girl like Charlotte would be perfect bait.

It had certainly given him something else to think about. He had been heading to the pub to drown his sorrows, so a bit of rat-catching had been a welcome distraction. He hadn't really wanted to go and get drunk. There had been a time in his life, in his mid-teens, when the answer to everything seemed to lie at the bottom of a can of Tennant's Extra, so Fitch knew that he had a weakness for alcohol, that it could easily take over his life, just as it had taken over his parents'.

The temptation to drink himself into oblivion was always particularly sharp on a Sunday. He was worried sick about Hayley. Correction, he was worried sick about Jade and Amber being in her care. When did a mother start becoming unfit? he wondered. When she began to put herself first, which Hayley undeniably did? He knew the girls would be looked after at the farm. Barbara would make sure they were fed properly (if you counted crispy pancakes as food) and their clothes washed and ironed. But it wasn't a healthy environment. The house, despite Barbara's best efforts, was a tip. The dogs – two collies, an Alsatian and a fluctuating number of rescued greyhounds – had the run of the house and shed their hairs everywhere. The sink was always piled high with washing-up, and even when you picked a clean cup out of the cupboard it was stained with tea or coffee rings and was slightly greasy. There was no proper heating, just a motley collection of night storage heaters and open fires, and Fitch was petrified that a blaze would break out one day: being thatched, it would gallop through the building with little hope of survivors. There definitely

123

weren't any smoke alarms. And the room the girls were sharing was damp, with two outside walls and rotten windows that the wind howled through. They might be the biggest landowners in the area, but the Poltimores lived in squalour.

How best to extricate Jade and Amber from the situation had been bothering him for weeks now. He had to tread very carefully. He knew they weren't in any real danger, but it wasn't the life he wanted for his daughters. And if he went steaming in, the Poltimores would close ranks. Hayley would make life as difficult for him as she could. He knew he only had the girls at the weekends because it suited her to be able to dump them and go to see Kirk, but she could soon make it difficult for him to have access just to spite him.

He still didn't know why she was so incredibly volatile these days. A result, no doubt, of guilt, tiredness and over-stimulation. Fitch couldn't reason with her, or get her to see that this was not the ideal way to bring up children. Barbara was spread thinly enough. All her offspring were demanding, bar Lesbian Lindsay who had been banished to Bamford. Jade and Amber deserved an environment where they were automatically the centre of attention. They shouldn't have to fight for it. He was pretty sure they fended for themselves when they got home from school. He had subtly tried asking their teacher if they were keeping up at school, and had been reassured, but somehow he couldn't see anyone sitting down and doing their reading or their spellings with them. He tried his best to have an input at weekends, but he felt strongly that they deserved a break as much as anyone else and he certainly didn't want to hothouse them.

Gloomily he went back into his house and switched on the telly for company. It was so quiet without the girls, he needed something to fill the silence. What should he do? he wondered. Should he try to talk to Hayley? Have a sensible, grown-up conversation where they put all their cards on the table and came up with the best plan possible for Jade and Amber? But he knew it wouldn't work. At the moment, Hayley seemed incapable of behaving like an adult, or thinking about anyone other than herself. He leaned back and shut his eyes, praying for inspiration, for a solution, for a way out of this mess.

Penny Silver cleared away the last of the supper dishes, feeling a Sunday-evening gloom descend upon her that she didn't deserve. The kids had slithered away from the table as quickly as they could, citing homework as their excuse, but Penny knew it was just that neither of them wanted her or each other's company. If she thought about it too much, it would make her cry, but she told herself it was just their ages. Teenagers just didn't *do* sitting around a meal table chatting. They wanted to go into their own space, inhabit their own self-centred little worlds, plug into their zones.

She had thought it would get easier. The loneliness, the sense of isolation. And, quite frankly, the boredom. But if anything it was getting worse, largely because she was losing hope. She had been so determined to manage, calling upon her endless reserves of optimism. But after three years the reserves were running dry. And she had proved nothing to Bill, except that he was right about moving to Withybrook being insane, but she was never going to give him the satisfaction of knowing she had made a huge mistake.

When he'd fucked off to Bristol with his new consultant's post and his bloody registrar, with her strawberry-blonde hair and her overbite, Bill had expected Penny to plump for one of the three-bedroom boxes on the Pickwell estate in Bamford with her settlement – she'd be near to the shops, the cinema, the railway station. But she would rather have died than live in one of those rabbit hutches, whose walls were so thin you couldn't put up a decent-sized chunky curtain pole. She didn't want the kids playing out in the street, or worse, the neighbourhood kids traipsing through her token patch of garden. Bill, of course, had set himself up with a very nice garden flat in a Victorian house in Clifton, but was very swift to point out that, if Penny insisted the children carried on going to Lodminster School, with its crippling fees, then she shouldn't be surprised if there wasn't much left over for a house. She resented him making out that it was her decision, because she knew perfectly well that he wanted what was best for Tom and Megan too, but he was mean-spirited enough to make it look like extravagance on her part. But Lodminster wasn't extravagance, it was a necessity, because of Megan being a child prodigy on the cello and Tom being, well, Tom – clever but difficult: impossible to diagnose by a child psychologist but definitely not quite right and in constant need of the sort of channelling you only get when you fork out for private education. But by making out it was at Penny's insistence, Bill absolved himself from any guilt that all she could now afford was a little stone cottage on the outskirts of Withybrook.

They had been here three years now, and Penny was still struggling. She was still not over the shock of Bill leaving her. She hated being on her own. And now the kids were teenagers, they hated being stuck out in the country, miles from their mates and the shops and the swimming pool. Was she going to have to capitulate and sell the cottage that she had strived so hard to make a home, and move back into Bamford, thereby giving Bill the satisfaction of knowing he was right?

She sat in the kitchen, and poured another glass of red wine. Then looked at the clock: half past eight. It was at least another two hours before she could go to bed. She didn't sleep well as it was. She'd be up at four if she tried to sleep now.

There was nothing on television. Penny had stopped watching medical dramas because they repeatedly taunted her by proving that consultants were inveterate shaggers, and she couldn't bear soaps. And reality television was anathema – why watch other people's reality when her own was hard enough to deal with? Curling up with a book was admitting defeat. It was ironic – when the children were little and she had been rushed off her feet, she had often longed for half an hour with the latest novel, but now it seemed like the most depressing option in the world.

She pulled her secret fag stash out of the little wooden box on the dresser. Only it wasn't a secret stash any more, because the children no longer cared if she smoked. When they were little, they used to find her cigarettes and snap them up to stop her filthy habit. Now she felt as if she had their permission to smoke herself to death if she so wished. She pulled out a cigarette, looked at it, then decided it wouldn't go any way towards suppressing her malaise. She snapped it in half herself, irritably.

She looked at the clock again. Three minutes later than the last time she looked. She picked her coat off the back of the chair. She'd pop down to the Speckled Trout, see if there was anyone in there.

She ran up the stairs.

The sound of Megan's cello came through the bedroom door. It wasn't right, to have a child who practised studiously without being nagged. She tapped lightly and walked in. Megan looked up, scowling that her near perfect rendition of Saint-Saens' 'The Swan' had been interrupted.

'I'm popping down to the pub,' Penny told her, and Megan nodded absently, pushing back her mane of dark hair and peering back at her sheet music to find her place.

She didn't knock on Tom's door, just poked her head round. The smell of paint and glue hit her, and she wondered if she should open the window. He was painting the hideous plastic models that all thirteen-year-old boys seemed to be obsessed with. She had been assured that, unless he was a total loser-freak, he would grow out of the obsession almost overnight some time in the near future. Which would seem rather a waste, Penny having spent the price of a small second-hand car on boxes of the stuff. Guilt money. A mutant army to make up for the fact that he came from a broken home and his father only saw him one weekend in four.

'I'm off to the Speckled Trout,' she said to him

brightly. But like Megan, he barely looked up from his task, just seemed mildly irritated that she had interrupted.

She ran back down the stairs. As she walked through the hall, she stopped at the mirror, unable to leave without checking for lines, wrinkles, slackness of jaw or openness of pore. She felt mildly reassured by what she saw. She wasn't classically beautiful, but Penny knew she was striking. She had a long, pale face, with pronounced cheekbones and brown, rather hooded eyes that spoke of hidden depths and dark secrets. She kept her brunette hair short and choppy, shot through with crimson-red flashes that some might have considered inappropriate for a GP, but she didn't care. She was tall, five foot nine, with long, rangy legs and a small bum, so she knew she could get away with the short skirts, dinky cardigans and opaque tights that were her uniform. She had a collection of arty silver jewellery – chunky rings and beaten necklaces and dangly earrings – which she'd collected over the last few years, buying trinkets for herself on her birthday because no one else ever did. OK, so her mum sent her a book token and the kids usually gave her a cellophane-wrapped basket from the Body Shop, but she never received anything of any significance. So she treated herself once a year, going to one of the trendy galleries in Exeter and finding a piece that suited her personality. Or rather, represented the person she longed to be. Not the world-weary, embittered, frustrated middle-aged woman who had once had so much to give but whose generous heart was being slowly frozen. She was well into her forties, even if, thanks to great skin and good bone structure, she barely looked thirty-five. There wasn't much time for her dreams to come true, she was beginning to realise. By the time Tom was ready to go to university, and she could realistically just think about herself, it would be too late.

As she walked down the road towards the pub, the chill night air settled around her. She tucked in her scarf, wishing she had put on her fake Uggs as the cold from the tarmac seeped through the bottom of her zebra-skin ballet flats. But her legs didn't look as good in stumpy sheepskin boots . . .

She was trying desperately to pretend to herself that she didn't care if he was in there or not. But deep inside there was that little kernel of hope, the one that kept one foot in front of the other. She knew she would feel either joy or despondency the moment she stepped over the threshold. A quick glance to the chair he always sat in at the end of the bar. He was usually in there on a Sunday night. Don't be disappointed if he isn't, she warned herself. Prepare yourself. But a little bit of her imagined him at the bar, turning to smile at her as she walked in, nodding at the seat next to him, pulling out a crumpled fiver to get her a drink . . .

Charlotte sat at the bar, not quite able to believe that one of the country's best known artists was digging a spare spoon into the citrusy yellow goo that oozed out of her lemon pudding. It had eventually arrived, hot and steaming, with a dollop of Devon clotted cream on the side, and Sebastian had eyed it hungrily.

'Can I have a bit?' he'd asked, grabbing a teaspoon from the glasses on the bar that held spare cutlery.

'Get your own!' chided Norman.

'I only want a spoonful,' he insisted, and Charlotte relented.

Sebastian proceeded to eat more than half.

The evening was definitely turning out better than expected, Charlotte decided. It had got off to a shaky start, but she found she was enjoying herself, bantering with Sebastian, trying to keep up with his capricious trains of thought. Of course, it was plainly obvious that he was self-centred and spoiled to death, but he was so open about the fact, and so charming with it, that one couldn't help but be . . . well, charmed.

'Go on,' she urged him. 'Finish it off. I've already had a huge steak and mushroom pie, remember?'

He didn't need any more encouragement. As he scraped up the last of the lemon sauce, the door opened, and a tall, dark-haired woman walked in, wrapped in a shearling coat. Sebastian raised a hand in greeting and the woman's face lit up.

'Hey! Penny! A glass of red for Penny, please, Norm. And another for Charlotte . . .'

Charlotte put up her hand to stop him.

'No, no. I've had enough. Honestly. I can't get drunk on my first night.'

'Hi!'

The woman came up to join them and leaned in to kiss Sebastian, who put a hand on Charlotte's arm to introduce her.

'Penny, this is Charlotte. She's just moved to Withybrook. She's run away, just like you and me.'

'Hello.' Penny gave Charlotte a polite but cool smile as she unwound the scarf from her neck and took off her coat.

'Penny is in Category C,' Sebastian informed

Charlotte. 'An incomer. But she's also very useful because she's a doctor. And she knows everyone.'

'It's lovely to meet you.' Charlotte tried to meet Penny's eye, but she was busying herself putting her coat on the back of a chair. She could tell she wasn't thrilled by her presence. Her eyes were guarded, and she had a nervous energy about her that made Charlotte feel tense. As she pulled up her chair to join them, Penny looked askance at the pudding bowl on the bar top. The two spoons lay incriminatingly close. Charlotte immediately felt guilty.

Sebastian waved to Norman.

'Actually, I might as well order a bottle for these two.'

'Honestly, not for me,' protested Charlotte.

'Just one more glass. An ice-breaker. You can't just leave now Penny's arrived. It would be rude.'

Charlotte couldn't help feeling that Penny would be perfectly happy for her to leave right this second, but Sebastian was very persuasive. And she really didn't feel like going back to Myrtle Cottage on her own just yet.

'Just one more, then,' she heard herself saying, against her better judgement.

The bubble of excitement Penny had felt at seeing Sebastian at the bar was quickly burst by the presence of the small curvy blonde at his side, a wide-eyed Patsy Kensit lookalike wrapped in cream cashmere. Penny tried hard to smile a greeting, and swallow down the choking bile that rose in her craw as she realised they'd been sharing a pudding. She wanted to pick up the bowl and throw it across the room. They had, apparently, only just met, but she felt as if she was intruding. There was an air of intimacy woven around them that was almost impenetrable. But then, Sebastian did that. Drew you in, made you feel as if you were his only ally, as if it were you and he against the rest of the world. No doubt he'd been weaving his spell on this hapless creature.

Penny had had a crush on Sebastian Turner ever since they'd got drunk together one Friday night two years ago. Bill had taken the kids to Centre Parcs for the weekend and Penny had faced the prospect of a weekend alone. She knew there was a band on at the Speckled Trout. She could see no reason why she shouldn't go. There would be a good crowd in there. She wouldn't stand out. Why shouldn't an attractive, middle-aged divorcee be allowed to have a good time? Yet it was an ordeal, to screw up your courage and face a pub full of people, trying to appear nonchalant. What if everyone ignored her, and she had to stand, self-conscious, with a drink she had clearly bought for herself, trying to look absorbed in the band? But she forced herself to do it. No one was going to come knocking at her door to sweep her off her feet. If she wanted to find someone else to share her life, she had to get out there.

In the end, it had been a wonderful evening. There had been plenty of people ready to greet her, buy her a drink and make her feel welcome. As a local GP she was well known and appreciated. She still didn't know why Sebastian had homed in on her. He'd been there on his own, miffed because his wife had phoned to say she wouldn't be able to get back down to Withybrook until the next morning. They'd sat in the corner with a bottle of Havana Club and a bucket of ice, talking and laughing and listening to the band. They were playing covers – Van Morrison, Leonard Cohen, songs from Penny's student days – and it was a half-pleasant, half-painful experience. She loved the music and the lyrics, but they reminded her of happier times, when she had been young and naïve and hopeful and totally innocent of the pain that lay ahead. She wished she'd worn something more glamorous than black jeans and a white T-shirt, but Sebastian told her she reminded him of Chrissie Hynde, so she supposed she didn't look that bad.

At the end of the evening, he offered to walk her home. He had to pass her cottage on the way back to Withybrook Hall. They linked arms as only the very drunk can do, meandering their way up the high street under the lamplight. Penny felt her heart thumping very loudly, knowing she was being ridiculous, but recognising the signs – she had fallen head over heels in love.

She wanted to smother him, mother him, inspire him. Smooth away the hunted look he seemed to wear, the one that had made him toss back drink after drink that evening. It would destroy him eventually if he carried on. The ferocity with which he devoured alcohol was nihilistic. He drank to escape his demons, to blot out reality. She knew it was eating at his insides. The hollow cheeks and huge eyes were not just a fashion statement. As a doctor, she should want to cure him. Only she wanted the cure to be her. She wanted to be his reason for living, the thing that gave him joy.

But most of all, she wanted to make love to him. She wanted that smooth, pale skin under her fingertips, to kiss the mouth that spoke of such preposterous things, to pull him inside her and help transport him to a place that released him from the torture he felt. But why would this angelic demon boy want to sleep with a woman of her age? She must have at least ten years on him. Though there had definitely been moments. Frissons. When he had looked at her with those clear green eyes, and she'd known he was thinking about it, and not rejecting it out of hand. There was chemistry. She hadn't imagined it.

Yet how could she want to sleep with another woman's husband, after what had happened to her? She didn't; not really. But a tiny little part of her thought, why not?

'Is this your house?' They had stopped by the little wooden gate that led to her cottage. Sebastian ducked behind the hedge. 'Don't want your husband seeing me and coming out with a shotgun.'

Penny realised that he thought she was still married. That they had talked all evening and, although she had mentioned her kids, she hadn't once referred to Bill, their marriage or their divorce.

'Don't worry. He's not an issue. He's long gone.'

'Really? You didn't tell me.'

'It's boring, isn't it?'

Sebastian looked perturbed by this latest information.

'So you're divorced?'

She nodded, feeling a lump of self-pity in her throat.

'And you haven't got anyone else?'

'Why would anyone want me?' Even as she said it, she cringed. Her self-pitying mew was more of a turn-off than a surfeit of cellulite, thread veins and greying hair.

'Why wouldn't they? You're gorgeous.'

'Yeah, right. They're queuing up.'

'Don't do yourself down. All the men in the pub were eyeing you up. You'd got the best arse in there.'

'Shut up!'

But she couldn't help grinning. He moved in close to her and she drew in her breath as he put his hands on her hips and pulled her towards him. She could feel the warmth of him as he pushed his pelvis into hers. It was suggestive, but not unpleasantly so, as their legs entwined.

'I'd do you.'

She blinked, surprised by his frankness.

'Easy to say,' she flashed back, because it was.

The next moment she was astonished to find him kissing her. Deep, sensual, controlled kisses that stirred feelings in her she thought had been long buried.

She breathed in shakily. They stood in silence for a moment, arms wrapped round each other.

'Do you want to come in?' she whispered.

He didn't answer for a long time.

'I better not,' he sighed. 'I might start something I shouldn't.'

She wasn't going to beg. She still had her dignity. She just gave him a kiss on the cheek and extricated herself from his embrace.

'Thanks,' she said in a small voice, not quite sure what she was thanking him for. Turning her upside down? Giving her a sympathy snog? Kick-starting her bloody libido? She'd have been much better off if he'd left her alone.

Ever since that night she had been tortured by the memory of his lips on hers. She fantasised about him non-stop, dreaming that he turned up on her doorstep having left his wife and declaring undying love. Of course, it would never happen, and in the meantime she had to settle for the occasional drink with him in the pub. But a woman could dream, couldn't she? What she couldn't cope with, however, was the thought that there might be a rival for his affections. Seeing him with Charlotte had shaken her, as in a flash she could imagine him only too well walking out on Catkin to be with this girl.

Penny felt the urgent need for a cigarette.

'Coming outside for a fag?' she asked Sebastian, knowing she was testing him and hating herself for it.

'Nah.' He shook his head. 'It's bloody freezing out there.'

'I'll have one.' Charlotte jumped off her stool. 'If you don't mind me pinching one.'

Penny was surprised. She wouldn't have had Charlotte down as a smoker. She looked far too wholesome.

'Course. I'll be glad of the company.'

Sebastian watched the two of them go. He felt guilty about Penny. He'd so meant to do the right thing that evening. Just restore Penny's confidence and give her a little fillip. She was attractive, and entertaining, and sexy, and he knew that he could tell her that all he liked but she wouldn't believe him. And so he'd kissed her, to prove it.

Yet as soon as his lips had touched hers, he knew he had made a terrible error of judgement. This woman was so fragile. She had melted into him so totally.

She couldn't cope with his vote of confidence. In his world, people distributed meaningless kisses all the time. In Penny's world, a kiss meant something. A commitment, a declaration. His slightly drunken, rather impulsive gesture had been meant as an act of kindness, which Sebastian realised now was not only patronising but dangerous.

He knew she hungered after him. He enjoyed her company, he really did. She was lively, funny and unpretentious. Her head wasn't filled with the posturing nonsense of the showbiz circles he and Catkin moved in. But he was careful to keep her firmly at arm's length. She didn't deserve to be damaged by the likes of Sebastian Turner, and he knew he would damage her. He always did. The only person who had ever been able to withstand his destruct button was Catkin, which was why he was married to her.

Only lately, their relationship was beginning to wear him down. His isolation during the week meant he was alone with his darker side. Rather than inspiring him, it inhibited him, his confidence seeping away until his studio became a prison from which he was desperate to escape. And so it was hardly surprising he ended up in the Speckled Trout, talking to all and sundry and trying to find solace.

Catkin tried to make up for being away all week by throwing elaborate house parties at the weekend, filling the house with people she thought were interesting and stimulating, or more to the point might be useful. She never invited Sebastian's old art-college friends, because she thought they were bad for him. Most of them didn't have even a modicum of his success and she felt they were hanging on his coat-tails. Not as much as the liggers and hangers-on that *she* invited, he wanted to point out.

This weekend, he'd had to tolerate the heart-throb from the latest soap opera and his girlfriend and a celebrity make-over artist, among others. Sebastian strongly suspected Catkin had a hidden agenda, and was angling for him to have a make-over. She was always going on to him about his scruffy clothes, the fact that he still wore stuff from his schooldays, and didn't get his hair cut properly. He insisted on going to the dodgy barber in Comberton when even he thought his locks were too straggly. But people didn't expect artists to ponce around in Armani, did they? Surely they wanted artists to be slightly bedraggled and unshaven?

He was starting to resent this nannying. Why did Catkin feel such a great need to change him? It had been fantastic in the early days. They had loved each other for what they were. She had fallen for him because he dressed like he didn't give a shit – and he didn't. She had adored his friends; they'd all partied like rock stars. They had adhered to no timetable, obeyed no rules, had no regard for mealtimes or bedtimes.

Now, she was trying to turn him into something he wasn't. She was trying to stop him drinking. She even controlled what went into the fridge, and had the supermarket deliver what she thought he ought to be eating – crudités and fucking hummus and fresh fruit and pro-biotic yoghurts. He let it all rot, and walked to the village shop for Pot Noodles and Mars Bars and tins of Campbell's condensed chicken soup and Jammy Dodgers.

'You can't eat like that for ever,' she warned him repeatedly. 'And if you don't eat fruit and vegetables you'll get scurvy.'

He argued back that he always put lime in his vodka and tonic.

She said it was all for his own good, but he knew it was for hers. She was worried about her profile. Now she had shot to fame, she was nervous that he would tarnish her image. Success had changed her. She had become uptight, inhibited, wary, manipulative. That wasn't the Catkin he had bought into. But the more he told her he wanted things to be as they had been, the more insistent she was that they couldn't stand still. The stakes were too high, she told him. They were public figures and they had to protect themselves.

Did that mean compromising themselves? he argued. Did they have to become something they weren't?

Sitting in the pub that evening, after their hideous guests had left and Catkin had climbed into the back of the people carrier she'd bought Tommy Yeo, Sebastian decided he was going to stop being ineffectual and compliant. What right did Catkin have to rule their lives?

Outside, the two women huddled together on a picnic bench, shivering in the cold night air. Penny pulled out her illicit cigarette packet and offered one to Charlotte.

'I shouldn't really,' said Charlotte, grabbing one eagerly. 'I gave up years ago. When . . .' She trailed off, and a strange look came over her face.

'When?' prompted Penny.

Charlotte shrugged.

'One New Year's Eve. When I realised it wasn't really doing me any good. But every now and then I give in. When I'm really drunk. Or stressed.'

'Are you stressed, then?' asked Penny lightly.

'You know. New people. New place. I'm not great on change. Though everyone seems really nice so far.'

'Oh, yes,' lied Penny effortlessly. 'Everyone in Withy-brook is lovely.'

Cigarettes extinguished, they went back into the pub, and Charlotte picked up her coat.

'I must go,' she said. 'I've got so much to do tomorrow.'

'Time lasts longer down here,' Sebastian reassured her. 'You'll have everything done by lunchtime.'

Charlotte pulled a little grey wool beanie onto her head. Penny thought sourly that it would make her look like a frumpy middle-aged fell-walker, but Charlotte looked like an adorable pixie.

Charlotte put her arms round Sebastian and hugged him.

'Thank you for all the drinks.'

He looked at her, suddenly sad she was going. She'd been a breath of fresh air. And there was something intriguing about her. She was soft and marshmallow sweet on the surface. Perfectly edible. Wide eyes, sugar-pink lips and that little mop of cropped curls. But did that softness go right through to the centre? he wondered. It was something that Sebastian had noticed about women. The tougher they seemed, the more vulnerable they were. While the ones that were sweetness and light often had an inner steel.

Impulsively, he decided to ask Charlotte to lunch next Sunday. He knew Catkin would be incandescent, because she planned her guest lists very carefully. But how could you not like Charlotte? She was adorable, and perfectly confident. She would fit in, he felt sure. And surely it was the neighbourly thing to do, if she had just arrived? Most pertinent of all, didn't Sebastian have the right to ask who he liked to his own house?

Before he could stop himself, the words were out of his mouth.

'Why don't you come for lunch on Sunday? Come and meet Catkin. She'll be glad there's someone her own age in the village.'

As soon as he said it, he realised his mistake. Penny was looking like a puppy that had been kicked. Fuck, thought Sebastian. He couldn't not ask her too. Not that he didn't want her company, but he instinctively knew that for her own good he shouldn't encourage her. He didn't mind chatting to her in the pub, but he'd never asked her to Withybrook Hall, sensing that would be a step too far.

'Why don't you come too, Pen?' he asked, trying not to sound lukewarm and praying desperately that the children had some immensely vital extra-curricular activity that couldn't be missed.

'I can't leave Tom and Megan . . .' she faltered.

'Why not?' Sebastian demanded, wondering why he couldn't just leave it at that. 'You're here now, aren't you? Let them fend for themselves.'

Penny bit her lip.

'I would ask them too, but Sunday lunch at our place can get a bit . . . well, I don't know if it would be suitable.'

Charlotte looked mildly alarmed.

'Nothing hideous,' Sebastian assured her. 'A bit of fruity language and the odd spliff. But not suitable for impressionable teenagers. Anyway, Penny needs to cut the apron strings.'

Why couldn't he shut up? Anyone would think he wanted her to come.

'Do you know,' said Penny, 'you're right. I'll leave them a stew and some jacket potatoes.'

'Bravo,' said Sebastian, thinking he really should have kept his trap shut.

'Well, that would be lovely,' said Charlotte. 'Can I bring anything?'

'God no,' said Sebastian. 'Catkin always over-caters.'

'That would be great. I'll see you then.'

Penny watched Sebastian watch Charlotte go with a sinking heart. He hadn't taken his eyes off her face all evening, except to surreptitiously examine her cleavage, which was annoyingly pert and inviting underneath her cream cashmere jumper. Her heart contracted with the pain. It was quite the most hideous feeling, and made her want to scream and cry and stab Charlotte in the ribs with the nearest sharp implement.

Charlotte stumbled slightly over the threshold of Myrtle Cottage. She couldn't remember the last time she had had so much to drink, but actually it had probably been the right thing to do. With the best part of a bottle of Shiraz inside her, she was anaesthetised and hadn't given the rat infestation a second thought all evening. Now she was back, she wasn't going to check the kitchen to make sure there were none there. Instead, she ran up the stairs to her bedroom, shut the

143

door firmly, stuffed a blanket across the gap under the door, and got into bed fully clothed, wrapping the duvet round her.

Despite the wine, sleep evaded her. She must be overtired. Too much had happened today. Added to which, she could see the moon shining in on her through the uncurtained window and couldn't remember if it was when it was new or full that it could drive you mad. And every time she shut her eyes she imagined the scrat-scrat-scratching of little claws.

As the cold seeped into her bones, she thought she had never felt so alone. For the first time in weeks, she wondered about Ed, what he was doing, how he was feeling, and if he was as miserable as she was. The last time she had seen him, when they emptied the house, he had lost over a stone and looked terrible, drawn, grey-skinned. He'd wanted to talk, but Gussie's husband had been firm and steered her away from him. Which to be fair, was what she had asked him to do. But now she wondered if maybe they should have spoken about things—

She mustn't think about him. That way madness lay. She had long resolved to shut him out of her mind, pretend he had never existed. She pulled the duvet round her, shut her eyes tight and fell into a troubled sleep.

By eleven o'clock that evening, Hayley could no longer keep her eyes open. She decided to go down and make a cup of hot chocolate then go to bed, where she could happily rerun the events of the weekend in her head. From the lounge, she could hear the boom of the television: her mother would be glued to some dreary

Sunday-night drama while her father dozed. She didn't bother offering either of them a drink.

The kitchen was the usual horror story. Under the window sat a massive tank containing a solitary terrapin, which floated eerily about in water green with its own faeces. Copies of *Farmers Weekly* were piled high, unread but untouchable, next to the ever-increasing mound of farm paperwork. Along one wall were the pet food bowls, filled with varying degrees of drying Pedigree Chum and Miaow Mix: the animals, it seemed, were allowed branded food while the humans were relegated to generic crap that her mother bought in bulk from the cash and carry – giant boxes of breakfast cereal, bottles of red and brown sauce, trays of translucent baby-pink sausages, brick-sized slabs of fatty bacon slices, bags full of broken biscuits. Feeding five hungry blokes was no joke, either physically or financially, and Barbara Poltimore had let the slow food movement pass her by entirely. Browning dishcloths harboured even more germs than the surfaces they occasionally wiped. An enormous, malevolent yellowing cat sat in a greasy armchair, letting out the occasional growl that passed as a purr. Hayley knew better than to try to stroke it. She flicked on the two-bar electric heater, but it was like pissing in the ocean. She could see her breath, and would be able to until April was out.

She hated this room, the room that had been the centre of her life for so many years. She thought longingly of Kirk's kitchen, with its limestone floors warm with under-floor heating; the double sink with the taps that delivered moussy filtered water; the fridge with the ice-machine and the integral wine cooler

145

stuffed with vintage champagne. She gave a shudder of dissatisfaction. She had to endure nearly a whole week of this dump before she went back up to her haven of luxury. It was penance indeed. The only way to get through the next few days was to sleep, she decided, as she flicked on the kettle that she knew without looking would be filled with limescale.

As she waited for the kettle to boil, she had a sudden burst of maternal responsibility and wondered where the girls' uniforms had got to. She ran down the corridor to the utility room, expecting to find them hanging over the drying rack or folded neatly into a washing basket. Instead, she found them in a heap by the washing machine, still damp and covered in a fine layer of cat hair. Swearing under her breath, she picked them up to shake them off and hang them over the nearest radiator in the hope that they might be dry by morning. But as she did so she caught a whiff of ammonia; one of the cats had done more than just sleep on them. Now she was going to have to put them back into the washing machine and stay up until they had run through.

She pulled her brothers' work clothes out of the machine and dumped them on the floor, stuffed the dresses and jumpers in, and realised there was no washing powder left. She threw the box across the room in a rage. What was she supposed to do now? Even she couldn't send the girls to school stinking of cat pee.

She was going to have to wash them by hand with washing-up liquid. She lugged the pile of clothes into the kitchen and over to the kitchen sink, only to find it brimming over with chipped mugs, some of them full, some of them containing dried tea bags. What the hell was going on? Didn't anyone clear up after themselves in this house? She cleared everything out of the sink and dumped it on the side, then ran the hot tap. Only it wasn't hot. It was stone cold. Hayley remembered that she'd run herself a scalding bath not long after the girls had had theirs. She'd obviously drained the tank. It would take hours for it to heat up again.

There was nothing for it. She'd have to go home. She stuffed the clothes into a black bin liner and went out to her car. Throwing the bag onto the back seat, she started the engine and drove out of the drive as if the hounds of hell were after her. Half a minute later she pulled up outside her marital home, opened the front door and crept in. The house was silent. Fitch must be in bed. She made her way into the kitchen, where the washing machine was thankfully empty. Not only that, but there was a plentiful supply of Ariel and a big bottle of sweet-smelling Lenor. She filled the machine, put it on quick wash, then went to the fridge to see what she could find to eat.

She was just sitting down with a bowl of fresh pineapple and cream when she heard footsteps behind her.

'What the hell do you think you're doing?' It was Fitch, with a face like thunder.

'My bloody mother forgot to wash the uniforms. And there was no washing powder, and no hot water.'

'So you thought you could just march in here and use mine, without even bothering to ask?'

Hayley put down her spoon carefully. She didn't want an argument, not at this time of night. But guilt, as ever, made her defensive.

'Yours?' she asked lightly. 'I distinctly remember choosing this with you in Comet.'

'The day you walked out of here is the day you gave up any right—'

'Stop right there.' Hayley put up her hand. 'I think you'll find I'm entitled to half. If not more. And presumably you want the girls to have clean clothes for the morning?'

'You should have left their uniforms with me. I'd have done them.'

'Well, aren't you a saint and a martyr?'

Fitch looked at her, puzzled.

'Why do you have to be such a bitch, Hayley? I go out of my way to be as reasonable as I can—'

'And then you shove it down my throat. Make me feel as guilty as you can.'

Fitch didn't reply. He knew very well he wasn't going to win any arguments, because Hayley wasn't capable of seeing anyone else's point of view. It was late, he was tired, and he didn't want to stay here while they slung insults at each other.

'Go home,' he said wearily. 'I'll bring their clothes up first thing.'

He put his hands on her shoulders to guide her out of the kitchen towards the front door. But she burst into noisy tears.

'Nobody understands,' she sobbed. 'Nobody understands how hard it is for me. No one does anything to help. I'm bloody exhausted and I don't need this at the end of the day.'

She began to sob even harder.

'Hayley, calm down.'

'It's not fair. Why do I have to be punished all the time? I'm trying to do my best . . .'

Fitch sighed inwardly. He knew the procedure. He was going to have to cajole and console Hayley for the next half-hour, to stop her going off into the stratosphere. This hysteria was her default mechanism when she knew she was behaving badly. She started blaming everyone else around her, when it was quite clear she was in the wrong. It was exhausting. But if he didn't calm her, there was no knowing what she might do or say.

'Come on. Come and sit down. Come and have a drink.'

He led her through into the living room and sat her down on the sofa, then went to pour her a glass of port. He'd hoped for an early night. Fat chance.

Hayley sat with her legs curled up underneath her, surveying her husband through her still-damp lashes. There had been a time when Fitch had represented the escape she needed. When she had thought he was glamorous and exciting. But now she had tasted real glamour and excitement, he seemed dull by comparison.

She had loved this house once as well. It was stripped back, minimal, but somehow snug. The end wall was exposed brick, the ceiling was beamed, and the rest of the room was fresh pristine white plaster. There was a wood-burner, and beside it a pile of sweet-smelling logs. The wooden floorboards gleamed golden with beeswax. Hand-built shelves groaned with books and CDs. On the walls were black-framed photographs Fitch had taken of the girls. A driftwood coffee table held a funky lamp that changed colour. There were two long, low sofas that were so comfortable you never wanted to leave them, strewn with striped cushions. Two old wooden apple crates held the girls' movie collection.

For a moment she wondered why she had left. Then she remembered how claustrophobic she had come to feel, how the house's womb-like cosiness had seemed to reproach her for her lack of maternal feeling. There was absolutely no questioning Fitch's masculinity, but he was a better mother to the girls than she had ever been. He was the one who nursed them when they were ill, oversaw their homework projects, took them shopping for new clothes, took them to the riding stables for lessons. And Hayley was left feeling insufficient, freakish. There was something missing in her, she was sure of it. All she felt was a slight sense of panic when the girls needed her. She almost recoiled when they reached out for her. Almost, but not quite. She usually managed an awkward embrace, but it made her feel uncomfortable. She envied Fitch his natural warmth, the way he scooped the two of them up and obviously took such pleasure in their physical presence.

What was wrong with her? It wasn't that she was frigid. She loved the feeling of a man's body, his arms around her, his hands on her. That was when she was at her happiest, when she was being consumed. But the demands these two creatures made on her was terrifying, when she didn't even feel she knew them. She understood how to please a man only too well. She did it instinctively. But children? She didn't have a clue.

Fitch brought her over a glass of port, and she sipped it, then leaned her head back against the cushions and closed her eyes. She was so tired. She could just doze off here, in front of the fire. Back at the farm, she'd be freezing, forced to wear three layers of clothing and bed-socks.

'Hayley.' His voice sounded serious. 'I think it's time we made things official, don't you?'

Her eyes snapped open. 'Official?' What was he on about?

'You know. We should sort things out with a solicitor. Start proceedings.'

Hayley panicked. She didn't want to make things official. She feigned puzzlement. 'Proceedings?'

'A divorce.'

'What?'

'Well, we can't carry on like this indefinitely.'

'I don't think we should rush into anything—'

'Rush?' He sounded surprised as he came to sit down on the sofa next to her. 'I don't call this rushing. You've been seeing Kirk for nearly a year now.'

Hayley sat very still. She was going to have to think quickly. She didn't like this at all. She liked to be the one in control, the one who dictated the pace. And she certainly didn't want to start divorce proceedings until she was certain of her future with Kirk. He was bound to ask her to marry him sooner or later. She'd make him the perfect wife, she knew she would. Once she'd got the ring on her finger, then she'd play ball with Fitch. She'd get a decree absolute before you could say small blue box from Tiffany.

She tried not to think about the ring Fitch had bought her. The pretty little antique ring with the solitaire diamond from the jeweller's in Comberton. She had been thrilled with it at the time, but she was embarrassed by it now. She had long taken it off and stuffed it in the top drawer of her dressing table. For a moment she felt a twinge of shame. But she told herself it wasn't her fault. She couldn't help it if the man of her dreams had walked into her life. Once she'd thought Fitch was that man, but somehow he wasn't enough any more. Not now she'd tasted what Kirk had to offer.

But she had to be careful. She didn't want to burn her bridges.

She put her glass of port down on the coffee table and turned to face her husband, her eyes soulful.

'I'm not ready for this, Fitch.'

He raised an eyebrow.

'Tough. This isn't about you, Hayley. It's about me. And the girls. I want a line drawn underneath everything. I need to move on. I'm not just going to sit here and wait—'

She put a finger to his lips.

'Shhh . . .'

She slid her arms around his neck.

'We don't have to have this conversation.'

'Yes, we do.'

She ignored him, brushing her lips along his neck. She knew he liked it. She used to feel him melt when she did it. But he seemed to have frozen in her embrace.

'Hayley . . .' He sounded awkward as he tried to extricate himself. But she wasn't going to be deterred. She slid her hands round to cup the back of his head, sliding her fingers through his long hair, then leaned in to kiss him. There. She had him. He was responding, kissing her back—

Suddenly, he pulled back sharply, jerking his head out of the way.

'Stop it!'

She flinched at the irritation in his voice.

'Don't play games with me, Hayley. It's not fair.'

He stood up, glowering. She folded her arms.

'You'd better go.' His voice was cold. 'I'll bring the washing up first thing, like I said. About half seven.'

His tone of voice was final. Hayley knew better than to argue. She had played her trump card, in the mistaken belief that Fitch would find her irresistible after nearly a year of abstinence. At least she presumed he was abstaining. Maybe she was being taken for a fool?

She decided that she was best off leaving. He'd taken her rather unawares. She needed time to think, to plan a strategy. She picked up her coat, kissed him chastely on the cheek.

'Goodnight, Fitch.'

'Night, Hayley,' he replied, rather drily.

After Hayley had gone, Fitch went back to bed, hunkering down under his duvet, unable to get to sleep. He was cross with himself. He had mentioned divorce just to test her, and he should have known what her reaction would be. Sex was Hayley's only currency. And quite often it worked. There had been a moment when he had almost given in. Both the lure of her warm body and the possibility of having his girls back under his roof had been very tempting. But he was pretty sure that this was one of her games, that she had just wanted to prove how irresistible she was, and he didn't want them all back on those terms. She had to understand how much hurt and damage she had caused her family.

Then he panicked. In rejecting her, perhaps he had lost his only chance? A woman spurned, after all, was a dangerous thing. He should have made it clearer that there was a chance for them, but it had to be conditional on certain things. Her getting rid of Kirk, for a start. The problem was she wasn't reasonable.

He knew she was still unhappy. He could feel it in her. Kirk might be giving her everything she wanted in material terms, but he didn't get the feeling their relationship was in any way stable or nourishing. Her head had been turned by his wealth and his lifestyle – things Fitch couldn't even begin to offer her. But until she realised that, there was no going back.

He wondered if there was hope. If there was any way he could make her truly happy. He would make changes if he had to. But he sensed there was some deep discontent in her that went beyond anything he could rectify. Looking back, they had become embroiled too quickly. They had married before they had really got to know each other, and the children had been born so soon afterwards, there had been no time to work on their relationship and figure out where things had gone awry.

Perhaps they should have moved away? He could have set up in business somewhere else. He'd done it once, after all, with success. Hayley might have flourished with a change of scene. She was so entrenched in Withybrook – apart from her stint at her uncle's factory, it was all she had ever known. And he supposed it was claustrophobic. It didn't bother him in the least what the other residents thought, but he wasn't related to half of the village, and hadn't been to school with the other half. There was barely anyone for miles around who didn't know the ins and outs of the Poltimores' business. And what they didn't know, they made up. Maybe it would get to you in the end. And maybe he had been selfish, with his contentment at finally fitting in somewhere, at being accepted and having a place in the pecking order at last, instead of being made to feel an outsider. Had Hayley's dissatisfaction and subsequent desertion been the price of his contentment?

Just how much *was* he to blame? he wondered.

Six

On Monday morning, Charlotte woke early. If she had thought living in Withybrook would be quiet, she was mistaken. The dawn chorus was deafening, and was mixed in with the jubilant crowing of someone's cockerel in a nearby garden. He was soon joined by the cows lowing, whether because they were hungry or needed milking she had no idea. Then the local schoolchildren gathered at the bus-stop, laughing and shouting, swapping sweets and forbidden cigarettes. A few foul oaths floated up to her window, until the bus finally arrived to take them away. Tractors trundled up and down the high street, then a milk lorry thundered past, followed by the recycling men throwing everyone's empty bottles with gay abandon into the back of their truck. She had intended to have a lie-in after her long drive and her late night, but in the end she gave up.

She clambered out of bed with a thick head; she had drunk more wine last night than she had for months. She leaned her head out of the bedroom window, breathing in the fresh air. It was cool and sharp. The day was fine – not sunny, but not the oppressive grey of the day before. Again she caught the scent of wood-smoke mixed with dung: a pleasant change from the smog-filled fumes she was used to.

She scrambled into her jeans, eager to explore the little house in the light of day. Her bedroom was fairly nondescript, with low-beamed ceilings and a small window, tired floral wallpaper and a mushroom carpet, but nothing that a bit of elbow grease couldn't sort out. The bathroom, however, was a disaster. A dark brown bath, a minute basin, a cracked and stained loo – none of it was salvageable, and the whole room had been tiled from top to bottom, which meant a lot of back-breaking work removing them, and no doubt the plaster would come off too. Charlotte tried not to feel daunted. She was going to have to do the donkey work herself, which she wasn't used to. But on her budget she couldn't afford to pay workmen for doing things she was actually perfectly capable of doing.

She brushed her teeth and washed her face, then peeped into the second bedroom: similar to the first. So far so good, and much as she had expected. She went down the stairs, with its threadbare cord carpet, and was pleased to see that the hall was flooded with light from the semi-glazed front door. That was half the battle, having a welcoming entrance, and with decent paintwork and new carpet, the place would be magically transformed.

The dining room was tiny. There wasn't much she could do about that, but she had plenty of tricks up her sleeve – a few optical illusions and clever use of mirrors, and prospective purchasers would think they were looking at a veritable banqueting hall. The living room, happily, was a decent size, although the fireplace was hideous and the light fittings bordered on the criminal.

As the most important room in the house, the heart

of the home, the kitchen was going to be the biggest challenge. It was dark and poky. The units were heavy mock-oak with ornate brass handles and latticed fronts. The floor was covered in nasty dark green hexagonal tiles. To make up for these shortcomings, the larder (which had housed the rats, of which thankfully there was no sign) was very spacious. She could imagine it lined with shelves, groaning with brightly coloured bottles and jars and tins, strings of garlic and chillies hanging from hooks.

There was a back door leading out into the garden with a huge cat flap hacked out of the middle. She pushed it open. Immediately outside the door was a depressing concrete area which held the bins, and what was obviously an old coal store. The garden was long and thin, with broken-down larch-lap fencing, a patchy lawn and a couple of empty flower-beds. Charlotte told herself that even Vita Sackville-West struggled to make a garden look inviting at this time of year, and noted an old wooden bench that she earmarked for renovation. She had to keep looking on the bright side, and not become daunted.

She had bought a new spiral-bound notebook, a sketch pad and a tube of fresh pencils. She felt rather as it if was the first day at a new school, filled with both excitement and fear of what was to come, wondering if she would make any friends, and if she would be able to cope with the workload. She began by sketching out a floor-plan of the cottage, measuring each room carefully, and was quite surprised by the square footage. It was, indeed, deceptively spacious, but suffered from being cluttered by awkward furniture, most of which she was going to get rid of at the first opportunity.

She commandeered the kitchen as her office, spreading her papers out on the work surface and using the wall as a noticeboard to display her plans. The trick for selling was to keep the house as neutral as possible, without making it seem bland. Fresh and light, but with a few quirks that enhanced its character to make it stand out from the next property. Thankfully, Myrtle Cottage was structurally sound, and so this revamp was just cosmetic. Its layout was perfectly practical; there was no need to start knocking down walls, the windows were in good condition, and the wiring and the roof were up to scratch just as Gussie had promised. Simple touches, like changing the doors from flat veneer with nasty metal handles to something more in keeping, would make the world of difference.

She lugged her box of paint samples out from the car, then found an old cardboard box to tear up. She carefully painted her chosen colours onto sizeable strips, which she could then take into each room and consider. The temptation, of course, was to paint everything white, but Charlotte knew that while it worked in certain spaces it could be cold and stark. She liked to mix her paints herself; she didn't like being dictated to by the paint companies, and she loved experimenting. Mixing and adding and stirring until she had the perfect shade was immensely satisfying. For the next hour, she played with warm creams and caramels, until she settled upon a rich but light golden hue which she could use throughout the house, bringing it to life while providing the perfect foil for any other colours she brought in.

But she knew she was displacing. It was always the temptation, to rush ahead to the detail when what really mattered was working out the cost. Sighing and putting the lids back on her pots, she picked up her notebook and began to walk around the house making a list of essentials.

New kitchen units
New bathroom suite
Interior doors × 7
Front door
Back door
Carpet throughout
Flooring – kitchen and bathroom
Fireplace – living room
Light-fittings throughout

She punched in numbers on her calculator as she went. She was disheartened to find that she had reached ten thousand before she had even got up the stairs. She was going to have to have a drastic rethink. The problem was she was used to clients to whom money was no object. They wanted the very best, and that's what she gave them. She rarely had to compromise. Decorating on a shoe-string was not her forte, but it was going to have to be – and quick. This was a whole different ball game, and she suddenly felt despondent. She wasn't qualified to pull this off at all. Perhaps she should phone Gussie now and tell her? What was the point of pulling in a princessy interior designer to do a cheap refurb? She didn't do budget.

Then she gave herself a talking to. Just because she was used to dealing with demanding clients who only wanted the best didn't mean she couldn't compromise. She was perfectly down-to-earth and practical. She was able to source a good deal. She had imagination. It pained her to cut down on quality, but at the end of the day she was only dressing the house to make it look palatable for prospective purchasers. Never mind if the carpet wore out in six months, or the kitchen cupboards fell off. She was creating an illusion. And although it went against the grain, and everything she stood for, she didn't have a choice.

By now it was midday, and her head was throbbing. Whether it was the stale air, the surfeit of wine or the stress, she couldn't be sure. Not having any breakfast probably didn't help. She decided to get out and explore the village and go in search of sustenance.

She came out of the front door and into the street, turning right, as she was pretty sure she remembered seeing a shop on the other side of the road from the pub. She inspected the houses along the way, surprised at the disparity. Some of them were almost derelict. The frames were rotten and she could see tattered curtains through the filthy windows. Some of them had prams and plastic toys scattered over the gardens, and cars up on bricks. Others looked as if they might be empty, or even harbouring an unnoticed corpse. At the other end of the scale were the houses that had been done up tastefully, with slate house signs, muted colours on the doors and windows and interesting beaten copper sundials and water features. There didn't seem to be anything in between.

The village shop-cum-post office was an extraordinary mixture of exotic and prosaic, which she supposed accurately reflected the demographics of the village.

You could get olives and tinned corn beef, but not Marmite. Dom Perignon and Carlsberg XXX, but not a reasonably priced bottle of half-decent red. A girl with ginger and white striped hair and a belly-button ring chewed gum behind the counter. A board boasted scrappily written index cards offering bunk beds and BMX bikes for sale, next to beautifully designed adverts for art exhibitions and garden openings. There was a pile of local papers on the counter, but no other papers or magazines. Racks of faded wrapping paper hung next to a carousel of gaudy greetings cards. A set of shelves displayed rows of homemade chutneys and jams with handwritten labels. Boxes of free-range eggs sat next to Tupperware cartons of penny sweets: fizzy cola bottles and chocolate mice and strawberry laces. The air was thick with their sugary scent.

'Do you sell . . . bread?' ventured Charlotte, thinking that what she really needed was several rounds of toast and a pot of tea.

The girl pointed to a shelf that contained a couple of sorry-looking sliced loaves.

'S'all we've got left. Thursday and Saturday, the baker comes. But you'd do best to order what you want, 'cos it goes quick, like.'

Charlotte picked up one of the loaves reluctantly, thinking that she had better go to a supermarket and stock up. She chose a pot of homemade strawberry jam, and was grateful that she had packed butter in her cool-box.

'What about milk?'

The girl wearily reached behind her and plonked a carton of UHT on the counter.

'Fresh milk you've got to order, too.'

Charlotte added a packet of ginger nuts to her purchases, and a tin of tomato soup. She needed something for lunch. As for supper, there was absolutely nothing in here that would serve as a meal. She wasn't a food snob by any means, but one look in the freezer and she had dismissed boil-in-the-bag curry and crumbed haddock fillets.

As she approached the counter, she decided she would do her best to ingratiate herself with her first villager.

'I'm Charlotte, by the way.' She smiled at the girl as she handed over her purchases. 'I've just moved into Myrtle Cottage.'

The girl stared at her, then managed a smile.

'I'm Nikita,' she finally offered. 'Have you got kids, cos I do babysitting?'

'Um, no,' said Charlotte. 'It's just me.'

Nikita frowned. 'What do you want to move here for, on your own?' she asked, stuffing Charlotte's shopping into a paper-thin plastic bag. 'You'll go mad.'

Charlotte pulled a ten-pound note out of her purse.

'Do you sell magazines?' she asked hopefully, thinking that what she really needed was to sit down with a copy of *Homes and Gardens*.

'You've got to order them,' Nikita replied, handing over the bag of shopping just as it split and the contents fell all over the floor.

When Charlotte got back from the shop, there was a letter from Ed's solicitor on the doormat. She recognised the cream vellum envelope. She felt slightly sick, as she always did when faced with something official. She hoped it wasn't a bill. She opened it carefully.

There was a letter, and wrapped inside it a form of some sort.

She scanned the letter quickly.

Ed has asked me to pass this on to you, in the hope that you might visit. If you do not feel able to do so, please return the order to me at your earliest convenience . . .

Her stomach turned over as she looked at the form. A prison visiting order. Did he really expect her to visit him? In prison? She had instructed his solicitor to pass any communications on, but she thought she'd made it pretty clear that she didn't want any more to do with Ed than was necessary.

She pinned the order up on the kitchen wall next to her sketches, and stared at it.

Ed was still her husband.

She was still his wife.

Did she owe him a visit, after what he had done? He'd reduced them both to nothing, literally and metaphorically. He was in prison, and she was in hiding, scrabbling to make a living, in fear of being discovered by her newfound friends. She was having to live under an assumed name, disguise herself; she had little hope of a future. Everything had been snatched from her: her home, her career, her marriage, her friends.

Most of the time, she operated on automatic pilot. But sometimes, like now, the grim reality closed in on her and her mind was filled with questions. Would she ever be someone else's lover again? Or someone else's wife? Or even . . . someone's mother?

This was the really painful question. But she had to consider that, without Ed in her life, there was a chance, a small chance, that she might conceive with another partner. She took in a tiny breath, allowing herself for the first time to give this possibility some real head space. No one had ever pinned down which of them was the cause of their infertility. Suppose it wasn't her . . . ?

She shook her head and told herself to stop. She couldn't go down that road. Not yet. After all, she was still married to Ed. They hadn't actually discussed the future of their marriage. It had seemed insignificant. And there had been so much other bureaucracy to deal with that Charlotte couldn't face divorce proceedings on top of everything else. Not that there would have been any doubt that she could do him for unreasonable behaviour. How unreasonable could you get?

Now, looking at the prison order, she wondered if she ought to visit him and discuss the future. Until she put Ed behind her, she wasn't going to be able to move on. She was living in the shadow of what he had done.

She deserved a future, surely?

'Hello?'

Lost in her reverie, she nearly jumped out of her skin. She looked up to see her rescuer of the night before standing in the kitchen doorway. What was his name? Something weird. Mitch? Fitz? Fitch . . . that was it.

'Fitch. Hi.'

He took up nearly the whole of the doorframe with his broad shoulders.

'Sorry. I didn't mean to scare you. I just thought I'd come and check there were no more visitors.'

'Not that I've seen so far. And thank you so much for last night.'

She moved automatically over to the kettle.

'I was just going to make another pot of tea. Can I tempt you?'

'Why not?'

He looked around.

'Looks like you've got your work cut out for you.'

Charlotte made a face. 'I think I might have bitten off more than I can chew.'

'It's pretty daunting. I did up the old bakery, down the road. It's still not properly finished.'

'I've got to get my skates on. The owners want this on the market in the early spring.'

'And you're doing it all yourself?'

'Well . . . there's stuff I can't do. Like plastering.'

'Give me a shout if you want a hand. I can turn my hand to most things.'

'Thanks.'

Charlotte smiled, not sure if he was offering out of the kindness of his heart or if he wanted paying.

'And if you want a fireplace, or a house sign, I'm your man.'

'I'll probably want both.'

She handed him a cup of tea.

'Do you want sugar? Only I don't have any . . .'

'No, no . . . that's fine.'

She could see the visiting order over Fitch's shoulder, and wondered if she would be able to take it down without him noticing. He was going to turn round any minute and spot it. It was unmissable.

'Actually,' she said hastily, 'you could come and look at my fireplace now and tell me what you think. Bearing in mind that I am on the tightest budget imaginable.'

He followed her obligingly into the living room. They both looked at the hideous fireplace and exchanged grimaces.

'Well,' he said. 'If it was me I'd just rip the whole lot out, plaster it up and have a plain slate hearth. Have it as a feature, stick a vase of flowers in it. Then if the purchasers want a real fire, they can put whatever they like in.'

Charlotte nodded. 'Good idea.'

He handed her back his empty cup.

'I better go. I'm on my way to pick up the girls from school.'

So he was married with children. Of course he was. Most people their age were.

'Monday nights is swimming. My wife refuses to take them.' He gave a small cough. 'My ex-wife.'

'You're divorced?'

'Not yet. Talking about it.'

Charlotte bit her lip. Part of her wanted to spill the beans and share her own dilemma with someone, and the temptation to share it with someone who was going through the same thing was huge. But she didn't want to reveal her life story to the first person that stepped over her threshold, so she kept quiet.

'Well, thanks for dropping by.'

'It's OK. I know what it's like being the new kid in town. The locals don't fall over themselves to be welcoming around here.'

'No?'

'You've got to have been here a long, long time before you're accepted. At least three generations.'

'I'm not planning on staying here that long.'

'You say that,' warned Fitch, 'but it gets under your skin. It's pretty hard to adjust to the real world once you've lived in Withybrook.'

When Fitch had gone, Charlotte plonked herself down on the sofa in the living room, stretched and yawned. She was absolutely exhausted and yet she felt she had achieved nothing of note. She picked up her notebook and tried to draft out a plan of action, making a list of people she needed to call – skip hire, telephone, internet provider – but she couldn't get the visiting order out of her head. She knew that unless she dealt with it, she wasn't going to be able to concentrate.

The quickest option would be to stick it straight in an envelope and send it back to Ed's solicitor. But somehow she felt that was the coward's way out, and would provide her no respite. What she needed to do was to visit Ed, outline her terms and conditions, and draw a line under the whole hideous affair. A divorce would mean freedom and a chance to start again. Pleased with her decision, she went to find the order and work out what she had to do. The instructions were firm and clear and not to be argued with. She was to phone the prison and make an appointment.

She found that if she went to the top of the house and leaned out of the bedroom window she could get two bars of signal – just enough to provide telecommunication with the outside world. She prodded in the prison number and stuck her head out of the window, looking out over the rooftops of Withybrook and watching the crows circling round the chimney pots.

'Hello,' she said tentatively. 'I'd like to make an appointment to visit a prisoner.' She took in a deep breath. 'Edward Briggs.'

'What's your order number, love?'

The man on the other end sounded disinterested. She imagined him, fat stomach straining against his uniform, sitting in a room of empty chairs that were bolted to the floor. As Charlotte gave him the details, she realised she was entering a whole new world, with its own rules and regulations, that was about as far removed from her experience as you could get.

When she put the phone down, her hand was shaking. Next Friday. She was going to visit her husband in prison next Friday. She swallowed down a gurgle of nervous laughter, and was astonished to find she felt rather elated. It was the first piece of positive action she had taken off her own bat. Coming to Withybrook was positive, but she had been goaded, persuaded, aided and abetted by Gussie and could hardly claim the idea as hers. But this she had done of her own free will, she'd grasped the nettle and she felt better for it. Maybe she was coming out the other side, at long last. She had spent so long floundering about in the chaos of what Ed had created, she had almost forgotten that she had choices.

Infinitely cheered, she decided to take the truck and go to find the nearest supermarket. When the fridge was full, she would feel a little more at home. And she'd treat herself to that copy of *Homes and Gardens* and a big bottle of expensive bubble bath. At the moment, it was the little things that made life bearable.

Penny typed up her patients' notes into her computer, pushed back her chair and sighed. It had been an exhausting afternoon. Mondays always were, as people had had the weekend to deliberate their ailments and were eager to get them off their chests. The surgery she worked in was on the outskirts of Comberton, and there were an awful lot of people on the poverty line on the register. It was funny; people always thought Devon was some sort of idyll, a place where nothing bad happened, but Penny had seen as much suffering here as she had in any inner-city practice. People grey-skinned from poor diets, both overweight and underweight, many of them with mental illness, depression, stress, kids with ADD. There were few employment opportunities, few facilities – breathtakingly beautiful countryside was all very well, but there was bugger all for a lot of these people to do. She did everything she could to help them empower themselves, but it was a losing battle when the clock was ticking and you had to rush on to your next appointment. You couldn't make much of a difference in five minutes.

She sat back in her chair and closed her eyes. She had ten minutes' tea-break. It should have been fifteen, but she had inevitably over-run. She breathed in slowly and let her mind drift. She knew exactly where it would go, because it always did.

It was her treat to herself, her little mini-fantasy. It was free, after all, and didn't do anyone any harm. The need to fantasise was always greater after she had seen him. Sometimes she had almost, *almost* got him out of her head, reduced thinking about him to a couple of times a day, but just as she thought she had cured herself — for she thought of her obsession as an affliction — then he would pop up in her life and fan the flames again. And she would be stricken once more, tormented by images of him day and night, allowing her imagination to run wild.

This time she allowed last night's turn of events in the Speckled Trout to take a totally different route. When she asked Sebastian if he wanted a cigarette, he agreed with alacrity. He followed her outside, and no sooner had she delved into her bag for her lighter than he grabbed her, pulled her to him, and devoured her with hot, passionate kisses. Oblivious to the cold night air, they had let their combined ardour carry them away. Within moments they were making love on one of the picnic benches. Sebastian was telling her he couldn't resist, that he thought about her constantly, that the torment was stopping him working . . .

Penny let the preposterously unlikely dream run its course with a smile on her lips. By the end of it, she was so turned on she didn't know what to do with herself. Woe betide her next patient, she thought. Her nipples were hard, and she could feel a throbbing between her legs, an incredible effervescence as minute bubbles of excitement danced around her loins. There was nothing she could do about it now; she could hardly stuff her hand in her knickers. Even though her door was shut people frequently barged in without knocking; that really would be the ultimate embarrassment. She fanned herself with a sheaf of paper, convinced that her thoughts were written all over her face. She couldn't carry on teasing herself like this. One day she would explode with the frustration.

It was tragic, really. A horny, middle-aged woman with no one to take it all out on. What would she prescribe if one of her patients came in and described her own symptoms to her? What would she recommend, to alleviate their suffering? A vibrator, she supposed, with a rueful smile. A buzzy little magic wand. A battery-operated friend that guaranteed satisfaction every time.

As she stood up on trembling legs to go to fetch herself a glass of water, she stopped in her tracks. Why not take her own advice? Why shouldn't she have a vibrator? If all the magazine articles she read in the surgery were true, every woman in England had one in her knicker drawer. Or carted one round in her handbag just in case the urge overtook took her. They were no longer taboo, but commonplace – as necessary in every woman's armoury as a good moisturiser and decent tweezers and a well-fitting bra. Some people had several – a different design to suit the mood. For heaven's sake, even *Good Housekeeping* had a Sex Toy of the Year. She had no need to feel ashamed or embarrassed, and every right to know what all the fuss was about.

She sat in front of the computer self-consciously for a few moments, before getting up the nerve to type 'vibrator' into the search engine. She was slightly worried that it would be embedded into her history for ever more, but not entirely sure anyone would ever be interested enough in her online activity to investigate. A dazzling range of websites came up, from the overtly graphic to the coyly twee. She chose one that seemed warm and intelligent, rather than sensationalist. It explained each piece of apparatus in a clear and non-threatening way, but was also amusing and self-deprecating. In browsing the site Penny realised that she had been leading a rather sheltered life, but her appetite had been whetted. If these little babies delivered the goods like they promised, then she wanted in.

In the end, she chose one that was substantial, but not alarmingly so. And expensive. And didn't make much noise. Her finger hovered over the mouse as she hesitated, wondering whether she really had the nerve to click 'buy'. Then suddenly she found she had done it, and her mouth went dry.

It promised next-day delivery, in a plain padded envelope, not one emblazoned with 'Sex Toys 'R' Us' in bright-red capitals. Nevertheless, she would have to whiz back from the surgery at lunchtime to find it, because if Tom and Megan got back first, they could not be relied upon not to rip it open. They had no respect for her privacy. For all she knew, her precocious daughter already had one in each colour. She wouldn't be surprised at all.

Feeling rather like a naughty schoolgirl, she closed down the website, smoothed down her skirt and buzzed in her next patient.

On her way home that evening, Penny decided to call in on Daisy Miller. Daisy was one of her older patients, and one of her favourites, but Penny had a sense of unease about her that wouldn't go away. Daisy had always been bright, alert and good-humoured, but on the last few occasions she had seen her she had a faint aura of bewilderment about her that she tried to hide with a smile. Even in old age, a pretty face could go a long way towards disguising ills, and Daisy had wide blue eyes and unlined skin, and a cloud of soft white hair. She was the sort of old lady you would choose to look like. But something wasn't right. Six months ago Daisy had fallen and broken her wrist, and had been into the surgery regularly while it healed. Penny had taken to calling in on her at the time, but she hadn't seen her for a couple of months since the plaster had finally come off. She thought it was high time to check up on her.

It took Daisy a while to answer the door, and as soon as she did so Penny's heart sank. There was a blank, worried expression on her face, and a total lack of recognition.

'Daisy? It's Dr Silver. Dr Silver from the surgery? May I come in?'

Daisy looked to one side, and Penny could tell that in the far recesses of her mind she was weighing things up, struggling to assimilate the information in her memory bank. Eventually she looked back at Penny and nodded, standing to one side.

'How have you been? I haven't seen you for a while.'

Daisy didn't answer immediately. She picked up a tea towel that was lying on the arm of a chair.

'The cat's been up on the furniture again.'

She flapped the towel ineffectually and gave Penny a smile. Penny swallowed. As far as she knew, Daisy didn't have a cat, at least not any more.

She didn't need to look far to know that Daisy was finding it hard to cope. In just six months the state of her little cottage had depreciated alarmingly. Once it had been spick and span and shiny as a new pin. Now there was the rather stifling smell of the unkempt. Not a nursing home smell, because that was always masked by disinfectant, but a rank, greasy staleness.

She inspected Daisy's dress, and suspected that she had been wearing it for some time, perhaps even at night as well as in the day. It was creased and stained, and Penny could discern sweat patches under the arms. She had no tights on, just slippers. Daisy had always dressed impeccably.

'Daisy, I wonder if I could go and get myself a glass of water?'

Daisy frowned slightly, as if in the back of her mind she recognised this as a trap, but she smiled and nodded.

Penny slipped into the kitchen, suspecting it would provide more clues. What she saw there made her heart sink further. There were dirty plates everywhere, opened tins with half-eaten contents, some of them mouldy. Apple cores and orange peel, toast crusts.

'Daisy,' she said carefully, 'I think we should see about getting you some help in the house.'

'I don't need help.' The little woman's riposte was stout.

'Perhaps someone who could come in and do a bit of washing-up and cleaning—'

'I do my own cleaning. Are you saying I'm not clean?' There was more than a touch of querulousness now.

'No. It would just be nice for you not to have to worry. Don't you think?' Penny tried to keep her voice as neutral as possible.

Daisy stood in the middle of the room, arms by her

176

side, mutinous in her silence. Penny wondered desperately what tack to try next. What she really needed to do was get Daisy into the surgery and have her properly assessed, but she felt fairly sure she wouldn't co-operate at this juncture.

'Have the family been to visit?'

Penny knew Daisy had a daughter who lived somewhere near Oxford, but who rarely came down to Devon.

'Yes, yes.'

Daisy nodded enthusiastically, but the lack of detail in her response made Penny suspect that she was either lying or didn't have a clue what she was saying.

'That's nice.' Penny took in the thick layers of dust – not that that was a crime, she was no slave to the duster herself – the greasy grime round the sink, the piles of newspapers, the empty milk bottles that hadn't been put out, some of which still had milk in that had gone rancid. She felt a surge of anger that it had to come to this, that no one else seemed bothered about Daisy's welfare, that if it wasn't for the fact that she was actually a caring doctor who happened to have the time to pop in on impulse, then this woman would probably fester in her own mess until she died, probably of some vile infection she would pick up from the lack of hygiene. How many other elderly patients were there out there, neglected and forgotten? She watched as Daisy walked over to the sink and squirted some washing-up liquid into the bowl.

'I've been a bit off-colour,' she admitted. 'But I'm feeling much better.'

She ran the hot tap and looked Penny straight in the eye.

177

'I'm getting on with it.'

She started gathering up the mugs that scattered the work surface. Penny sighed. She wasn't going to get Daisy to admit there was anything wrong. In fact, to all intents and purposes, she probably didn't know there was a problem. She must be living in a hazy approximation of her previous existence, where reality was slightly blurred and memories slipped out of the mind's grasp like quicksilver. But no doubt there would be a tiny, constant nag of fear, a sensation that there was no going back and nothing to be done, like going on a fairground ride and regretting it as soon as the chairs started swinging too high.

Penny decided sensibly that there was nothing she could do now without distressing Daisy any further, but resolved to bring her plight up at the practice meeting. They could draw up a plan of action, and at least she would have the support of other professionals, who might be a bit more objective about the situation. Perhaps she was reading too much into it. Perhaps Daisy had just been a bit off-colour, and was simply slowing down. She hoped so. She wouldn't wish dementia on anyone.

As she drove back through the village, Penny saw the lights on in Myrtle Cottage and wondered if she should pop in to see how Charlotte was getting on. The sensible GP and mother of two told her that would be the right and kind thing to do. But the frustrated, embittered and jealous middle-aged divorcee saw Charlotte as competition, and couldn't quite bring herself to stretch out the hand of friendship. It wasn't Charlotte's fault that she had managed to elicit an invitation to Withybrook Hall within five minutes of meeting Sebastian, but Penny felt aggrieved. OK, so she had been asked too, but only by default, and she had known Sebastian for much longer. Chumming up with Charlotte would be tantamount to sleeping with the enemy. Although, on the other hand, there were those who said keep your friends close, but your enemies closer . . .

In the end, however, she just felt too tired, and if she was to go round she should at least bring a bottle of wine or a box of chocolates. She would earmark her visit for later in the week, when she felt less oppressed by the world.

What did the evening ahead hold for her? Two grumpy, argumentative teenagers, who would turn their noses up at what she had cooked for them, would just about deign to tell her what had gone on in their day, and would start making their demands for the week ahead. All without any concern as to how her day had gone. She loved Megan and Tom dearly, but she sometimes wished they would go against type and buck against their stereotypical behaviour. It would be such fun, she thought wistfully, if she could make spag bol and they could all sit round the kitchen table munching on garlic bread and talking and laughing. If she felt more fulfilled and less taken for granted in her home life, perhaps she wouldn't be quite so desperate for an escape. But for the foreseeable future that's what she was stuck with. And if she was honest, the house without them in was even worse; she hated the weekends Bill took them to his flat in Bristol. Forty-eight hours of freedom, and nothing to do. More to the point, no one to do it with.

She pulled up outside the small patch of gravel that

served as a parking area next to her house. She sat for a minute before going inside. Something would have to change before long, or she would go completely stir-crazy.

Seven

Catkin slid stealthily through the door of Sebastian's studio. She was desperate to see what he was up to, and it looked as if subterfuge was going to be the only way she could manage it. The studio was usually out of bounds to everyone, even her, because Sebastian didn't want anyone judging his work in progress in case he found their opinion inhibiting. She was allowed to see it when it was finished, and not before. But she needed to have a look, just for peace of mind.

She couldn't see anything. There were no canvasses on the easels, no smell of paint, no brushes thrust into pots of turps. She felt a cold chill in her heart. She was reminded of the scene in *The Shining*, where Shelley Duvall discovers that Jack Nicholson has been writing 'All work and no play makes Jack a dull boy', over and over again.

'What the fuck are you doing?'

She jumped out of her skin, to see Sebastian standing in the doorway, glaring at her accusingly.

She gave him a winning smile.

'I just wanted a look,' she explained hastily. 'I'm so excited about what you're doing. I couldn't resist.'

He looked at her evenly.

'Well, you won't find it here,' he replied. 'Most of it's gone to be framed.'

'Oh.'

She looked down at the floor, not sure whether to believe him. It was a plausible enough explanation.

'So what's the title?' she asked brightly. 'The theme?'

'Don't Stick Your Nose In Where It's Not Wanted.' He walked towards her, a smile on his lips. 'Please, Catkin, don't interfere. You know it does my head in.'

'OK. Sorry. I just . . .'

She starting edging her way out, knowing she was guilty of breaking one of their golden rules.

'By the way,' Sebastian added, 'I've invited a couple of people for lunch.'

Catkin stopped in her tracks, unable to believe what she had heard.

'What?'

'It's OK. I've told Stacey. She's going to lay another couple of places.'

'Who?' Catkin knew her tone was sharp, but this could spell disaster.

'Oh – Penny Silver. And a girl I met in the pub on Sunday. She's an interior decorator or something. Doing up a house in the village.'

His response was irritatingly casual. Catkin drew in a deep breath. She mustn't lose it. If she did, there was no knowing what Sebastian might do in retaliation. Bugger off and not turn up to lunch at all, very probably.

'Right,' she managed faintly. 'I better go and have a look at the seating plan.'

'Oh, for fuck's sake.' Sebastian rolled his eyes. 'Just let everyone sit where they want.'

'I can't do that!'

'What? In case they enjoy themselves?'

Catkin swallowed. 'Don't take the piss,' she pleaded. She wanted to ask him to wear something decent for lunch, but she knew that would be pushing it. He'd be in jeans with baseball boots if she was lucky, a scraggy shirt and bare feet if she wasn't. His parents had brought him up to wear exactly what he wished, not what social niceties dictated. At their table, you could have found people in white tie at one end and semi-clad at the other, and no one seemed to mind which end of the sartorial spectrum you chose.

She'd better go and get ready herself. It was less than an hour before the guests were due to gather in the drawing room, which would give her just enough time to make herself presentable. As she hurried across the lawn, she wondered if Sebastian had been telling the truth or if he'd been fobbing her off. If he really hadn't done any work then they'd be in deep trouble. But she knew she'd never get him to admit it if he hadn't. It was going to be up to her, as usual, to get them out of the shit.

Charlotte spent a long time debating what to wear to lunch. She hadn't brought a huge amount of dressy stuff with her, but although Sebastian had insisted it was casual she had spent so long this week in grubby jeans and sweatshirts that she wanted to make the effort. She settled on a red silk polka-dot frock which she always felt comfortable in, dressing it down slightly with flat black suede boots.

She surveyed herself in the mirror. It was a relief to feel human again. The week had been exhausting. She'd spent it pulling up carpets, chipping off tiles, peeling off wallpaper, and years of dust and dirt had come with it. She felt as if it was engrained in her skin and her hair. She'd soaked for hours in the bath, and rubbed herself all over with exfoliating scrub. Her nails were a disaster; she could never be bothered to wear rubber gloves, and now she was paying the price. There were small patches of childhood eczema on her palms where the cleaning products had irritated her skin. But at least she had a shell now. The house was a blank canvas, ready to be transformed. She'd decided that she couldn't manage the kitchen and bathroom herself, that she would have to get someone in to fit them, but by keeping the units plain and simple she would just about be able to keep in budget, as long as there were no disasters along the way. But there was no doubt it was a daunting task. She had hugely underestimated how long everything was going to take, and it was far more tiring than she had thought, especially as the nearest builders' merchant was more than twenty miles away, which meant a trip there could wipe out a whole morning.

Her body ached. She had muscles in places she didn't know she had. And she hadn't been sleeping all that well. She thought she would fall into bed and pass out, but she found she was restless, easily woken by the strange sounds of the countryside – owls and foxes – and when she did sleep she had disturbed dreams.

So all in all her reflection didn't please her. She looked pale, tired, and she'd definitely lost weight. Usually that would delight her, but it made her look even more drawn. She did the best she could with some tinted moisturiser, a lick of mascara and some lip-gloss.

For a moment she wondered if she was being foolish

accepting Sebastian's invitation. There were going to be other guests there, people from London. Might she be recognised? Probably not – people usually didn't recognise people out of context, she was using her maiden name, she had a convincing cover story. She was going to risk it. After all, why should she have to spend her life in exile when she wasn't actually guilty of anything?

Catkin pulled the towel off her head impatiently and rough-dried her hair, still seething from Sebastian's latest bombshell.

She knew Penny Silver; she'd been to her a couple of times with minor ailments and she thought she was perfectly pleasant, but she didn't want a middle-aged GP at her lunch table talking about bunions and pubic lice, for heaven's sake. And the other was some misguided creature who thought she could make a fortune by slapping a bit of emulsion around. Bloody Sebastian. Why did he always have to go and put a spanner in the works, just when she had worked out the perfect table plan? Now she had two spare women – two! – both as dull as ditchwater with nothing to bring to the party.

Deep down Catkin knew she was being vile and control-freakish, and that really she should be laid-back and chilled and welcome in any of Sebastian's waifs and strays. She knew that was how the house had been when he was younger. His parents were wealthy drop-outs who had ushered all and sundry into their lives, and it had been an enriching experience. From tramps to tsars, you could have fallen over anyone at

Withybrook Hall in its heyday. Catkin had seen the pictures and heard the stories.

But that wasn't how it worked these days, sadly. You couldn't drift around associating with any old Tom, Dick or Harry if you wanted to get on. Success meant mixing with success, and you had to be very careful to keep your finger on the pulse of who was in the ascendant and who was about to fall out of favour. It was suicide to be linked with failure. You had to cling to the ones who were on their way up, ditch those on their way down. And it was a full-time job keeping tabs on it all.

Catkin was ruthlessly ambitious, and she had a dream: for herself and Sebastian to be the king and queen of all A-list couples, the ones whom everyone looked to for the next direction. She wanted the nation to hang on their every word, the papers to follow their dress, their décor, their eating habits, their holiday destinations. But she didn't want to be seen courting this exposure. She wanted it to be an organic process, a discreet and seamless ascendancy. Charles Saatchi and Nigella Lawson rather than David and Victoria Beckham. And she didn't see why it couldn't happen. Sebastian was already renowned, if not infamous, and she was becoming better known. She was desperate to move on, however. It was time she had her own show, something with a little more gravitas. Teenage dilemmas on daytime television were all very well, but she wanted a vehicle that had more depth, that allowed her more searching questions. Celebrity counselling. *On the Couch with Catkin* was her working title. It wasn't quite *In The Psychiatrist's Chair*, but to be a major star you had to dumb down a bit, and she couldn't remember ever seeing Dr Anthony Clare in *Hello!*. She had a vision of herself on a plush purple velvet sofa, sporting Christian Louboutins and horn-rimmed spectacles. Sexy and brainy, that was her selling point.

And this weekend, she had finally snared the man she wanted to sell herself to. Martin Galt was an independent producer whose company specialised in high-rating, personality-led reality television. Catkin was going to present him, discreetly, with her well-thought-out, carefully written proposal, having spent the last twenty-four hours softening him up, pampering him and his rather insipid wife Inge.

Catkin's house parties were legendary. London people always seemed very amused by the idea of an English country weekend, and were only too eager to accept her invitations. The parties were a mixture of traditional country pursuits and sybaritic self-indulgence. She organised clay pigeon shooting on the lawn, or croquet matches, or fishing trips. The evening was a lavish, six-course dinner accompanied by the finest wines. She made sure her guests had a weekend to remember, that her skills as a hostess were branded on their brain. She wanted them to come away feeling as if they could never repay her hospitality, because there would come a day when she would call in the favour. She certainly hoped Martin Galt was feeling indebted. She had arranged an afternoon's shooting the day before with a local syndicate, and it had cost her an arm and a leg. Personally, she didn't see the point of standing about in a freezing bit of countryside taking pot-shots at birds that had been bred to be killed. But it was a prestige sport, with immense snob value, and had seemed to impress her guests.

If Catkin paused long enough to think about it, she realised that she had no true friends. She didn't invite anyone just because she wanted their company. That was where she and her husband differed. Sebastian would not give a second thought to how useful someone was. And she could never tell who he would take a liking to, and who he would shun. If he didn't like someone, he was impossibly rude, either ignoring them point-blank or goading them mercilessly. He was unrepentant, and insisted that at least he wasn't superficial and false and two-faced, which Catkin took as a personal insult. She insisted that if they wanted to get on he had to play the game. He just laughed.

It was wearing her down, the constant tussling between them. It was almost as if he took pleasure in sabotaging her efforts. He had absolutely promised to be charm personified this weekend, and now he'd gone and dumped two unwanted guests on her. There was nothing she could do about it now.

She threw open her wardrobe to decide what to wear. She wanted to look stunning, but not over-dressed. It was only Sunday lunch in her own house, after all. She selected some Sass & Bide jeans and a black polka-dot Marc Jacobs blouse, finished off with some large gold hoop earrings. Along the corridor, she could hear the sounds of her guests getting ready: baths running, hairdryers blowing, footsteps up and down the corridor as they endeavoured to paper over the cracks left by the rigours of last night's partying. As well as Martin and Inge, she had also invited Jonathan Elder and his wife. Jonathan was a publisher who had expressed an interest in Sebastian's autobiography, even though Sebastian had insisted time and again that he had no intention of spilling his guts for the vicarious pleasure of the middle classes. But the figure that had been muttered as an advance was a substantial one, and would go a long way towards balancing the books in the Turner household. If, as she suspected, Sebastian wasn't coming up with the goods in the studio, then he might just have to share his innermost secrets with the world.

To counteract these heavy hitters, and as a bit of light relief, she had invited Boz Mayhew, the chirpy cockney florist who had a slot on *Hello, England,* and who was working his way into the hearts of the nation with his cheeky banter and light touch with gerberas. Boz was her ally at the studio, and she knew she could depend on him to keep her illustrious guests entertained and not be too contentious. And who knows, he might come out of it with his own show or a book deal. Catkin was fond of Boz, and didn't view him as competition. They were like chalk and cheese, which was why they got on. Boz had brought his boyfriend Lee; Catkin wanted as few spare women as possible, for she knew Martin's reputation as a bit of a lech and a Lothario, and she didn't want his eye off the ball for a second. Or his wife upset.

All in all, the stakes were pretty high this weekend, and Catkin really didn't want to worry about Penny Silver and some two-bit decorator who thought she was Kelly Hoppen. But to go against Sebastian at this stage was futile. They were probably trotting up the drive even now, clutching a box of Quality Street and a bottle of Jacob's Creek. She couldn't turn them away. She would just have to pray that they wouldn't be too mind-numbingly dull, or worse, get drunk and come out of their shells. She'd have to make sure their glasses weren't topped up too frequently. Normally she didn't stint on alcohol, but she was dealing with an unknown quantity here.

Dressed, coiffed and made-up, she went down to the kitchen, where Stacey and her daughter Nikita were preparing lunch. Stacey lived in the village with her six children, and Catkin had taken her on as a cook-cum-housekeeper as soon as she and Sebastian had arrived in Withybrook. It had taken her a while to train Stacey up, but after two years she had licked her into shape. Nikita, her oldest daughter, who did the waitressing and washing-up, was more of a lost cause. She was wearing a grey zip-up hoodie and ridiculously wide jeans that trailed along the floor, her hair all over her face.

'Nikita,' Catkin cooed, 'come up to my bedroom and let's see if we can get you into something more suitable . . .'

Nikita didn't mind being bossed about, and the rate Catkin was paying was well over what she would get anywhere else, so as far as she was concerned she could ask her to serve topless if she wanted to. She followed her obligingly up to her bedroom, and stood looking round it in unashamed awe as Catkin flipped through racks and racks of clothes, all neatly colour coded and hung on padded hangers. The room was bigger than the whole council house she and her five siblings were crammed into. The bed itself wouldn't have fitted into Nikita's room, which was no bigger than a cupboard, but at least she didn't have to share it.

After several false starts, Catkin put Nikita in a black linen shirt dress and flat red pumps, and tied her hair back in a smooth ponytail. A flick of black eyeliner over her lids and some red lipstick and she looked perfect. Subservient, but sexy. Almost as if it were possible for her to be called Nikita, whereas before the notion had been risible.

'Wow,' said Catkin. 'You look amazing.'

Nikita just rolled her eyes and chewed on her gum.

'Gum out, please,' said Catkin, holding out a bin.

Nikita gobbed it out obligingly. Catkin shuddered. She didn't have time to do the whole Eliza Dolittle thing on her now. She'd just have to pray that the guests didn't notice her ragged fingernails, or the love bite on her neck. Though arguably there were some men who liked that kind of thing.

Nikita's make-over accomplished, Catkin went down into the drawing room to make sure that everything was as it should be. It was a beautiful room, with French windows facing out onto the lawns. But Catkin thought that it was faded and old-fashioned. The whole house, in fact, felt as if it had been preserved in aspic. In some ways that was good, because they couldn't actually afford to refurbish it, and it was still impressive in a faded-grandeur sort of way. Besides, Sebastian wouldn't countenance any changes whatsoever, no matter how minor. It was almost as if he wanted to keep the house as a shrine to his parents and their Bohemian lifestyle. Rather unexpectedly, he adored both of them, which was slightly at odds with his snarling, world-weary image. He wouldn't have a word said against them, or what they stood for. They were sacrosanct. Catkin struggled with this, especially as she felt no real loyalty to her own parents. She didn't bother to keep in contact with either of them, not even a Christmas card. It seemed hypocritical. What had either of them ever done for her, after all?

She stood by the French windows for a moment, so close to the glass she could feel the cold air pulsing through. She looked out at the lawn, and the incredible landscape beyond – a small wooded valley leading to the moors behind, unfolding their way towards the dark purple sea, which could just be glimpsed in the far distance. It was almost infinite. You couldn't look at the view and not gasp with admiration.

Catkin picked idly at one of the window frames. It was crumbling. If she poked hard enough, the wood and the paint would fall away, so she stopped. It was a little bit how she felt herself – that if someone poked her hard enough, she would crumble. It was such hard work keeping it all afloat, but she was so close, so close . . . she couldn't give up now. Catkin wanted to live life to the full. She craved fame, wealth, recognition, influence. She had married Sebastian not because he was a ticket to this, but because he was bloody impossible, her biggest challenge. She knew the day she broke his spirit and tamed him was the day it would be all over. There was a constant battle between them. She was the sensible adult, the one who kept it all together, while he was the naughty child. She had to find a way of getting what she wanted without breaking the magic that had brought them together. She didn't want to impose her will upon him. She couldn't. But for them to be in partnership, and rule the world, that was her dream . . .

She heard a footstep on the oak floorboards behind her.

'Catkin . . .'

She turned. It was Martin Galt. His very success floated into the room before him. He had steel-grey hair cropped very short, and a Bermuda tan. He wore a well-cut suit with a blue shirt underneath, no tie, and a white-gold band on his wedding finger that fooled no one. A supremely confident man. But Catkin was a supremely confident woman.

She crossed the room and kissed his cheek. He smelled of Tom Ford. He put a hand on the small of her back and pulled her in to kiss the other cheek, lingering a fraction too long. She drew back, and fixed him with a dazzling smile.

'So, Martin, have you enjoyed your weekend?'

'Enormously. Though I was hoping for a chance to talk to you in private at some point.'

'Oh?' She looked at him archly, managed not to become flustered. Her heart was pattering. Was he going to suggest the very thing she wanted?

'You're amazingly charismatic.' He held her eyes in a steady gaze which, despite all the skills she had honed over the years, she couldn't quite read. 'Your eyes are stunning.'

She blinked, suddenly self-conscious. 'Thank you.'

'They remind me of the sea just off Turks and Caicos.' He reached out and touched her cheek with the back of his forefinger, a light touch that said it all. She did her best not to jerk away. She knew this type. She would have to play along, at least for the time being. 'We should have dinner. Discuss possibilities.'

'You've got my number.' She dropped her voice to a husky whisper.

'Yes,' he replied. 'Yes, I have . . . got your number.' He paused for a moment, nodding gravely. 'In fact, I know *exactly* what your game is. I know *exactly* what this is all about. Frankly, Catkin, I prefer a more direct approach. You needn't have gone to all this trouble. You should just have come straight out with it.'

She told herself to stay calm. He was just trying to unnerve her. She put up a hand to brush back her hair and gave what she hoped was an enigmatic smile.

'Why don't you tell me what it is you want?' His voice was low.

She could feel unease floating into her guts. He was testing her, pushing her, and she couldn't quite work out how to play him. Men like Martin had gargantuan egos. One step wrong and she could screw her chances for good. But she knew instinctively that he would value balls and nerve above everything.

'You know exactly what I want,' she countered. 'My own show. Prime-time exposure. And if you don't give it to me,' she finished bravely, 'then someone else will. It's up to you.'

He laughed, showing a flash of expensive dentistry. Then stopped, leaning into her. She could smell his recently used Rembrandt toothpaste.

'How far would you go, Catkin, to get what you wanted?'

This was the make or break moment.

An image of her name emblazoned on the screen flashed into Catkin's mind. She looked at Martin. He wasn't unattractive. It wouldn't take long . . .

What the hell was she thinking? It was out of the question. No – she had to gain his respect, but not offend him. A flirtatious rebuff was what was needed. A lightly teasing refusal would keep him interested without compromising her. With maybe just a hint that she could be persuaded if he persevered. It was a fine balance. It would all have to be in the eyes. Catkin widened hers slightly.

'I've never slept with anyone to further my position, if that's what you mean.'

'Oh?' He allowed his gaze to flick around the room. 'How did you end up with all this, then?'

She gave an involuntary gasp. He was implying that her marriage was a sham. She tried to keep her voice steady. 'I love my husband very much.'

'Really?' His tone was beyond disparaging.

'Yes. She does.' A languid drawl from the doorway made them both start. 'Christ, Catkin. I don't know how you deal with these tossers on a daily basis.'

Sebastian strolled into the room. Her heart melted. He was wearing a white shirt and jeans, and his beloved Berluti calf-skin moccasins. He'd made the effort, and she knew it was just for her. How could she have wavered, even for a moment? Because she couldn't deny to herself that there had been a second when she had entertained the idea of sleeping with Martin Galt, if it meant getting what she wanted.

Martin remained as cool as a cucumber.

'Don't pretend it doesn't happen in the art world, Sebastian,' he shot back. 'No one in the fame game is whiter than white.'

Catkin's heart sank. All the effort she had gone to, and it had all gone up in smoke. She might as well cancel lunch right now. She'd known from the outset it was going to be a disaster. But just as she was about to snap to Martin that she'd phone for the minibus now if he wanted to leave, Nikita led Penny Silver into the room.

Sebastian leaped across the room to give her a hug.

'Penny!' he greeted her warmly. 'Welcome to the lions' den. This is Penny,' he turned to Martin. 'And if you try anything on with her you'll have me to answer to.'

Penny looked rather startled by this unconventional introduction. Martin didn't turn a single steel-grey hair. Catkin felt as if she might be about to pass out.

'Nikita,' she said faintly, 'could you bring in the champagne? I think we could all do with a drink.'

Charlotte pulled on her camel coat with the faux fur collar and snuggled it round her neck. She decided to walk to Withybrook Hall. It was only half a mile up the road, and she craved fresh air. The village was sleepy and quiet as she strolled up the high street. She'd heard the bells ring out at about half past ten, but everyone must be back from church by now. She imagined the families inside their houses, sliding their Sunday joints into the oven, peeling potatoes, rolling out pastry for apple pies . . . She hurried on to where the houses dwindled away and the road narrowed, twisting up a hill lined with a traditional Devon bank wall. It wasn't long before she reached the entrance to Withybrook Hall – a set of double gates which led to a long, sweeping drive that curved around an expanse of lawn surrounded by beech trees, oaks and acers. At the end of it stood the house. It was a classic Georgian rectory. Long and low, painted white with a grey slate roof, it had two large bay windows either side of a pillared entrance approached by wide stone steps.

It was idyllic and stopped Charlotte in her tracks. The November breeze ruffled her hair, and she could smell the distant sea. She gave the smallest of sighs. This would have been Ed's dream. This must have been what he had in mind when he made his massive error of judgement. She could picture him imagining them in a house like this, their children frolicking on the lawn, swinging from the branches of the massive oak. She remembered all the brochures she had found over the years. Tears stung her eyes for a moment. Where were they now? He was stuck in prison, and she was working on the hardest job she had ever done in her life, for the smallest return, and with no idea where she would go and what she would do once it was finished.

She gave herself a little shake. This was her day off, and she was determined to enjoy it. She ran up the steps and took hold of the lion's head knocker, giving two sharp raps. She had to move forward. She wasn't going to let her past spoil her future.

The girl who answered the door seemed vaguely familiar. Charlotte couldn't place her until she greeted her with a croaky Devon burr and a shy smile.

'All right?'

Charlotte peered at her more closely. It was the girl from the post office; she'd popped in several times this week for baked beans, fresh eggs and fish fingers from the dodgy freezer when she couldn't face the thirty-mile round trip to the supermarket.

'Nikita?'

The girl nodded, embarrassed. 'I feel like a right div.'

'You look gorgeous.'

'If Brindley ever saw me, he'd take the piss something wicked.'

'Brindley?'

'My boyfriend. He'd laugh his head off.'

'I doubt he would.' Charlotte couldn't believe the difference in her.

'May I take your coat?' Nikita held out her hand and smiled, as Catkin had taught her. Charlotte slithered out of her coat and handed it over.

'I didn't know you worked here.'

'Weekends. Me and Mum. My sister Montana has to look after the kids. But it's OK. Mrs T pays good money, and we get to take the leftovers home. They last us till Wednesday, usually.'

Having heard voices, Sebastian shot out into the hall.

'Charlotte. Thank God you're here. I'm surrounded by complete tossers.' He handed her a glass of champagne with a grimace. 'Get this down your neck. You're going to need it.'

He led her through into the drawing room. Charlotte's experienced eye took in her surroundings; traditional English, nothing but the best though nearly thirty years out of date. Yet somehow it was timeless, with its plump sofas, occasional tables scattered with trinkets and photo-frames, the club fender in front of the fire. It wasn't at all what she had expected. She'd imagined stark punk-rock minimalism – ironic stags heads next to brightly coloured works of art, high-concept lighting and pony-skin rugs. Nothing redolent of family life. This room felt happy, cosy, welcoming, unthreatening.

A striking woman with a sharp bob glided across the room.

'You must be Charlotte,' she gushed. 'I'm Catkin. Let me introduce you to the rest of the suspects . . .'

Penny stood awkwardly by the fireplace, furious with herself for feeling so out of place. It wasn't as if she wasn't a perfectly attractive, intelligent woman with something to say for herself. She'd spent years mingling with consultants and eminent surgeons and specialists who were far more talented and gifted in their own fields than any of this lot, for heaven's sake, and she'd always managed to hold her own. But she felt rather tongue-tied. There was a smug arrogance to these media types. She could almost see their eyes glazing over when they realised she was a mere mortal. Even their wives had perfected the rather dismissive smile, the disinterested nod, and what the hell did they do with their lives? Bugger all, as far as she could make out. Just spent the vast amounts of money their smarmy husbands made, judging by their tans and their jewellery. Trophy wives, both of them. Small-boned, doe-eyed and dim. Martin Galt made her flesh creep. Jonathan Elder wasn't so bad, but incredibly pompous − pseudo-intellectual, and for no good reason, for as far as she could make out he published kiss-and-tell celebrity memoirs, which were hardly edifying. But then, that was where the money was.

Add to this was the stress of being in the same room as Sebastian. He always made her feel light-headed, weak-kneed, dry-mouthed. Her brain turned to mush and her words came out all wrong. And a moment ago, Catkin had given her a small, patronising and knowing smile from across the room, as if to say she knew exactly what Penny was feeling, and that she should join the queue. After all, who wouldn't find him irresistible?

Thankfully, the little gay florist – Foz, Boz? – was coming over to her now. He and his boyfriend had been bounding round the garden, admiring the box hedging and the mossy statuary, imagining it in the summer months when the herbaceous borders would be pulsating with colour. She managed to engage the pair of them in conversation, actually made them laugh with her descriptions of some of her patients and their complaints. At least they had the manners to pretend they were interested, even if they weren't.

And then Sebastian came back into the room with his arm around Charlotte, and she felt quite sick with jealousy. She could feel herself turn green. It was the worst feeling in the world. Why was he so intimate with her, when they had only met briefly? He was introducing her to the others, laughing, his hand touching her waist as he ushered her into the group, and she seemed completely at home. Confident. Even though Penny was sure she had never met any of these people before. How did Charlotte manage to be so sparkly and radiant? Both Jonathan and Martin had perked up visibly at her arrival, and were gawping at her cleavage. Penny wished she had worn something more inspiring than a round-neck leopard-skin cardi and black denim miniskirt.

Shit. Sebastian was coming over to her now, with a bottle of champagne, to top up her glass. She felt panic. Frozen to the spot. She had no idea what to say or do.

'Hey, Pen, relax. No one's going to eat you. Drink up, there's a good girl.'

She held out her glass and realised her hand was shaking. Only slightly. But Sebastian clocked it, and curled his fingers around her hand to steady it as he poured. She felt his warmth, and she felt herself melt.

'Thank you,' she managed to stammer, and he looked into her eyes. She blushed scarlet, couldn't meet his gaze. Could he read in them what she had done the night before? she wondered.

The vibrator had arrived in the post on Thursday morning, just before she left for work. She'd snatched it off the doormat before either of the children could see, and thrust it into her dressing-table drawer, where it lay for the next two days. Though she could see it in her mind's eye all the while, distracting her while she worked. Would she ever have the nerve to use it? More to the point, would she ever have the opportunity?

Serendipitously, on Saturday both children announced they were going on sleepovers and wouldn't be back till Sunday night, which had the dual convenience of allowing her time to experiment and meant she wouldn't feel guilty about going out for Sunday lunch. Once the house was empty, she felt slightly self-conscious. She moved around doing her chores, stacking the dishwasher, loading the washing machine, until she could no longer put off the fact that she had a hot date with her new mechanical friend.

Once she had accepted it, she felt incredibly self-aware. Her body felt alive as she prepared herself, as if her blood was slightly nearer the surface than usual. She had a long, relaxing bath, pouring a generous dollop of Champneys bath oil under the tap, and lighting several scented candles. She was going to be her own lover, but she had to get herself in the mood.

She slipped on a silk kaftan she had bought from the market in Bamford. The emerald green suited her colouring, and the feather-light fabric caressed her skin as it slid down over her limbs.

She looked at herself in the mirror. She'd moved the candles from the bathroom to the bedroom, and the light they gave off was soft and flattering. She was quite pleased with what she saw. Her legs were long and still brown from a summer spent in shorts, her breasts were small but firm and she could see the outline of her erect nipples under the silk. She turned her back to the mirror then looked at herself over her shoulder, giving herself a little moue of a kiss. Not bad, Penny Silver, she thought.

For a moment, she felt sad. She longed for a lover to appear in the reflection behind her, to slide his arms around her waist, then nuzzle her neck. Then lift her up and carry her to the bed. But he wasn't going to appear. She only had herself for company tonight. Well, herself and her new best friend. She wasn't going to let her mood spoil their first encounter.

She held her purchase in her hand. It was smooth, and slightly heavier than she'd expected. She twisted the base that activated the vibrations, and it buzzed into life. She ran it over the palm of her hand, enjoying the gentle, tickling sensation. The noise was negligible, the most discreet of hums, for which she was grateful. She didn't want to go waking up the house with her night-time shenanigans. She started by running it over her body, getting used to the feeling. The unfamiliar attention made her purr with pleasure and she began to relax.

She spread her legs and watched herself in the

mirror as she rubbed in a little body lotion – the leaflet had recommended lubrication, but she was surprised to find herself already quite wet. Anticipation, it seemed, was a powerful aphrodisiac. She slid the vibrator tentatively between her legs. She manoeuvred it gently, over her labia, her clitoris, finally dipping it inside her. It was like coming alive inside, a deep but subtle renascence. Flickers of intensity shot through her loins. She could feel it in her very fingertips. Then suddenly, an incredible explosion that she could hardly bear but never wanted to end, a sweetness that devoured her from the inside. It made her cry out with surprise and pleasure, and she thanked God she hadn't risked her adventure with the children at home.

Christ, she thought, looking at the little implement with awe. Who the hell needed men? She fell back onto the pillow, laughing, and drifted off into a delicious, much-needed slumber.

Hours later she'd woken with an immense sense of loss. She looked at the vibrator sitting innocently on her bedside table. It might have given her the most explosive, mind-blowing experience, but what wouldn't she give to be simply lying in the arms of someone who wanted to be with her? Never mind post-coital tristesse. Post-masturbation tristesse was enough to make you want to slit your throat.

Now, as Catkin announced lunch was ready, Penny took a large gulp of champagne to blot out the memory of the night before and hopefully give her a little Dutch courage. She wondered about feigning a sudden illness and taking flight, so she didn't have to face the ordeal of lunch, but the lure of two more hours looking at Sebastian won out. Just to breathe the same air he was breathing was enough.

Catkin managed to corner Sebastian before they went into the dining room.

'Sebastian,' she pleaded, 'please try to talk to Jonathan at lunch. I wouldn't be surprised if he'd got a contract upstairs in his suitcase. He's desperate to sign you.'

'How many times do I have to tell you?' Sebastian's eyes were cold. 'I'm not writing a bloody book. I'm not selling my family, my friends or my secrets down the river. Why don't you understand?'

'Why don't *you* understand?' she hissed back. 'We're talking high six figures here. And unless you've got any better ideas – like maybe doing some fucking work – we're going to have to start selling off your precious family silver.'

Sebastian gave a shrug. 'Or you could just spread your legs for Martin Galt.'

Catkin gave a gasp. 'I would never do that.'

'No?' Sebastian gave a smile and swayed slightly. Catkin realised he had drunk more than she thought. 'You thought about it. I could see it in your eyes.'

'No, I didn't—'

'It's funny. I'm the one who gets all the bad press. But actually, my morals are quite high, in comparison to yours.'

He ambled off, through the hallway and into the dining room, where she could hear him mingling with the other guests as they took their seats. Catkin stood for a moment, stung. Why was it so hard? They should be having a wonderful time. They were both young, gifted and beautiful, with the world at their feet. So why were they at each other's throats all the time?

Charlotte felt increasingly awkward during what was the most delicious meal she had eaten for days. Crispy pork, roast parsnips and potatoes, carrots tossed in fennel seeds and petits pois à la francaises, served with homemade apple sauce and rich, dark gravy. She felt slightly self-conscious at being the only woman who seemed to be enjoying her food. The two wives were open about avoiding fat and carbohydrates, and just had a sliver of meat and restrained portions of vegetables. Catkin and Penny both toyed with theirs, but made up for it by drinking copious amounts of the delicious wine that Nikita kept pouring.

Boz and Lee, bless them, kept the conversation flowing with wicked anecdotes and topical jokes. Sebastian sat darkly at the foot of the table, drinking steadily, pointedly ignoring Jonathan Elder's wife on his left and repeatedly whispering in Penny's ear on his right. At one point Charlotte saw Catkin remonstrate with Nikita, clearly telling her not to fill Sebastian's glass up so often, but he responded by standing up and fetching the bottle himself. You could have cut the tension between them with the carving knife that sat on the platter bearing the positively medieval leg of pork.

Over apple crumble and Devon clotted cream, Charlotte found herself the object of conversation, as Boz began to ask her about her job. She was hesitant, and supplied only half-truths. To admit to her past clients, many of whom were wealthy and well known, might mean revealing her own identity. Not that she was a celebrity designer, but someone might deduce she'd been working for Breathtaking Designs, and a link might be made from there. She didn't want to leave any trail. So she played her work down, made out that her clients were less illustrious than they really were.

And all the while Catkin observed her shrewdly, eventually leaning forward with eyes that glittered.

'So, Charlotte,' she said, 'how would you like to come and redecorate Withybrook Hall? I think it's long overdue.'

At the end of the table Sebastian banged his glass down. Catkin smiled sweetly.

'I know Sebastian disagrees. And maybe swags and tails will come back in if we wait long enough. But really – it's all a bit *Howards' Way*, don't you think? What would you do in here?'

'Well,' said Charlotte carefully. 'It all depends on what you wanted. I usually work to a brief.'

'Say you were given free rein?' demanded Catkin. 'How would you give it the kiss of life?'

Charlotte swallowed. She felt as if she was betraying Sebastian somehow. 'I'd keep it really simple. High-gloss acid yellow walls, maybe? And lots of black framed pictures. Sort of Giverny with a twist.'

Catkin looked around the room, trying to imagine the transformation.

'I think you should come and give us some ideas,' she enthused warmly.

Sebastian pushed his chair back from the table. 'This is my family home,' he said stiffly. 'I don't want it messed about with.'

He stalked out of the room and everyone looked at each other.

'Think you've touched a raw nerve there,' observed Martin.

Catkin sighed. 'There's retro,' she said. 'And then there's hideous.'

Charlotte looked down at her plate, feeling guilty that she had effectively been the start of the argument.

'Maybe you can talk Sebastian round?' said Catkin. 'He seems to have taken to you.'

Charlotte didn't know quite what to say.

There was absolutely no denying that a commission like this would be a life-saver. As well as being a high-profile, dream job. If she wanted to re-establish herself, it would be an impressive start to her portfolio. But it was clear Sebastian wanted nothing to do with it, and her loyalty at the moment was to him. He'd befriended her, invited her to lunch, made her welcome in his home. She couldn't just ride roughshod over his finer feelings. And although the house was crying out for a make-over, and her mouth watered at the prospect of being allowed a free rein, she had her principles. So she smiled politely.

'I'm up to my eyes trying to finish my current project,' she replied. 'But perhaps after that . . .'

'Have you ever considered a career in television?' Martin intervened smoothly. 'Maybe you should come and do a screen test and throw some ideas around? There must be something new we could do with interior decorating that doesn't involve men with double-barrelled names and flouncy sleeves.'

Catkin felt like plunging the cheese knife into his heart. He was deliberately goading her, she felt sure of it. Next he'd be offering Penny Silver a slot as a celebrity doctor.

But Charlotte turned to him with the sweetest of smiles.

'Absolutely not,' she said firmly. 'I'm very camera shy. And I love what I do. So there'd be no point.'

'Everyone,' objected Martin, 'wants to be famous.'

'Actually, no. They don't.' Charlotte corrected him. 'It doesn't interest me in the least, I can assure you.'

She could feel her cheeks redden. Any minute now someone might start grilling her even more closely, and she didn't feel up to any sort of interrogation. Luckily at that moment, Nikita came in with a tray of tiny silver espresso cups and a plate full of dusted chocolate truffles, and so the attention was turned away from her.

Narrow escape, thought Charlotte. Narrow escape.

At the other end of the table, Penny felt sour. No one had offered her a bloody screen test. She wished she had the nerve to go and find Sebastian and console him. Slide her arm around his shoulders and murmur a few words of solace. He had been whispering in her ear conspiratorially throughout lunch, bitchy but witty remarks about the other guests, and Penny had felt her insides turn to syrup at his proximity. But now his mood had blackened, she no longer felt like his partner in crime. One thing was certain: his wife was a nightmare. A self-serving control freak. What the hell was he doing with her? He was a free spirit, a mischievous, puckish creature who needed the lightest of reins to keep him on track, not an overbearing harridan cracking the whip.

'OK, everybody. Make-over time.'

Everyone's head swivelled. Sebastian was standing in the doorway, grinning. He was holding a selection of paint pots in each hand.

'Let's see what we can do, shall we?'

No one breathed a word as he sauntered over and stood in front of the main wall with its outdated self-striped paper.

Catkin clutched the table. She knew there was no point in remonstrating with Sebastian when he was like this. He was like a child. Any attention and he simply behaved even worse. The best tactic was to ignore him.

The gentleman in Jonathan Elder started to rise to his feet to stop him, but then thought better of it. Why stop a bad boy in the middle of behaving badly? This could be history in the making.

Martin Galt sat back in his chair with a smirk. He was going to enjoy this.

And so everyone at the table watched in horrified disbelief as Sebastian took each can of paint and sloshed it against the wall. Arcs of colour shot through the air, hitting their target with a satisfying splat.

After a few moments, he stepped back and surveyed his handiwork with satisfaction.

'What do you think?'

Nobody quite dared reply.

Sebastian tipped his head to one side and nodded approvingly.

'Jackson Pollock, eat your fucking heart out.'

Eight

On Monday morning, Sebastian lay in bed, the duvet pulled up to his chin. He knew he had behaved appallingly at the weekend and had undermined his wife at every opportunity. Of course, he knew what he should do was pick up the phone to Catkin and apologise. But she never accepted apologies graciously, she always made him feel worse, so there was no point.

The lunch party had disintegrated pretty quickly after his little one-man show. The only person he felt had been on his side was Penny, who gave his hand a squeeze and whispered 'Well done' as she kissed him goodbye. He and Catkin hadn't even had a showdown. She'd merely packed up her things and called Tommy to take her back to the station early, her silence speaking volumes.

In the end, he had gone into the dining room and tried to clean up the mess as best he could, because otherwise Stacey would try to do it. She'd been quite happy to tell him what she thought.

'Having a tantrum, were you?' she'd asked him. 'Well, I hope it was worth it.'

She made him feel thoroughly ashamed, but then she'd had six children, so she was used to bad behaviour.

The underlying problem, the reason he was being so utterly vile and antagonistic, was he still couldn't think of a single thing to paint. Every time he squeezed a blob of raw umber or ultramarine or crimson lake onto his palette and started to dabble, he froze inside. It was all futile. He didn't see the point. Catkin would tell him soon enough. The point, she would say, was cold hard cash. But Sebastian had never found money a motive. On the contrary, it was positively inhibiting. The success of *Alter Egos*, which he had meant to destroy but had ironically been such a triumph, had repressed him even more. And now he felt boxed in, claustrophobic, frustrated, angry – and of course he ended up taking it out on Catkin, because he was frightened.

He couldn't admit it to anyone, but he hadn't actually put brush to paper since that last exhibition. He had four white walls in a gallery waiting to be filled just after Christmas, the art world were holding their breath, and he had nothing, not even a germ of an idea. He spent his days lying in bed playing poker online, smoking a bit of weed, wandering down to the post office to collect the various magazines and newspapers he had on order – *Q*, *Art Monthly*, *Sporting Life*, *Vanity Fair* – in the hopes that one of them might stimulate him to have an idea, that one of them might contain an article or an image that might unlock his creativity. But so far they had only served to inhibit him further. He veered between feeling scathingly critical of other people's work to thinking everyone else was a genius and he was a fraud.

When he was little, he had wandered the countryside with a tin of watercolours and a pad of paper, doing slightly surreal paintings of his surroundings:

wild, exuberant work that showed no restraint, just raw talent. Looking back, that was when he had been happiest. When he had painted for the sheer pleasure of it, with no pressure, no demands, no expectations. And he was angry that the thing he loved had been tainted. When he looked at a blank canvas now, his head filled with questions: would it be good enough for the public? Would it be well received? Would it make money? Time and again he told himself those things didn't matter, but of course they did. Catkin had spelled it out to him time and time again.

He lay in bed until midday feeling crippled with malaise. Why the hell was he such a coward? Why couldn't he just march into the studio and get on with it? What was he so terrified of? He only needed to make a start, and he needn't show anyone else, after all. But then Sebastian knew he was his own harshest critic, that to execute anything that pleased him even remotely would be a Herculean task, especially the way he was feeling.

Eventually, he managed to roll out of bed. He could hear Stacey dragging the Dyson round, eliminating all evidence of the weekend's merriment. He decided to walk into the village. He had a craving for a Tunnock's caramel bar. He wanted to feel its shiny red and gold striped wrapper, slide his fingers under the flap and unwrap it, then bite into the gooey, wafery concoction that would stick his teeth together. He wondered fleetingly about doing a series of paintings based on iconic British food products – Marmite, Ribena, Bisto – but of course Andy Warhol had got there first with his bloody soup tins. He could imagine the reviews already – *'derivative, unoriginal, ersatz'* – and his heart sank. Everything had always been done before. It was impossible to pull something new out of the hat. He pulled on his parka with the fur-lined hood and stomped off down the drive.

He wandered back up the high street later, his booty in a plastic bag. A brace of Tunnock's bars, a copy of *Fur and Feather*, a pouch of tobacco and a bottle of Panda pop. As he went past Myrtle Cottage, he wondered if Charlotte was inside, and whether she would mind an interruption. He needed to purge himself of his shame for the day before, and he felt strongly that although she didn't approve of his behaviour, she wouldn't judge him too harshly. He was drawn to her, and wondered if he could confide in her. He knew, after their conversation in the pub last week, that she could relate to his predicament, and he wanted to explain. He wouldn't get sympathy from any other quarter: his wife, or his gallery owner, or his accountant, or his former tutor. To a man, they would tell him to grow up and not be so self-indulgent. He could always phone his parents – they were unconditionally supportive and always had been – but long-distance phone conversations were unsatisfying and what he needed was someone who genuinely understood his dilemma, so he could feel less bloody guilty.

She answered the door in a pair of outsize blue men's overalls, her head wrapped up in a silk scarf knotted on top of her head. She smiled when she saw him.

'Excuse my attire. I'm painting,' she told him. 'And before you ask, I don't need any help,' she added impishly.

Sebastian hung his head in mock shame.

'I know, I know. I behaved like a wanker.'

'You were being wound up.'

'Do you think so?' he said hopefully.

She laughed. 'Don't come to me for absolution,' she warned. 'But you can come in and talk to me while I work, if you want to get it off your chest.'

She stood to one side and ushered him in. He followed her into the dining room.

'I wasn't very nice to Catkin. I know I wasn't.'

Charlotte picked up her brush.

'She puts you under pressure.'

'She does?' Sebastian knew he thought this, but it was nice to know someone else had the same opinion.

'You didn't want all those people in your house.'

'Well . . . only you and Pen.'

'And Catkin didn't want us . . .'

Sebastian slid onto the floor and sat under the window, then pulled his tobacco out of the bag.

'Mind if I smoke?'

Charlotte shook her head.

'She's very ambitious, isn't she? Catkin, I mean?'

'She never stops. It's full-on the whole time. She pushes herself, and she pushes me. And all she ends up doing is pushing us apart.' He licked his cigarette paper. 'You don't want to hear all this.'

'It's the pursuit of perfection, isn't it?' Charlotte daubed globs of paint onto the wall and worked it in with careful strokes. 'We're just not satisfied any more, are we, our generation? We've got to have more. We've got to have it all.' She stood back to view her handiwork. 'If we could just be content with our lot . . .'

Sebastian looked at her through a plume of smoke.

'So are you content with your lot?'

She looked down at him for a moment. 'I was,' she said quietly. 'I'd told myself to be happy. That I might not have it all, but I had more than most. But then . . .' She trailed off, then walked over to her pot of paint to reload her brush.

Sebastian didn't say anything. He sensed that to push her would be crass. As she walked back across the room she gave him a small, sad smile, a smile that said that the subject was closed.

'Do you think this colour works?' she asked anxiously.

Sebastian surveyed the walls.

'Yes,' he nodded. 'It's like old parchment. Pale, antique gold. It's nice.'

'Good,' she replied. 'And you might as well help if you're going to just sit there. There's a spare brush.'

She nodded over to her trestle table. Sebastian got to his feet. Next to the brushes sat a pad of paper and a clutch of pencils. Charlotte had been sketching out her ideas for the cottage. Sebastian leafed through them idly, not really interested – her drawings were skilful, but the subject matter didn't interest him in the least. Why would he care where the sofa was going, or what sort of lights she had planned? But as he put the pad of paper down, he found his fingers were itching. The longing to pick up one of her pencils and start to draw was suddenly overwhelming.

He cleared his throat rather awkwardly.

'Um, actually . . . Would you mind . . . ? Would you mind if I sketched you?'

She looked at him, slightly surprised.

'Go ahead.'

His heart thumped as he began to draw. He could feel it flow through him, the sheer unadulterated pleasure of drawing for its own sake, of drawing something because you wanted to. That deep down need to capture a feeling, a moment. The spirit of a person who moved you.

Charlotte carried on painting, feeling slightly awkward, but as she got engrossed in her work she eventually lost her self-consciousness. As the wall in front of her gradually lost its grubby paleness and took on the honeyed glow of the paint she had mixed, she felt an increasing sense of satisfaction. She wanted to finish the room today, so that it had a chance to dry properly overnight and she could see if the colour really did work. You could never tell until a room was finished, until every surface was covered. It could be either too insipid or too oppressive. Then again, it might be perfect.

For half an hour, the pair of them worked in silence, a comfortable silence, with neither of them interrupting each other's flow. Then Sebastian put down his pad with a contented sigh.

'Can I have a look?' asked Charlotte.

He nodded, holding the pad out wordlessly, drained by the first piece of work he had done for months that hadn't made him want to slash his wrists.

She looked at the drawing in awe. There were hardly any pencil marks at all. The charcoal had barely flirted with the paper. But there she was, looking back at herself, as clear as her own reflection in the mirror. She gasped, putting her hand to her mouth. What she hadn't realised, and what Sebastian had made as plain as day, was how haunted she looked. Her expression was wary, her eyes guarded. She looked like the keeper of a very dark secret. Which, of course, she was.

'What's the matter?' he asked anxiously. 'Don't you like it?'

'It's . . . incredible. But I didn't realise . . . I didn't realise I looked so . . .'

She wasn't sure how to explain it.

'I look as if I've got something to hide.'

'You do.' Sebastian nodded. 'That's the essence of you. That's what I wanted to capture. You're so . . . beautiful and pure on the surface. But there's something underneath . . .'

She felt trapped, suddenly. She tried to smile, as if a smile would wipe all traces of the secrecy from her face.

'It's just stress, I suppose. Trying to get this place into shape.'

She could feel him looking at her again.

'I don't think it's just stress,' he said softly. There was a pause, and then he spoke again. 'What is your secret, Charlotte?'

She stood very still for a moment, hands clasped in front of her face as if in prayer. It was so tempting to confess her murky secret to Sebastian. But if she couldn't keep her own counsel, then she could hardly expect anyone else to.

'I know there's something,' he persisted. 'I can feel it in you. You've come here to run away from something. Haven't you?'

'Don't interrogate me.' It was a plea rather than a command.

'I thought I might be able to help. Whatever it is,

I'm pretty unshockable. No one ever behaves worse than I do.'

She had to smile at that.

Yet he knew. He knew there was something.

Equivocation, she decided, was the only solution. To offer him a tiny bit of the whole truth. She knew he wouldn't give up.

'OK,' she said, her voice shaking. 'You want the truth? My husband and I couldn't have babies. And . . . our marriage couldn't take the pressure any more.'

There. She'd told him. Not a lie. Just a tiny kernel of the story. The beginning, really, of the whole sorry tale.

Sebastian looked aghast. She could see in his face that he wished he'd kept his mouth shut.

'Shit,' he said. 'Shit, Charlotte. I wish I hadn't asked. I never know when to stop.'

She looked down at the floor. He walked over to her and took her in his arms. Squeezed her tightly to him. She could feel the compassion roll off him, and she felt comforted.

'Just tell me to fuck off the next time I start prying.' His voice was slightly muffled in her ear. 'I didn't mean to upset you. Honestly. It's just . . . I could see it all in your face. I wanted to know. Because I wanted to make it better. I really did.'

'Well, now you know. And you can't.'

Her head was on his shoulder. He took her hands in his and squeezed.

'You're very brave.'

'No, I'm not.'

'Coming here like this to start again—'

'It's just running away.'

'So? There's nothing wrong with that. Why stick around if it's bad?'

He smoothed back her hair out of her eyes, and wiped the few tears that had trickled out from her cheeks. She felt strangely comfortable with him. Even though his gestures were incredibly intimate, they were in no way invasive. He held her in his arms again and they stood in the middle of the room, in the tightest embrace, neither of them moving.

Eventually, she pulled away.

'Thank you,' she whispered. 'I feel better for telling someone.'

'It's nothing to be ashamed of.'

'No,' she agreed. 'But I haven't quite dealt with it yet. So I'd rather it wasn't common knowledge.'

'I won't say a word,' promised Sebastian. 'I might be a tactless prick, but I know how to keep a secret.'

He dived for the carrier bag he'd got from the post office, rummaged about in it and produced the two Tunnock's bars.

'What about a cup of tea?' he asked. 'And I defy you not to feel better after one of these.'

Later, Sebastian walked back up the road slowly, thinking about Charlotte. The incredible, sweet, brave girl with the broken heart had touched something deep inside him. What a self-indulgent little prick he was. There was a creature who really did have something to cry about, while his turmoil was totally of his own making. He felt thoroughly ashamed, but also intrigued by her predicament.

Having children wasn't something he and Catkin had given much thought to as yet. It was obviously out of the question while she was building her career, but now he thought about it, he realised he had assumed it would just happen one day when the time was right. After all, Withybrook Hall was made for children. He had been so happy there. And he had taken it for granted that one day the old nursery would be filled with his offspring; that they would gallivant across the lawns and scramble up the trees. But it wasn't going to happen as if by magic. And even then, what if they were presented with the same problems as Charlotte and her husband? Not that he was trying to turn Charlotte's predicament round to himself, but it had jolted him out of his lethargy. The tangible sadness inside the girl, the brave front she put up, her fragility had woken him up.

As he turned in through the gates, and glimpsed the roof of his studio, his heart stopped for a moment. Usually, he would recoil at the sight of his prison. But today, he hurried towards it, feeling in his pocket for the key. He couldn't get the door open quickly enough. He hurled his bag of shopping to one side, pulled off his coat, ran his hands through his hair and took a deep breath in.

This was the moment all artists waited for. The burst of inspiration that was more important than breathing. The tingle that slid along every vein and made you feel alive. It was in such incredible contrast to the moribund sensation Sebastian had been feeling for the past few months. How could he flip from one state to the other, just like that? It wasn't something you could force, because God knows he had tried to force it often enough. But a single experience, a single moment, could help you slide from a stifling, barren restlessness to joyful exuberance.

He rushed over to the roll of linen canvas he kept on the wall and pulled out a length, slicing it with a Stanley knife. He knew the size he wanted exactly. He pulled out four stretchers and laid them out on the floor, tapping the mitred edges together to get the size and shape he wanted, laying an extra one across the middle for strength. Then he spread the canvas over the table-top and placed the frame gently on the top. It might have been a while since he had done this, but it was second nature to him. He was totally absorbed as he made sure the grain of the linen was parallel with the sides of the frame, then folded the canvas over the edges, making sure the linen was taut. He started to put in the tacks, using his trained eye to position them exactly, one in the centre of each side. Once they were in place, he added more at half-inch intervals, and finished by folding neat hospital corners, as if he was making a bed.

He hesitated before preparing the canvas. He was in such a hurry, he wanted to start straight away, but he still had to prime it and wait for it to dry properly, which would take at least six hours. But he told himself it would be worth the wait. He applied the first coat, then pulled out a sketch pad, found his favourite 6b pencil, and started to put down his ideas. He felt slightly crazed. Almost obsessional, as if he had to pin her down before she flew away.

All night long he worked, flitting from stretching canvasses to priming them to sanding them down, and in between he drew. He couldn't work fast enough for the ideas that were flooding his mind. He was drowning in the essence of her. Just before dawn, he fell exhausted onto the futon he kept in there and fell asleep. It was the sweetest sleep he'd had for months, untainted by alcohol or drugs. He hadn't even stopped for a cigarette all night.

She was the first thing he thought of when he woke. And he tried to identify his feelings for her. It certainly wasn't a sexual feeling – he wasn't fantasising about her in a weird way. She was just so unlike any woman he had met before. She was so self-contained and un-needy – yet she probably needed emotional support more than anyone. There was a purity about her, an innocence. It made him want to protect her and keep her safe from harm. He had never felt like that about anyone before. Which possibly said more about him than anything.

Maybe, thought Sebastian, for the first time in his life he was worrying about someone other than himself.

He rolled off the futon and got to his feet. There, scattered around the studio, were the six large canvasses he had prepared the night before, stretched, primed and ready for him. For a second he felt frozen with fear. What if the desperate need to paint from the night before had been an aberration? What if it had evaporated, leaving him with the same torpor he had been suffering for months? But no – already he could feel the urge to get started.

He looked around and realised the studio was a disgrace. The air was stale, the surfaces thick with dust, littered with ashtrays and abandoned magazines. He felt a sudden puritanical need for order and cleanliness.

He didn't want his work to be sullied with his former chaos. This was going to be a fresh start. He threw open the skylights and let the sweet morning air in. He stacked the wood-burner with fresh logs. He collected up all the mugs and glasses and stacked them in the dishwasher, threw all the empty bottles in the bin, sorted through the magazines and newspapers, put all the loose CDs back in their cases.

Suddenly there was an almighty banging on the front door. His heart leaped into his mouth – perhaps it was Charlotte, in trouble, needing him. He rushed to open it.

It was Stacey, red-faced and anxious.

'Thank God you're here,' she gasped. 'The missis has been phoning and phoning you all night. I just spoke to her. She told me to see if you were here. She thought . . .' She trailed off, not wanting to voice Catkin's fears. Sebastian couldn't keep the irritation out of his voice.

'I'm fine, Stacey,' he told her. 'I was working. I slept in here last night.'

Stacey peered into the room over his shoulder, not quite believing him, as if she wanted evidence of some sort of debauched orgy that she could report back.

'Oh,' she said flatly, clearly disappointed. 'Well, you'd better ring her. She was talking about coming back home, she was that worried.'

The last thing Sebastian needed now was to hear Catkin's censorious tones. He turned to Stacey with his most charming smile.

'Could you call her for me?' he asked. 'Only . . . I'm under rather a lot of pressure. Tell her I'm absolutely fine and I'll call her tonight.'

For a second, he considered asking Stacey to come in and clean up. But no – he didn't want anyone contaminating his air, or to listen to her burbling away about her six children. He didn't usually mind at all – he was happy to listen to the minutiae of her life that was so far removed from his, even though she lived barely two hundred yards down the road. No, he needed to keep the place sacrosanct and his mind clear. Sebastian wanted to stay inside his little bubble for as long as he could. Any contact with reality might burst it.

He could tell by the way Stacey pursed her lips that she didn't approve of the fact he wasn't calling his wife himself. But eventually she waddled off. She knew him well enough not to argue, and to mollify her he'd agreed to let her bring him over some lunch at one. Stacey wasn't happy unless she was cleaning under your feet or providing.

Once Stacey was out of sight, he went over to the first canvas and placed it reverentially on the easel in front of him. His heart was beating so loudly he could hear the blood pounding in his ears. He felt sick with excitement and anticipation. This was like meeting a secret lover for the first time – the greatest thrill mixed with the greatest fear, not knowing what was going to happen, waiting for the first move to be made, not wanting to go too fast or too slow but desperate to begin.

With trembling hands, he set out his palette and began to squeeze the tubes of paint that had sat untouched for so many months. The squirls of colour oozed their way out reluctantly at first, then flowed more freely. The smell hit him, so familiar and evocative. How he could have left it so long he didn't know. This was the stuff of life to him. This was what he was meant to do. How could he have spent so many months idling, letting his creativity atrophy? And as his creativity withered, so had his soul, until he had become someone he despised. It was only now that he recognised just how hateful he had become.

He ran his fingers through the oils, stirring, mixing, adding little dots of colour to create the perfect flesh tone, a creamy pinky-white, then he began to smear it over the canvas, his fingers darting all over the surface, creating curves, sinews, muscles. It was as if he was caressing her himself, bringing her to life with his touch – her shoulder, her neck, her spine . . .

In a mere twenty minutes, the whole canvas was smothered in Charlotte-ness; impressionistic strokes that were at once light but bold, like the loudest of whispers. Now he had captured her whole, it was time to put in the detail. He'd barely known her a week, but he felt as if he had known her a lifetime, as he worked in the curve of her lips, the set of her brow and the light in her eye.

She was perfect.

Nine

On Friday, Charlotte woke feeling as if she had greasy washing-up water sloshing about in her stomach. Perhaps it was the paint fumes accumulating. She should have opened more windows while she was working.

Or perhaps it was because today was the day she was going to visit Ed.

She ran to the bathroom and threw up in the sink, tendrils of hair sticking to her sweaty forehead. She'd better phone the prison to cancel. After all, if she had a bug they wouldn't thank her for bringing it with her.

She clung to the sides of the basin as she ran the tap to rinse away the contents of her stomach. Now she had been sick, she felt a bit better. She looked in the mirror as the colour slowly came back into her cheeks. Cancelling her visit would just be prolonging the agony. She had to confront Ed and, although it sounded corny, get closure. She felt strong enough now, after a few months on her own. She'd started building a new life for herself. She felt as if she had a future; even though it wasn't exactly rosy, it wasn't entirely bleak. But she had to shed her demons in order to move on.

'Come on, girl,' she told herself, going back into the bedroom and pulling open the wardrobe door. What did you wear to visit your husband in prison? In the end, she decided on jeans and a grey cable-knit hooded jumper. She didn't want to stand out as the posh bird and get her head kicked in on the way out. Or look as if she'd gone to any great effort. She drank a quick cup of tea and managed two slices of toast. If she was going to be sick again, it was better to have something to throw up.

She'd calculated that it was going to be nearly a four-hour drive. The prison was in Warwickshire, so it was straight up the M5, but she wasn't looking forward to driving her tank all that way. It had been rattling rather ominously of late. She packed her handbag swiftly, sticking in a banana and a can of Diet Coke to swig on the way. She referred to the complicated list of instructions from the prison. She remembered her visiting order, and her passport, for identification. She wasn't allowed to bring much in the way of presents, but then she didn't feel inclined to.

As she walked through the hall to the front door, she felt her heart lift just a little. The whole feel of the house had changed, even though all she had done was lift up the carpet and paint the walls. It felt cleaner, fresher, lighter, warmer. She had made some headway. She had achieved something, in the face of adversity. Visiting Ed was the next obstacle, and she could get over it. She knew she could.

There was a hideous amount of protocol to get through at the prison, though Charlotte couldn't help feeling that a lot of it was in place to wind up the visitors. She was searched, her paperwork was checked and double-checked, her bag was taken away to be stowed in a locker until she came back out, and there wasn't so much as a smile or a please or thank you. She felt sorry for the other women who had come to visit loved ones, some with children in tow. Their expressions were dull with the tedium of it all. They were obviously used to this treatment, and accepted it wordlessly.

As they were ushered like cattle into the room to wait, she felt a gloom descend. The cheap grey corded carpet, the orange plastic chairs, the strip lighting – this was no atmosphere in which to discuss the future. She sat down awkwardly, feeling slightly self-conscious, even though she knew no one else gave a stuff about her or who she was.

And then Ed walked in. She wasn't prepared for the way she felt. Disembowelled was the only word to describe it. She had meant to be so strong. She had thought she no longer cared, that she would be able to discard him. But when she looked across the room at him, she saw the man she had once loved. The man she had been through so much with. As he walked over to her, it was as if a film of their life together was playing out in front of her. She saw him feed her chocolate-covered fruit on their first date. She saw his eyes as he looked at her during their wedding vows. She saw his face above her as they made incredible love in their house. She saw his face as they looked at scan after hopeless scan . . .

He looked at her warily as he sat down.

'Hi,' she managed, her eyes roaming his face to discern what emotion he was feeling. He just nodded. She was surprised to see he looked well. His hair was cropped close to his head. He looked lean and muscular, and his shoulders seemed broader. Somehow when she'd imagined him in prison he'd been small and shrivelled. This guy looked tough, like a survivor. Someone not to be messed with.

'So – what made you come?' His voice was flat.

'Didn't you want me to? Isn't that why you sent the . . . ?'

'I thought maybe we should talk. Discuss the future.'

She nodded. She hadn't expected him to be hostile. She'd expected him to be relieved. Grateful, even, that she had come to visit. She put her fingers on the table between them, drumming them nervously.

'So . . . how is it?'

He raised an eyebrow.

'Fucking shite. Fucking boring. The food sucks. The conversation isn't exactly stimulating. And the décor's dire, as you've probably noticed.' He gave her a hard look. 'Oh. The gym's not bad. That's the one bonus.'

For a moment she wanted to snap back that it was his own fault, not hers, that he was in here. That he had had a choice. And the choice he had made was his. But she guessed he'd had plenty of time to reflect on that. This wasn't an opportunity to rub salt into his wounds. She'd done enough of that. This was about giving them both the chance to move on.

She cleared her throat. 'I thought perhaps we should talk about . . . um, a . . . divorce.'

Again, the eyebrow went up and he gave her a twisted smile.

'Let me guess. Unreasonable behaviour?'

'I haven't really thought about it.'

'I suppose you just want it over and done with as

quickly as possible. After all, it's not like you can screw any money out of me, is it?'

This was horrible. Why was he punishing her like this? She felt tears stinging her eyes and she looked up at the ceiling, as if by defying gravity she could stop them falling.

'Ed . . . Please . . . It doesn't have to be like this.'

'But this is exactly the way it is. I fucked up. You couldn't forgive me. End of marriage. End of story.'

She felt as if the rug had been pulled out from underneath her. She hadn't expected to feel so drawn towards him when she saw him. And she hadn't expected him to be so hard. She felt ashamed. She had thought she had all the cards, but it seemed she had none.

She stood up.

'I can't deal with this.'

'Oh, lucky you,' he snapped back. 'You can run away.'

'Why are you being like this?' As she spoke, she knew she sounded childish, whiny.

'I've had time to think about things. And I don't think I deserved the way you treated me. OK, so what I did was wrong. Fair cop, as they say. I did the crime, so I'm doing the time.' He spoke disparagingly. 'But look at all these other women . . .'

He indicated round him. There were couples in intense conversation, some chatting animatedly, some looking into each other's eyes. But Charlotte was surprised to see there was no hostility between the other couples in the room.

'A lot of these guys did far worse than me. But their women have stood by them.' He put a finger to his lips, feigning an attempt to remember something. 'What was that old cliché again? For better, for worse . . . ?'

Charlotte sank back down into the chair.

'So . . . what are you saying?'

Ed stared back at her. His eyes were dead, devoid of emotion. He'd never looked at her like that before.

'I've got nothing to say.'

She reached out a hand to touch him. This was unbearable. But he put up a warning hand, speaking in a mockney accent.

'No bodily contact, sweetheart. This is prison, remember?'

She pulled back her hand quickly.

'So,' he went on. 'Shagging anyone yet? Is that why you want a divorce?'

Charlotte felt a sudden surge of anger. Who did he think he was? Bloody Ray Winstone? Maybe he'd been brainwashed by the other prisoners. Maybe he thought he was some misogynist hard nut. What the hell was going to happen to him when he came out? She felt totally confused.

'I'm trying to rebuild my life,' she said, keeping her voice as steady as she could. 'After you managed to take everything I'd got away from me.'

They stared each other out for a moment.

'After I was arrested,' he said, his voice dropping almost to a deadly whisper, 'you said thank God you hadn't got pregnant, because you wouldn't want a monster like me fathering your child. Well, I would just like to say the same,' he went on, 'because I wouldn't want any child of mine having such a hard-hearted bitch for a mother.'

Charlotte recoiled from the harshness of his words. She got to her feet once again, her legs shaking.

'I didn't come here to be spoken to like this.'

'Then why did you?' he snarled back.

'I don't know,' she managed to reply. 'I just thought we could talk.'

'We had all the time in the world to talk. Before I got banged up.'

'Maybe I wasn't ready then.'

'Well, maybe I'm not ready now.'

She looked at him for a moment. The angle of his cheekbones that she had always loved to stroke. His nose, slightly broken and bent. His jaw, his neck . . . She felt an immense urge to reach out and touch him, as if her fingers might be able to impart what her words couldn't.

'I better go.'

He turned away. She thought she caught the glitter of tears in his eyes. So he did still care.

'Shall I come again?'

He shrugged.

'See you, then. Maybe?' she ventured again.

'See you . . .'

He didn't look at her as she backed away from the table, and then turned to walk towards the door. When she reached the exit, she looked round. He was sitting, staring down at the table with his head in his hands. All around him the other prisoners and their wives chattered and laughed as if they hadn't a care in the world.

If Charlotte thought she had hit rock bottom before, she was wrong.

*

233

The journey home was terrible. She veered between wild sobbing to teeth-clenching fury. She had to stop twice at a service station to pull herself together, comfort herself with a hot chocolate, splash her tear-stained face with cold water. And all the while she questioned herself. Had she been wrong to be so judgemental? Should she have stood by Ed?

No one else had ever suggested that she should. It had been a given, that they should separate. But then, she hadn't talked to that many people about it. Mostly Gussie and her husband, who were staunchly protective of her. She had been too ashamed to bring it out into the open and discuss it with anyone else.

Maybe what Ed had done *had* been an aberration. Maybe the stress of the past few years *had* caused him to make his huge error of judgement. Just because it wasn't his body going through the treatment didn't mean he hadn't suffered the pain and grief as much as she had. Perhaps she should have empathised with him more – put herself in his position, instead of judging him. As an alpha male, he must have felt emasculated, demoralised, powerless to change their situation, and when an opportunity arose – an opportunity he had thought was bullet proof – perhaps it was no wonder he hadn't been able to resist.

Was she shallow and disloyal? For a moment, she wondered what would have happened if it had been the other way round, if in a moment of desperation *she* had embezzled the charity funds. Would Ed have stood by her?

She looked at herself in the service-station mirror. Her eyes were bloodshot, her skin blotchy. She looked terrible. As she met her own gaze, she had her answer.

Ed would have stood by her till the end.

She rushed into the loo to be sick again. All she could taste was sour shame. She leaned against the wall of the cubicle. It was too late. The damage had been done. She had felt the hostility rolling off Ed. His dead eyes. His flat voice. There had been no indication that he wanted to make things right. She was no longer the woman he would go to the ends of the earth for. It was over.

On the way back into Withybrook she stopped at the petrol station outside Comberton to get some milk and bread. Fitch was there, filling up his red Land Rover Defender.

'Hey.' He gave her a wave. She didn't feel like talking, but she knew it would be rude not to after he had been so friendly, so she stopped for a second.

'Hello.'

'Are you OK? You look exhausted.' He looked at her, concerned.

'I just feel a bit peaky. I think it's all the paint fumes. I haven't stopped all week.'

He pushed the petrol nozzle back into its holder.

'Why don't you come down to the Trout for a drink later?'

'Oh . . . no, I don't think so.'

'It's always a good laugh on a Friday. The shoot's been out, so it's stuffed with beaters and gamekeepers filling their boots. They're quite entertaining.' He dug in the pocket of his combats for his wallet. 'I haven't got the girls till tomorrow. I could do with a night out.'

He looked at her hopefully.

Charlotte hesitated. The choice was to sit in all

evening crying into her soup and going over and over the horrible events of the day. Or to go out with Fitch and have a few drinks, maybe meet some new people. She wasn't sure if she felt strong enough for idle chit-chat after what had happened. But he had been so kind before, and he obviously wanted company.

Fitch shrugged, walking off backwards towards the kiosk to pay.

'It was just a thought.'

'No – wait. I'd love to come. Just give me a couple of hours.'

She needed to lie down for a while, then have a hot bath. Press a cold flannel to her face to bring down the puffiness. Eat something – apart from the morning's toast and two hot chocolates nothing had passed her lips all day.

Fitch smiled, and the warmth of it was reward in itself.

'I'll bang on your door at nine.'

The Trout was bursting at the seams. The shoot had been out all day, tugging their forelocks and kowtow-ing to the bankers and magnates and entrepreneurs who thought they could swoop into Devon for the day in their helicopters and Range Rovers and take owner-ship. Little did they know that the serfs who looked after them gave not two figs for who or what they were, and put two fingers up as they left, happy that the vast amount of money they had spent during their day's sport sustained the local economy. If someone was misguided enough to pay thousands of pounds for the privilege of shooting a bird too dumb to get out of the way, they deserved to be ridiculed. It was a contest as to who was more stupid: the shooters or the shot.

Now, however, after a day's hard physical exercise and the strain of being pleasant to people with more money than sense, the beaters and the gamekeepers were letting their hair down. Red faces and green clothing were de rigueur; the beer flowed. The game-keepers' wives, who prepared the lavish lunch in the shooting lodge and organised the beaters, held court in one corner, now resplendent in cleavage-revealing sparkly tops and jeans. Norman behind the bar took orders for plates of ham, egg and chips to be sent out. Acres and acres of ground had been covered today on foot in the biting November air and appetites were sharp.

Fitch pulled Charlotte through the throngs to the bar. She had managed to revive herself: a half-hour nap, a big bowl of porridge with banana and maple syrup, followed by a wallow in the bath and ten min-utes carefully applying her make-up had made her look and feel almost human. She was glad she had just put her jeans back on, as high fashion clearly had no place in the Speckled Trout.

The sense of camaraderie was overwhelming. It was the perfect environment to wash away the memory of the sterile, hostile prison. And a few drinks would soon fade the image of Ed and his burned-out, men-acing demeanour. Fitch bought her a Sloegasm which, he explained, was part of the initiation if she wanted to become a proper regular. She sipped it appreciatively. It went straight to her nerve centre, dulling her anxiety, lifting her mood.

As the pair of them stood by the bar, she soon

found herself noticed, and quickly surrounded by the shooting fraternity, who fired questions at her and bought her drink after drink. Fitch watched on, quietly protective, as two lads in particular seemed to adopt her as their own, showering her with compliments. He couldn't step in and claim her. For a start, she was a free agent, and besides, it wasn't the sort of evening where you expected to spend time as a couple and engage in quiet conversation. It was a free-for-all. Anyway, he suspected it would do Charlotte good to fraternise. She'd obviously been stuck in all week working on the house. But that didn't mean he wasn't going to keep an eye on her.

He watched as Darren and Bradley closed in on her. The pair of them were nice enough sober, hardworking and honest, but give them a few drinks and they were loose cannons. Fitch kept a wary eye. They both had the gift of the gab, broad-shouldered, bright-eyed country lads.

'Are you with Fitch, then?' they asked Charlotte.

'Not "with" with. I'm just having a drink with him.'

The two of them exchanged glances.

'Wouldn't fancy your chances if his missis finds out.'

Charlotte bit her lip. 'I thought they were separated.'

'Yeah. But I wouldn't want to cross Hayley. She still thinks Fitch belongs to her, even though she's shagging this other bloke.'

'Right.'

For a moment, Charlotte felt anxious. She didn't want to cause trouble or step on anyone's toes. And she could sense that the news was going to get back to Hayley, one way or another, that she had been in here with her husband.

'Where are you from, then?' Darren demanded.

'London.'

'Posh, then,' countered Bradley.

'Not really.'

'You talk posh.'

'I can't help that.'

They both affected lugubrious expressions.

'We haven't got a chance with you.'

'Either of us.'

'You wouldn't touch muck like us.'

'Not with a barge pole.'

Charlotte laughed. 'You don't know, till you try. I might fancy a bit of rough.'

Oh my God. Had she really said that? Those Sloegasms were even stronger than they looked. She was flirting outrageously. There was no harm in it. The boys were enjoying the banter and so was she. They knew she didn't mean it. There was no malice in any of these people, and no pretensions. They just wanted her to muck in and have a good time. There was certainly a party atmosphere. An impromptu band were gathering next to the piano, tuning up their guitars.

'Right,' said Darren. 'You going to join in the talent contest, London Lady?'

Charlotte's eyes widened in alarm. 'Talent contest? I didn't see any signs.'

'There's no signs. It's just what we do on a Friday. Everyone lobs a fiver in the bucket to enter. Winner takes all. Simple.'

Fitch leaned forward.

'You've got to, I'm afraid. You won't be accepted into the village until you've done something.'

She watched, rapt, as contestant after contestant

went up and did their thing, the acts getting more and more shambolic as the alcohol took a grip. There were magicians and Shirley Bassey imitations, juggling, a duet of 'Islands in the Stream'. Some were surprisingly talented, others dreadful, but whatever the standard it was entertaining and the audience were onside, clapping and cheering regardless.

Fitch stormed the stage and did a rendition of 'Mustang Sally'. What he lacked in tunefulness he made up for in enthusiasm, and the crowd roared their enthusiasm, not least Charlotte.

'That was fantastic!' she told him as he climbed off the stage, his long hair slick with sweat.

'Bit of a cliché.' He grinned. 'But it's the only song I can sing. I do it every time.'

'Come on, London Lady.' Darren urged her forwards. 'Show us what you're made of.'

Charlotte was determined to do just that. She was no wet blanket, and she loved a challenge. Besides, she had a party piece. She'd performed it many a time among friends. And anyway, all these people were her new friends. She was sure of that.

Buoyed up by her Sloegasms, she shimmied over to the pianist.

'Do you know "Makin' Whoopee"?'

He gave her a thumbs-up and struck up the opening notes. Undaunted, Charlotte scrambled on top of the piano and struck the infamous pose Michelle Pfeiffer took in *The Fabulous Baker Boys*. She smiled at her audience, and began to sing.

Another bride, another June
Another sunny honeymoon

Another season, another reason
For makin' whoopee

The onlookers whooped and hollered, delighted by the turn of events. Undaunted, Charlotte slithered and writhed on top of the piano, her bum in the air, her face in a sultry pout, crooning the words:

He's washing dishes and baby clothes
He's so ambitious, he even sews
But don't forget, folks, that's what you get, folks
For makin' whoopee

Across the room, Fitch looked concerned and put his pint glass down on the bar. Charlotte dropped her voice down for the final stanza.

You better keep her
I think it's cheaper
Than makin' whoopee

There was uproar. Fitch shut his eyes. He knew what was coming next. He'd seen the film often enough. But Charlotte didn't have the benefit of several days' rehearsal with a choreographer, or a kind cameraman or editor. Instead of the graceful slither off the piano, she perched on the edge, looked down, swayed from side to side and fell through the air.

In two bounds, Fitch was at her side and caught her in his arms to a round of rapturous applause. Charlotte smiled drunkenly up at him.

'Shit,' she slurred.

The rest of the pub cheered as Fitch carried her

effortlessly across the room and out of the door. The freezing night air hit her lungs and she gasped as if she'd had a bucket of cold water thrown over her. She went to struggle out of his grasp.

'Put me down.'

'No way.'

'I want to stay. I'm having fun!'

'You have no idea what those blokes are capable of.'

She would be mincemeat in her condition. He knew Darren and his cohorts only too well. When they'd had a skinful they could talk anyone into anything, and Fitch didn't want to see Charlotte toyed with.

He strode purposefully up the high street and there was nothing she could do. She tried wriggling but he held her tight, like a naughty toddler, until he reached the front door of Myrtle Cottage and put her down. She slumped against the door jamb.

'Key?' he asked her hopefully.

She started helplessly patting at her pockets, but as soon as she moved away from the support of the wall it was obvious she couldn't stand up. Fitch grabbed her by the scruff of her neck and fished about until he found the keys. As he unlocked the door, Charlotte fell over the threshold.

'I think,' she slurred, 'I might have had a bit too much to drink.'

And she passed out.

When she woke the next morning she sat up gingerly. She didn't know which was worse, the hideous thumping pain in her head or the memory of what she had done the night before. A little bit of her hoped it wasn't true, that she had just dreamed it, but no – she felt fairly sure that she had done her best Michelle Pfeiffer impersonation in front of the whole village. What on earth had got into her? The few other times she had done it had been in front of friends, not three sheets to the wind, and she had been on a decent-sized grand piano, not an upright. God, they must be splitting their sides in Withybrook this morning. Her cheeks burned with the humiliation. She would have to face them, in the street, the post office – not in the pub, she was never going in the pub again. She was never going to drink again—

'How are you feeling?'

'Jesus!'

A deep voice made her jump out of her skin. She looked round, and realised that Fitch was sleeping in the armchair at the foot of her bed with his coat pulled over him.

'Fitch?'

He stretched and yawned.

'Good. You're alive.'

'I don't know . . .' she groaned. 'Just about. What are you doing here?'

'I thought I'd better stay here. Make sure you didn't choke on your own vomit. I managed to stay awake till about four, but I must have fallen asleep.'

He fixed her with a look that was half amused, half reproachful.

'How many Sloegasms?'

'People kept handing them to me.'

He shook his head in fond exasperation.

'By the way,' he added, 'Darren texted me. You won, hands down. Sixty quid.'

'You're kidding?'

'It was unanimous.'

Charlotte slumped back on her pillows, not knowing what to think.

'Oh my God,' she groaned. 'My head.'

He got up and pulled on his coat.

'Right,' he said. 'You get up, get yourself ready. You're coming with me.'

'No way!' she protested. 'I'm staying right here. I'm going to sleep it off.'

'No, you're not,' he said firmly, pulling back her bed covers. 'The best cure for a hangover is fresh air and exercise. If you stay in bed you'll still feel rough at lunchtime. If you come with me you'll be miraculously cured. Trust me.'

He looked down at her, grinning.

'You've got twenty minutes. I'll meet you outside my house. Bring your coat.'

Charlotte whimpered and pleaded, but Fitch was having none of it. She stumbled blindly into the bathroom to do her teeth, vainly trying to recollect the night before. She couldn't remember coming home, or getting into bed. Thank goodness she had woken up fully clothed. Not that Fitch would have tried anything on, she was sure, but the thought of him trying to undress her inert drunken body was beyond the pale.

Twenty minutes later she obediently turned up outside his house, to find him already waiting in his Defender. She could see two figures in the back seat, and Dido bobbing up and down in the boot, excited.

'I've been to collect the girls,' he explained. 'I always have them at the weekend. Jade and Amber, this is Charlotte.'

Charlotte climbed into the front seat and turned to smile at Jade and Amber. They were sweet – all pink and orange striped tights and felt pixie hats, with long pigtails and gaps in their front teeth. They chirruped away at her.

'Daddy says you're from London.'

'Yes.'

'We've never been to London. Is it nice?'

Charlotte considered her answer carefully.

'Parts of it are very nice. Like Big Ben. And the Thames. And London Bridge. But some bits of it aren't very nice at all. You'll have to see for yourselves once day.'

'Do you live near Big Ben?'

She didn't live anywhere any more.

'I used to live . . . quite near.'

'Cool.'

Charlotte was quiet for a moment. It seemed a million miles away, the metropolis that had been her home for so many years. That she had never imagined being without. That she had taken for granted. It was so removed from Withybrook, and although she was becoming fond of her new home, she missed London dreadfully. In the old days, she and Ed would lie in on a Saturday morning, then cook a huge breakfast before going off shopping to buy food for their dinner guests, or to buy nice wine and chocolates and flowers to take to someone else, and maybe something new to wear. Superficial, self-indulgent stuff to make up for the fact that they both worked so hard all week. She had loved Saturdays . . . Stop it, she told herself. Those days were gone, never to return.

As Fitch pulled away, Charlotte wasn't sure if her

stomach was going to survive the journey, but Amber offered her a Polo and it took her mind off it. They drove out of the village, over the cattle grid across the moor, then along a tortuous road that to Charlotte seemed endless, although it was probably only a couple of miles until they finally stopped in a car park in the middle of nowhere.

'Where are we going?' asked Charlotte, scrambling out of the car and shutting the door.

'Follow me.'

Fitch led her along a path up a scrubby slope as the girls ran on ahead. As they climbed over the crest, Charlotte gave a gasp. The landscape opened up to a vast expanse of gorse-covered moor, before dropping vertically down to a shimmering, deep green sea that stretched as far as the eye could see. The cliffs stood out against the sky. They looked as if they were covered in flock velvet, as if some model railway enthusiast had carefully moulded their every curve. Beneath, jagged rocks jutted out of the water, their cold, hard surfaces in direct contrast to the grassy knolls above. The waves crashed, their white spume providing a frill around the coastline.

'My God,' breathed Charlotte. 'I'd no idea . . . It's . . . incredible.'

She was staggered. She hadn't a clue that this was practically on her doorstep. Yes, she knew that Withybrook was a stone's throw from the sea, but not that the scenery was so jaw-droppingly, mind-blowingly dramatic. The panorama made her feel incredibly small and insignificant, as if the cliffs and the rocks and the ocean had been here since the dawn of time and she had only been dropped on the planet as an afterthought.

Fitch stood next to her.

'Kind of puts things into perspective, doesn't it?'

Charlotte breathed in the air, great gulps of salt-tinged oxygen.

'It's pretty levelling. I feel like nobody. But somebody, at the same time.'

'I come here when it all gets too much,' admitted Fitch. 'It makes you realise that no matter what you decide, the world is going to carry on.'

'That we're just mere mortals, whose problems are insignificant?'

'Yes,' agreed Fitch. 'But it also makes you realise life is worth living. How could you not stand here and want to live?'

Charlotte looked down at the sea. It was impossible to tell how deep it was from here. It could be two, twenty, two hundred feet deep. She shivered.

'I don't know,' replied Charlotte. 'It's given me a terrible urge to jump.'

'Please don't,' said Fitch. 'It's bloody freezing at this time of year. I don't want to have to fish you out.'

Charlotte laughed. 'You've been chivalrous enough already.'

They gazed down at the water.

'So – why the urge to jump? Primeval instinct?'

'I don't mean it. It's just . . . life doesn't always turn out the way you expect, does it? And I don't know if I can cope with any more surprises. Sometimes I just want it all to go away.'

Fitch put an arm round her and squeezed her to him. Charlotte leaned against him, feeling comforted.

'How's the head?'

'Do you know what? I feel much better. You were right.'

'Just think,' he teased, 'you could still be snoring your head off in bed. Come on.'

She followed him obediently as he strode off with Dido still on her lead; the moors were covered in sheep that even the best-behaved dog couldn't resist chasing. Jade and Amber had scampered on ahead, sure-footed. This was clearly their territory. Charlotte picked her way more carefully along the narrow footpath. It would be terribly easy to lose your footing and go tumbling down the cliff.

Eventually the two girls stopped some way ahead of them. Fitch waited for Charlotte to catch up. She was slightly breathless, unused to the strenuous exercise. They watched Jade and Amber, who were sitting on a low stone wall, lobbing stones down the cliff-side, competing to see who could throw the furthest.

'They're gorgeous.'

'I know,' he said. 'And they don't deserve the shit they're going through.'

'They seem very happy.'

'Kids are resilient, aren't they? And I do my best to give them a stable time when they're with me. But their mother will pull every trick in the book to get what she wants. Even at their expense. I shouldn't be telling you all this . . .'

Fitch was angry with himself. It was all very well thinking those things about Hayley, but it was a different matter sharing his private thoughts with a girl who, let's face it, he barely knew.

'I'm sure they'll be fine—'

'It's just I don't know how things are going to end up,' Fitch burst out, suddenly. 'Is she going to marry this bloke? And if so, where are the girls going to end up? Bloody Watford or wherever it is he lives? I don't want them to have a stepfather – some creep with more money than sense who can just buy them stuff to keep them quiet . . .'

'Maybe it won't come to that,' said Charlotte gently. 'Maybe Hayley just needs to get it out of her system.'

Fitch gazed at the horizon. He'd said too much.

'Come on,' he said. 'Let's go. You need some serious hangover food.'

He whistled for the girls to follow, then turned and headed back the way they had come.

Fitch had cooked a big ham the day before. He served it up with huge chunky homemade chips that he cooked in the oven, and a delicious crunchy coleslaw. The girls insisted on baked beans too, and he bartered with them that as long as they ate some salad he would concur.

They chattered incessantly all the way through the meal, and Charlotte watched how patient Fitch was with them, pandering to their whims and rituals: making sure they had their favourite glasses to drink their squash, how he put Jade's ketchup carefully on the side of her plate and squirted it liberally all over Amber's chips, just as they liked. He was so calm and confident with them. She thought of her friends who had children: the husbands she knew didn't have a clue what to do with their own kids – none of them would have been able to rustle up a meal like this without making a terrible fuss and suborning every female in the vicinity to help them out. But Fitch's capability didn't make him any less masculine – in fact, quite the opposite. Fitch was no wuss reluctant to get his hands dirty. He'd got it sussed. He was prepared to make the effort in order to make life easy for everyone.

After lunch, Charlotte helped to wash up then sat on the sofa in the living room while the girls went out into the garden to play and Fitch made tea. She picked up the *Saturday Independent* magazine and started to leaf through it, but her eyelids became heavier and heavier. She fought against sleep, but she felt so relaxed and comfortable, it wasn't long before she'd drifted off.

She woke with a start to find a dark-haired woman standing over her.

'So it's true,' said Hayley, with a triumphant smirk. 'Darren and Bradley couldn't wait to tell me you'd been pouring drinks down her throat all night in the Speckled Trout. And you were seen coming out of her house this morning.'

Fitch stood in the doorway with a mug of tea in each hand.

'I wasn't pouring drinks down her, Hayley. Darren and Bradley were. And I stayed the night to make sure she didn't choke to death.'

'Yeah, right,' chortled Hayley. 'You must think I'm an idiot.'

Fitch frowned. 'I think what you've forgotten,' he said patiently, 'is that under the circumstances I'm entitled to do whatever I like with Charlotte. Even though I've done precisely nothing.'

'I . . . think I'd better go,' said Charlotte awkwardly, getting to her feet.

'Don't go on my account,' said Hayley.

'Stay right there,' commanded Fitch. 'I've made you tea.'

'Honestly,' said Charlotte, 'I've got lots to do. Thank you for a lovely lunch.'

'Shouldn't that be a lovely night?' Hayley couldn't resist a dig. Fitch threw her a warning glare and followed Charlotte to the door.

'You shouldn't let Hayley frighten you off.'

'I just don't want to cause trouble.'

Fitch rolled his eyes. 'She's frustrated because lover boy was busy this weekend, so she's looking for trouble.'

'Will you be OK?'

Fitch nodded. 'Fine. I can handle her.'

Charlotte leaned forward and gave him a kiss on the cheek.

'Thanks. You've been a real life-saver. And you should copyright your hangover cure – you'd make a fortune.'

Fitch smiled and shut the door, then went back to confront his wife for spoiling what had been a very pleasant and perfectly innocent afternoon. She was on the sofa drinking Charlotte's cup of tea.

'Oh well,' she said lightly, 'what's sauce for the goose . . .'

'There's nothing in it and you know there isn't.'

'I just don't know what Jade and Amber are supposed to think.'

'They enjoyed having someone else to talk to at lunch.'

'It's confusing for them, though, don't you think? Parading her in front of them like that. I've deliberately kept them away from Kirk so they don't get confused.'

Fitch slumped in his chair. Hayley's vision of what was right and wrong was always skewed. Her explanations for her behaviour were preposterous. If she'd kept the girls away from Kirk it was because she didn't want them cramping her style. Nothing to do with protecting them. Hayley only ever acted out of self-interest.

'For the last time, there's nothing going on between me and Charlotte. She came for lunch, that's all.' He spoke wearily, knowing his denial was almost pointless, because Hayley would believe what suited her.

Hayley plonked her cup down and put her feet up on the coffee table, waggling her bare toes and admiring her navy blue nail polish.

'By the way,' she said casually, 'I might as well tell you my plans. We're going to Dubai for Christmas.'

Fitch shrugged. 'Good for you.'

'I mean me and Jade and Amber. Kirk's offered to take us all. Club class. To a five-star hotel. We've got a suite.'

Fitch jumped up immediately.

'No way. You are not taking the girls away for Christmas.'

'Too late. It's booked.'

'You can't do that!'

'It's a fantastic opportunity. When have they ever been abroad on a luxury holiday?' She was goading him now, getting at him for not being a good enough provider. 'You can't deny them the chance of a lifetime.'

'Watch me.'

'I know.' Hayley stood up and crossed her arms. 'Let's ask them, shall we? See where they'd rather be?

A luxury hotel on a sun-drenched beach? Or stuck in bloody cold and boring Withybrook?'

Fitch clenched his fists. There was no point in arguing with her while she was in this mood.

'OK,' he said, trying to keep his voice even. 'Maybe you're right. They're very lucky. And Kirk's very generous.'

'He certainly is,' smirked Hayley. 'I'll send you a postcard.'

As soon as Hayley was gone, Fitch rushed up the stairs to the filing cabinet on the landing which held all their paperwork. He pulled open the drawer and rifled through the files until he found the one marked 'Passports'. He flipped it open and his heart leaped into his mouth. There was only one in there: his.

Hayley was obviously cleverer than he'd given her credit for.

Ten

Catkin pulled in the belt of her red Diane von Furstenberg wrap dress, tied the knot with a flourish and slipped on her patent leather boots. She nodded approvingly at her reflection. It was the perfect outfit – chic, a little bit sexy, but not too much. It was, after all, only the Withybrook Christmas Fayre she was opening, not switching on the Oxford Street lights.

She hoped she wasn't going to be expected to stay all afternoon. She was exhausted. As well as her usual daily slot, she had been filming some extra inserts for the run-up to Christmas about the stresses and strains of the festive season. Some of them had been trivial – how to deal with family feuds and competitive present-giving – but others had moved her deeply. People who were alone at Christmas, for example. It was these deeper, more thought-provoking inserts that had convinced her even more that it was time to move on from the superficiality of *Hello, England* to something more edifying, but her schedule had been so frantic that she hadn't had time to follow it up.

One thing was good, though: Sebastian seemed to be working his socks off. When she had arrived home the night before it had been all she could do to coax him out of his studio. He eventually emerged, paint-spattered, looking as if he hadn't eaten, slept or washed for days. Normally that would set off warning bells, but he didn't smell of booze and had assured her it was the unkempt façade of the motivated artist.

'Nothing matters when I'm absorbed,' he told her.

She'd frogmarched him into the bath quickly enough, and phoned Tommy to fetch them a Thai take-away from Comberton.

She called to see if he was ready. It had been Sebastian who had talked her into opening the Fayre. His mother had been instrumental in starting it nearly twenty years ago, and he still seemed to feel weirdly responsible for its success. He always sold hand-painted Christmas cards, which Catkin told him off for. People only bought them because they hoped they might be worth millions one day, not because they wanted to send season's greetings. But Sebastian told her she was cynical. Besides, he pointed out, all the money raised went to the local children's hospice, so surely what he was doing was a good thing.

The village hall was heaving, full of festive cheer and the fug of mulled wine that Fitch was selling by the gallon. He had built a faux Alpine hut to serve it from, strung with fairy lights, and was doing a roaring trade as the scent of cinnamon and cloves lured customers over. Jade and Amber were dressed as elves, and sold bags of roast chestnuts.

He had been astonished to find that Hayley was here. When he'd queried her presence, she'd looked back at him with wide-eyed innocence. She wouldn't miss the Fayre for all the world, she'd told him. It was all part of the run-up to Christmas. He'd managed to bite his tongue and not mention Dubai. He never wanted to be accused of sniping.

Jade was pulling his sleeve. They'd run out of chestnuts. He left the stall to go and put some more to roast in the ancient oven in the kitchen.

He found his mother-in-law washing teacups.

'Hi, Barbara.'

The two of them were always polite to each other. And they'd never really discussed his marital situation. It was the elephant in the room. They discussed arrangements for the children, but they hadn't touched upon the sticky subject of Hayley's infidelity once. Fitch had no idea what Barbara's attitude was.

But today, it seemed, she was ready to talk. As Hayley flitted past in her skimpy Miss Christmas outfit, Barbara pursed her lips and turned to him.

'She will come round, you know.'

'What?'

'Hayley. It's one of her phases. She does this, when she feels trapped. She's done it all her life. She runs away when things get what she considers to be boring. I was hoping she'd grown out of it, that having children would make her less selfish . . . I don't know what I did wrong.'

A look of bleakness shadowed her face.

'Just give her time. She'll come back. I know she will.'

She turned away, and went to fetch a clean tea towel, obviously thinking she had said too much.

Fitch didn't know what to think. He looked over at Hayley, in her short red skirt trimmed with white fur, her stocking tops visible, her cleavage on display. She flitted from person to person with her book of raffle tickets, charming them, beguiling them, divesting them of their hard-earned cash.

What did he want? he asked himself. Did he want her back?

What he wanted was the old Hayley back. Not this tainted version, with her skewed sense of morality, who played games with him when of course she was the only one who could win.

Charlotte was selling gingerbread men. She had made ten dozen, decorating them in funky bright colours, with squiggles, spots and stripes. At fifty pence each they were going quickly.

For the past few weeks she had thrown herself into her work, desperate to bury the bitter memory of her visit to Ed. The house had come on in leaps and bounds in that time. Although to an outsider it would seem like chaos, as every single room was in turmoil – strips of wallpaper, dust sheets and pots of paint scattered everywhere – she could feel it taking shape. She worked long hours and weekends, and in her time off she curled up with a DVD rented from the post office. More often than not she fell asleep before the end, but Nikita was very lenient about when she finally returned them and didn't fine her if she was a couple of days late. That, Charlotte had to concede, would never happen in London, where fines were draconian and the shopkeepers showed no mercy.

She had taken Nikita on as an extra pair of hands when the girl had complained to her one day about not having enough cash to buy Christmas presents. Charlotte could only afford a very basic rate of pay, but Nikita was grateful and eager to help. And she turned out to be extremely dextrous and careful. Charlotte had thought she would only be up to the most menial of tasks, but in the end she had her doing the banisters and the newel posts on the staircase, a time-consuming and tedious task that nevertheless required precision. Nikita was painstaking and neat, taking pride in her handiwork. It meant that nearly all the woodwork on the staircase was finished while Charlotte could forge ahead with other tasks. If she'd had to do the staircase herself, it would have held her up for at least a week.

Nikita was fascinated by what Charlotte did. During their coffee breaks she pored over Charlotte's magazines. One day Charlotte got out her portfolio. Nikita leafed through it in awe, sighing over the wondrous settings: the palatial loft apartments, the elegant drawing rooms, the cutting-edge kitchens.

'You're so lucky,' sighed Nikita. 'I'd love to do this.'

'You could,' Charlotte insisted. 'I haven't got any proper qualifications. Only art A level. Surely you could do that at college?'

Nikita shook her head gloomily.

'I've got to work, haven't I? We can't afford for me to go to college. Not with six kids.'

'But they aren't your responsibility,' objected Charlotte. 'They're your mum's. It's your life, Nikita.'

'No, it isn't. Not since my dad walked out on us. It's up to me to see they're all right.'

'But if you got some qualifications, then you could get a better job.'

Nikita sighed. 'That's not how it works. '

'Night school,' said Charlotte. 'You could do evening classes. It would take you longer, but you'd get there in the end.'

She jumped up and went over to her laptop.

'Let's have a look and see.'

'Forget it,' said Nikita. 'It won't happen. Anyway, how would I get to college? We haven't got a car. Bamford's miles away, and there's no regular bus.'

It worried Charlotte that Nikita was so determined that she wouldn't be able to succeed. She put up every barrier imaginable to Charlotte's suggestions, even though she was obviously a very capable girl. Charlotte hated to see her potential go to waste. How could she accept her lot, working for a pittance in the post office and skivvying for Catkin Turner, stuck in Withybrook for the rest of her life? Yet at the same time she admired the girl's incredible loyalty to her family. She never complained about her duty to her younger brothers and sisters. Charlotte decided not to give up. She would keep badgering her, encouraging her, enticing her. She might come round eventually.

'Anything's possible,' she insisted. 'You can do anything you want with your life. It's up to you.'

Nikita just frowned and shook her head.

Charlotte could see her now on the other side of the hall, with a clutch of her brothers and sisters, rooting through the jumble. The Fayre was wonderful. Every person in the village seemed to have contributed something, and everyone was here to buy. It was heart-warming, and certainly encapsulated the spirit of Christmas, unlike so many of the events she used to attend in London, which had been so commercial, all about profit. Although this was about raising money, it wasn't for personal gain. Every single penny went to the local children's hospice.

Charlotte looked over at the big chart that displayed

how much money had been raised so far. For a moment, she had a memory of the giant cheque that Ed had held up that fateful night, but she suppressed it. She wasn't going to let her past spoil today. She was going to enjoy being part of the community, get into the spirit. She turned to her next customer and was delighted when they bought six gingerbread men. Another dozen and she would have sold out.

Penny pushed her way through the crowds, increasingly anxious. She could see Megan in a quartet with some other villagers, churning out carols, lengths of garish tinsel wrapped around their music stands. But where was Daisy? The old lady had been there a moment ago. Had she wandered off? Then she spotted her, standing stock-still by a man selling holly wreaths and mistletoe. Penny pushed her way over.

Penny had taken it upon herself to bring Daisy Miller to the Fayre. The old lady had nodded enthusiastically enough at her suggestion, and had been ready when Penny knocked at the door. Maybe her dementia had been temporary, Penny thought hopefully. But as the afternoon went on, she realised that this wasn't the case. Daisy became confused and muddled by the simplest things. She seemed to have quite forgotten the concept of paying for things, which led to some embarrassing interludes when she just helped herself to what was on offer. In the end, Penny had persuaded Daisy to let her have her purse, and then settled up for whatever items took Daisy's fancy. Which were curious items indeed: a plate for serving garlic bread, some slug repellent, a pair of earrings that flashed on and off, and a huge bag of coconut ice. Who was she to argue? thought Penny. No doubt there was some sort of logic to the purchases. Though deep down she knew that wasn't the case. Daisy was losing it, big time, as Tom and Megan would say. The thought depressed her, and she realised that the time was getting closer when she would have to involve the authorities. Sadly, she had little choice.

She stopped at Fitch's stall and bought them each a glass of mulled wine. For a moment she debated the wisdom of giving Daisy such a potent brew, then decided what the hell. It couldn't make her much worse. And Penny definitely needed a drink. Looking after Daisy was worse than looking after small children.

At the end of the afternoon, Catkin drew the raffle.

Charlotte won. The prize was Christmas dinner. A huge free-range turkey. A sack each of potatoes and carrots. A net of Brussels sprouts. A handmade pudding. Two dozen mince pies. And a cake.

It was no use to her whatsoever. She was going up to London for Christmas Day, to see Gussie. And so she donated it to the children's hospice, to a round of applause. They might not clap so enthusiastically, she thought wryly, if they knew who she really was, and what her husband had done. But it went a small way towards assuaging her still guilty conscience.

Eleven

Any idea that anyone in Withybrook had of going elsewhere for Christmas was put paid to on Christmas Eve morning, when snow started falling thick and fast out of the still skies, smothering the moors within minutes. It would be madness to attempt to go anywhere. The gritters never came this far. Most of the roads across the moor were blocked. Sheep were left to fend for themselves as farmers gave up the futile attempts to get their Land Rovers out with bales of extra hay. They just had to pray their flocks had the stamina to outlive the weather.

The bells of the church rang out to its own flock for midnight mass. Charlotte could hear them, sitting in her little house, and suddenly felt the need for company, for the comfort of strangers. She had been planning to go up to Gussie's for Christmas. It would be the first time she had returned to London since she had left, and she thought she felt strong enough to return and face her past. But now it was out of the question. She was stranded in Withybrook. Completely cut off. Maybe it was for the best, she thought miserably. Being in the bosom of Gussie's exuberant, madcap family would probably only highlight the hopelessness of her own situation. And although Gussie had absolutely insisted they would love to have her, she would still feel like an outsider, the one who didn't belong. And at least if she stayed here she wouldn't have to worry about bumping into someone she knew and being snubbed.

She slipped on her coat and shut the front door. She'd attached a holly wreath to the knocker, woven through with white organza ribbon, in a nod to the festivities, but she hadn't bothered with a tree. And she'd had no cards. After all, no one knew where she was. She wondered if any had arrived at their old house in Parsons Green. There might have been a few misguided souls left in the country who hadn't heard the scandal, and had sent her and Ed season's greetings. She imagined the new owners consigning them to the bin. The thought depressed her, and she tried to shake it out of her head as she made her way up the high street to the church. The snow crunched satisfyingly underfoot. It had remained crisp and hard and white, not yet reduced to the greying mush that London snow quickly turned to. She turned in through the gate, and walked through the churchyard, surrounded by the proudly erect tombstones of former villagers, many bedecked with floral tributes left by relatives heedful of the time of year as Christmas pricked at their conscience.

Inside, the church was warm, glowing with candlelight, the organ gently wheezing out 'It Came Upon a Midnight Clear', while the congregation stamped the snow off their feet and compared notes on the weather. It was surprisingly full, given that only those within walking distance could make it, but the inclement conditions had brought out a sense of community in the inhabitants of Withybrook. They felt the need to come together and bemoan their lot.

Charlotte spotted Sebastian, lolling in a pew at the front, tucked up in a preposterous Afghan coat and a pair of mirrored sunglasses that gave him the air of a dissolute seventies rock-star. He patted the seat next to him when he saw her.

'This is the family pew,' he said. 'But I'm the only bloody one here. Catkin's stuck in London. She went to some terrible C-list party last night and couldn't get down the M5 this morning. Or so she claims. She'd probably far rather spend Christmas with her showbiz friends than be stuck down here with me.'

Charlotte slid onto the pew next to him and stroked the arm of his coat admiringly.

'Excuse the stench,' he grinned. 'It was my mother's, when she went through her hippy phase. It stinks of patchouli. But it was the warmest thing I could find.'

'I wouldn't have thought this was your scene,' Charlotte said.

'You're kidding?' Sebastian pushed up his sunglasses and looked at her. 'I love it. I've been to every midnight mass here since I was born. I'd never spend Christmas anywhere else.'

This was true. He loved the ritual. The way the service never changed, although the vicar might. The one thing he wished was that his parents were here. Really, thought Sebastian, he was a sentimental old fool, the polar opposite of the public's perception of him. But this was where he belonged. He still couldn't quite understand how his mother and father preferred to be in Barbados at this time of year, though he knew the weather suited them much more than the icy Exmoor draughts.

Charlotte spotted Fitch coming in the door, in a Russian hat and a greatcoat. She waved him over, and he slid into the pew next to her, reaching out to shake Sebastian's hand. They'd chatted in the pub often enough on a Sunday night, and Fitch had fitted some granite work surfaces in Sebastian's studio.

'I never usually come to church,' he whispered, 'but I suddenly felt the urge for company.'

Charlotte touched his arm in a gesture of sympathy. She knew that Hayley and the girls had flown off to Dubai two days before, and that he must be missing them dreadfully.

Sebastian was craning his neck to see who else was in the church, and spotted Penny coming in, tentative and anxious. He waved her over too.

'All God's little lost lambs,' he said happily, as she hurried over, grateful for a friendly face.

'Bill was supposed to drive the kids back down from Bristol this afternoon,' she explained. 'He couldn't even get across the Downs. Looks like I'm stuck on my own for Christmas.'

'Join the club,' said Sebastian. 'We've all been abandoned by our nearest and dearest.'

As the organist struck up 'Oh Come All Ye Faithful', Sebastian gave a little smile. He might not have his family here, but his pew was filled with friends. And having Charlotte near him always lifted his heart. He thought of his studio, filled with her likeness, then turned to look at her profile. Had he done her justice? That little nose, sprinkled with freckles? Those frank, green eyes with the long lashes? She turned to look at him, slightly disconcerted by his attention, and he looked down at his hymn-book. He wasn't a weirdo, a stalker, but he'd have to be careful not to behave like one.

After the service ended with a rousing 'Hark the Herald Angels', a couple of ladies from the village served mulled wine from a big punch bowl, and passed around mince pies. Charlotte, Sebastian, Penny and Fitch huddled together at the top of the aisle.

'Well,' said Fitch, 'if we're all on our own for Christmas Day, why don't we get together? I'm happy to cook. You're welcome to come to me for lunch.'

The four of them looked at each other. Nobody wanted to spend the day alone.

'I've got crates and crates of booze,' said Sebastian. 'What do you want – Bollinger? Veuve?'

'You can have my turkey,' offered Penny. 'It's not huge, it was only going to be for me and the kids, but it's going begging. And I've got a pudding.'

'I've got some things I was going to take up to my friends,' finished Charlotte. 'Christmas crackers. And loads of nice cheese.'

'Perfect,' said Fitch. 'Shall we say midday?'

He felt a huge sense of relief. He had been dreading a silent, lonely day in the house, waiting for the phone to ring. Now he had a project, and company, and something to think about when he went to bed later.

As Charlotte left the churchyard, she saw Nikita kissing a lanky young lad of about seventeen by the gate. She deduced it must be Brindley. Then she watched as three of Nikita's little brothers and sisters swarmed round, and the five of them set off for home, mittened paws in gloved hands, pom-poms bobbing. Who was she to meddle with the status quo and tantalise Nikita with the promise of a better life? The girl looked quite happy as she was, bossing her siblings about, arm in arm with her boyfriend, greeting the rest of the villagers she'd grown up with. She was safe and secure in this environment. There would always be someone to watch out for her. That was the advantage of a tight community like Withybrook. They looked after their own. Not like people in London, who turned on you like a pack of dogs when something went wrong. She was lucky to be here, she decided.

The next morning, Charlotte slept in. She had left the heating on all night because of the snow, and was so warm and snug she didn't wake until half past ten. After all, it was Christmas Day and she didn't have to work, so her body had allowed her to relax. She walked over to the window and looked out. It was so silent, a gentle snow still falling, the flakes drifting towards the ground aimlessly. The snow in the road was pristine; no one had attempted to drive through it yet. It was ridiculously pretty; a Christmas-card cliché. It was hard to believe there was anyone else awake in Withybrook, but Charlotte presumed there must be by the tell-tale plumes of smoke. She imagined children emptying out stockings, tearing at wrapping paper, squeals of excitement, and felt the usual tug at her heart.

She hadn't sent Ed any sort of Christmas message. And now she wondered if she should have done. He must be feeling dreadful, banged up with all the other inmates, institutional jollity forced upon them in the guise of soggy sprouts and paper hats. But then, she reminded herself, he was the reason she was stuck in exile. If it wasn't for Fitch and his kindness, she'd be on her own with nothing but her radio for company.

She turned away from the window sharply. She wasn't going to waste any more time feeling sympathy for Ed, especially when he had so adroitly turned the tables on her. Instead, she was going to enjoy the day with her new friends. She ran down to the kitchen, made herself a pot of tea, then packed up a basket with the things she had been going to take up to Gussie as an offering: local cheeses wrapped up in greaseproof paper, smoked trout, a huge pork pie and some jars of chutney, and a bag of handmade chocolates. She scooped up the clockwork snails she had bought as stocking fillers for Gussie's four children and wrapped them in some white tissue paper, tying them with a length of velvet ribbon. They might provide a bit of light relief later in the afternoon.

Then she ran back upstairs to have a hot bath. She put on a short cream wool kilt and a cream cashmere sweater. She blow-dried her hair properly and realised it had grown quite a bit. She put her pale butterscotch suede boots in the top of her basket of goodies and slipped on the wellingtons she had finally managed to acquire as they were a total necessity in Withybrook, then headed out of the door to pick her way carefully down the road among the snowflakes.

Catkin sat cross-legged in the middle of her bed, staring at her BlackBerry.

She had phoned every mainline train station, every cab firm, and had even, in a moment of madness, contemplated a helicopter, but the bottom line was there was no way out of London. And now, if she wasn't going to spend the day alone in her flat with whatever was available in the corner shop, she was going to have to take Martin Galt up on his invitation.

He had been at yesterday's party: Christmas drinks thrown by the producer of *Hello, England*, a typical media free-for-all with drink flowing like the Thames and the odd canapé which everyone ignored. She had panicked when she'd seen him, but he had been more than friendly. Obviously Sebastian's appalling behaviour hadn't prejudiced him against her.

'Why haven't you been in touch?' he chided.

'Why haven't you?' she countered bravely, then wished she hadn't been so bold, because he was a man who loved a challenge and she'd seen a glint of more than just amusement in his eye.

'If you're still stuck here tomorrow,' he'd murmured, 'I've got a table at Claridge's. There's a few of us going. Inge's up in Scotland – I'm not even going to try to get there.'

She'd nodded politely, certain at the time that by morning the snow would have melted and she would be on her way back down to Withybrook, but as she had made her way home, dizzy with too much cheap Sauvignon Blanc, more snow had fallen, sealing her fate.

Claridge's it was.

She phoned Sebastian.

'Happy Christmas, darling,' she said, trying to keep her tone light. 'I'm so sorry. There's absolutely no way I'm going to get down.'

'What are you going to do, then?' he asked.

'Um – there's a gang of us going to Claridge's.'

'Very nice,' he replied mildly. 'I've been asked to lunch in the village. With Fitch — the stonemason? Penny and Charlotte will be there.'

'All the losers, you mean?' The words came out before she could stop herself, a little bit of her cross that he didn't sound as bereft as he might have done.

'Well, all the ones that aren't as lucky as we are,' replied Sebastian drily. 'Who are you going with?'

She named a few people that he may or may not have heard of. 'Oh, and Martin Galt,' she added, as if the name was of no consequence.

Sebastian's response was quite robust. 'That tit?' he said cheerfully. 'Rather you than me.'

'It's either that or sit in the flat with Pot Noodles.' Catkin felt the need to defend her decision. 'Anyway, have a lovely day. I'll try to call you later.'

She rang off, then dialled Martin's number.

'Martin, it's Catkin Turner. Merry Christmas. And if your invitation still stands, I'd love to come to lunch . . .'

Two hundred miles down the road, Sebastian chucked the phone back on its cradle, unsettled. Catkin wasn't the sort of girl to let a bit of snow stop her. She obviously had better fish to fry, like that slimy Armani-clad producer. She couldn't take a day off networking, not even on Christmas Day, he thought gloomily. He couldn't help noticing how casually she'd slipped Martin's name into the conversation, as if Sebastian wouldn't notice. He hoped she'd be careful. He trusted Catkin — at least he thought he did — but he didn't trust Martin one bit.

Well, he wasn't going to let it spoil his day. He went

looking for some wrapping paper – he'd drawn each of them a little picture of Withybrook the night before. They could chuck them in the bin if they wanted, but he couldn't turn up empty-handed.

Fitch got up early on Christmas morning to put the turkey in the Aga. He'd collected it from Penny's house the night before, lugging it home and leaving it on the work top to come up to room temperature overnight, making sure it was safely out of Dido's reach. He hadn't cooked Christmas dinner before – they had always gone up to Hayley's parents' – but he reasoned it was no harder than a roast, which he was used to doing. He cobbled together a stuffing by defrosting some sausages and squeezing out the insides, then mixing the sausage meat up with onions and some dried apricots and pecan nuts he found in the cupboard. Not exactly Gordon Ramsay, but it was the best he could do under the circumstances.

He had tried to make the house as festive as possible for when Jade and Amber got back. There was a tree with twinkling lights, and paperchains, and Christmas cards perched on every available surface. He wanted it to feel atmospheric for their return, so they didn't feel cheated out of a traditional English Christmas. Though they probably wouldn't, he thought glumly. He personally couldn't think of anything worse than Christmas in a Dubai hotel, but no doubt they were having the time of their lives with Kirk's bottomless wallet to pander to their every whim.

Fitch tried not to wonder what they might be doing as he peeled the potatoes. Hayley had promised that she would get them to phone at some point during the day, but he was more than used to her not keeping her word. He knew the girls would want to speak to him, but Hayley was quite capable of fobbing them off by saying the phone wasn't working. Though no doubt Kirk's state-of-the-art phone would be able to get through to the moon if he so desired it. He imagined that Hayley would be making full use of the hotel children's club so she could lounge about by the pool or in the spa. Or in the bedroom. He hoped she and Kirk weren't demonstrating their affection for each other too openly. He shuddered as he imagined the man's hands straying over Hayley's fulsome breasts. Please let them have the decency to keep it to the privacy of their own room, he prayed.

Penny was the first guest to arrive, pink-cheeked from the cold and looking stunning in a short red sweater dress that showed off her long legs and rangy figure. It felt strange welcoming her into the house as a visitor. Fitch had been to the surgery with the girls on a number of occasions, so he knew Penny quite well, but he still felt slightly awkward, and he could see she felt a little on edge. She was so warm and reassuring in the surgery, but today she was out of her comfort zone.

'This is so weird,' she said, putting down a big box on his work surface. 'I've never spent Christmas without the children . . .'

'Nor me,' agreed Fitch, and they shared a rueful smile, neither one wanting to admit quite how much it hurt.

'Bill won't be at all prepared,' she went on. 'He won't have crackers, or chipolatas, or stuff for their stockings . . .'

She felt tears sting her eyes. Tom and Megan might pretend to be all grown-up and not care, but they were still children at heart.

'Hey,' said Fitch. 'They'll survive, you know. And it's not like it's your fault. You didn't make it snow.'

'No,' agreed Penny, but she still couldn't help thinking of her children trying to have fun with Bill and his po-faced girlfriend, whose nose would be right out of joint.

Luckily Sebastian arrived at that point with a half-case of vintage champagne, and by the time Charlotte arrived five minutes later, the first cork had already been popped. And actually, because they only had themselves to please and it had been an impromptu arrangement, there were none of the usual tensions and expectations and crises that Christmas heralded. Everyone mucked in. Penny laid the table, while Charlotte prepared canapés with her smoked trout. Sebastian lit a roaring fire and kept everyone's glasses topped up, then rifled through Fitch's music collection before putting on the Beach Boys.

'It's happy music. I defy you not to be happy while the Beach Boys are on,' he explained, defending his choice, and after a while everyone had to admit it was strangely appropriate as it lifted their mood and made them dance around the kitchen. By two o'clock, when the turkey was dragged ceremoniously from the Aga to a round of applause, they had all drunk the best part of a bottle of champagne each and had forgotten their woes.

As dusk fell, the uproariousness of lunch subsided into a sleepy, post-prandial slump. Resplendent in their gold crowns, they all took up a position in front of the telly, dozing off in the warmth of the fire, the girls clutching Baileys, the boys Remy Martin.

Sebastian watched Charlotte hungrily from across the room as her lashes fell onto her cheek and Fitch gently removed the glass from her hand. He wanted to observe her at close quarters, drink in her every nuance, commit every little detail to memory. He watched as she fell against Fitch's broad shoulder and snuggled instinctively into his arm. Were they sleeping together? Sebastian wondered. And if so, was he jealous? Surprisingly not. He just hoped that if they were, Fitch would be careful with her. She was so fragile. It wouldn't take much for her to crumble, Sebastian knew.

She was the antithesis of Catkin. Tough, calculating Catkin, who despite her promises hadn't called him back, and when he'd called her BlackBerry it had gone straight to voicemail. Was she really too busy hobnobbing and brown-nosing to bother? Was she, even now, bubbling and sparkling for the hideous Martin Galt? His heart gave a little lurch. He had always felt safe in the knowledge that he was the most important person in Catkin's life. But perhaps not. He remembered the look she had given Martin Galt when he had walked in on them, open invitation in her eyes. Maybe she was more than capable of sleeping with another man to further her career, and he'd been a fool not to realise it.

He let his imagination run on. He pictured Martin and Catkin alone at a table for two in Claridge's – not part of a big party, as she'd claimed. The empty glasses, the meaningful glances, the walk upstairs to the room the slimy bastard had already booked . . .

Sebastian took another swig of Remy and realised

that he was in danger of becoming maudlin. So when Penny stretched and yawned and declared it was time she went, Sebastian jumped to his feet and offered to walk her home. They said their farewells quietly to Fitch, not wanting to wake Charlotte who was still tucked under his arm, Dido on her other side resting her chin on her lap.

They stepped out into the stillness of the high street. Penny stumbled on the icy pavement and Sebastian put out a hand to steady her, then slipped his arm into hers. It was a gentlemanly gesture, reminiscent of another age.

'Don't want you falling and breaking an ankle. I know for a fact the local doctor's completely sozzled,' he joked.

They walked up the street arm in arm, like a Regency couple taking a promenade. She swayed against him every now and then. He slid an arm round her waist, and she felt her pulse quicken as his fingers stroked her hip gently. They arrived at her cottage and stood under the street lamp, bathed in its golden glow as snowflakes drifted lazily past them. It was like being in a snow-globe, thought Penny dreamily, as Sebastian tilted up her chin with his forefinger and kissed her. She had longed for this moment so many times, since the first time he had kissed her in the very same place.

'Come in with me,' she murmured. 'Keep me warm.'

This time, he didn't demur. She led him by the hand up the garden path, fumbled for a moment with the lock, then drew him inside the door. Dropping her coat to the floor, she led him up the stairs to her bedroom.

Never in a million years had she guessed that Christmas Day would make her dream come true. This was the best present ever. The man she had fantasised about all this time, in her bed. Little did he know how many times she had rehearsed this moment, lying between the sheets, bringing herself to the brink of ecstasy again and again, whispering his name in the dark. And now it was going to happen for real.

He was taking off his clothes, stumbling slightly in the gloom – she had only switched on the bedside lamp, not wanting him to view her imperfections. She slid out of her dress, letting it fall symbolically on top of his pile, and stood before him in her underwear.

He groped for her, feeling for her breasts. They fell back onto the bed. She wanted to kiss him, but he was eager to get on with the job in hand, pulling at her knickers. Never mind, she thought. He was obviously overcome with desire and couldn't wait. They could have a quick, frenzied fuck to get it out of their system, then spend the rest of the night exploring each other's bodies at leisure.

He rolled on top of her, pushing her legs apart with his knee, insinuating himself into the optimum position as he entered her.

'Hey,' she whispered. 'What's the hurry?'

But he was in no mood to slow down. Suddenly he gave a small, guttural groan and slumped on top of her. She lay for a moment feeling the rapid beat of his heart on her chest. She felt filled with desolation and disappointment. This wasn't how it was supposed to be. It was like going to bed with some randy, selfish teenager who had no idea that sex was a two-way street. She shifted uncomfortably under him, and realised he had gone to sleep. She suddenly felt angry: with Sebastian, for being so inconsiderate; with Bill, for leaving her so vulnerable, and with herself, for being a silly, obsessive middle-aged woman with a crush on a boy who didn't have the means to satisfy her.

She prodded his back. 'You'd better go.'

But he showed no signs of waking. He was out for the count. She managed to push him off her. He rolled onto his back and carried on sleeping, oblivious. Once she would have given anything to have him lying naked next to her. She would have lain there, feasting hers eyes on his body, that mouth whose lips she craved, that lean torso. Now, she just wanted to get away.

She left the room and slipped into her daughter's bed. She savoured the smell of innocence in Megan's room – the freshly laundered sheets she'd changed as soon as the children had left for Bill's, the J-Lo perfume she had bought her just before Christmas to wear to the school disco, the strawberry-scented candles that lined her window sill. God, thought Penny, as she lay there willing sleep to come. What wouldn't she give to have her time all over again, so she could do it right?

It was nearly midnight when Charlotte woke. She looked up, blinking, into Fitch's kind face smiling down at her.

'What's the time?' she murmured sleepily.

'Nearly twelve.'

She rubbed her eyes, then leaned back. His arm was still around her – he had sat still for the past two hours so as not to disturb her. She leaned her head on his shoulder and gave a contented little sigh, then slipped a hand around his waist.

'Thank you for a lovely day,' she said dreamily.

They sat curled up together for what felt like a lifetime. Then Fitch lifted a hand to stroke her blonde curls gently, and she nuzzled against him, enjoying the contact. She turned her face to look at him, eyes wide with anticipation, and he bent his head to kiss her. Just one gentle, tiny kiss that could, at a push, be interpreted as a gesture of affection between friends. Their eyes locked in the moments that followed, uncertainty hanging in the air, and then she raised her face and kissed him again, only this time it wasn't the kiss of mere friends.

He tasted of brandy and Terry's Chocolate Orange. Quite, quite delicious.

She felt his large hands circling her ribcage as he pulled her towards him. She put up her hands and twisted her fingers in his hair. It was surprisingly silky. His mouth was brushing her ear, and she shivered in delight. She tipped back her head, and as his lips traced their way over her throat she felt the pulse in her neck double, triple in time. Then they were kissing again, slow, slow, languorous, deliberate kisses that made her melt. She pulled him into her, wanting to feel the weight of a man's body on her, revelling in his masculinity. It seemed only natural that they should roll off the sofa and onto the rug in front of the fire. He slid his hands under the softness of her sweater, and she relished the warmth of his fingertips, shivering as they danced lightly over the surface of her skin.

It had been so long since she had thought about

anything physical. It was funny how you could just shut your mind to it. She hadn't really missed sex at all since she'd arrived in Withybrook. Only now she was simmering with desire, revelling in Fitch's touch, desperate to feel her body against his. His hand was under her skirt, stroking the inside of her leg so gently, snaking its way up her thigh, each caress weakening her resolve. She knew that once he had found his way inside she would be lost; that there would be no way back.

Is this what she really wanted? Even though her body was screaming out for him not to stop, there was a tiny warning bell that told her to stop and think. She was confused enough, about her future, her marriage, her feelings for Ed. And Fitch wasn't really over Hayley; she felt sure about that. They were both too raw for sex to be a sensible idea . . .

He had reached her knickers. She felt him stroke the soft silk, his thumb running over her and awakening such exquisite sensations. Her longing was overwhelming. For a second she pressed herself against him, letting out a soft moan. It would be so easy, to slither out of her clothes, to give herself to him, to devour every inch of him.

But how would they both feel afterwards?

She grabbed onto the front of his shirt.

'I can't!' she gasped. 'I can't do it, Fitch. I'm . . . so sorry. It's not that I don't want to . . .'

'Hey. It's OK.' He extricated his hands as soon as he sensed her discomfort.

'It's . . . complicated. I'm . . . kind of in a relationship. It's sort of over but . . . we haven't quite resolved things yet. I don't think it would be fair . . . I wouldn't want to lead you on.'

A little tear slid down her cheek. The feelings Fitch had released had been so intense, and though Charlotte knew it was all too easy to get carried away in the throes of passion, she also knew there was more between herself and Fitch than just animal attraction. But to give in to booze-induced lust would create more trouble than it was worth. They each had enough problems already. They were probably both just feeling in need of a bit of love and attention. This was a rebound skirmish for each of them. No, decided Charlotte. Sleeping with Fitch would really mess things up. He was, after all, her greatest ally. The best friend she had in Withybrook. And she didn't want tongues wagging or people speculating every time she walked down the street or into the Speckled Trout. They'd both probably be mortified the next day, unable to meet each other's eye.

Charlotte tried to brush away the tear surreptitiously.

'You're crying . . .' Fitch looked at her in concern.

'Sorry. I'm just being stupid. It was so . . . nice.' Nice? What a ridiculous word.

And then more tears escaped. And when he put his arms around her and squeezed her to him, shushing her gently, the floodgates opened. The trauma of the last few months, the uncertainty, the loneliness, all closed in on her. She was so tired of being brave. It would be so wonderful to let Fitch scoop her up, make love to her, to be a part of someone else just for that short time.

As she sobbed, Fitch just held her, rocking her in

his arms. He didn't question her, he just let her cry herself out. Eventually, she managed to stop.

'I'm sorry,' she gulped. 'Probably too much to drink. And bloody Christmas – it always makes me emotional.'

'Ssh,' he replied softly. 'You don't have to explain.'

She stayed in his arms for a moment. She could feel his heart, slow and steady, beating at half the rate of hers. He was in control. She wasn't entirely sure that she was. She would only need to feel his touch on her bare skin again and she would capitulate.

'I think I better go home,' she sighed, and he let her go. Charlotte hesitated for a moment. If only they could spend the night together and then erase the evidence. She hadn't realised how much she missed the comfort of another body. She opened her mouth to express what she was feeling.

'It's OK,' said Fitch, gently stroking back her hair. 'I know . . .'

She walked away from him, afraid she might cry again. She grabbed her coat, fished for her wellingtons then busied herself gathering up the rest of her belongings. She felt terrible, plunged into the abyss of gloom that comes when the party's over.

'Shall I walk you back?'

'I'll be fine,' she gabbled, edging away from him. The sooner she was out of his reach, the better. If she was near him, she would be able to smell him, feel his warmth, and she knew she wouldn't be able to resist. She opened his front door, breathed in the crisp, cold night air and stepped out onto the pavement. Behind her the door closed gently, and she set off up the road, not daring to look back.

Catkin let her Chloe frock fall to the floor before sliding into bed without brushing her teeth or taking off her make-up. She felt hideously depressed. On the surface, it had been a glamorous and wonderful day. There had been a whole gang of them at Claridge's, all refugees whose plans had been thrown awry thanks to the weather. They had drunk themselves stupid, eaten their way through a magnificent lunch, flirting, arguing and competing with each other for attention. They had been the most sparkling table in there, everyone looking at them with envy and awe. Catkin had glittered in their midst, she knew she had. Several people had stopped and asked for her autograph, and she had scrawled happily on their napkins – 'Merry Christmas love Catkin xxx'.

None of this had gone unnoticed by Martin. She felt happy that he had witnessed the attention she got, and would realise that she had real star potential. But at the end of the evening, he had gone off without saying goodbye, without making a plan, without any hint that they should do business together. And she felt ashamed, because she knew that if he had crooked his finger, had suggested a quiet drink together, or even something more, that she would have been unable to resist.

Now, she felt rock bottom and paranoid.

All her fears came flooding in. Where the hell was she going in her life? And what about her marriage? She and Sebastian were far from being the team they needed to be, and it was going to be their downfall. She felt fear. A great gnawing fear in her stomach that it was all going to go horribly wrong, and that she was going to lose everything. And maybe it was going to be her fault, for wanting too much, for pushing too hard, for being over-ambitious and greedy. She knew her expectations were eating away at the foundations of her marriage. It was never going to be an easy relationship; they were both strong personalities who didn't like compromise. Yet she couldn't for the life of her figure out how to make it work.

They could have the world, if only she could figure out where they were going wrong. She turned her pillow over for the tenth time and thumped it back into shape. What kind of agony aunt was she, if she couldn't figure out her own mess?

At four o'clock that morning, Sebastian slunk out of Penny's cottage and back up the lane to Withybrook Hall. What the hell had he done? He should never have treated Penny like that, like some cheap date who was asking for it. What a selfish, arrogant tosser he was. He was thinking that more and more about himself these days, he realised. He felt unanchored, insecure. He was drifting through life with no idea where he was going, and now he was hurting people en route.

Poor Penny. She'd just wanted him to show her a little bit of love and affection. He knew that, but he had been too afraid to give it to her, because he knew he shouldn't. But he'd fucked her all the same. Why? Out of spite? Because his wife hadn't been there when she should have been?

And Catkin. He'd been unfaithful to Catkin, because he had become paranoid about where she was and what she was doing and why, and she was quite possibly guilty of nothing. Even though she still hadn't called him.

He stood at the top of the drive. Only the thought of the next blank canvas stopped him from going into the house and opening another bottle. Instead, he headed for his studio. As he opened the door and stepped in, the smell of oil and turps hit him and gave him a lift. This was where he should be. He should be concentrating on his painting. It was only a matter of weeks till his next exhibition. And he had to admit that this was the first time he had ever really cared about what he had done. Without any hesitation, he pulled out the next canvas and set to work while the image of her was still fresh in his mind.

For the next four hours, he pored over his vision of purity and perfection. She was an angel, he decided. An angel that he knew would never be his, because he didn't deserve her and she certainly didn't deserve him. But it didn't stop her from inspiring him. Charlotte was going to save him from himself.

Twelve

In due course, the Christmas Day revellers each had an invitation to Sebastian's private viewing. A large, thick, stiff white card with bold black writing in a stark font that just bore his name, the name of the gallery, and a date and time.

Charlotte pinned hers to the kitchen wall, next to all her sketches, wallpaper samples and the pictures she had pulled out of magazines. It was definitely time she went back to London. She wanted to show Gussie the photos of everything she had done to the house – obviously she could email them, but she felt the need to see her friend face to face and make sure she was happy with her progress. She could have a look around a couple of showrooms, bring herself up to date. She might even buy some new clothes. She hadn't bought a single thing since she had been in Withybrook, and she missed the rush of a new purchase. She must be feeling better about herself, she thought, smiling, if she could contemplate retail therapy.

Fitch plonked his on top of the pile of papers that sat on his kitchen table – invoices, quotes, VAT forms – and promptly forgot about it. It was at the weekend, so it was out of the question as he would have the girls. He wouldn't have dreamed of asking Hayley to have them just this once. She had been even more impossible since they had got back from Dubai. Over-confident, bossy, inconsiderate. And she had brought up the subject of divorce.

'I think perhaps you were right. We should make things official,' she'd said, and Fitch's heart sank. If she had come round to the idea, it must mean things were serious with Kirk. He would have to go and see a solicitor to find out where he stood in terms of custody. He would not, absolutely would not, coun-tenance Jade and Amber living under that bone-head's roof, but he knew the law didn't always come down on the father's side.

Sebastian brought Penny's invitation round to her in person, and apologised for his atrocious behaviour on Christmas night.

'Please forgive me,' he begged. 'I can only blame the drink. It turns me into a lairy old goat. It was inexcusable.'

Penny blushed scarlet, embarrassed that he could even remember their ungainly coupling.

'It's fine,' she assured him, hoping he'd drop the subject. It was something she had tried to block out of her mind. But he persisted. And what was worse, he picked up her hand and caressed the back of it with his thumb as he spoke. Self-preservation told her to snatch it away, but she loved the feel of his fingers on her.

'I know there's a really strong attraction between us,' he continued, 'but I don't want us to have some mucky, clandestine affair. It would be really easy, to slip down here in the week and spend time with you – and don't think I'm not tempted. But you deserve better than that. And I don't want to betray Catkin. She's my wife, and I love her.'

Penny fixed him with a look.

'You already have betrayed her. Technically.'

Sebastian looked pained.

'Yes. I know. And I feel terrible about it. I took advantage of you, and I cheated on Catkin. Which makes me weak, spineless, despicable—'

'Human?' offered Penny.

He shrugged. 'I've always found it hard to resist temptation. Especially when I've had a drink.'

Penny jerked away from him.

'Right,' she said, unable to hide the hurt in her voice. 'So you quite fancy me, and chanced your arm because you'd had a few too many?'

He wrapped her up in his arms.

'Penny,' he soothed. 'Penny, Penny, Penny. I just don't want you to get hurt. And you would.'

'What you mean is,' she said sadly, 'I'm not worth sacrificing what you've got.'

He sighed. 'Don't do this to me,' he pleaded. 'We might be a bit rocky at the moment, me and Catkin, but we're going to come through. She's the one who keeps me going. She's the one who supports me; keeps me on track. I can't jack in my marriage.'

'You'd have a lot to lose, after all,' Penny pointed out wryly.

'Don't be bitter.' He looked into her eyes imploringly, and she felt herself drawn into his gaze. 'And don't think that, given a different set of circumstances . . .'

'Who says I'd be interested?' Penny tilted up her

chin. If she didn't fight, she'd cry. 'It was just a drunken Christmas shag.'

And not a very good one, at that, she wanted to add.

Sebastian looked chastened. 'We are still mates, aren't we?'

'Course,' replied Penny, because she couldn't bear the idea of not seeing him again.

'And you will come to the exhibition?' he pleaded. 'It would mean so much to me – to have you there.'

'Really?'

'Yes.' He put an arm round her shoulders, and she felt herself go warm at his touch. 'You've been a fantastic friend to me, and I've treated you like shit. Come and have a wild time at my expense.'

'I don't know. I wouldn't know what to wear for a start.'

'Oh, for God's sake,' said Sebastian crossly. 'You women. Wear what you normally wear. You always look great.'

Penny rolled her eyes. He had no idea. She couldn't turn up to the Rhombus Gallery in one of her usual outfits. She'd have to nip over to Exeter, see if one of the boutiques there could come up with something sufficiently trendy.

'So, I'll put you down as a yes, then, shall I?' Sebastian was nothing if not persuasive.

'OK,' she laughed, and as he left her kitchen with a backward wave she realised one thing. She hadn't been cured of him at all. His boyishly charming apology had melted her inside. Catkin didn't know how lucky she was. More than anything, Penny longed to be the person Sebastian turned to, the person who supported him, the person who spurred him on. She picked up his empty teacup and stroked the rim where his lips had touched it. She suspected he was even more out of reach than ever. She rinsed the cup under the tap hastily, telling herself to get a grip. It wasn't going to happen, and the sooner she got over it, the sooner she might have a chance of inner peace. Possibly even happiness.

Sebastian, meanwhile, was on a roll, even more so now he had made his peace with Penny. His conscience had been pricking him, but now he felt he had atoned for his thoughtless, selfish crime, and so, with the weight taken off his shoulders, he was able to get back to work with a spring in his step.

He was, for the first time in his life, genuinely happy with the pieces he had produced for his exhibition, because he felt they were pure and from the heart, and because they harked back to his original love of figurative drawing. There was no need to search for any hidden meaning in what he had done. The paintings were purely representative. If they meant something to him personally, then that was his secret. All that mattered was that his creativity had been unleashed, and he had been able to enjoy his work, instead of feeling as if he was working under some hideous sword of Damocles that was forcing him to perform. If he'd thrown out the rule book in the process, then so be it. Maybe his statement would allow other artists to break free from the tyranny of modern art and the apparent need to say something startlingly original if you wanted to succeed. In Sebastian's view, controversy wasn't art. He knew that, because he had courted it and peddled it and it was bollocks.

Surely just beauty was enough? He was determined that this exhibition would prove that. As Renoir said, 'Why shouldn't art be pretty? There are enough unpleasant things in this world.'

He was pleased, too, that he and Catkin seemed to have reached a truce. She had come back the minute the snow had melted away, and thrown herself into his arms, clearly distraught she had missed Christmas with him. They'd enjoyed a couple of days of domesticity together before she had to rush back to the studio, going for long walks and eating the casseroles that Stacey had left them, tucked up in front of the fire. He realised they rarely spent time alone with each other, and they both agreed they should do it more often. At weekends, there were always manic preparations for whichever guests were arriving, Catkin tense with pre-match nerves and Sebastian cantankerous because he didn't feel like socialising. Usually by the time Catkin was due to go back to London, they had got on each other's nerves so much neither of them could wait for the driver to arrive. But this time, she had clung to him, tears on her lashes, not wanting to leave.

She was also thrilled that he was being so industrious, although she was peeved that he wouldn't allow her a sneak preview of what he had done.

'Not until it's properly hung,' he insisted.

Instead, she threw herself into the organisation of the preview party. Sebastian frankly didn't give a toss who came, and so he was quite happy for her to take over the guest list, the catering, the flowers . . .

He drew the line when she started fretting about his outfit.

'Why are you women so obsessed with clothes?' he demanded. 'I'll probably just wear jeans, as usual.'

'You can't just wear jeans. You're the artist.'

'Exactly,' said Sebastian. 'I can wear what I like.'

Catkin wound her arm around his neck.

'If I choose you something,' she purred, 'will you wear it?'

Sebastian eyed her thoughtfully.

'If it makes you happy,' he finally concurred, and she clapped.

Ozwald Boateng, she decided. Or maybe something with a bit more edge. Galliano . . .

The week before the exhibition, Charlotte decided to visit the doctor. Her eczema had really flared up over the past few weeks, thanks to all the strippers and thinners she'd been using and the fact she couldn't be bothered to wear gloves. Even though she liberally applied aqueous cream every night her hands were cracked and red and raw, and in some places looked in danger of becoming septic.

By chance she found she was booked in with Penny, who immediately prescribed her some steroid cream and told her off, mildly, for letting it get so bad.

'Are you going to Sebastian's exhibition?' she asked, as Charlotte folded up her prescription.

Charlotte nodded. 'How about you?'

'Maybe,' said Penny, doubtfully.

'Oh, do,' said Charlotte. 'Sebastian would be disappointed if you didn't.'

'I doubt it.'

'No, really,' Charlotte insisted. 'I think we're his only mates. He can't stand that pretentious air-kissing brigade. Oh, go on,' she urged. 'I won't know anyone else otherwise.'

Penny shrugged and laughed. 'If I can find something to wear,' she promised.

As soon as Charlotte had gone, Penny typed up her notes on the computer, then frowned. The records stated that she was registered as Charlotte Briggs, yet Penny was certain she'd always introduced herself as Charlotte Dixon. She looked back through her notes, then spotted something that caught her interest. Fertility treatment? Why was Charlotte having fertility treatment? As far as she knew, she wasn't married. Not that you needed to be married to have fertility treatment, of course, but it was more usual.

Penny scrolled back even further, looking for clues. She felt a little bit guilty, snooping like this. But Charlotte obviously had a secret. Was it breaking the Hippocratic oath, to snoop through her past like this? Penny reassured herself that any good doctor would familiarise themselves with a new patient's history, but deep down she knew she was just prying.

Well. According to the records she was married, with unexplained infertility. And she was called Charlotte Briggs now, not Dixon. Dixon was her maiden name.

Penny sat back in her chair, frowning. The name Charlotte Briggs was bothering her. It rang a bell, somehow. She typed the name into her search engine. She was surprised when a whole page of newspaper articles came up. She leaned forward to read them, clicking through all the articles carefully, astounded at the pictures of a glamorous Charlotte with her hair long, standing next to what must be her husband. Penny read on hungrily.

Bloody hell. Charlotte had always looked as if butter wouldn't melt. But there she was, in black and white for all to see, apparently embroiled in a hugely distasteful fraud case. Her husband had run off with the profits from a charity ball, and lost the lot on an insider deal that went wrong. He was now inside.

There was a picture of them dressed up for the ball, Charlotte in a figure-hugging black dress, her hair pinned up, her husband next to her in black tie. With them was the man whose son had died of leukaemia, whose hospice the ball had been raising money for. The money Ed Briggs had embezzled. In the photo, they looked like a dazzlingly successful and wealthy couple. Charlotte looked a million miles from the girl she was down here, who was rarely seen in anything but jeans and was usually splattered in paint.

No wonder she had done a runner from London. No doubt she had been shunned by all her friends, sacked from her job, excommunicated from her social circle. Penny wondered if she had colluded with her husband in the scam. The articles in the paper indicated not, and her gut feeling told her it wasn't the sort of thing Charlotte would be party to. But then you never knew with people. She, after all, had had no idea her husband was shagging his registrar until he'd announced he was leaving.

Penny rather hastily shut down her browser, feeling as if she was poking her nose into Charlotte's private life. Which of course she was. And she had to admit she was rather shocked. She was dying to know more, but she could hardly ask Charlotte about it. For a moment, she felt a visceral desire to share her discovery with somebody else. There was nothing more pleasurable than imparting scandal, after all. Yet tempting though it was to spill the beans, Penny wasn't a natural gossipmonger, and somehow she didn't want to betray Charlotte. She'd never done her any harm, after all. And she'd obviously been through a lot. The revelations certainly shed light on what a girl like her was doing holed up in Withybrook.

Brooding slightly on what she had discovered, she called up her next patient's notes before buzzing them in.

Thirteen

The Rhombus Gallery was so-called because it was shaped like a squashed diamond, each of its four walls the same length. It had a high pointed glass roof, like the spire of a cathedral, which let the sunshine flood in, and the natural light made it a favourite with artists. The walls were matt chalky white, and the floor black elm, and most of the people who entered its hallowed interior matched themselves to the monochrome colour scheme.

Tonight it was heaving with artists, actresses, authors, models, rock stars, glitterati, literati, media whores and pundits. They were all gathered in the spacious reception hall, waiting to be ushered through into the inner sanctum where Sebastian Turner's latest exhibition would be revealed to them in all its glory.

To oil the social wheels, waitresses in black hot-pants and high-necked sleeveless tops were handing round gin and tonics muddled with crushed blackberries and crème de Mure, which made most of the guests insensible within minutes. To soak it up, platters of exquisite sushi were passed round, as well as cups of beetroot gazpacho and Devon Ruby Red steak tartare. There was no point in serving anything resembling a carbohydrate to this crowd.

Catkin wore a deep-yellow silk dress held up by a

thick gold chain round her neck and a deadly pair of YSL sandals, her trademark bob shorter and sharper than ever. To her delight, Sebastian had slipped into the suit she had chosen for him without demur, though he had refused to wear a shirt underneath and insisted on rolling up the sleeves. He was right, of course. He looked charmingly dissolute. The artist in control of his own destiny.

At nine o'clock, when people were starting to go cross-eyed from alcohol, he gave a short speech in front of the ceiling-high stainless-steel doors that led to the gallery.

'Every now and again someone comes along in your life who gives you a fresh way of looking at things. They inspire you. They make you want to create. They give you vision. Confidence. And sometimes they do this without even knowing it. This person has given me the courage to paint what I believe in and to be honest to myself, when the pressure to create something just for effect and impact is overwhelming. I hope you think the results are as beautiful as I do.'

With a small nod of the head, he indicated to the security guards to open the doors. The crowds swarmed in.

On each of the four white walls were hung three canvasses. A dozen altogether. Six foot square, each bore an exquisite oil painting of a woman. A girl with a curly blonde crop and wide, green eyes. In one, she was curled up on a huge sofa. In another, she was clasping a glass of red wine, in another engrossed in a battered copy of *Madame Bovary*. In one she was asleep, her head resting on her arms. Two depicted her devouring a plate of fruit, her fingers tearing at the flesh of a juicy orange. In the final painting she was simply smiling, looking straight at the observer, her eyes alive with promise.

From a distance, it seemed as though the artist had barely touched the canvas. But up close, it was evident that he had painstakingly built up layer upon layer of paint to get the depth and the texture, working and reworking with his brush to achieve a thick crust of palest pink and creamy white and gold, interspersed with smudges of grey. Sinuous strokes laid their contours across the canvas, snaking their way over the girl's hips, breasts, neck, mouth . . . And in the midst of each, except in the paintings where she was sleeping, two verdant eyes gleamed out. On close inspection, the irises contained tiny dots of green and gold, applied with the finest brush so they glittered like jewels, hypnotising the viewer.

The work was exquisite. The work of a master. The work of a man who understood a woman's body, and who wanted nothing more than to relay her beauty to his audience. Even though she was fully clothed in all the paintings, it was if she was laid bare. They were sensual, almost erotic, but not lascivious in any way. The curve of her lips, the delicate bone on her ankle, the shadows at the base of her collarbone – the detail was so perfect it was almost as if she was going to slide off the canvas and walk among the guests.

Sebastian held his breath for the reaction. You could usually tell within the first thirty seconds whether an exhibition was going to be well received. There was an initial silence as the spectators drank in painting after painting. Then the sound of a slow hand clap started across the room, joined by another, and

then another, until the gallery was filled with thunder-
ous applause, interspersed with cheering and wolf-
whistles.

Sebastian smiled. He never usually gave a toss what
anyone thought of his work. But this time, he was
proud of what he had done.

Charlotte stood in a corner of the room, horrified.
Thank goodness her hair had grown since the paintings had been done. She'd had it blow-dried sleek and
straight, with a long wispy fringe. Her black cocktail
dress was a million miles from the scruffy clothes she'd
been depicted in. And she was wearing quite a lot of
make-up, over-compensating for the fact that she'd
hardly worn any for months. She didn't look at all like
the fresh-faced, curly-haired creature replicated all
around her. The guests were all so self-absorbed and
excited, they didn't notice her anyway – she'd have had
to walk round the room naked to have got any
attention.

How could this have happened? This was her worst
nightmare, to be on public display for all to see when
she had been so careful to hide herself away. And what
the hell was Sebastian thinking of? These pictures
implied that there was something between them. They
were so intimate and personal. She'd had absolutely no
idea that he had been observing her so closely. Apart
from the day when he had sketched her in her house,
he had never been more than . . . well, just friendly,
she had thought. Affectionate at a push. There had
never been any suggestion from him of a deeper
relationship between them. But these pictures told
another story. How could she deny it, looking at what

stared back at her from the four walls? No one could walk away from this exhibition without thinking they had been embroiled in some affair.

She pushed through the crowds, keeping her head down. She was going to run outside and get a taxi. As she made her way back through the huge double doors into the reception area, she saw a figure in a yellow dress, running down a corridor.

Catkin.

Her heart leaped into her mouth. She hesitated for a moment by the exit. What on earth was Catkin going to think?

Penny stood at the back of the room, clutching the blackberry cocktail which had now started curdling in her stomach.

Had she really spent three hundred pounds on a dark red silk dress for this? To have Charlotte bloody Dixon-slash-Briggs shoved in her face? To have the whole world know that this was who Sebastian Turner put on a pedestal, adored and adulated, when Penny was the one he had fucked on Christmas Day? She felt incredibly bitter as she remembered him begging her to forgive him for his behaviour, how he couldn't betray his beloved wife. And all the time he was banging some gangster's moll. Penny was sure Sebastian didn't know Charlotte's true identity, or her dark secret. The saccharine-sweet portraits of her made her look the picture of bloody innocence, as if butter wouldn't melt in her mouth. They made Penny feel sick.

Why had Sebastian asked her to come to the exhibition? Was it just to humiliate her? Or to prove that she meant nothing, whereas Charlotte – Charlotte! Not Catkin, as he had protested – meant everything? Whatever had she done to him to deserve such cruel treatment? Did he have no feelings for anyone else on the planet except himself?

All around her, the press were going wild. Critics were scribbling; flashes were going off left, right and centre. Adjectives and epithets were being bandied around – 'luminous', 'incandescent', 'coruscating' – and references were being made – Renoir, Degas, Fragonard, Ingres. And the question on everyone's lips: 'Who is this girl?' No one seemed to have any idea.

Penny did it before she could stop herself. She pushed her way out of the room, her fists clenched at her side. She found a likely journalist phoning in his copy from the reception area. She had no idea which paper he was from, nor did she care. Once the first one knew, the others would soon follow. It would be splashed all over the Sunday papers. Just like before, thought Penny spitefully. History repeating itself.

'If you want to know who she is,' she murmured *sotto voce*, 'her name is Charlotte Dixon. Also known as Mrs Charlotte Briggs, whose husband is currently inside doing time for fraud. I'm sure you'll have all the details on file.'

The journalist looked at her, surprised. 'You sure?'

Penny nodded. 'Absolutely.'

He lifted his phone and gave her a nod of appreciation. 'Cheers, love.'

'It's a pleasure,' she replied, and with the utmost dignity, she walked out of the gallery, down the steps, and hailed a taxi back to the station.

Catkin stood in the pink marble of the ladies' bathroom and threw her glass at the wall. How the fuck could Sebastian have humiliated her like this? He couldn't, if he had tried, have done anything worse to undermine her. How could she have been so taken in by him? She'd been so filled with hope when he had finally got it together for this exhibition. She'd thought they were working as a team at last, working towards her dream, that he'd banished his demons. Instead, he had unleashed them. She was going to be a laughing stock. The whole world was going to know that her husband had a two-bit painter and decorator on the side.

His very thoughts about this girl were entirely apparent. They were the most sensual paintings that anyone could ever see. The simple tasks were more erotic than something more blatant. They literally took your breath away with their beauty. She knew it was the best work he had ever done. The collection told an incredible story that no one could fail to relate to. That the artist was head over heels with his subject was totally undeniable. Every brushstroke was a loving caress. They were masterpieces.

It took a lot to shake Catkin. But as she stood in the middle of the ladies' room, she began to gasp for breath, panic overwhelming her. She had no idea what to think. She had no idea what to do.

The door opened. Although she knew she should flee into the nearest cubicle and try to regain her composure, she couldn't move. She found herself rooted to the spot. The glass lay shattered on the floor at her feet. She sank to her knees, sobbing.

'Catkin . . .'

She looked up, her shoulders heaving. Straight into the anxious face of her nemesis. If she could have spat, she would have. But she was crying too hard to summon up the saliva.

'Get out,' she snarled. 'Get out!'

If she'd had another glass, she would have thrown it at her.

Charlotte looked at the shards surrounding Catkin, and went to get some paper towels out of the dispenser.

'We better get this cleaned up. Or you'll cut yourself.'

'Don't be such a fucking Girl Guide,' spat Catkin. 'We all know the truth now.'

'Listen,' said Charlotte. 'I don't know what it's about any more than you do. As far as I'm concerned, Sebastian is a friend. That's all. I absolutely promise you, I absolutely swear, that nothing has ever happened between us. The most intimate thing we have ever done is share a Tunnock's bar.'

Catkin looked at her askance and Charlotte smiled ruefully.

'Hand on heart, this is a total shock. It's completely freaked me out. I don't know what he's playing at, but as far as I'm concerned the most important thing is that you know there was nothing going on between us.'

Despite herself, Catkin couldn't help but believe the girl. Why else would she have had the courage to come straight in and face up to her? She put her hands up to her face, wiping away the streaks of mascara that were tracking down her cheeks.

'Why did he do it to me?' she asked tearfully. 'It's so cruel . . .' Charlotte handed her a paper towel to wipe her face. 'I've got to get out of here.'

'No. That's the last thing you should do.'

Catkin looked up at her, startled.

'Don't let yourself come out of this looking like a fool. Or a victim,' Charlotte urged. 'The press will love it if they think there's something going on, or that you're upset. Get out there, circulate, charm everyone. If you want to go and smash glasses afterwards, feel free. But don't show them your belly, or they'll stick the knife in.'

Catkin grabbed at her arms.

'Will you come out there with me? If people think we're friends, they might believe there's nothing going on . . .'

Charlotte thought for a moment. Catkin was right. If they fronted everyone, they would defuse the rumours. But if she did that, there was no way her identity wouldn't be discovered. The pressure would be too intense. She wouldn't be able to keep the press at bay. She couldn't risk it.

'I'm really sorry, Catkin.' She hugged the woman to her. 'I can't.'

'But why not?'

'I can't tell you. Just go back in there on your own. You'll be fine. Come on. Dry your eyes and get your make-up back on. There're important people out there you need to impress.'

She pulled Catkin to her feet, and brushed the last few pieces of glass off her.

'Where did you learn all this PR spin?' demanded Catkin.

Charlotte gave a twisted smile. 'Bitter experience. Which is why I'm getting out of here before the shit hits the fan.'

Catkin peered at her. 'Who are you?'

'I'm nobody. And nothing. And you never saw me.'

Charlotte opened the loo door, pulled her coat collar up around her face, and strode out of the entrance hall to the exit as quickly as her trembling legs could carry her.

Fourteen

The exhibition was a sensation. Editors, journalists, collectors and critics gushed ecstatically, queuing up to congratulate Sebastian with an enthusiasm that was uncharacteristic of their usual world-weary ennui. He was initially wary of the praise. He knew only too well the emperor's new clothes syndrome could have a sudden backlash and come back to bite you when you least expected it. But by the time the whole room had unanimously lauded him, he was starting to think that he really was a success. And this success was so much sweeter than before. He was, he realised, proud of what he had accomplished.

Catkin was amazing. She worked the room like the professional she was, resplendent in her yellow dress, lavishing praise upon her genius of a husband, targeting the most illustrious collectors and critics and charming them, knowing they would be dually responsible for the final price to be fetched for each piece. But the moment the viewing was over, the moment the last guest trickled out of the door and the staff started clearing up the mess, she closed down. Sebastian came over to hug her, and saw immediately that the light that had been shining in her eyes all night had been snapped out like a bedside lamp.

'Catkin – you were wonderful.'

She looked at him with contempt, and immediately he started to shrivel.

'I think we're done, Sebastian.'

He chose to misinterpret her.

'Yes – I guess we can go on somewhere else to celebrate—'

'I don't mean done here,' she snapped. 'I mean we're finished.'

'What . . . ?'

She gestured round the room, at the dozen Charlottes.

'How do you imagine this made me feel?'

He held up his hands.

'They're paintings. They could have been of anything: fruit bowls—'

'Jesus Christ, Sebastian. Have you looked at them?'

Sebastian stared round, confused. Of course he'd looked at them. He'd spent all his waking hours looking at them for the past few weeks.

'This is a love story. On canvas. You're fucking obsessed. Can't you see that?'

Sebastian felt panic creep over him as a slow realisation started to dawn.

'Catkin, I'm not in love with her if that's what you think.'

'You might as well have got up and wanked all over them in public.'

He recoiled at her crudeness.

'You don't understand—'

'What? That you've just painted twelve of the most stunning paintings of this century? Of some little two-bit decorator? And I'm supposed to believe you don't give a toss about her?'

'Not in that way. Not really.'

'Uh-huh?' Catkin put her hands on her hips, always a bad sign.

'She just touched something in me, that's all. She's vulnerable, fragile, kind of . . . innocent. I wanted to capture that.'

Catkin nodded. 'Right.' Her tone said it all. She didn't believe him.

'She made me want to paint. It's as simple as that.' Sebastian wasn't sure why he was having to defend himself.

'So she's your muse?' She spat out the word as if it was an obscenity.

'To use an over-rated cliché, yes, I guess she is.' Sebastian was starting to get angry. 'There's nothing wrong with having a muse.'

'No.' Catkin's voice was very small all of a sudden, which frightened him more than her shouting. 'But I guess the problem I'm having is . . . I thought I was your muse. After everything I've done for you, trying to get you in the studio. Supporting you. Encouraging you. It was kind of a shock to walk in here and find out somebody else was pushing your buttons all along.'

She started wiping away tears. Sebastian looked at her, aghast. He'd had no idea that this was how his work was going to be interpreted. To him they were simple portraits of someone who'd inspired him. But now, looking round, he understood their impact. The exhibition as a whole was incredibly intense. Twelve immensely powerful paintings of the same woman. Was it any wonder that people, including Catkin, might think he was ever so slightly besotted?

Had he been? He looked back over the past few

weeks' feverish creativity. He hadn't been besotted with Charlotte herself, as everyone seemed to think, but he had revelled in the creativity she had released in him. She'd freed him from his own tyranny, the total apathy he had felt. It had been such a relief to *want* to paint something, to know exactly how he envisaged each piece, and for that piece to have come out perfect every time. Twelve times. Was that a crime?

Of course it was, he realised now. He'd had complete tunnel vision. He hadn't given a second thought to anybody in all the time he had been working, right up to the moment when he had given his speech. A speech which he now realised could have been completely misinterpreted.

Catkin was picking up her bag, going to find her coat.

'Catkin—'

'Fuck off,' she replied. 'And you needn't think you're staying at the flat. I'll send a truck down to Withybrook for my stuff.'

And she walked out of the gallery, his beautiful wife in her glorious yellow dress, with her long, long legs in those high, high heels, and he wondered why it was that she'd never inspired him to paint, despite her endless encouragement, and what it was that caused the chemistry, what it was that flicked the switch between paralysis and inspiration. What it was that evoked the gloriously hedonistic pleasure of creating something for the sheer love of it. And he realised that if he had the answer to that, then he'd be an even richer man than he already was.

Penny saw Charlotte running down the platform to catch the Bamford train just as the last whistle blew.

Her make-up was smudged, and she looked distraught, running along in her high heels. The guard beckoned her urgently towards the door he was about to slam shut, and Penny saw her as she jumped on board. She prayed she wouldn't get into her carriage, that she would turn right and not left. She breathed a sigh of relief as she saw Charlotte head towards the front of the train, swivelling her head from side to side to find a spare seat.

Penny felt terrible. The evening had been a disaster. She knew she shouldn't have come. She realised now that Sebastian had only asked her to be polite and to salve his conscience, because in fact he had no feelings for anyone except himself. He was a narcissistic little shit. He hadn't betrayed her. It wasn't even as interesting as that. She was nothing in his life. He'd got his leg over on Christmas night because Charlotte had been tucked up under Fitch's big, strong arm, and Sebastian couldn't handle it. All that crap about his wife. He had no loyalty to his wife. Even Bill, who had behaved like a complete bastard, wouldn't have rubbed Penny's nose in his other woman like that.

She sipped at her watery hot chocolate. It trickled down and settled uneasily on top of the blackberry mush. Penny badly wanted to be sick, and she knew what it was. Not what she'd drunk, but guilt.

She shouldn't have told the journalist about Charlotte. It was confidential information she'd got from Charlotte's medical records, which she shouldn't have been privy to in the first place, and she had had no right to divulge it. Of course, there was no way anyone could trace the leak back to her, but that wasn't the point. She'd acted impulsively and now she regretted it. Whatever Charlotte's relationship with Sebastian was, she would have had no intention of hurting Penny, she was sure. And now Penny had done the one thing that meant Charlotte's life was ruined. She'd obviously come to Withybrook for a fresh start, and Penny had blown the whistle on her.

She stirred the remnants of her hot chocolate miserably with the white plastic stick, wishing that she'd been stronger. How were you supposed to protect yourself against falling in love? Once the seeds of passion were planted, it was very hard to shut your mind to it. And then it made you behave like a lunatic. She'd slept with another woman's husband, shafted someone big time, and now she was filled with self-loathing.

She laid her head against the back of the seat and shut her eyes. She'd try to sleep. Although she might miss her stop and end up in Penzance. Frankly, she didn't care if she did.

Fifteen

The post office in Withybrook opened on a Sunday from ten till twelve for people to come and fetch their newspapers, and to buy the annoying things they had forgotten to get for lunch, like mint sauce or gravy browning.

Fitch eyed the various photographs of Sebastian's exhibition on the front pages of the papers that were lined up ready for collection. Obviously there wasn't much else in the news today as they all seemed to have picked up on it. He fished out his copy of the *Independent* while studying one of the tabloids. 'The Man with the Golden Brush!' it proclaimed, and went on to eulogise about Sebastian being the saviour of the British art scene.

Most of them had chosen the painting of Charlotte staring out of the canvas to represent the exhibition. It made the hairs on Fitch's neck stand on end. It depicted her so exactly – the wide eyes, the half smile. He had to agree. The man was a genius. It was as if he had captured her soul on canvas—

'I never had a clue,' said Nikita, breaking into his thoughts.

'What?' asked Fitch absently.

'That she was at it with him.' Nikita pursed her lips to show her disapproval. 'Or that she was on the run.'

'Sorry?'

'Haven't you read the article?' Nikita thrust a copy of the *Mail on Sunday* at him.

It was just the sort of aspirational, celebrity-driven tale the *Mail* loved. By the time Fitch had read their version of events, he felt sick. So that's what Charlotte was doing in the wilds of Withybrook. She was in hiding because her husband had failed to pull off a rather tacky scam that he should have known better than to attempt. And now, it seemed, she was embroiled with everyone's new favourite artist, Sebastian Turner. At least, that's what the media were speculating, although they were all swift to point out that Sebastian's wife Catkin had been firmly at his side throughout the exhibition. There was a photo of the two of them together, Catkin looking chic and triumphant, Sebastian just looking . . . well, like Sebastian. Slightly rumpled and burned out, but annoyingly attractive.

Fitch slid the paper back to Nikita with a little shrug.

'It just goes to show,' she said, 'that you never really know people, do you?'

'No . . .' agreed Fitch. He remembered Christmas night, how she'd told him things were complicated. He felt rather hurt that she had pulled the wool over his eyes so completely. He thought they had built up an element of trust between them. He'd confided his fears and worries about Hayley to her, and she'd kept silent in return. Not that she owed him any explanation, of course, and if she wanted to keep her past a secret that was up to her. But he felt disappointed nevertheless.

And he was rather shocked she'd been having an affair with Sebastian all the time. She'd certainly hidden that well. But the paintings told the story. It was written in her eyes. Fitch felt a bit of a fool. What had he been to her? Just a useful cover? Had she left him on Christmas night to go slithering up to Withybrook Hall, once Sebastian had dropped Penny off? Poor Penny – was she a cipher as well? Had they both been used to put everyone off the scent? It wasn't a pleasant thought.

He was cross with himself for caring about Charlotte a little bit more than he should. He couldn't deny it. He felt immensely drawn to her. There had been that moment when there could have been something between them. He'd replayed it in his mind over and over again since Christmas, wondering how wrong of him it had been to kiss her. And whether, if he had persisted, it could have gone further. And what would have happened then?

Now he was glad it hadn't gone any further. If it had, he'd be in rather deeper than he was now, and today's revelation would have been even more of a shock.

He handed Nikita his money. Jade and Amber were further down the shop, filling little paper bags with sweets.

'Jade! Amber!' he called, and they came running up with their booty. His heart melted. They were the only girls that mattered to him, he reminded himself. They would always remain loyal to him, and he would love them unconditionally for ever. Perhaps that was it, he thought. Perhaps he should restrict his affections to his children from now on. It would certainly make life a lot simpler.

*

Hayley lay dreamily in bed, luxuriating in that heavenly moment after waking before you actually opened your eyes, and wondered how it could be that she had got so lucky.

The day before, she and Kirk had been to the Grove. Billed as London's country estate, it was a five-star hotel of incredible luxury. Kirk had spent the day on the golf course, while Hayley lounged in the state-of-the-art spa. She had a blissful massage and a facial, then snoozed the rest of the afternoon away in the relaxation room – dark and womblike, it was furnished with comfortable beds separated by dark purple organza curtains, lit with flickering tea lights and scented candles. This was the life. This was exactly what she wanted. To be pampered, and luxuriate.

Why hadn't Fitch been able to see that? It wasn't as if he didn't earn good money. They could easily have spent the weekends somewhere like the Grove. Her mother would have had the girls. But instead, her stubborn husband wanted to go and hunt minnows up at Landacre bridge, or just walk down to the Speckled Trout for a ploughman's lunch, or wander round the bloody farmers' market in Comberton, snapping up venison or peculiar-coloured cauliflowers and drooling over the cheeses. He told her she was irresponsible when she complained: as a farmer's daughter, she should appreciate the lease of life the resurgence of the market had given them. He could be so self-righteous at times. He just didn't under-stand her needs. She'd grown up in Withybrook, for heaven's sake. She was bored to death with it all.

Whereas Kirk . . . he understood her needs. He'd given her more stimulation in the past few months than she'd ever had. He loved taking her shopping, buying her whatever she wanted. Pulling out the most amazing dresses in the most fabulous boutiques, urging her to try them on, telling her she looked gorgeous. And then buying them for her! Then sliding them off her at the end of the night. Doing things to her body she had never even dreamed about.

She slid out from between the satin sheets. She was going to go and shower off last night's excesses. She reeked of sex, and although it turned her on, she wanted to make herself sweet-smelling for him, so they could do it all again.

She bent down to scoop her clothes up from the floor, sweeping under the bed to retrieve every last thing. As she pulled her stockings towards her, an item of clothing she didn't recognise came with them.

It was a pair of knickers. If you could call them that. A wispy little rolled-up knot of pink ribbon and lace that had clearly been worn and hastily removed. They were tiny. Barely a size eight. She imagined some dinky little honey blonde wriggling out of them and throwing them out of his bed with abandon. She swallowed. She'd been totally naïve to think that he spent the weeks alone, saving himself for her. A man of Kirk's appetites didn't do abstinence.

She straddled him, sitting just above his cock. He opened his eyes and smiled.

'Hey, baby. You got something for me?' He caressed her flank, running his hand up to her waist, then higher, reaching out for her breast. But she pulled away.

'I certainly have,' she replied. 'Shut your eyes and hold out your hand.'

She saw the flicker of lust in his expression before he obeyed. Gently she placed the offending article in his palm.

'Now open,' she breathed.

He frowned as he looked at her offering. She put her head to one side and smiled at him, then gave a little shrug.

'I found them under the bed.'

He shook his head in bewilderment.

'What am I supposed to do with these?'

'I just wondered whose they were?'

'Yours. Aren't they?'

He was good. He didn't miss a beat. She took them out of his palm and held them aloft disdainfully to show him their full size.

'I don't think so. Do you?'

'They must belong to the cleaner.'

She glared down at him.

'You must think I'm an idiot.'

Seconds later she was seeing stars, as she felt his rock-hard knuckles connect with her lip, and her teeth break the tender skin on the inside of her mouth. Metallic blood flooded onto her tongue moments before she felt the pain; a sharp, agonising explosion. She screamed at him to stop but no sound came out.

'Don't get arsey with me, you bitch.' His voice was hoarse with rage. 'I've spent a small fortune on you this weekend. That leaves you with no rights at all.' He grabbed both of her arms, his fingers digging into her flesh. She tried to move but his grip was like a vice. 'I've bought you, lock, stock and barrel. And I don't answer to you. Got that?'

She nodded, terrified. She could feel her lips swelling, and she didn't think she could speak.

'I'm sorry,' she blabbered. 'I just—'

'Well, don't . . . *just*. Not ever.'

He pushed her over onto her back, pinning her down onto the bed. She shut her eyes as he entered her. He seemed excited by the violence. As he rode her he swore explicitly, his anger spilling over into his epithets. Hayley's instinct was to fight, but she knew she stood no chance. His arms were as thick as her thighs, the muscles bulging from his workouts. He was relentless. He seemed to be lasting for ever. She prayed for him to come quickly, and tried to tense her muscles to encourage his ejaculation, but he was in another place, responding to some other stimuli.

Eventually he reached his peak with a final foul oath, and fell onto her.

'Was that good for you?' he asked with a malevolent smile, and she nodded, knowing that if she wanted to get out of here alive that was the only answer. He'd never let her go out looking like this. He wouldn't want her out in public, bearing evidence that he had walloped her. If she wanted to escape, she'd have to be very careful.

She waited until he was in the shower. He always spent at least fifteen minutes in there, and he wouldn't be able to hear her departure over the noise. She didn't bother to pack, just pulled on her clothes from the night before, grabbed her handbag and ran down the stairs. For a terrible few moments she couldn't find her car keys. Perhaps Kirk had hidden them? She'd have to run, out of the house, down the road as fast as she could, try and find a way to the station . . . She thought her heart was going to explode it was pounding so hard. Then suddenly she saw her key-ring poking out from underneath a tea towel. She grabbed it, hearing the shower upstairs stop. She only had moments to get away. He'd be stepping out of the shower, reaching for a towel, walking back into the bedroom.

She ran out of the front door. If he walked over to the window, he would be able to see her. With trembling hands she unlocked the door, leaped into the driving seat, and plunged the key into the ignition. Thank God the car started straight away. She turned it round quickly and headed off down the drive, then pulled up in front of the remote-control gates. There was always a hesitation before the sensor recognised there was a car there and started to activate. It was the longest few moments of her life. What if Kirk had spotted her, and had got to the panel that controlled the gate, locking her in? Would she have the nerve to use her car as a battering ram? It would be her only means of escape. She was just about to put her foot down on the accelerator when the black wrought-iron gates began to twitch and then swing open, painfully slowly. She shot out of the drive before they were fully open, spraying gravel in her wake. She imagined Kirk must have heard the screech of her tyres. She probably had three minutes on him. He'd have to get dressed, grab his keys, get to his car . . .

She got to the end of Kirk's road. Which would be the best way to go? The quickest and most obvious route was west, towards the M25, then the M4 and M5. But if he was going to follow her, he would assume that would be the route she would take. He'd catch up with her in minutes. So she turned left, not entirely sure where she would end up, but fairly sure it was safer than being predictable. Her heart was still hammering, and she had no idea how she was able to think so clearly and logically. She eyed her petrol gauge. Nearly on empty. She'd have to stop. Oh God, what had she got herself into?

Six hours later, Hayley drove into Withybrook. She felt faint with exhaustion. Except for the petrol, she hadn't dared stop once. Her mouth was dry with fear and lack of fluid. Her face throbbed. Her stomach was churning. As she drove up the familiar high street, she felt as if the houses on either side were reaching out to embrace her and welcome her home. She immediately felt reassured and more confident. This was her territory. Kirk couldn't get to her here.

She pulled up outside the Old Bakery and sat in her seat for a moment. Instinct had told her not to go to her brothers. They were so reactive. They would be straight into their souped-up Astras and back up the motorway to kick Kirk's head in. And the last thing Hayley wanted was a protracted battle. She just wanted to feel safe.

She pulled down the sun visor to look in the vanity mirror and gasped in horror at her appearance. Her lip was bloody and swollen; her right eye was completely closed. She looked almost unrecognisable. She pulled a tissue out of her handbag and tried to dab at some of the dried blood, but it wouldn't budge. She thought about trying to cover up the damage with some foundation, but worried about infection. So she just pulled out her sunglasses and put them on, even though the day sported no sunshine.

She climbed out of the car wearily. Her body ached from the tension of driving as fast as she could, while keeping one eye on the rear-view mirror in case Kirk tried to run her off the road. She knocked tentatively on the door, racking her brains for a believable excuse for her appearance, but none of them would convince even a child, so she prayed neither Jade nor Amber answered.

Luckily Fitch opened the door. He looked at her in dismay.

'Jesus, Hayley. What happened?'

'Don't let the girls see me.'

She put up her hands to cover her face. Fitch stepped to one side to let her past and pointed up the stairs.

'Go straight up to my bedroom. I'll make sure they don't come up.' It was a command that brooked no argument. He strode back into the house as Hayley obediently fled up the staircase and into the room she had once shared with Fitch. She threw herself onto the bed, curling herself up into a ball and burying her face in the pillows. She longed to pull the duvet over her and hide for ever.

She sank into the comfort of his bedding. It smelled of him. It wasn't unpleasant. Just a faint trace of manliness, and the lavender soap he used. It was familiar, comforting. A safe smell. Kirk spent so many hours making sure he was odourless. Showering and scrubbing in his industrial-strength power shower. Changing his shirt three times a day. Then slathering himself in expensive aftershave. Now, she realised it was all to rid himself of the scent of evil. Fitch's scent was the scent of an honest man. A man who had nothing to hide. She rolled onto her back and stared at the ceiling. My God, she'd been a fool.

She looked around the room, and realised that every trace of her had been eradicated. Of course it had. Why would Fitch want any reminder of her whatsoever, after the way she had treated him? Her dressing table had gone. And all the rugs and cushions. The curtains had gone, and in their place were dark wood slatted blinds. It was a masculine room. Plain white sheets. A charcoal-grey blanket, folded neatly at the bottom of the bed. There were some photos of Jade and Amber blown up and put into plain black frames. There were two paintings she'd never seen before – impressionistic views of Exmoor, swiftly but expertly executed. His shoes were lined up against one wall – work boots, and walking boots, and Timberlands. Not like Kirk's range of pointed, shiny, leather-soled brogues and loafers in every colour, every finish.

She shut her eyes, longing for restorative sleep to bring her oblivion. But as she heard Fitch's footsteps on the stairs, she knew that wasn't going to be possible. She was going to have to face the consequences of what she had done and hope, pray, that he had it in him to find forgiveness, even though she knew damn well she didn't deserve it.

'Did he hit you?' Fitch voice was flat, emotionless.

Hayley sat up.

'How did you know?'

'It's obvious that's the sort of bloke he was.'

'Is it?'

Fitch had to bite his tongue. The temptation to say

it was blindingly apparent to anyone with half a brain was huge. But he didn't want to get embroiled in a scrap straight away.

'Let me clean it up.'

He turned on his heel and went out of the room. Hayley waited until he came back with a basin of hot water, a flannel, and some antiseptic, as well as some painkillers and a glass of brandy, which she swallowed gratefully.

Fitch set to work on her face. She'd forgotten how gentle he was, and how at odds it was with his size. But it hurt like hell nevertheless. She winced as the antiseptic bit cruelly into her wounds.

'What did you do to deserve this, anyway?'

Tears sprang into her eyes at the memory.

'I found some knickers under his bed. He didn't like it when I asked whose they were . . .'

Fitch said nothing as he finished off by applying some arnica, sweeping his fingertips across her swollen skin.

'There,' he said. 'It'll take a few days to go down. We'll tell the girls you had a car accident. That the air bag went off.'

Hayley nodded, feeling a wave of shame. To think that she'd let that monster near her children. That they had spent a week in his company. Had been swimming with him, and sat on his knee playing games on his mobile phone. She had even fantasised about them being bridesmaids at their wedding. Because, of course, that had been what she wanted: only the day before she had dreamed about a huge reception at the Grove. It had only taken one wallop to bring her to her senses. He had it in him to kill her. She felt sure of that. The look in his eyes had been murderous. But she was safe here. Fitch wouldn't let him get to her.

She started shaking uncontrollably. All her limbs were juddering, her teeth clattered.

'You're in shock,' said Fitch. 'I think I should get the doctor.'

'No,' said Hayley. 'Just hold me. I'll be fine if you . . . just hold me.'

Fitch stood and looked at her for a moment. She could see doubt and consternation written all over his face, and she didn't blame him for hesitating.

'Please . . .'

He relented, pulling her into his arms, and she burrowed into his strength. His embrace was safe and comforting, not the vice-like grip she had experienced earlier that day, but a cocoon of masculinity that offered protection.

'I'm calling the police,' he said.

'No! For God's sake. Please—'

'This is assault, Hayley. This is grievous bodily harm. He should go down for this.'

Hayley shook her head. 'You don't mess with his kind. He's got contacts. And even if he did get banged up, someone would come and get us.'

'What were you doing with him, Hayley?'

'I don't know.' Her sobs came harder and harder. 'I'm so sorry, Fitch. I didn't know what I was doing. I was depressed. He seemed to know who I was and what I wanted.'

'A punch in the face?'

'Please, Fitch. I know I've been stupid. I know I was wrong . . .'

'Jesus, Hayley. Have you got any idea what you put us all through? Me and the girls. And your family?'

'I know. I know! I just couldn't help it.' She clutched at his arm in panic. 'Please. Don't make me go. I know I don't deserve to stay. But I need you.'

She clung to him, sobbing. Fitch stared at the wall over her head. What was he supposed to do? Hurl her out onto the streets? How could he do that to the mother of his children?

He had no choice but to let her stay.

'Of course you can stay,' he soothed.

Gradually her sobs subsided.

She was safe now, Hayley thought as she drifted off. Fitch was the kindest, most wonderful and loyal man on the planet. He'd just been waiting for her to come to her senses. She had thought Kirk had understood her, but it was Fitch who knew her through and through, and he wasn't going to let her down. She gave a little sigh, and he rubbed her back to reassure her that he was still there. Moments later she was fast asleep.

When Hayley's breathing was the deep and even of the unconscious, Fitch turned down the dimmer switch, shut the bedroom door gently, then went downstairs to send Jade and Amber up to bed. Then he called Hayley's mum to tell her Hayley had been delayed and the girls were staying here another night. He poured himself a hefty Scotch, and downed it in one.

What he had seen made him feel sick. What kind of an animal had she been consorting with? Deep down he suspected that she was right, that the likes of Kirk were beyond the law, that to try and seek justice would only result in more trouble for them. For a moment he thought about jumping into the car and driving hell for leather up to wherever it was Kirk had his hideous playboy mansion. Fitch wasn't afraid of physical confrontation. He'd had to use his fists often enough when he was younger. But it was obvious this bloke didn't play by the rules. If he was prepared to smack a woman in the face, he wasn't going to fight a duel like a gentleman. He probably had knives, guns, henchmen – he'd make sure the opposition was eradicated. Fitch was no coward, but he was no fool either.

What was he going to do? Was he going to have Hayley back, after the way she had treated him? If he did, then he would have his girls back too. Which was what he wanted more than anything. He could forgive her, if it meant they could be a family. To know that Jade and Amber could be under his roof every day was worth the sacrifice. And he and Hayley had loved each other once. Surely they could again?

The best thing he could do was look after Hayley, nurse her back to health and restore her confidence. Then find a way to make them both happy. Maybe find a way to give her whatever it was she had been craving – he supposed he should be taking some responsibility for what had happened. They needed to talk, and be honest with each other, if they were going to make a go of it.

Before he went to bed, he looked in on the girls. He wondered if there was anything they needed from the farm for school the next morning, then decided he could always drive up and fetch it if needs be. Their uniforms were washed and ready, and their homework done. Thank God they weren't in that horrible damp house. Dido ran between the two beds, checking up on them as she always did. The little dog hated it when they weren't here.

Fitch went back along the corridor and stood in the doorway of his bedroom, gazing at his wife lying under the duvet. It was Sunday night. His family were back under his roof. This was what he had wanted for so long. But was he doing the right thing, letting Hayley back into his life? She had gone to such a dark place, would she really be able to find her way back?

It was up to him to help her, he decided. It was his duty. He slipped off his clothes, brushed his teeth, then climbed into bed beside her. She rolled into his embrace, curling herself into him. For a moment he tensed, not sure if he wanted bodily contact.

Then he relented, curling an arm around her waist. Tentatively at first, but then she snuggled into him and he tightened his clasp. It was as if she had never been away.

Sixteen

As downers went, this was pretty spectacular, thought Sebastian. Worse than the plummet after any drug-induced high, and he'd had plenty of those. But this was different. This was proving harder to recover from. A day in bed had no effect. Three days in bed and the low was more suffocating than ever. And he knew why. Because he'd brought it upon himself. He had unwittingly engineered his own downfall, and he couldn't see a way out.

On paper, he was a triumph. On paper, he had peaked. The exhibition was sold out, and could have sold ten times over. The reviews were unanimously glowing, from the tabloids to the most esoteric, snotty art magazines. The phone rang non-stop with requests for him to do interviews, features, documentaries. Jonathan Elder had to join the long list of publishers badgering him for his autobiography. Someone had even approached him to record an album, wanting to tap into his wild-boy, rock 'n' roll image. Never mind that he couldn't hold a tune – they had equipment that could deal with that.

He was a phenomenon, by anyone's definition. But in his heart, he'd screwed up. By unlocking himself, he had sacrificed everyone he loved and cared about. He was an absolute fool, a self-absorbed, self-indulgent, self-serving waste of space. So here he was, locked up in a prison of his own making, with nothing but the walls to look at.

Never had Withybrook Hall felt so empty. It had always been empty during the week, but now he knew Catkin wasn't coming back it felt emptier. The rooms echoed his footsteps mockingly. The air was cold. It was as if the house itself was chastising him. The home he had always loved was determined to teach him a lesson and refused to offer him any comfort or succour. His refuge had turned its back on him. He had always, always felt safe here. But now, he just felt very afraid, and there was nowhere else to run.

He'd sent Stacey away. He'd given her a fortnight's paid leave, although she had protested volubly. But he couldn't bear her presence. She was so . . . ordinary. Her very presence made him realise what a luxury it would be, to be ordinary. Because let's be honest, who was happier? Sebastian Turner, alone in his mansion with his millions? Or Stacey Humphries, with her cramped council house over-spilling with children, with every last penny accounted for?

Stacey, of course. She'd got it right. She earned an amount of money that was entirely proportionate to what she actually did, and therefore she valued it. She worked herself to the bone to better the lives of the people she loved, and for that they loved her back. That's not to say they didn't squabble and bicker and fight, and give her a hard time occasionally, but she gave as good as she got and as a result she had respect. She would never wake up with a sinking feeling, thinking melodramatically, God, there is no way I can pick up a Hoover today, as he did a paintbrush. She had no option. Her world was entirely objective. She had few, if any, choices.

He paced the corridors, the rooms, looking for respite. He couldn't rest in his bed, on a sofa, on the floor. He didn't want to eat. He drank himself into oblivion, and then stopped, because he knew the alcoholic cocoon was false, and what he was desperate for was an answer. Grey Goose would supply him no resolution. He had to find a way out for himself. He had to purge himself of his shame, and figure out a way to get through the rest of his life. And hopefully restore the travesty that his relationships had become.

Firstly, of course, his marriage. He felt sick at what he had done to Catkin. He had allowed his own cowardice, his own niggardly fears about what he could and couldn't achieve, to seep into their relationship, eating away at the foundations until it had collapsed just at the point he had reached his nadir.

They should be enjoying his success together. Catkin would have revelled in the media attention. She would have loved helping him choose which magazines and programmes to go with. She would have dressed them both, played up to the cameras, showed the world how gripping the Mr and Mrs Turner Show was. They would have eaten out and drunk at other people's expense, been ushered to the front of the queue for every glittering occasion. And even now, designers were sending him samples of clothing, begging him to wear their exclusive ranges. She would have adored every second of it.

And no doubt Catkin would have reaped success off the back of him. She was talented and clever herself, but there was nothing like being associated with success for propelling your own career forward. Her exposure next to him on the screen and in the papers would have brought any number of offers out of the woodwork.

But Sebastian hadn't done a single interview, or returned a single call. He had become a recluse. Luckily, his money was automatically transferred into his account, because he wouldn't even have been bothered to bank the cheques. The only person he had called was Catkin, but it wasn't long before he realised she had barred his calls from her phone. She was refusing to have anything to do with him.

He'd taken to watching her on television, flipping on the morning show hungry for a glimpse of her. He was chagrined to find that she looked fantastic; glowing and animated. She didn't look as if she was pining. And she did her job so well – listening intently to the viewers when they phoned in their problems, never judging them, but providing them with well-considered and appropriate solutions. She never belittled or patronised them. She was a star, his wife. And he'd trodden all over her in his quest for gratification. No wonder she had cut him out of her life. He deserved everything he'd got.

It wasn't just Catkin he had screwed over. There was Charlotte and Penny. He had abused both of them too. He had totally exploited the two people who had made his life bearable over the last few weeks. He hadn't known about Charlotte's past, and couldn't have predicted that her cover would be blown, of course, but nevertheless he had given no thought at all to the effect the exposure might have on her. He had used her, prostituted her image, captured her likeness for his own ends. Not once had he wondered whether what he was doing was an infringement of her privacy.

And Penny. He'd seen her across the room as she'd walked into the exhibition. Seen the hurt and shock on her face as she'd realised who it was on the walls. He hadn't given a thought to how she would react when she saw Charlotte emblazoned all around her, when he knew she had a crush on him.

He was barely human, he thought in disgust. Because to be human you had to empathise. But not once had he been able to put himself in someone else's position. All he'd been able to think about was himself.

Now, he stood in front of an empty fridge in the kitchen. He hadn't slept, bathed, shaved or eaten for three days. He thought he had probably reached his lowest point. He stared out into the back garden, at the sweeping lawn he had played on so many years ago, when he'd had no idea that such a bleak future lay ahead of him.

Bleak? Who was he trying to kid? There was absolutely nothing bleak about his position. Any despair he was feeling was totally of his own making. He was standing in the middle of a beautiful house, looking out at the most staggering view, his name on the lips of some of the most powerful people in the country, and he expected pity?

He gave a derisory snort, and the noise made him jump. He hadn't heard a sound for days. He had a choice: do the world a favour and slash his wrists, so they could all forget about him and move on to the next flavour of the month, or pull himself together and enjoy the fruits of his success.

He looked at the Sabatier knife block. The black handles with their brass rivets offered themselves to him invitingly. He turned away. That really would be the ultimate act of self-indulgence. Not to mention sadly predictable: the tortured artist taking his own life.

It was the horrifying prospect of being considered a cliché that made Sebastian walk up the stairs and run himself a bath.

It was, therefore, an entirely appropriate place to have his eureka moment. He was lying in the cooling suds, surrounded by stubble-studded scum, thinking that he really should get out and pour himself a fresh tub, when his eyes spotted a crack in the ceiling. He followed the crack down to the tiles, which he suddenly noticed, for the first time, were an unappealing grey with an art deco abstract border that had probably, at the time of application, been quite the thing but which were now horribly dated. So, too, was the enormous corner bath in which he was lying, and the dolphin taps. Although it was large, and the fixtures and fittings had been top of the range at the time, the whole room suddenly struck him as shabby and outmoded. Catkin had tried to tell him as much many times, but he had refused to see it. This had been his parents' bathroom, where his ravishing mother had prepared herself for party after party, and for Sebastian it was part of who he was.

But now he was searching for answers, about who he was, and why, and how he could change himself, he realised that his environment had probably had an enormous influence on him. By preserving Withybrook Hall in aspic, he was selfishly clinging on to the happy memories of his childhood, in the vain hope that he could replicate it in adult life. Of course he couldn't. He had to make his own way in life, not live in the past.

He clambered out of the bath and wrapped a towel round his waist. He then gave himself a tour of his home being as objective as he possibly could, trying to detach himself from any sentimentality. As he wandered through the rooms, it was as if he was seeing Withybrook Hall for the first time, and he began to see why Catkin had constantly complained. It was dated, tired, almost decrepit in places. And as much as he loved it as it was, he realised that the house deserved better. You wouldn't keep a beautiful woman in clothes that were faded and out of date, so why a house?

He finally stopped in the kitchen. He had to admit, it had absolutely nothing going for it, except its size. But all that could be changed. All it would take was a bit of imagination, and he certainly had plenty of that. He pictured it flooded with light, a haven of polished elm and limestone, warm natural materials interspersed with the very best in culinary appliances. A dream kitchen. No. A dream home.

He felt a burst of excitement. The house was going to be his next project. It would be a showcase for the various pieces of art he had collected over the years, which were racked up in his studio waiting to be hung. He would redecorate the house from top to bottom to surprise Catkin. A grand gesture, perhaps, but a heartfelt one. One that would prove to her that he knew he was wrong, and that he was sorry.

And the one person to help him do this was surely

Charlotte. He trusted her taste. He'd seen what she had done to Myrtle Cottage. Her drawings were imaginative, fresh, not self-consciously over-stylised. She would keep the essence of the house while giving it a total face-lift. And at the same time, he could atone for treating her so badly. He'd had no idea how he was going to even begin to approach her and apologise, but now he had a valid excuse for knocking on her door.

Sebastian felt exhilarated. He pulled on his jeans, nearly tripping over them in his haste, grabbed a sweater, some socks, dug out his Converses from under the bed. He was still tying his laces as he fell out of the front door. He raced down the drive and along the lane, slipping on the slippery surface of the frost-encrusted road, his breath coming out in cloudy white gusts.

By the time he reached Myrtle Cottage he was gasping, with a stitch in his side. But he banged urgently on the door nevertheless. The moments before Charlotte answered seemed like a lifetime.

He was shocked at how dreadful she looked: even worse than he had looked when he woke up that morning. Her face was pale and gaunt; her eyes huge, with dark circles underneath. She was wearing tattered jeans and an old polo shirt, and her hair looked wild and unkempt, as if it hadn't been near a brush for days.

She looked at him warily.

'Charlotte . . .' he began, not sure where to start. 'Jesus, you look terrible.'

She gave a wry smile. 'Thanks.'

'I've come to apologise.'

She stood to one side to let him in.

'What for?'

Sebastian slunk in through the door.

'Thinking about myself, as usual. I honestly didn't think. The exhibition – I didn't realise how creepy it looked. And how incriminating. And I really had no idea about . . . you know, your husband and stuff. I didn't know that was all going to come out . . .'

'Listen,' said Charlotte, 'forget it. The exhibition was amazing. And you weren't to know about my lurid past. It was stupid of me to think I could hide for ever. It was going to come out eventually. Though I must admit I didn't imagine it would be quite so dramatic when it did happen. Splashed all over the Sunday papers.' She managed a slightly mirthless laugh. 'Again.'

The two of them stood in the hallway, surrounded by ladders and paint pots and dustsheets. Sebastian scratched his head awkwardly.

'So . . . are we still mates?'

'Of course we're still mates!'

Sebastian looked at her in amazement. 'How can you be so good?' he asked. 'So . . . forgiving?'

'I'm not always.' She motioned him to follow her. 'Come and have a coffee. And see what I've done to the kitchen. I'm really pleased with it.'

He followed her obediently. She obviously didn't want to go over old ground, so he decided he would leave things at that, and be grateful that he had emerged unscathed.

As he walked into the kitchen, he was astonished. The little room was totally unrecognisable. The ugly old units had been ripped out, and in their place were a row of tongue-and-groove cupboards painted white, with cup handles, topped with beech work surfaces.

The floor was covered in bright green rubber; the tiles on the wall were a matching green shot through with silver. It was simple, fresh and modern, but with some traditional touches that kept the cottagey feel – a huge butler's sink, the original drying rack that she had stripped back and waxed, a series of prints photocopied from an ancient Mrs Beeton that she had hand-tinted and framed up.

'Wow.' Sebastian gazed around admiringly.

'I'm quite pleased,' she admitted. 'And I've managed to keep the cost right down. Less than two thousand pounds for the whole room.'

Sebastian was impressed. If she could work this magic on a tight budget, imagine what she could do given free rein. He felt a surge of excitement.

'Listen,' he said. 'I've got a proposition. I want to do up Withybrook Hall. From top to bottom. No expense spared. Catkin's been going on and on about doing it for ages – as you know. So I wanted to do it for her, as a surprise. And I'd love you to do it for me. It seems only fair that you should reap some of the profits.'

Charlotte looked at him in surprise. 'Well . . . thank you. I'm really flattered.'

'So what do you think?'

'Obviously, I'd love to. But—'

'Don't say but. But's never good.'

'The thing is, Myrtle Cottage is nearly finished. It's going on the market next month, with a bit of luck. So I'm going to have to move on.'

'Where are you going to go?'

'I don't know yet. I'm thinking about travelling.' She put her fingers up in quote marks. 'Going to "find" myself.'

Sebastian looked crestfallen.

'Anyway,' Charlotte went on, 'I don't suppose Catkin would be too thrilled with my input. Under the circumstances.'

'Maybe not.' Sebastian hadn't considered that. Yet again, he hadn't thought his plan through. Was he ever going to learn?

'At least let me take you for lunch,' he offered finally. 'You look as if you haven't eaten for days.'

'No way. I'm not going into the Trout with you. Not after all those terrible articles—'

'Do you know what?' Sebastian interrupted. 'The funny thing about down here is actually nobody gives a toss. They might be inveterate curtain-twitchers, and know the intimate details about your business, but they're not actually bothered. They don't judge. It's not like London, when people give you the cold shoulder or cut you dead.'

'Really?' Charlotte looked doubtful.

'Honestly. It's why my parents moved here. All their friends used to behave dreadfully, but it didn't matter in Withybrook. They could get up to all manner of nefarious activities and still be given the time of day. Basically, I don't think people here understand the nuances, so they just let you get on with it.'

'I haven't dared go out for days, for fear of what people might be saying.'

'You shouldn't care anyway,' said Sebastian stoutly. 'You're not actually guilty of anything.'

'True. But there's guilt by association, I can assure you.' Charlotte still remembered the ignominy of being blanked in Sainsbury's car park, and the churning feeling it had given her in her stomach.

'Come on.' Sebastian wasn't going to be dissuaded. 'You need one of the Speckled Trout's game pies, and some lemon pudding.'

'OK,' she relented. 'But let me go and put something decent on.'

'No!' said Sebastian. 'I keep telling you. It doesn't matter. No one cares.'

'I do,' said Charlotte firmly. 'At least a clean jumper and some lipstick.'

Twenty minutes later they were ensconced at a table by the inglenook fireplace with a gin and tonic each. The pub wasn't full of people whispering and nudging, as Charlotte had imagined. Everyone seemed quite open about it. Norman hadn't batted an eyelid at their appearance, just took their order cheerfully and poured them their drinks.

'Hey, London Lady. Saw you in the paper.' Darren walked past on his way from the bar and raised his glass to her with a cheeky grin.

'Yes, and just for the record, I'm not shagging her,' Sebastian informed him, tipping back in his chair.

Charlotte blushed scarlet. Darren dug Sebastian in the ribs.

'Wouldn't blame you if you were,' he declared.

'Excuse me!' said Charlotte. 'I am sitting here.' But she couldn't help laughing. Sebastian was right. No one in Withybrook gave a monkey's about her past. Or her present, for that matter. Suddenly she felt as if she could breathe again. She'd shut herself in the cottage for days, only scuttling out when she had to, filling up at the petrol station the other side of Comberton for fear of bumping into anyone. Particularly . . .

She banished that thought from her head. She didn't want to know what Fitch might think of her. Not a lot, she suspected. She had been steeling herself to go and see him and set the record straight, but hadn't quite plucked up the courage. But now she thought perhaps she would.

She realised that Sebastian had asked her something, and snapped back to attention.

'What?'

'How am I going to get Catkin back?' he asked plaintively. 'She won't even answer the phone to me. How am I going to get her to believe that I didn't set out to hurt her?'

He looked utterly anguished.

Charlotte realised she'd seen that expression before. But not on his face. On Ed's. The agonised expression of a man desperate to be understood. She picked up her knife and fork and cut through the crust on her game pie.

'I'm sure she'll come round eventually,' she told him, knowing that she sounded totally unconvincing.

'She'll never forgive me.'

'Of course she will.'

Sebastian stared at her intently. 'Do you really think so?' he demanded. 'Women aren't all that forgiving, you know.'

'Yes, they are. She probably just needs time. And a bit of space. To think.'

'Like you?'

'What?'

'Isn't that why you came here? To give yourself time and space?'

'I suppose so . . .'

'So. Have you forgiven your husband for what he did?'

Charlotte was floored for a moment.

'Why the interrogation?'

'I'm interested. Have you?'

'What he did was different,' she protested.

'In what way?'

'He knew exactly what he was doing. And it was despicable. Totally premeditated.'

'So why did he do it? Just because he thought he could get away with it?'

Charlotte looked down at her plate.

'Because he wanted us to have a new life,' she managed finally. 'He wanted me to stop work, and get a house in the country. Because he wanted . . . to keep on trying for a baby.'

She swiftly put a piece of pie in her mouth so she could swallow down her tears with it.

'Jesus,' breathed Sebastian, enthralled. 'He must have loved you very much.'

Charlotte had to lie down after lunch. Two double gin and tonics, a heavy meal and all the emotional upheaval had exhausted her. Talking to Sebastian had silted everything up again. She just didn't know what to think any more. She lay on her bed, her mind racing, trying to sleep. But sleep eluded her, just as it had the last few nights. She was physically and emotionally exhausted.

One thing she had to do, she decided, was talk to Fitch. She knew he'd have seen the news. And the longer she left it, the harder it was going to be to talk to him about it. She decided she would walk down to his workshop on the pretext of choosing a bit of slate for the fireplace in the dining room. She slid back out of bed and went to look at herself in the mirror.

She looked awful. She'd have to spend at least an hour on her appearance to look even half decent. She decided not to bother. She was only going to see Fitch to explain things. She pulled on her coat and stuck on her boots, then went out into the high street.

Fitch's workshop was adjacent to his house. She tapped on the door and stepped inside. He was slicing up pieces of stone with a circular saw. All around him were pieces of marble and granite waiting to be cut up into headstones or fireplaces. Everything was covered in a fine layer of stone dust. The noise from the saw was tremendous, and totally drowned out the afternoon play on Radio Four that was burbling from a digital radio perched on a shelf. Dido jumped up as soon as she saw Charlotte and came running over. Fitch turned off his machinery and took off his mask.

'Hey.'

He smiled. Politely, Charlotte thought. He didn't look exactly thrilled to see her.

'Hi.' She stuffed her hands in her pockets. It was freezing in the workshop. 'I came to see about a piece of slate. For the fireplace.'

'No problem. Have you got the measurements?'

She nodded, pulling a scrap of paper out of her pocket on which she'd written the dimensions. He took it from her, studying it carefully, not meeting her eye.

'And . . . I came to say sorry.'

He looked up, raising an eyebrow. 'Sorry?'

'You must have seen the papers.'

'Well, yes. You couldn't exactly miss them.'

'I should have told you.' She sighed. 'Christmas night. I should have explained.'

He shrugged. 'It's none of my business.'

'No. But you trusted me with *your* business—'

He put a hand on her shoulder. She felt a warm tingle.

'Charlotte, it's not a problem.'

'And I haven't been shagging Sebastian,' she blurted out. 'In case you thought I had.'

He laughed at that. Properly laughed, and she saw the wariness go out of his face.

'What are you laughing at?' she asked indignantly.

'You,' he replied. 'You worry too much.'

Charlotte felt a little bit disgruntled. Here she was swallowing her pride and trying to apologise.

'Well, I'm glad you think it's funny. I didn't want you to get the wrong end of the stick, that's all—'

'Of course I didn't.'

'Well, good.' Flustered, she looked down at the cement floor, not knowing where to go with this next.

'Come here, you.'

Fitch pulled her to him and enveloped her in a big hug.

'The important thing is,' he said, 'are you all right? It must have been awful.'

She sank into his warmth. The softness of his thick padded shirt. She loved the comfort of his arms. She rested her head on his shoulder.

'It *was* awful. But it's over now. I can try and get back to normal. The house is nearly finished. You should come and have a look.' She shut her eyes, wondering if she dared ask. Yes, of course she did. 'In fact, why don't you come for supper? I've got a proper kitchen now—'

'Actually,' said Fitch, 'I've got some news myself.'

Something in his tone of voice made her step back and look at him. She couldn't quite read his expression.

'What?'

'Hayley's back,' he said finally.

There was an awkward pause.

'Oh,' said Charlotte brightly. 'That's good. Isn't it?'

'Yeah.' Fitch nodded. 'I think so.'

Charlotte suddenly felt like crying. She blinked hard.

'The bastard lamped her one,' Fitch explained. 'She came home with a black eye. But at least he knocked some sense into her. She wants us to make a go of it. Get back together.'

'Right.'

'The girls are thrilled.'

'Of course they are.'

'I guess it's what I wanted.'

Charlotte looked at him doubtfully. 'Even after what she did to you?'

'Hey,' said Fitch. 'Everyone's allowed one mistake.'

'Really?'

'Of course. We're only human.'

Charlotte started to shiver. The air in the workshop was icy and the floor was freezing. The cold was seeping up into her bones.

'That's great, Fitch,' she said. 'I'm really happy for you. Anyway, I've got to go.'

'I'll drop the slate up. Tomorrow?'

'Whenever. Thanks.'

She nearly tripped over Dido in her haste to get out.

As she shut the door behind her she heard the sound of his saw start up.

She huddled herself into her coat, keeping her head down against the east wind that was blowing down the high street. She didn't want to meet anyone. Didn't want to talk to anyone. She didn't trust herself not to cry.

Fitch's news had totally rocked her. She realised now she had been pretending to herself that she didn't have feelings for him, but as soon as she saw him she had desperately wanted to feel his arms around her. He made her feel so safe, and warm inside. He made her feel as if nothing bad would ever happen again. She'd wanted him to sweep her off her feet, take her into the warmth and cosiness of his little house, tell her everything was going to be all right and then . . . maybe . . . kiss her . . . But now, there was no chance of that. He had made that very clear. He had gone back to his wife, the wife he had loved all along, even though she had treated him appallingly. Charlotte just hoped Hayley knew how lucky she was, and that she had learned her lesson.

There was one blessing. At least she hadn't made a fool of herself and declared her true feelings before he'd dropped his bombshell. She'd never have been able to live that down.

She woke in the middle of the night with the moon shining down on her. She had got used to sleeping without curtains. It made her feel connected to the world outside. When she couldn't sleep, she counted the stars splattered across the inky-black sky.

But tonight, she wasn't counting stars. She lay in the

moonlight, thinking about the conversations she had had that day. Both of them, with Sebastian and Fitch, had made her realise the power of forgiveness, and how cruel it was to withhold it from someone you loved. She had never really looked at the situation from Ed's side. She had only judged what he had done from her position. And perhaps she was wrong.

Maybe it was time to forgive Ed.

After all, if Fitch could forgive Hayley, whose crime was committed out of total self-interest, and hadn't been borne out of love, then who was she to carry on judging her husband? He had, after all, just been desperate to give her what they both wanted, the thing that was a God-given right for most people. They had loved each other passionately once. Up until the moment he had committed his crime. She remembered them making love the night of the ball, and how intense it had been. She had loved him more than ever at that point, so why couldn't she just come to terms with what he had done and return to that point?

She could. The more she thought about it, the more obvious it seemed that it was time to forgive him and move on. They could start again together. He was due out of prison in a few months. They could move here. To Withybrook. They could rent a little cottage – there were always plenty in the area available to let. She could take up Sebastian's offer to redecorate Withybrook Hall. The money would be good; it would be six months' work at least, and they could live off that while Ed decided what he was going to do. He'd probably be pretty unemployable, with a prison record, but he could start up his own business down here. And with Withybrook Hall in her portfolio she would soon pick up more business. And then maybe, eventually, they could buy their own place – something like Myrtle Cottage, which they could do up and sell on.

Charlotte became increasingly excited. It would be a whole new life for them. And Ed would love it down here – the moors, the sea. She could imagine him going into the Trout for his pint every evening. They could get a dog – a Border terrier like Dido. Or something bigger – a retriever. A gun dog.

Yes, she decided. They could start anew, with none of the shadows of their former life hanging over them. She could hardly wait until daybreak. She would phone the prison, speak to Ed, ask him to send her another visiting order.

Fitch was so right. Everyone was allowed one mistake. Hers had been not being able to forgive. But now she had looked deep in her heart, she could. Until Ed had made *his* mistake, she had loved him unreservedly. There was no reason why they couldn't go back to how they were.

Seventeen

The morning of Charlotte's second prison visit dawned bright and breezy, with a tingling crisp air that whipped colour into your cheeks.

This time, she decided she wasn't going to apologise for her presence and try to remain inconspicuous. If she wanted to dress up, she would. She put on a stripy dress that Ed had bought her in Jigsaw and had always loved her in. Her hair was long enough now to pin up in a clip with a few wispy tendrils hanging down. She put on her make-up carefully. Then she went to her dressing-table drawer and slid her wedding ring back on. She hadn't worn it for months, and it felt strange on her finger. She looked at it, wondering if she was over-egging the omelette by wearing it. She decided to keep it on. It was symbolic, after all, of the gesture she was about to make.

For better or worse. Those had been their vows. And it didn't get worse than what they had already been through. So, by that argument, the only way was up. And she couldn't wait.

She ran down to the kitchen to make some coffee, then heard the front door go. It was Nikita, who had come to help finish off the grouting in the bathroom.

'You look smart,' said Nikita suspiciously.

'I've got a business meeting,' Charlotte lied effortlessly. 'I'll be away all day. Will you be OK?'

Nikita nodded, then brandished a prospectus.

'I've found a college course,' she said eagerly. 'I'm going to apply, to go in September. I wondered if you could do me a reference.'

'Of course I will,' said Charlotte. 'I'd be delighted.'

She picked up her handbag. She felt guilty leaving Nikita when she was obviously so keen to talk, but she knew if she was late to the prison they'd be difficult about letting her in.

'I better go, or I'm going to be late. '

'See you then,' said Nikita. 'Good luck with your meeting.'

The sun was dazzling as Charlotte left Withybrook, and she felt the light fill her heart as she drove through the village. She negotiated the narrow street carefully as she'd learned to – you never knew when you might meet a tractor or a herd of cows or a muck-spreader. She reflected how she had grown used to life in the country, and how she'd learned to do without so many things that she had once relied upon – two-hour dry cleaning, twenty-four-hour petrol stations, eight-screen cinemas. Life was simpler here, but somehow richer. There was so much more human contact. She reflected on the people that had come into her life. Not just Fitch and Sebastian, but Sid from the garage who had changed her tyre when she'd a slow puncture and panicked, and refused to charge her for it. And Darren from the pub, who had come and chopped the tree down in the back garden that was blocking the light into the kitchen, and also refused to take any money.

And Norman, the landlord at the Trout, who had dropped her off a bag of daffodil bulbs, though God knows where he had come by them. She had learned not to ask. She also knew that one day she would be able to repay them all in some way, because that was how village life seemed to work – a system of barter, with your favours on credit indefinitely, with no one keeping tabs as such.

Yes, she thought, she had done right to come here. It had healed her in so many ways, and restored her faith in human nature. And it would be just the place for Ed to start again, after everything he had been through. Withybrook would be the perfect antidote to prison, with its live and let live attitude.

The truck flew effortlessly up the motorway, as if it knew how important the meeting was. She sang at the top of her lungs as she drove, playing Ed's favourite REM cassette over and over again. As the familiar tracks came on, they reminded her of all the good times they had shared. She could picture him dancing in their old kitchen as they waited for friends to arrive for dinner, opening another bottle of wine, sharpening the carving knife, stopping to kiss her on the nose as he walked past . . . That could all happen again. They'd make new friends. Get a social life. Not on the scale they used to, perhaps, but Charlotte was all for keeping it simple this time around.

She didn't find the red tape at the prison intimidating this time. She dazzled the guards with her radiant smile and they looked at her slightly askance, not used to visitors being friendly. She could hardly wait, jiggling with impatience in the queue as they waited for the door to the visiting room to be unlocked.

*

Ed looked even more gaunt than he had last time. His face was set hard; his eyes like granite. As she walked towards him, Charlotte thought how she would feed him up when he got out, and take him for lots of walks – he would love the freedom of the moors, the wildness of the coast. He would soon lose his prison pallor.

'Hi,' she said, sitting down with a smile.

He nodded curtly in reply.

'So,' he said. 'What's the occasion? What's so important? You brought divorce papers for me to sign or something?' His voice had an edge. He was putting on an act, playing the tough guy to prove he didn't care.

'No,' she told him. 'The exact opposite.'

He scowled. 'What do you mean?'

'Oh, Ed,' she sighed. 'I know it's taken me ages to get my head round it. And I'm really sorry. But I've finally managed . . . to understand what you did. And why you did it.' She leaned in as close to him as the rules allowed. 'I'm not saying it was right. I'll never say that. But . . . it doesn't matter. Not any more. It's history. So what I've come here to say is . . . let's start again.'

His face remained deadpan.

'You what?' he said. 'You mean . . . us?'

'Well, of course *us*. It's not going to be easy, I know. You're going to be in here for a while, for a start—'

To her total consternation, he started to laugh. Not a laugh of joy and relief, a nasty, bitter, mirthless sound.

'What's so funny?'

'It would be funny, if it wasn't so fucking tragic.'

His eyes bored into her mercilessly. She swallowed nervously. This wasn't quite the reaction she had expected.

'I know you're probably angry with me for taking so long to see the light. I can understand that. But we can work through it. Talk about it.'

'Don't give me that bloody counselling shit.'

Charlotte put up her hands.

'OK, OK. It's going to take time—'

'No, it isn't.'

'Oh.' She managed a smile. 'Good.'

'It's not going to take any time at all. Because it's not going to happen.'

Charlotte put her face in her hands and breathed in for a moment. She realised she had been hopelessly optimistic, thinking she could just waltz in here and forgive him magnanimously. He'd had all the time in the world to brood on how she had treated him, after all, and he was bound to be harbouring some resentment. No doubt the other inmates had poisoned him; they were bound to swap stories, and they had probably vilified her to make him feel better.

'I'm sorry. I shouldn't have just swanned in and expected it all to be hunky-dory. The thing is, I can't imagine what you've been through over the past few months.'

'No. You can't.'

'It hasn't been easy for me either.' Charlotte wasn't entirely sure she should be grovelling quite so much. 'But I think we should try our best to put the past behind us and look to the future.'

Ed nodded thoughtfully. 'That's what you think, is it?'

'Not that we should forget what's happened. That wouldn't be healthy.'

Another bark of mirthless laughter.

'Have you been to a shrink or something?'

'No. It's common sense.'

'Right. Well. Delightful though your proposition is, I'm afraid it's not going to work out.'

He looked away for a moment. When he looked back, the expression in his eyes had changed. There was something like pity lurking in there. And . . . guilt? And a bit of defiance. It made Charlotte uncomfortable.

'Why not?' she demanded. 'We can make it work, if we want to.'

'Charlotte . . . I might as well tell you. There's someone else.'

For a moment, you could have heard a pin drop.

'Someone else?' Charlotte stammered. She hadn't expected this. 'Well, who? You can't have met someone in here.' She looked wildly round. Surely he hadn't turned gay. Though she supposed it could happen.

'It's not someone I met in here. It's someone I knew before.'

She could see he was struggling with his confession. She felt a tightness in her chest, a sense of impending doom.

'Just tell me.'

He looked down at the table.

'It's Melanie.'

Charlotte's mouth went dry.

'Melanie?' she whispered.

Melanie. The podgy little pop-eyed assistant who had followed him around like a lap dog. She had always fawned over Ed, hung on his every word. He couldn't be serious about her. She'd probably been sending him sickly sweet letters on pink notepaper written with a scented gel pen. Adorned with stickers and signed with hearts and kisses. Charlotte cast her mind back to the last time she had seen her. It was at the ball. Melanie had worn white. White to defy Charlotte. White to draw attention to herself.

Charlotte remembered Melanie and Ed in the doorway, talking urgently. She had felt at the time she had been fobbed off, that there had been more to their conversation than Ed was admitting to, that they were colluding in some way. But she had been so preoccupied with the ball she hadn't given it a second thought. Now it made perfect sense. Melanie adored Ed. She'd been after him from the beginning. She would have got her claws into him as soon as she could. Well, she could bloody well take them out again. Melanie wasn't a threat. She was no contest.

Charlotte gathered up all her strength.

'You'll just have to let her down gently. Tell her it's over.'

'I can't.'

'Ed, for heaven's sake. She's just your assistant. I'm your wife!' She could hear her voice rising in panic. A few people looked round, wondering what the problem was. She put her head down, embarrassed, and put her hands up to mask her face.

Ed didn't flinch. He leaned forward, speaking low. 'It's a pity you didn't remember that six months ago. Or think it was important.'

Charlotte glanced at the clock, thinking fast. She didn't know how she was going to talk him round in the few minutes they had left. She'd have to arrange to come again.

'I'm sure Melanie's been very supportive,' she ventured. 'But—'

'Listen to me, Charlotte.' Ed looked straight into her eyes. 'Melanie has been amazing. She didn't judge me, not for one second. All the time following my arrest, she was there for me. While I was awaiting trial, she stood by me. She comforted me, encouraged me, looked after me. In my darkest hours, when I felt like jumping out of the window, she talked me out of it. She was there in court for me. She's been to visit me every week. She writes to me, sends me presents. She records my favourite shows for me for when I get out. Little things. But when you're stuck in here, little things matter.'

Charlotte opened her mouth to try to speak, but Ed put up his hand to stop her. As he finished his speech, Charlotte realised he was fighting back tears.

'Basically, Charlotte, Melanie taught me that life without you was worth living.'

Charlotte felt a horrible falling sensation, as her future slipped out of her grasp.

'But . . . you can't give up on us. Not without giving it a chance.'

'You didn't give me a chance, Charlotte. You made me feel like shit. You made me feel like I wasn't fit to walk this earth.'

'I'm sorry. I'm sorry! And, Ed – you've got to remember you did a terrible thing—'

'You see? You still can't let it drop.'

'I can't believe this. You're giving up on us for *her*?'

'Yes.'

'Please, Ed. At least let's talk about it again. I've got such great plans. Amazing ideas. I've found us a place to live. You'll really love it.'

'Enough!'

He slapped his hand down on the table. Startled, Charlotte stopped in mid-flow.

'I'm not giving up Melanie. Not now. For one very simple reason.'

'What?'

He paused. Swallowed. Looked at her uncertainly.

'She's pregnant.' There was a long pause. 'I'm sorry.'

Charlotte sat very, very still.

Around her, the noise of the prison receded. All she could hear was the pounding of blood in her head, and the sound of Ed's words.

Melanie. Melanie was having Ed's baby.

She felt her heart crack. For in that moment, not only did she realise that Ed had betrayed her beyond forgiveness, but that their unexplained infertility was down to her. That he could now go and procreate as many times as he wished but that she, short of a miracle, never would.

If he had wanted to destroy her, annihilate her, tear out her heart and stamp on it, he couldn't have found a better way.

She could forgive infidelity.

But she couldn't forgive him for taking away her hope.

She didn't want to cry in front of him. Not here, in front of all the other inmates. She didn't want them speculating as to why she was weeping. No doubt they would have worked it out for themselves. She imagined Melanie coming to visit, her bump more than apparent. She'd be one of those women who thrust themselves into maternity frocks when they were just two days late. She could picture her in a Laura Ashley dress with a Peter Pan collar.

'Well,' she said sadly. 'I guess that's it, then.'

'This isn't how I wanted it,' said Ed.

'Don't worry about it. Looks like it's my fault, not yours,' replied Charlotte, with an uncharacteristic bitterness.

And it was her fault. If she'd been able to get pregnant in the first place, none of this would have happened. They'd still be in their house in Parsons Green, with a fat little baby lying on a rug on the floor, and maybe another one on the way.

Ed looked anguished. 'It wasn't your fault. Don't think that.'

Suddenly he looked like his old self again. Gone was the hard-nut jailbird image. He must have put that on as an act to protect himself, and to distance himself from her.

Charlotte got to her feet. She couldn't cope with pity at this juncture.

'I suppose you'll want to marry her. I'll get things started.'

'I haven't asked her to marry me.'

'Well, you should. It's only fair on the baby.'

They looked at each other. They were husband and wife, yet they were miles apart. How the hell had it come to this, wondered Charlotte, when they had once loved each other so much? It just wasn't fair. Would it have been too much to ask, for her to have got pregnant? Just the bloody once?

'I better go,' she said, before she started crying.

Ed gave the bleakest, most fleeting of smiles.

She hurried out. As she collected her bag from one of the prison officers, he gave her a friendly smile.

'Cheer up, love,' he said. 'It might never happen.'

That was, Charlotte thought, just the problem. It hadn't.

Eighteen

The Wolseley was packed, even at quarter past seven in the morning, filled with people, beautiful people, who clearly had very important business with each other indeed. With its grand pillars, arches and stairways, it wasn't the place for mere tittle-tattle, but somewhere to broker life-changing deals and cement strategic relationships. Catkin toyed with her pancakes and maple syrup. The excitement in her stomach had taken the edge right off her appetite.

Martin Galt sat in front of her with a plate of eggs Benedict. She tried to concentrate on what he was saying, but she wasn't really interested in the detail. All she cared about was the fact he'd called her, told her he loved her proposal, and that the broadcasters were interested in an initial six-episode run, subject to pilot.

'I want to shoot it as soon as possible. So if you can fax my office your availability, we can get going. I'll start work on a script, get the researchers moving.'

Catkin couldn't believe it. After the hideous fracas of the exhibition, she had been thoroughly shaken. It had knocked the stuffing out of her. The public humiliation had been almost more than she could bear. She had felt like running away. She didn't want to face the outside world, especially the one she moved in, that was so judgemental, so happy to believe anything bad when it happened, so filled with *schadenfreude*. But she'd pulled herself up by her boot straps. She reminded herself that she was in control of her own destiny. If she wanted to sink into a mire of self-pity, then she could, but if she wanted to succeed, she needed to take positive action. People would be waiting for her to fail, and so she had to prove them wrong. She'd taken the bull by the horns, swallowed her pride and couriered her proposal round to Martin. No one got anywhere by moping. You had to make things happen. And she had.

Her own show! She still couldn't believe it. Of course, there were plenty more hoops to jump through before they got the green light, but she'd jumped through the biggest: getting a big-name producer to take her seriously. He was sitting right in front of her, talking contracts, schedules, transmission dates. She remained coolly professional, as she had trained herself to do. But inside, she was jumping up and down with glee.

By eight o'clock they'd shaken hands on a deal, finished their breakfast and were both on their way to their places of work. It had been that simple. Catkin felt as if she was walking on air as she made her way along Piccadilly looking for a cab.

Half an hour later, as she walked into her dressing room, the smell of orchids hit her. Someone had put them in a vase. Without even stopping to read the card nestling among the blooms, she pulled the bouquet out and shoved it in the bin. Then she sat down in front of the mirror and surveyed her reflection.

Perhaps a change of image? Perhaps a totally new

look, to show this was the new Catkin. The woman who had moved on. The woman who was going to be the next big thing. She looked at her profile, wondering about changing her bob to a crop.

No, she decided. The bob was her brand, her look, her trade mark. She'd keep it. She was perfect as she was.

Sebastian was at his wit's end. He had tried everything he could think of. Lavish bouquets of white orchids sent to her dressing room. Texts, emails, letters, all unanswered. A tiny heart-shaped gold locket, with a photo of each of them inside, which came winging its way back by courier the next day, unopened.

Every morning he watched Catkin on the television. He felt like a stalker as he scanned her face for signs of misery. But there was none. She looked as radiant as ever. Of course, she would have spent a good hour in hair and make-up before going on, so any dark circles or worry lines would have been smoothed out. But she didn't seem to have missed a beat. She came across as on top of her game. Not a woman who was pining for her husband in the least.

The only thing he hadn't dared do was approach her in person. He didn't think he could face the humiliation of an outright rejection. He didn't want to see the look of contempt in her eyes.

He lay back on his bed. He had barely moved from it for days. He'd been living off pasta and grated cheese. Stacey would have a fit if she could see the place, thick with dust, curtains unopened, clothes littering the floor. He'd regressed to his student days. Three empty bottles of Grey Goose were lined up on the floor. He'd been sipping at it gradually, just so he had a permanent level of anaesthesia, not total oblivion. He had to be on the ball in case she ever did call, or come back.

The television was blaring out the theme music for *Hello, England*. The bland, moon-shaped face of the presenter came on, beaming cheerfully.

'Coming up in the next half-hour, Catkin Turner is with us, providing her usual common-sense solutions to your problems. If you have a problem and you think Catkin might be able to help, call us right now on this number . . .'

Sebastian stared at the screen.

Why the hell hadn't he thought about it before?

It was the perfect answer.

And it rather appealed to his artistic nature.

With one eye on the number on the screen, he picked up the phone and dialled.

It didn't take much for Sebastian to fob his way onto the show. He knew exactly the sort of personality and back story the researchers were looking for when people phoned in. After all, he'd lived with Catkin's job for years; he knew all the tricks of her trade. He called himself Steven Tate, rather pleased with the artistic reference. He affected a slight East London accent, harking back to his art college days, where to talk as if you'd been within fifty miles of a public school was death. And he laid his tale of woe on with a trowel. Not that any of it was insincere. He genuinely didn't know where else to turn.

The researchers had lapped it up.

'We're putting you through to Catkin in the studio

now, Steven,' the producer told him. 'Just be yourself. She's very sympathetic.'

Moments later, he was outlining his problem to the nation at large. Well, those of them who were sad enough to watch *Hello, England*. Which was a good couple of million.

'I made a terrible mistake, and my wife won't forgive me,' he informed the studio audience and the viewers. 'She thought I was having a fling with someone I work with, and I wasn't. It was all a misunderstanding. But now, she won't talk to me or have anything to do with me. She refuses to listen to my side of the story, or accept my apology. And the thing is, I never meant to hurt her. I just want the chance to explain.'

Catkin's face was filled with compassion. She looked into the camera, her gaze sincere.

'Steven, we all do things we shouldn't sometimes. And we can't always expect our partners to understand when we make a mistake. What your wife probably needs is time to come to terms with what you did and work out how she feels. But in the meantime, perhaps you should try a romantic gesture. Women love to feel pampered. Maybe a large bunch of flowers with a message attached?'

'I've tried that,' Sebastian replied gloomily. 'Six bunches to be precise.'

Catkin exchanged glances and raised eyebrows with her co-presenters, who shook their heads sorrowfully to show what a sad case this was. Catkin clasped her hands between her knees and leaned forward, adopting a concerned expression.

'Steven, how long have you been married?'

'Over five years.'

'Well, that's quite a long time. I think your wife owes you at least the chance to explain, so that you can decide together if your marriage really is over. Or maybe try some counselling.'

'I know,' said Sebastian. 'But she won't talk. This is my last resort. My only chance to communicate with her. You're my last hope, Catkin.' He couldn't help the pleading tone that came into his voice. And he'd dropped the accent. A slight frown appeared on Catkin's brow. 'I just want to tell her that without her I'm nothing. I can't work. I can't sleep. I don't eat. I just lie here waiting for the phone to ring. Or the door to open. I just want to take her in my arms, and kiss her. Never let her go.'

This was the real him speaking now. A heartfelt plea.

You could have heard a pin drop in the studio. Catkin sat bolt upright, her eyes wide. She seemed unable to speak for a moment.

'Catkin?' prompted the presenter. 'Can you offer any advice on Steven's plight?'

When she spoke, her voice was trembling slightly.

'I think,' she said, 'that you'll find that your wife will listen. I think she's probably been hurting, trying to prove to herself that she can live without you, and that you don't matter. But it sounds to me as if you're meant to be together. Try phoning her again, just one more time. My gut instinct tells me that this time she'll answer.'

There was a pause.

'Thank you,' said Sebastian. 'I'll do that. And I'll let you know what happens. Thank you, Catkin.'

'You're welcome,' she replied. 'Steven . . .'

She looked straight into the camera and smiled, then wiped away a tear. The studio audience broke into applause.

The camera homed in on one of the presenters.

'Coming up after the next break . . .'

Sebastian gave Catkin three minutes to leave the studio and get back into her dressing room before he called her.

'Catkin?'

'Sebastian?' She sounded breathless. 'You're a madman! You could have got me sacked.'

But she didn't sound cross, not at all.

'Shall I come up to you?' he asked.

'No,' she said. 'Don't move an inch. I'll get a driver. I'm coming down.'

Sebastian hung up the phone and threw it in the air with glee. Then he jumped off the bed and looked round at the chaos. He lunged back onto the bed, picking up the phone and dialling hastily.

'Stacey? It's Sebastian. Tell me you're not busy. I need you. Now!'

Today had been a perfect nightmare from start to finish. If Penny could have chosen to eradicate one day from her memory, this would be it.

The surgery had finally been forced into making a decision about Daisy. After the Christmas Fayre, Penny had felt obliged to call her state to their attention, and they had been monitoring her closely. Since New Year, her condition had deteriorated even further, to the point where she was quite unable to look after herself. The real tragedy was that there was no family to care or bother or make the decisions that needed to be made. Penny had tried to contact the daughter, but she was abroad in Germany, and merely sounded distant, both literally and metaphorically.

'I'm sure you'll make the best decision,' she'd told Penny, who had been incredulous that someone could be so hard-hearted and uncaring. But then, Daisy didn't have a bean to leave: she lived in a council house, on a meagre pension. Usually if there was property or money involved, the relatives flocked round. So it had been up to Penny to find suitable accommodation, a care home that was willing to take on Daisy in her state of dementia, and the choices had been utterly depressing. In the end she had had no option. There was only one home with an NHS place available that had the facilities to deal with her. It was a grim, forbidding place, housed in a rundown building on the outskirts of Comberton, with no grounds, few facilities, and surly staff. Penny's heart had sunk as she made the arrangements, feeling as if she had betrayed Daisy's trust.

They had moved her this afternoon. Penny would never forget Daisy being ushered into the back of the taxi as long as she lived. She had shuffled out obediently in her sad little squashed-down shoes. She obviously had no idea where she was going, or that she would never be coming back to her house. A nurse from the home carried out her suitcase. The rest of her life was being left behind. The house would be emptied, and then the council would send someone round to decorate it from top to bottom and a new tenant would be installed before the paint was dry. As if Daisy had never existed.

Which she almost didn't. The Daisy Penny saw now was a shell of her former self. The beautiful twinkling blue eyes were now blank. Her cloud of white hair was straggly and lank. She had a habit of flapping her hands in front of her, as if she wanted everything to go away. How long, wondered Penny, would she be stuck in that hellhole waiting to die? With no one to care whether she did or not? And what was going on in her mind? Did she have snatches of lucidity, where she recognised the full horror of what was happening, but then couldn't communicate? Or was she blissfully unaware? Did she live in the present, or the past? Or have any concept of the future? Would she be able to look forward to the tea trolley coming round? Because that was about as exciting as it was going to get.

Penny knew there was no point in her resolving to visit Daisy on a regular basis. It would be a futile, sentimental gesture conceived to salve Penny's own conscience. And she would never keep it up. The days would slip by, there wouldn't be time, and Daisy would sit there, forgotten. Better not to make the resolution than fail to keep it.

She sat at her desk, her shoulders slumped in submission. There was a bottle of red wine on the side that one of her patients had given her as a Christmas present. She swilled out her coffee cup in the sink, unscrewed the cap and poured herself a hefty measure, then gulped it down. It made her feel a tiny bit better. Well, not better, just numb at the edges. As she typed up her report on the computer, she kept topping herself up. It seemed to help her keep her objectivity, and reduced the impact of seeing Daisy's tragic plight in black and white on the screen in front of her.

By the time she left the surgery, she realised she had drunk the whole bottle. It had slipped down so easily. She rinsed it out guiltily and slipped it into the recycling bin as she sidled out into the car park, hoping no one would notice her. She'd be OK to drive. It was eight o'clock at night – the police wouldn't be out looking for drunk drivers yet. Anyway, the station in Comberton was notoriously under-staffed.

She drove incredibly carefully. Statistics drifted through her brain – like the fact that most drink-driving incidents occurred within three miles of departure. Well, she'd gone five, and she was all right, she thought, as she sailed past the sign that indicated Withybrook was another two miles. She was nearly home. Her mobile rang, distracting her momentarily. It was probably Tom or Megan, wondering where she was, why she wasn't home yet dancing attendance on them. She looked down to see if she could spot the name. In that split second, another car came round the corner. Penny swerved to avoid it, overcompensated, then sailed straight on and crashed into a tree.

She sat at the wheel, motionless. She didn't want to get out and see what she had done. The other driver had climbed out and was coming over.

Shit. It was Charlotte.

Penny smiled to herself. Well. What would you call that? Poetic justice? Just as she had dobbed Charlotte in, now Charlotte could dob her in. And it would be all over the local papers. GP in drink-driving accident. She'd lose her licence. Her job.

An eye for an eye.

She rolled down her window and gazed at Charlotte dully.

'Penny! Are you all right?'

Penny nodded as Charlotte pulled her door open, anxiously checking for any sign of injury.

'Are you hurt? Can you speak?'

'Just about,' Penny slurred. 'Fuck . . .'

'It's fine. If nobody's injured, it's not a problem. It's just a car. You're insured . . .' She frowned, concerned at Penny's lack of response. 'Are you sure you're OK?'

Penny gave her a lopsided smile. 'Completely anaesthetised.'

Charlotte's eyes widened. 'You're drunk. Oh my God . . . Penny . . . !'

She started looking round her, not sure what to do.

'We better get this off the road before anyone else arrives. You get out. I'll drive.'

'Aren't you going to call the police?'

'Of course not. You didn't hit me, so I'm under no obligation.'

Penny stared out through the windscreen, which had a large crack in it.

'Come on,' urged Charlotte. 'Let me drive it into that gateway. You can leave it there overnight and get someone to pick it up in the morning.'

Penny got out of the car obediently. Charlotte jumped into the driver's seat.

'Go and sit in my truck,' she ordered. 'I'll move this, then I'll give you a lift home.'

Penny sat in the cab of Charlotte's truck. She felt terrible. She couldn't believe her stupidity. What if she'd killed someone? They'd bloody lock her up and throw away the key. That would be the end of it. Her career, her life. Tom and Megan would have to go and live with Bill. And by the time she came out of prison they would have left home. She began to shiver. And she felt sick, which was hardly surprising: a whole bottle of cheap red wine down her neck in the space of an hour.

She opened the door of the truck in the nick of time, spewing onto the verge, just as Charlotte arrived back.

'Sorry,' she croaked, wiping away drools of spittle. How humiliating. A supposedly respectable GP retching her guts up in the gutter.

Charlotte reached into her glove compartment and passed her a packet of tissues. Penny dabbed at her face.

'Sorry . . .' she apologised again, weakly.

'It's OK,' said Charlotte. 'We've all been there.'

Penny couldn't imagine Charlotte had. She didn't look like the sort of person who lost control. And lost her dignity. She felt a wave of despair sweep over her. Her life was a disaster.

She slumped back into the passenger seat and began to weep.

'Hey,' said Charlotte. 'It's OK. There's no harm done. No one was hurt.'

'It's not that,' Penny sobbed. 'I'm so frightened. I'm afraid I'm going to end up like Daisy. A sad, batty old woman with no one to care about her. Stuffed in a nursing home and forgotten . . .'

Charlotte put an arm round her.

'Don't be silly,' she soothed. 'That's not going to

happen. Your kids love you. You've got loads of friends. We're all your mates.'

Penny looked at her. She couldn't bear the burden of her secret any more. She couldn't live the lie.

'You wouldn't be,' she sniffed, 'if you knew what I'd done.'

Charlotte looked puzzled.

'It was me,' Penny admitted. 'I told the press who you were. At Sebastian's exhibition.'

'What?' Charlotte looked flabbergasted. 'Why? And how . . . how did you know?'

'I saw your married name on your medical records. And I looked you up on the internet. It was all in there . . .'

She put her head in her hands.

'But why?' asked Charlotte. 'That's what I don't understand. Why?'

'I was jealous – sickeningly, horribly jealous that you meant something to Sebastian when I didn't.' She looked up defiantly. 'Have you got any idea what it's like, to be so totally head over heels in love with somebody that you don't know what you're doing? To have it eating away at you until it turns you into a bitter and twisted maniac, full of resentment and spite—'

Her face was twisted into a terrible grimace as she spat out her words, then came to an abrupt halt. She really did sound like a madwoman, some crazy demented Mrs Rochester figure.

Charlotte was gazing at her in horror.

'You poor thing,' she said finally.

'What?' Penny looked at her in surprise. This wasn't the reaction she'd been expecting.

'It must have been awful.'

Penny shook her head in amazement. 'How can you not want to punch my lights out?'

Charlotte shrugged. 'I know you didn't mean it,' she replied. 'And I know you're sorry.'

'If I was you, I'd call the cops and grass me up. And laugh while they drove me away.'

'What would be the point of that?'

'It's what I deserve.'

'No, you don't,' replied Charlotte. 'You've had a shit time. And it's not like you go driving round pissed every day. This was a one-off, and you were unlucky. Yeah, OK, so technically what you did was stupid and dangerous and maybe you should have your licence taken off you. But I'm not going to be responsible for that happening. As far as I'm concerned, you've probably learned your lesson.'

Penny gazed at her in awe. No wonder Sebastian had been besotted. This girl was a walking angel. After everything that had happened to her, she was able to see reason. And good in people.

'You're amazing,' she exclaimed. 'How can you be so accepting? After everything that's happened to you. If it was me I'd be a basket case—' She broke off. Charlotte was looking as if she was trying very hard not to cry.

'You don't know the half of it,' she said, her voice breaking.

'Charlotte?'

Charlotte shook her head. She put on her seat belt, put her hand on the keys in the ignition, then burst into tears.

'Oh, God,' said Penny. 'I'm *so* sorry. I really am. I didn't mean to upset you. Shit.'

'It's not that.' Charlotte grabbed for the tissues she'd given Penny and wiped her eyes. 'I've had a bit of a shock today, that's all.'

'Of course you have. You probably thought I was going to plough straight into you. Just take a few deep breaths—'

Charlotte shook her head. 'It's not the accident,' she gulped. 'It's . . . my husband.'

'The one who's in prison?' asked Penny, realising that sounded rather stupid. 'What's happened to him?'

'Not to him. To his secretary.' She gripped the steering wheel, shutting her eyes tight. 'She's pregnant.' Tears were streaming down her face. 'With his baby . . .'

Penny stared at her in disbelief, taking in what she had said.

'Oh, you poor sweetheart,' she said. 'You poor angel. Come here.'

She took Charlotte in her arms and squeezed her tight. And as Charlotte cried her heart out, Penny began to cry too, at the bloody injustice of life, and how some people got what they wanted, and how others were just shoved to one side. Was it destiny? Luck? Or was it about the choices you made? Could you go from being a loser to a winner?

Eventually Charlotte started to laugh through her tears.

'Look at us,' she said. 'If the police came along now, they'd definitely arrest us.'

The two of them sat in the front seat, sniffing,

wiping away their tears, looking at each other and laughing at the absurdity of it all. Charlotte shoved her tissue into the side pocket and started up the engine.

'I'd better get you home, or your kids will be worried.'

Penny sat back in her seat, drained. Her head was pounding with the revenge of cheap wine. She needed a dose of painkillers, a litre of water and something to eat. Then she was going to sit down and decide what to do with her life.

By the time she got home she felt quite sober, literally and metaphorically. Love. Who needed it? The only thing that really mattered, Penny decided, was the love of your own children. She was going to turn over a new leaf, concentrate on Tom and Megan while she still had them. Not that she neglected them. On the contrary, it was usually them that made it clear they didn't want to fraternise with her. But she was going to put her foot down. Make sure they did things together. Walks, movies, meals out, trips away . . .

It was the only antidote. She wasn't going to spend her time pining and prodding her sores. She was going to be the perfect mother. So that when her time came, if she hadn't found her soul mate, her kids would choose her final destination with care, and would visit her because they wanted to, not because they felt they had to.

Megan was in the kitchen, her long dark hair tumbling to her waist. She had on a tiny flowery dress with a little cardigan, and footless tights. Her toenails sparkled with newly applied bright pink polish.

'Hey, Mum,' she said.

Tom looked up from the table.

'Where've you been, dude?' he asked. 'We were getting worried.'

'I had a bit of a prang,' admitted Penny. She went to the sink to get a glass of water.

'No shit,' said Tom. 'Is it a write-off?'

Penny shrugged. She didn't want to think about it. It was going to be a pain whatever – endless phone calls to the insurance company, arguments over whether she was entitled to a replacement vehicle. And a paltry cheque if it was a write-off, which would mean she couldn't afford a new car.

Bollocks to it, she thought. She'd get a loan, do one of those low-interest deals. Get something a bit sexy. Maybe a soft-top. She earned a decent salary. Why didn't she ever treat herself? She always put herself last, put herself down.

Maybe if she lived like the person she wanted to be . . .

'We made macaroni cheese,' announced Megan. 'But it looks like puke.'

She proffered a bowl full of yellow, congealed pasta.

'Yep,' grinned Penny. 'It sure does. Come on. Let's go down to the pub.'

Tom and Megan gawped at her.

'What's got into you?' asked Megan.

'It's a school night,' said Tom.

'What the hell?' replied Penny, grinning. 'Let's have some fun while we still can.'

*

The driver had been frustratingly slow, the journey interminable because he had steadfastly refused to break the speed limit on the motorway. He didn't want to lose his job. Which was, she supposed, fair enough, but nevertheless Catkin had found her foot pressing an imaginary accelerator all the way, as if she could make the car go faster.

It had taken her big break to make her realise what it was she really wanted. Every time she had thought of her exciting news, something had prevented her from really relishing the fact. And when Sebastian had pulled his crazy prank, she realised what it was. Hearing his voice, she suddenly knew how much she had missed him. And how much she wanted to share her triumph with him. Success was bloody meaningless without someone you love to share it with.

For the past few weeks, she had felt like half a person. Although she had tried to shut him out of her mind, he was always there, in the background. When she heard something funny, she wanted to tell him. When someone in the studio drove her nuts, she wanted to offload it onto him. And her future, her dazzling future, was nothing without him.

Now, at last, they were turning into the drive of Withybrook Hall. The sun was just going down, slipping behind the house and bathing it in a red-gold-glow. And as they pulled up to the front, Sebastian came out of the door, standing at the top of the steps.

He'd obviously been waiting, looking out for her.

Her heart skipped a beat.

Sebastian. Her Sebastian.

She threw the car door open and jumped out, running up the steps to greet him.

'Hey, Mrs Turner,' he smiled, and she fell into his arms.

Nineteen

Trying to resuscitate a moribund marriage is incredibly hard work, as Fitch was finding out. He was doing his utmost to smooth Hayley's path back into family life. He had avoided recriminations. He made sure she didn't have to do too much around the house. He cooked wonderful food. But it didn't seem to make any difference. She was miserable. She seemed permanently on the verge of tears. And listless.

He supposed it was the shock. After all, being lamped by a bloke as big as Kirk would knock the stuffing out of most people. But even a week after her arrival back home, when her eye had gone down and she was able to go out in public, she showed no sign of recovery. She sank back into her usual diet of daytime television, soaps and lurid gossip magazines. She spent hours on her phone texting – God knows who. Fitch supposed he could have flicked through her messages but he didn't have the energy to deal with what he might find.

He knew he was pussyfooting round her. He didn't want to antagonise her because of the girls. They were so happy that she was back, and that they were living at the cottage again.

'Granny's house smells,' Jade confided to him. 'And her food is horrid. And Grandad's grumpy.'

'And it's cold,' added Amber. 'Freezing.'

'It's OK. You won't have to go back there,' promised Fitch.

In the end, he decided he wasn't going to take any more. The tension was intolerable.

'Hayley, if you're really depressed, maybe we should think about getting you some medication. It's just not fair. On you, me, or the girls.'

She looked up at him. Her eyes seemed dead. Her skin was pasty. Gone was the vitality of the girl he had married, the girl with the brightest eyes he'd ever seen, the girl with a sense of mischief, a sense of self. He wondered if she'd been taking drugs while she was with Kirk, and if she was suffering some sort of withdrawal. It could explain a lot.

She looked as if she was about to say something. Maybe she was going to reveal what was troubling her. If only she would confide in him. He would do anything to help her and get their marriage back on track.

'I suppose I'm just . . . ashamed,' she said. 'Of what I've done. Of what I could have lost.'

He came to sit down beside her.

'Moping about it isn't going to help,' he said. 'If you carry on like this, you will lose us. Look,' he went on, putting a fatherly hand on her arm, 'go and see Penny Silver. Tell her how you're feeling. There might be something she can do. And she won't judge you. She's had a pretty tough time of it herself.'

To his surprise, Hayley did as he suggested. Penny was incredibly understanding. She'd talked everything through with Hayley, right back before she'd even met Fitch. The two of them agreed that perhaps what

Hayley needed was some antidepressants. Not long term, just while she sorted her head out. Something to help her see over the parapet.

'I know what it's like, when you can't see the wood for the trees,' Penny told her. 'You'd have to be a pretty amazing person to pull yourself together without any help.'

From that day on Hayley seemed to turn a corner. She got back her zest for life. Her skin began to glow and her eyes began to sparkle. She made an effort with her clothes. And she communicated with the girls. She wasn't quite running round in a pinny making cup cakes, but she made an effort. She started taking them riding, even talked about getting them a pony they could keep at her parents.

Encouraged by her blooming, Fitch suggested a party. Hayley had always been such a sociable creature. If they started to entertain, perhaps she would start to come out of her shell again.

'Not a dinner party,' he assured her. 'Just a few mates round for supper. We can do a big chilli or something. Get some beers in.'

To his surprise, she was enthusiastic, and threw herself into the preparations. They only asked a dozen people: a few of their old mates from the pub, Penny and Charlotte, Sebastian and Catkin. She seemed really excited about Catkin coming – a proper celebrity.

The night of the party, Hayley came downstairs looking stunning, in a red sweater and jeans, her hair done in glossy curls that fell around her face. Fitch's heart stopped as he looked at her. He thought maybe, just maybe, she was back. The girl he had fallen in love with. But he had to be cautious. She was still very fragile, given to bouts of weeping at the drop of a hat. And dark moods, when she withdrew, although she had got better and didn't do it in front of Jade and Amber any more.

His gamble paid off. The party was a huge success. Hayley and Catkin, in particular, hit it off, putting on music and getting everyone to dance once the food had been devoured. The only slight cloud was that Charlotte had seemed a little withdrawn and had left early, but she explained that she had been working hard and wasn't feeling a hundred per cent.

The hard core stayed until half past two. When everyone had gone, Fitch and Hayley stood in the living room, surrounded by the detritus of a good party – empty glasses and bottles, ashtrays, CDs all over the coffee table.

'Let's leave it till the morning,' said Fitch.

'Good idea,' she replied, looking at him.

He took a step closer. She smiled.

They hadn't made love in all the time she'd been back. He still didn't feel able to, because that was the ultimate moment of forgiveness, and he couldn't pretend that it hadn't been a hard journey. Sometimes he felt that he was doing all the giving and she was just taking.

But tonight, all his misgivings melted away. She looked as she had that first day he had met her, her dark eyes full of mischief and promise, her mouth so inviting. He couldn't resist.

Within an instant, they were on each other. Within seconds, their clothes were discarded. They made love with an intensity that purged them of everything that had happened over the past few months.

And as Hayley came, she wept. He kissed her tears away.

'Hey. Shush,' he whispered. 'It's supposed to be nice. You're not supposed to cry.'

The next morning Fitch got up early, despite a bit of a hangover, and cleared up the party mess. He put the bottles out for recycling, opened the windows to disperse the smell of smoke, and loaded the dishwasher. It was a bright and sunny morning that matched his mood. When Jade and Amber came down, he made them bacon sandwiches. He settled them at the kitchen table, then made a sandwich and a cup of tea for Hayley.

'Go and get your things ready when you've finished. I'm just going to take this upstairs for your mum,' he told the girls.

The two of them nodded, munching happily.

Fitch ran up the stairs, careful not to spill the tea. He looked at the clock – fifteen minutes before he was supposed to take the girls swimming in Comberton. They were meeting some friends. He grinned to himself. There was a lot a man could do in fifteen minutes.

As soon as he walked into the bedroom, he could tell something wasn't right. Hayley was sitting on the bed, fully dressed and made up, staring dully into space.

'Are you coming to the pool?' he asked hopefully. 'We could go for fish and chips afterwards?'

She sighed in reply. 'I'm sorry.'

'That's OK,' said Fitch. 'I'll be back by two. We could—'

'I've tried and tried,' she interrupted him. 'But I can't get him out of my head.'

Fitch put the cup and the plate down.

'What do you mean?'

'He wants me back.'

Four deadly words.

'Kirk.' Fitch's voice was flat. It was a statement, not a question.

She nodded. 'He's sending a limo for me. It should be here any minute.'

'Kirk, the guy that gave you a black eye and a split lip and threatened to kill you?'

'He didn't mean it. He lost it because I thought he was unfaithful when he wasn't. He didn't know what he was doing. He's promised to make it up to me.'

Fitch clenched his fists. Was she insane?

He looked out of the window where a long, low white limousine was pulling up outside the front door.

'You get into that limo,' he said, 'and we're finished. You don't get a second chance.'

She looked at him sadly.

'I'm sorry,' she repeated, and walked out of the door.

Fitch stood for a moment in the bedroom, unable to believe what he had just heard. Had he dreamed last night? The fun they'd had? The incredible sex they had had? Did that count for nothing in Hayley's world? Or had that been the catalyst for her decision? Had it made her realise that this was going to be as good as it got with Fitch, and it wasn't good enough?

He ran down the stairs, and out of the front door.

'Hayley . . .'

She was about to get into the back. He could smell

the leather of the seats, hear the soft music playing, see the bottle of champagne that the creep had sent down for her. She was about to slip into another world, the world that she believed was so exciting and glamorous, but which he knew was just a façade. A façade that could fade away at any moment.

'Please,' he begged. 'Don't go. Surely we can work things out? Please. Not for me. But for Jade and Amber.'

'I'm sorry,' she replied. 'I just can't do it any more. I can't pretend.'

'What do I tell the girls?'

'Tell the girls . . . that they're lucky to have you. Because they are.'

She was in the back seat now, looking up at him. He could see her eyes were brimming with tears. He was surprised. It was the nearest she'd come to showing any real emotion.

'You probably hate me, Fitch. But I hate myself even more. For being weak. For not being able to resist. But that's just the way I am. And you're better off without me.'

She reached out and shut the door. He could no longer see her through the blacked-out windows. He watched in disbelief as the limousine glided off, insinuating its way up the street, totally out of place. He wondered what the village would make of that. It certainly made a change from the usual tractors and beaten-up hatchbacks.

He turned back to go into the house. Jade and Amber came bounding out of the kitchen, clutching their swimming bags, and sat down in the hall to put on their shoes.

'Are we ready to go?'

'Is Mummy coming with us?'

Two little faces looked up at him expectantly.

'Um,' said Fitch. 'Mummy's had to pop out. But I thought we could go out for fish and chips afterwards.'

The two girls high-fived each other in triumph.

It was so easy to please them, Fitch thought with a heavy heart. It was just a pity it wasn't so easy to please their mother.

He wasn't sure how he was going to get through the weekend, but he did. He didn't have the bottle to sit down and tell the girls where Hayley had gone, or why. He couldn't begin to make sense of it all himself, let alone come up with a rational explanation for a five- and seven-year-old. Why bring their little worlds crashing down? So he made sure the three of them had as much fun as they could, because deep down he was hoping that Hayley wouldn't have such a fantastic time with Kirk as she seemed to think she would, and that she would come back with her tail between her legs and ask to start again. A leopard, after all, doesn't change its spots. Kirk was a bona fide thug and the sooner Hayley realised that the better. He would just have to sit it out.

In the back of his mind, however, was also the fact that life was so much easier without Hayley's oppressive presence. He had become weary of constantly having to bolster her up. Why should he have to worry about her state of mind every minute of the day? She certainly hadn't seemed to worry about his, he realised now. Looking after her had been exhausting, both mentally and physically. With her out of the house again, Fitch felt free. Unencumbered.

Maybe what they needed was a clean break. She could go off and live in sunny Watford in Kirk's shag palace and swan around in designer dresses being taken to swanky restaurants. And they could get on with their life in Withybrook. For Fitch it would be an admission of failure, but was it really worth trying to keep a marriage alive for the sake of pride and your own values? Maybe the grown-up thing to do was admit that they'd made a mistake, that they were incompatible and wouldn't ever be able to make a go of it, because they both wanted different things out of life.

Whatever happened, whether Hayley stayed or went, the only important thing to Fitch was keeping Jade and Amber. He would never let them go. He would fight tooth and nail to keep them. They belonged here, in Withybrook, with him, and he was confident he could manage. It might be a struggle, but he could organise his work so that he could be with them after school and during the holidays. It might mean a bit less cash coming in, but money wasn't everything. He certainly had plenty of work lined up, and the most obvious solution was to take someone on to help him with the donkey work, someone he could train up and delegate to.

Yes, decided Fitch. If being a single dad was the way forward, then he could handle it. He never resented a moment spent with his daughters. He didn't feel the urge to go off on wild nights out with the lads, or weekends away. And Hayley's parents were always there in extremis, if he got snowed under or delayed.

Not that it wasn't tiring. They jumped into his bed at half six in the morning, and were still on the go when he urged them back into bed at eight. But they were tidy, they weren't fussy eaters, and they didn't squabble too much. And anyway, it would only be a few years before they were able to look after themselves. Then, in the blink of an eye, they would be young women, with their own lives. And then they'd be off and gone. He only had them for a very short time, and he was determined to make the most of them.

With or without his wife.

On Sunday, he took the girls to the beach at Mariscombe. Just over ten miles away from Withybrook, it was a stretch of golden sand fringed by a deep blue sea of rolling waves. In the summer, it was filled with holidaymakers, crammed with scantily clad bodies and ice-cream vans, but in the winter it was an exhilarating paradise peopled with just a few intrepid surfers, the odd kite-flyer and dog walker. Fitch never tired of its beauty. He remembered discovering it not long after he had moved to the area, and marvelling at its wild perfection. He loved coming here on a summer's evening with a disposable barbecue and a dozen sausages from the local butcher. He would cook while the girls frolicked in the waves, and then they would devour hot dogs smothered in tomato sauce, Dido hopping round them hoping for a tail end.

Today was too cold for either paddling or barbecuing. Behind the beach were the dunes, and the girls spent the afternoon rolling down them, their screams of laughter bringing smiles to the faces of passers-by. Why the fuck wasn't Hayley here? wondered Fitch darkly. You'd have to be completely heartless not to enjoy the scenery and their joy. He realised that he didn't even know if she was coming back this evening or not. She used to come back on a Sunday night, but there had been something final in the way she had driven off yesterday without a backward glance.

He'd get the girls into bed early tonight, he decided, then call Hayley on her mobile. Tell her that they needed to talk, and come to a decision about their future. He wasn't prepared to live in limbo any more. It wasn't that he wasn't able to compromise, but he couldn't let things drift. It was time to get tough.

The girls grumbled as he herded them back into the car and drove home. There was no sign of Hayley as they came back into the house. He made a quick supper of spaghetti hoops on toast, then the girls each had a shower while he gathered their sandy clothes off the floor and shoved them in the washing machine. Half an hour later, they were tucked up in bed.

'Is Mummy coming back?' asked Jade. She was the more anxious of the two. Being the elder, she was more aware of atmospheres and moods.

'Not tonight,' Fitch replied, thinking that if Hayley did turn up later he could easily say she had changed her mind.

He saw the two girls exchange a knowing glance, and was shocked. They obviously understood more than he gave them credit for. It made him feel incredibly sad. He'd failed them. He and Hayley had failed them. He felt a surge of frustration and anger, the sudden need to go and get completely shit-faced and forget the guilt that niggled at him morning, noon and night.

He compromised by pouring himself a Scotch, slinging in a couple of ice cubes, enjoying its fiery warmth as it hit the back of his throat. He picked up the phone, and scrolled through until he found her number.

There was no reply. He could imagine her taking a cursory glance into her handbag, seeing his number come up, then turning to simper up at Kirk as they drank a bottle of some flashy champagne. He threw the phone down onto the sofa in disgust. What if he had been phoning because one of the girls was ill? Though what she would do about it he didn't know. She didn't know Calpol from Cuprinol.

He leaned back and stretched, his body aching slightly from the strenuous walk on the beach and the climb up the dunes. He reached for the remote. There would be some anodyne Sunday-night drama on that might take his mind off things; something in period costume with an undemanding plot.

He was just nodding off when the doorbell drilled. He jumped up, startled. Maybe she'd come back after all, and forgotten her key. He tensed. Was she expecting confrontation or reconciliation?

As soon as he answered the door he knew that neither was on the cards for that evening. Hayley's father stood on the doorstep, flanked by two of her brothers. Fitch took a step back, suddenly nervous. What had she told them? They looked serious, as if they had come to remonstrate with him over his behaviour.

Shit – had they come to get Jade and Amber? They

bloody better not have. But why else would there be three of them? One to hold him down, the other two to carry the girls from their beds and up to the farm. Well, they weren't going to get away with it.

'What is it?' he asked gruffly, and was disconcerted when Hayley's father's face crumpled and he broke down in front of him, terrible sobs racking his body.

'It's Hayley,' offered one of the brothers.

'What?' asked Fitch.

'She's had an accident,' the other one told him.

'She's dead.' Her father's voice was that of a broken man. 'My little girl. She's dead . . .'

Twenty

When Jade and Amber scampered into his bedroom the next morning, Fitch felt as if he had only just got to sleep. It had been a terrible night. Eliciting the exact details from the Poltimores had proved a struggle, but eventually a picture emerged. Hayley had been driving Kirk's Mercedes when a car had jumped a red light and ploughed into the side of them. Hayley had been killed outright. Kirk had escaped without a scratch.

Fitch had spent most of the evening on the phone, as Hayley's father seemed totally unable to deal with the situation, just sat at the kitchen table in a daze. They had wanted Fitch to go back to the farm with the girls, but he refused to wake them, so one of the boys had gone to fetch Barbara, who completely fell apart.

In the end, Fitch had called Penny, who came over straight away.

'I'll give her something to knock her out,' she told him. 'The best thing they can do is take her home and put her to bed. There's no point in her staying up all night hysterical. Everyone's got to deal with this nightmare.'

She gave him a hug as she left.

'I'm so sorry, Fitch.'

He knew she didn't just mean about the crash.

He finally got to bed at about four, but he couldn't sleep. He was sick with worry about how he was going to deal with this latest nightmare. And now the girls were awake, bouncing on his bed, sliding under his duvet, fighting to get the closest to him. He had to tell them.

'Jade. Amber.'

They looked at him warily, unused to the strain in his voice. He held out an arm for each of them and they slid into his embrace. He held them tight, trying to control his voice.

'I've got some very sad news. You're going to have to be very brave, both of you. And I know you will. You're big girls . . .'

They looked at him solemnly.

'Is it Herman?' asked Jade. Herman was the terrapin in the Poltimores' kitchen, a creature they inexplicably adored.

'No,' said Fitch carefully. 'I'm afraid it's Mummy. There was a terrible accident. Someone drove into the side of her car.'

'Is she hurt?'

'Will she have a scar?'

'I'm afraid it was worse than that. She . . .'

Fuck. There was just no other way of saying it. There was no euphemism he could use. He had to come straight out with it.

'She died.'

Jade and Amber looked at each other.

'It didn't hurt her,' he went on hastily, even though he wasn't sure if this was true. 'She didn't feel anything. It was just like going to sleep.'

Jade's chin began to wobble.

'So are we orphans?'

'No, sweetheart. You're not orphans. I'm still here.'

Amber buried her face in his chest. Fitch felt his throat tighten. If only there was something he could do to take away their pain. He squeezed the two of them as tight as he could, pouring every ounce of his love into them in the hope that it might help.

Jade squealed in indignation. 'Daddy, you're hurting.'

Amber sat up suddenly, as if she had thought of something important.

'Can we have pancakes?'

The pair of them looked at him hopefully.

Fitch lay there for a moment, startled by their reaction. He supposed the truth would hit them later.

'Why not?' he said, and got out of bed to face the day. 'Why not . . . ?'

The estate agent strode through Myrtle Cottage nodding with approval, pointing his state-of-the-art tape measure at the walls and noting the period features down on his laptop. He'd been to see it months before, when Gussie and her brothers had asked for a valuation, and he had to admit that it was unrecognisable from the dingy, poky little abode that it had been.

This was now a delightful little home. It was flooded with light, painted in warm but muted colours, the woodwork fresh and gleaming. The hallway was airy and inviting rather than oppressive, with the floorboards stripped and waxed, a striped coir runner snaking up the stairs. The sitting room was cosy, with an oversized velvet sofa, shelves crammed with books and artefacts, a wood-burning stove and a wall smothered in paintings of the countryside all in different frames. The dining room was a particular delight, with silver and white rococo wallpaper in the alcoves either side of the fireplace, a pretty chandelier, and lace curtains fluttering at the windows. And although the furniture obviously wouldn't go with the house, it had been dressed to show any prospective purchasers just what effect they could achieve. A mixture of antique and modern, it was contemporary but not off-putting, and yet in keeping with the period features it had retained.

This girl knew what she was doing, he decided as he tried to calculate a fair asking price, one that would please the vendors but was achievable and wouldn't leave the house stagnant on the market for months because it had been over-valued. You had to be careful in Withybrook. Too high and you priced the locals out of the market, leaving it only open to out-of-towners and weekenders, which inevitably reduced the number of viewers. But at the same time, you didn't want to let a property like this go for a song. It was a peach.

He explained all this to Miss Dixon, adding that he would send his valuation in writing to Gussie in the post, but that he thought she would be pleased. And as he left, he asked for her card.

'I reckon I could get you loads of work, if you're interested,' he said.

She declined, politely. 'I'm not staying in the area once this job's finished,' she told him.

'Shame,' he said. 'We could do with more talent like you round here.'

Talent in more ways than one, he thought, as he closed down his laptop. She was a very pretty girl, even if she didn't make the most of herself. A bit of make-up and some decent clothes wouldn't go amiss. He hoped she'd make the effort when the viewers came round. It was an aspirational business, selling houses, and anything you could do to entice a purchase always helped. Including managing to get yourself out of your pyjamas by eleven o'clock in the morning.

Charlotte shut the door on the estate agent with a sigh of relief. He'd seemed favourably impressed, but she was nervous about what price he would finally give Gussie. She desperately wanted the house to do well for her friend. She was pleased with what she had done, but she hoped all her work was worth it, and had increased Myrtle Cottage's value. She would hate it to have been all in vain.

There were only a few little jobs left to do, as she'd explained to the agent. The slate in the dining-room fireplace, a couple of light fittings she had ordered on the internet but which hadn't arrived yet, and some etched glass to replace the horrible frosted glass in the front door, which would be so much more in keeping. Then her job was done. She could go when she wanted. Gussie had said she could stay on while the house was sold – in fact, it would be doing her a favour, to have it lived in, and to have someone to keep it clean. But Charlotte wanted to get away.

The past couple of weeks had been grim. She hadn't been able to come to terms with the shock of Ed's news. She vacillated between terrible anger at the injustice, raging fury at Melanie's treacherous behaviour, and sheer desolation, when she plummeted into the depths of despair, wondering what on earth she had done to deserve such heartache. To keep her mind off it, she'd thrown herself into finishing the cottage, jet-washing the little patio she had fashioned out of some end-of-range slabs, washing the windows until they shone, putting up the curtains, arranging bowls of fruit and vases of fresh flowers so it felt like a proper home and not just a show house.

And it did feel like her home. She had poured her heart and soul into it over the past few months. She had been able to decorate it to her own taste, choosing the colours she felt drawn to. And she had used her own furniture and bits and pieces to dress it – the things she had been able to salvage from the house at Parsons Green because they were officially the tools of her trade. She'd used remnants of fabrics from other jobs for curtains. And thus Myrtle Cottage was almost a reflection of her. Her ideal home. But she knew she couldn't stay here. She would have to find herself another job. Connor had given her a decent reference. She'd have to start sending off her CV, she thought wearily. She'd just started taking photos of the rooms on her digital camera to add to her portfolio when the door knocker went.

It was Nikita, who'd brought the last set of curtains up – Stacey had gone over them with her industrial steam iron until they were pristine.

'Terrible, isn't it?'

'What's terrible?'

'Haven't you heard?'

Charlotte shook her head. 'I haven't heard anything.'

'Hayley Poltimore.' Nikita announced the name importantly.

'What about her?'

'Dead! Crashed her lover's car last night. They reckon she was half cut.'

'No!'

Nikita nodded, obviously relishing being the bearer of bad tidings.

Charlotte felt sick. What a grisly, terrible thing to happen. She thought about Jade and Amber.

'Those poor girls,' she said, stricken.

Nikita made a face and shrugged. 'She wasn't much of a mother, was she?'

'You can't say that!' Charlotte was horrified. 'She was still their mum.'

'They'll probably be better off without her.'

'Nikita!'

'Everybody's saying it. Everybody knows he's the one who does everything in that house.'

Fitch. Poor, lovely Fitch. What on earth must he be going through? Charlotte knew his biggest worry would be Jade and Amber. What a terrible thing, to have to support your children through the death of their mother, no matter how self-absorbed she might have been.

She didn't hesitate. She didn't even stop to get her coat.

'Just take the curtains up to the bedroom. I'll be back as soon as I can.'

She flew out of the door and down the high street. She didn't stop until she reached the Old Bakery, where she banged on the door.

Fitch answered. He looked ashen. He hadn't shaved that morning. His hair was tousled, the sleeves of his shirt undone.

'Fitch. I've just heard . . .'

401

Words seemed superfluous. What on earth could she say? Instead, she flung her arms around his neck and pulled him to her. Instinctively his arms went round her, and she held him tight, all the sorrow and sympathy she could muster implicit in her embrace.

'I can't believe it,' she murmured into his neck. 'Are you all right?'

'I'm fine,' he replied. 'Well . . . relatively speaking. It's a nightmare, to be honest.'

'I just wanted to say I'm so sorry. I won't interfere. I'll let you get on . . .'

'No. Come on in. Please.'

Slightly reluctantly, not wanting to intrude, she followed him into the kitchen.

Jade and Amber were sitting at the table.

'Mummy died,' said Jade.

'We're having pancakes,' said Amber.

Charlotte went over and gave each of them a hug. They looked a little bewildered by this demonstration of affection, but didn't object.

'Tea?' asked Fitch.

'Let me,' replied Charlotte.

'It's OK,' Fitch reassured her. 'I'd prefer to have something to do.'

The phone rang. Fitch rolled his eyes.

'It hasn't stopped ringing all morning.'

'Do you want me to get it?'

'No. It'll be me they want.'

He went off into the hall to answer it. Charlotte looked over at Jade and Amber. She picked up the whisk in the bowl of pancake mix and gave it a stir.

'Right,' she said brightly. 'Who wants to give me a hand?'

A few minutes later, Fitch came back into the room.

'It was the undertaker,' he said quietly. 'They're going to fetch . . .'

He couldn't say the words. Charlotte just nodded her understanding. The body would be brought back home today.

She watched as a knob of butter melted in the saucepan, then poured in a dollop of batter.

'Not too much,' said Jade. 'We like them thin.'

Charlotte looked up and caught Fitch's eye. She realised he was looking at her oddly.

'Were you planning on getting dressed today?' he asked.

She looked down and realised she was still in her spotty pink pyjama bottoms and a white granddad shirt. And wellies.

'Um . . .' she said with a rueful smile. 'You never know, it might catch on.'

Charlotte offered to stay with the girls while Fitch went up to the farm to see Hayley's parents.

'I don't want to take the girls with me,' he explained. 'They're pretty cut up. It's going to be harrowing.'

'Listen,' said Charlotte, 'I've got nothing important going on. Consider me at your disposal. Whatever you want me to do, just ask.'

'Thanks.' Fitch rubbed his stubbly face. 'I'm just so knackered. I hardly slept.'

'I'm not surprised.'

'There's so much to do. So much to think about . . .'

He was already being asked questions that he didn't have a clue about. And he had a strong suspicion that the rest of the Poltimore clan weren't going to be much help. It was with a heavy heart that he went up to the farm.

It was lucky that he managed to hold it together, because the Poltimores fell apart before his very eyes. They simply had no idea how to deal with Hayley's death on either a practical or an emotional level. Her mother was distraught, verging on hysterical. Penny's medication had clearly worn off. Her father just retreated even further into himself. It became impossible to get a word out of him. The brothers were angry, and fought and swore among themselves. Fitch felt like the only adult in the middle of a nightmare situation.

In the end, he had to be firm.

'Come on,' he urged. 'We've got to get through this. We've got important decisions to make.'

But they seemed incapable of making any decision whatsoever, arguing and disagreeing among themselves over the most trivial matter. Fitch tried to keep calm. He supposed it was grief making them behave like this, but it didn't make things any easier.

Eventually, he decided to leave them to it and sort things out for himself. He made his way back home. It was such a relief to see Charlotte. She was so calm and non-judgemental. A voice of reason among the chaos.

'How are the girls?' he asked anxiously.

'They've been fine,' she reassured him. 'Jade's been a bit weepy, but then they just go off and play.'

'I'm really grateful to you,' he told her.

'Hey,' she said lightly. 'That's what friends are for.'

On her way home, Charlotte decided to pop into Withybrook Hall to see Sebastian. She couldn't face going back to an empty house. It had been a difficult day. Not that the girls had been any trouble, but she had felt so protective of them, had shadowed them round the house anxiously to make sure they were all right. As for Fitch. Poor Fitch. She felt drained.

Sebastian greeted her at the door, wide-eyed. He'd heard the news in the post office that afternoon.

'I can't believe it,' he said. 'It's so awful. She seemed so great at their party. She was the life and soul. I really thought they'd sorted it.'

He led her into the kitchen and poured her a brandy. She drank it down in one gratefully.

'I don't think Fitch knows where he is,' Charlotte told him. 'One minute his wife's there. Then she's left him. Then she's dead.'

'You just never know, do you?' Sebastian agreed. 'What's round the corner. God, what a cliché . . .' He laughed at himself.

Charlotte looked down into her glass.

There was something she wanted to ask him, but she couldn't quite bring herself to say it.

Was she wrong, to be helping Fitch the way she was? Because she couldn't deny that she had feelings for him. Was she taking advantage of the situation? Or was she doing what any friend would do in the circumstances?

Of course she was, she told herself finally. She would do exactly the same for Sebastian if it happened to him.

When Charlotte had gone, Sebastian phoned Catkin to tell her the news. He remembered Hayley and Catkin at the party dancing together, beautiful the two of them, hands high in the air, partying like girls should.

'Oh my God!' Catkin's voice was high with shock.

'Catkin . . .' said Sebastian. 'It's made me think. It's kind of put it all into perspective. Let's have a baby.'

There was silence at the end of the phone.

'It's what this house needs,' he went on. 'It's what we need. Let's forget all this career nonsense. We need a family.'

Catkin laughed for a second, then stopped.

'But I'm about to film a pilot. I'll be filming a series . . .'

'So what?' he said dismissively. 'You can still do it with a bun in the oven. And you can bring out your own range of maternity clothes. Think outside the box, Catkin . . .'

Fitch fell into bed that night, exhausted.

He tried not to think about the image of Hayley lying in the undertaker's in Comberton. The body had been brought down from Watford that afternoon. He couldn't imagine it. And he wasn't sure if he wanted to see it.

He was desperately trying to come to terms with his feelings. Mostly, he felt numb, because his emotions about his wife were so confused. He wanted to grieve, but he wasn't sure at what level to pitch his grief. Had he still loved her when she died? He couldn't answer that question. He'd certainly loved the girl he married, but there had become a point where she had become someone else, and he had to admit that he wasn't so enamoured of the new Hayley. But he had never lost hope of getting the old one back, of rekindling the passion they had once shared. He felt dazed by the whole thing, operating on automatic pilot, becoming very calm and businesslike and organised. It was his default mechanism. No doubt the shock would hit him before long.

Sleep evaded him. Five times he got up in the night to check on Jade and Amber, but they were sleeping peacefully. He prayed that they would come out of this unscathed. Their short little lives had already seen such disruption and upset. Maybe when all this was over he could restore a sense of calm, give them a routine and some stability. He could give them all of that. He knew he could. He could manage on his own . . .

Twenty-One

By Wednesday, the girls were begging to go to school. Fitch reeled at the idea at first. But when he thought about it, maybe it wasn't such a bad idea. What was the point of them staying at home with him, when he had so much to arrange, so many calls, so many decisions to make? School might provide the normality and security they needed. So he picked up the phone to the headmistress, who was always at her desk an hour before school began.

'I think it's probably best to keep their routine as familiar as possible,' she told him. 'The staff have all been appraised of the situation, and we've prepared the rest of the children for Jade and Amber's arrival. Children are surprisingly resilient, you know,' she added kindly.

So he dropped them off, and the headmistress assured him that she would ring him if they showed any signs of distress. Walking back through the playground, he was stopped by an endless stream of other parents, all offering their condolences, as well as offering to have Jade and Amber if he wanted.

As he walked back home, Norman shot out of the Speckled Trout. He grabbed him by the hand.

'Mate, I am so sorry.'

'Thanks.'

'And listen – if you want the Trout for the do after, just say the word. I'll lay it all on for you. You won't have to worry about a thing.'

Fitch considered his offer. The Trout probably was the most appropriate venue. The pub had been such an integral part of Hayley's life, and it meant that those who wanted to stay on and get plastered after the formalities were over could do so. The alternatives were the Poltimore farm or his own house, neither of which struck Fitch as suitable. The Poltimores simply weren't capable of pulling it together, and he didn't want his home tainted with the memory of such a traumatic event. He wanted the cottage to remain a haven for the girls.

'Thanks, Norman,' he said. 'That would be great.'

'Just leave it all to me: the catering, the booze. And don't worry about the bill. We can sort that out when the time's right,' Norman told him, and Fitch was touched.

All in all, the whole village had been incredibly supportive. There was a sort of reverent hush wherever you went, out of respect for his bereavement, but people certainly weren't afraid to come and give their condolences. Time and again they offered their help. Casseroles had turned up on the doorstep, and tins of homemade biscuits. Letters and cards poured through the letterbox. Darren and Bradley had turned up, subdued, and offered to take him to the pub, the only cure they knew for sorrow.

And Charlotte. Charlotte had been a pillar of strength. She'd taken over, really – sorting out the washing and ironing, the cleaning. Going through his correspondence and putting it into neat piles. Keeping the girls entertained while he was yet again on the phone.

'Tell me to fuck off if you think I'm interfering,' she'd said.

'You're not interfering,' he assured her. 'I don't know what I'd do without you.'

She'd even taken some of the surplus food they'd been given up to Hayley's parents, and spent an hour talking to her mother. Which was more than Fitch could face. He found his in-laws a strain. They were making a distressing experience even more harrowing.

The only thing he was grateful for was that Kirk hadn't decided to put his oar in. He had had the good sense not to make himself known in any way. Fitch prayed he wouldn't want to come to the funeral. It seemed entirely inappropriate, even though no doubt he had had feelings for Hayley. Even though he had been the bad guy in all of this, it can't have been easy for him, especially when he'd been involved in the accident.

Charlotte told him sharply not to lose any sleep over Kirk's feelings.

'If it wasn't for him, none of it would have happened,' she pointed out, but Fitch didn't necessarily subscribe to that point of view. How the hell could you apportion blame? Where did you start and where did you stop?

In the end, he decided he would have to take each day at a time, and just get through the funeral. He sat in the kitchen, surrounded by paperwork.

'I can't believe all the decisions I have to make. It's such a bloody responsibility. I mean, how am I supposed to know what hymns Hayley would have wanted? And what coffin do I go for?' Fitch put up his hands in mock despair. 'I mean, it would be funny if it wasn't so . . . not funny. Hayley would have wanted the designer range, lined with red silk. But it does seem a waste. Not that I'm trying to economise,' he added hastily. 'Shit, I'm sorry. You don't want to hear all this. It's morbid.'

'It's OK,' said Charlotte. 'It's fine. It's probably good to get someone else's input.'

He sat down on a bar stool and began to tap a pen against the pad he'd been writing on. Charlotte could see his nerves were jangling, that he was stretched to the limit. 'My biggest worry at the moment is whether the girls should go to the funeral or not. It just seems like such a terrible thing to put them through.'

Charlotte shook her head. 'I don't think you should. It's not the place for children. Everyone will be upset; they won't understand.'

'That's what I think. But the family are putting me under pressure. My mother-in-law wants them there.'

Charlotte put a hand on his shoulder.

'They're your children. You should do what you think is right. But for my money, I think you should wait until after the burial. Then go to the grave, just the three of you. You'll be able to give them your undivided attention and explain it all to them.'

Fitch gave her a wintry but grateful smile.

'You're so right,' he said. 'Of course that's what I should do.' His face screwed up again with worry. 'But what do I do with them? I can't just send them to school while their mother's being buried. It doesn't seem right.'

Charlotte thought about it for a moment.

'I'll look after them,' she offered. 'I'll come here.'

'Would you really do that? Would you really do that for me? Because I can't think of anyone I'd rather be with them.'

'Of course I'd do that for you, Fitch,' said Charlotte. 'Anything.'

There was a small silence. Fitch looked down at the floor, not sure how to express his gratitude. He ran his hand across his stubbly chin.

'Christ,' he said. 'I must look a mess.'

'Well,' said Charlotte, tipping her head to one side as she surveyed him. 'You do quite suit the dishevelled look. But if you want to go and have a shower, I'll make some supper.'

Fitch looked at her.

'Thanks for all your help,' he said softly. 'I couldn't manage without you.'

Charlotte went to open the fridge. She didn't want Fitch to see that her cheeks were a tiny bit pink. 'Omelette?' she asked. 'Or scrambled eggs?'

Twenty-Two

The day of the funeral was appropriately grey, with a fine mizzle that set in after breakfast and showed no sign of letting up. In some ways, Fitch was grateful. It would have been strange laying Hayley to rest in bright sunshine. He spent the morning looking for an umbrella, and came to the conclusion that he didn't own one. It wasn't his sort of thing. A spot of rain had never bothered him in the past. But somehow he didn't feel he could stand at his wife's graveside and let rain pour down on him.

Charlotte had two. A typical banker's umbrella, large and black, and a pink flowery one. It didn't take him long to choose.

Charlotte and Fitch had decided that the best way she should deal with any questions from Jade and Amber during the funeral was to tell them the facts. No airy-fairy nonsense about Mummy just being asleep and being able to watch them from heaven. It wasn't brutal; they just didn't feel that giving them any false sense of hope would do them any good in the long run. Platitudes and sentimental false truths would only confuse them further.

'The important thing for them to know,' said Charlotte, 'is that she loved them and always will.'

'It's just so hard,' said Fitch, as he pulled on the

jacket of his best dark suit. 'It's so unfair. They've been so good.'

It had broken Charlotte's heart to watch the three of them over the past few days, each equally helpless and bewildered. Sometimes crying, sometimes laughing, sometimes just being quiet. She'd tried to keep things normal, to keep a sense of routine so they would understand that life still goes on, that their whole world hadn't fallen apart.

'Will I do?' Fitch stood there in the middle of the kitchen, awkward in his smart clothes. He looked amazingly handsome, his dark hair touching the collar of his jacket, his shoulders broad.

Charlotte swallowed down the lump in her throat.

'You'll do,' she nodded.

He took a deep breath in to steel himself for the afternoon ahead.

'I don't know what time I'll be back,' he said. 'I expect it will go on a bit. And I need to be there for the family.'

'Don't worry. I'll put the girls to bed. I'll be here.'

She rushed across the room to hug him, wishing she could take some of the pain away. She breathed in the smell of him, then felt him kiss the top of her head lightly.

'Thanks,' he whispered, then quickly let her go.

She watched him leave the room. She felt filled with emotions she couldn't quite identify. Then she told herself sternly that she was bound to feel strange. It had been a gruelling time, with everything slightly heightened, slightly surreal. If she felt closer to Fitch, it was because they had been thrown together by the tragedy. Nothing more.

She took a tray of sandwiches into the girls for lunch. They were in the living room, half-heartedly watching television. They barely ate.

Eventually Jade turned to her, eyes wide.

'We're worried that we might forget what Mummy looks like.'

'Well,' said Charlotte carefully. 'You've got lots of photos, surely.'

'Not really,' said Amber. 'There're no really good ones of her. We've looked.'

Charlotte racked her brains, horrified by their plight. They needed some reminder of their mum, something to hold on to, something to comfort them when they were missing her.

'I tell you what,' she said. 'Why don't we do a picture? I'll help you. A nice big picture that you can put up in your bedroom and look at whenever you want.'

Their faces lit up.

'Go and get your paints,' Charlotte told them. 'I'll get some paper.'

They scampered out of the room to do her bidding. Charlotte sighed, hoping that she was doing the right thing. Of course she was, she told herself. The wrong thing had already happened. Hayley was dead. Anything, anything at all she could do to help from now on was going to be the right thing.

The funeral service went as well as could be expected. The entire village seemed to be there, as well as most of the hunt and the shoot, shuffling in wearing rain-spattered wax jackets. The air smelled of wet wool and damp dog.

Catkin stood out in purple velvet, a touch of glamour amidst the drabness. She refused to wear black to funerals. She did a wonderful reading, the congregation rapt as she recited the words to 'Every Breath You Take', one of Hayley's favourite songs. It had been Charlotte's idea, and Fitch knew that Hayley would have got a kick out of a celebrity at her funeral. She went in for that kind of thing.

The burial, by contrast, was horrendous. The wind whipped cruelly through the graveyard. The rain had fallen harder than ever, making the grave slippery and waterlogged. As the first soggy clods of earth had hit the coffin, Barbara had given a keening wail and collapsed onto her eldest son. The noise had continued throughout the vicar's carefully chosen words. No one could wait to escape to the warmth and comfort of the pub. The rush to leave the graveside was almost indecent.

Fitch lagged behind, wanting to thank the vicar and the undertakers for making sure everything ran smoothly. He was in no rush to get to the Trout and be faced with more commiserations. Not that he wasn't grateful for people's kind thoughts, but he was tired of it all. It was time to move on. He was clinging on to the thought of tomorrow, when he could get back to normal.

As he left the churchyard, a man fell into step beside him. He looked up, brow furrowed.

Kirk.

'What the hell are you doing here?' Fitch growled.

'Listen, mate,' Kirk said urgently. 'I know I'm the last person you want to see. And I'm not going to make any trouble. There's just something I think you should know.'

Fitch tensed his fists. What was the bastard going to come out with? Some fucking plot twist worthy of a Martina Cole novel? Was he after money?

'She was coming back to you.'

Fitch wasn't sure he had heard correctly.

'What?'

Kirk sighed, and passed a hand over his face. He looked terrible. Gaunt and red-eyed, not the smug picture of rude health that Fitch remembered.

'We'd been out to dinner. She told me it was all over. That she wanted to make a go of it with you.' There was a slight crack in his voice, and Fitch realised that he was struggling to hold it together. 'She did love you, you know. And the girls. Me and her, it was just one of them things. Chemistry, you know. It was never going to last . . .' He trailed off, clearly choked. 'I'm sorry if . . .'

He turned away, and Fitch watched him put the crook of his elbow to his eyes, to staunch the tears.

'You're all right.' Fitch put a hand on his arm.

'I wasn't going to come,' Kirk spoke in a rush, suddenly defiant. 'But she'd have wanted you to know.'

'Thank you,' said Fitch. 'I appreciate it.'

And he did. It must have taken a lot for Kirk to drive down here and approach him. He needn't have told him anything, could have kept Hayley's secret to himself for ever more.

'I know I wasn't always as good to her as I could have been,' Kirk was saying. 'And I'm sorry for that. Really sorry . . .'

Tears were streaming down his face now,

unstaunched, and his shoulders began to heave. Fitch watched in disbelief as this huge brute of a man sobbed, understandably reluctant to console him but moved nevertheless.

'I better go,' choked Kirk eventually through his tears.

Fitch held out his hand.

'Cheers, mate,' he said, that anodyne blokey phrase that said everything and nothing.

And the two of them shook hands, Hayley's husband and her lover, united in their grief and their disbelief as the rain fell relentlessly on.

In the Trout, Norman had done them all proud, serving big mugs of cream-topped hot chocolate fortified with brandy. Plentiful trays of food were passed around all afternoon and into the evening as the residents of Withybrook came together to remember one of their own, telling tales that grew increasingly bawdy as the drink flowed. Fitch had stood on the sidelines, not sure of his role, especially in the light of Kirk's revelation.

The news had stunned him. His mind was whirling. Hayley had been coming back to him. How did that make him feel? He didn't know. All he did know was it made her death even more futile, more tragic. And the knowledge didn't stop him asking himself what he could have done differently. He would never stop asking himself that.

At nine o'clock the band struck up, and the music and dancing began. Fitch had to admit that it was a fitting tribute to his wife. She would have been there in the middle of it all, the party girl, flitting from man to man. For a moment he imagined her amidst the mêlée, her flashing eyes, her smile. That come-hither look she gave everyone she came into contact with, the look that promised so much.

And in that moment, he knew. Even if she had come back, he would never have been able to trust her. Not really. He would always be afraid that she would be seeking the next thrill, because she thrived on drama and controversy. And he wondered if her telling Kirk she was coming back was just another one of her games, a ploy for more attention. He knew it was awful, thinking about her like that when she wasn't here to defend herself, but he doubted he would have believed her if she was.

At ten, Fitch swallowed down a final brandy and slipped away. His in-laws would be fine. They had their extended family around them. They didn't need him for support.

Inside, the house was quiet. He looked into the kitchen. On the work surface, he saw a large painting. He took a sharp breath in. It was a picture of Hayley, remarkable in its likeness. She was smiling, wearing her jeans and a blue flowery shirt that she was always fond of. Charlotte must have drawn it, he realised, with some input from the girls. One of them had written 'Mummy' in spidery black writing underneath. He touched the surface in wonder. The paint was still wet. He drew his hand away, not wanting to spoil it.

He looked in the living room, but it was empty, then crept up the stairs. The girls' bedroom was empty too. He felt slightly anxious. Perhaps they had gone back to Charlotte's house?

He found the three of them in his bed, Jade and

Amber under the duvet, Charlotte on top between them, fast asleep with a copy of *Dr Seuss* in her hand. They must have asked to sleep in there; they had taken to sharing his bed since Hayley's death and how could he refuse them?

He reached out and touched Charlotte gently on the leg to wake her. She woke immediately, then smiled when she saw him. She scooted to the bottom of the bed, careful not to wake the girls. He put a finger to his lips, indicating that she should follow him downstairs.

He took off his jacket in the living room, throwing it onto the back of the sofa, then sitting down with a sigh, stretching himself out.

'How did it go?' Charlotte asked.

'OK,' he said. 'OK . . .' He put his head back and shut his eyes, suddenly exhausted. He had got through the day on adrenalin, he realised.

'I'll make some tea.'

He nodded, managing a smile. 'Tea would be great. How were the girls?'

'They were . . . amazing. We did a picture – for them to remember.'

'I saw. It's fantastic. Thank you . . .'

He didn't know how to express his appreciation. He'd tell her tomorrow. How he'd never have been able to get through it without her . . .

When Charlotte came back with the tea, Fitch was fast asleep. She gazed at him, his dark lashes resting on his cheeks, all the stress and worry gone. She swallowed. She was supposed to be leaving Withybrook at the end of the week. She'd booked a fortnight in Portugal, hoping for some sun and relaxation while she decided what to do next with her life. But how could she leave this little family, just when they needed her? She wasn't flattering herself. At least, she didn't think so. They needed someone around to take their minds off things, to do the mundane things that they couldn't put their mind to, provide a distraction . . .

She decided she'd call Sebastian in the morning. See if his offer still stood. She could stay on for another couple of months while the house was on the market. Even if it sold tomorrow, it would be a while before contracts were exchanged. Yes, she decided. That was the right thing to do. It would give her something to get her teeth into, and she could keep an eye on Fitch. Just while he got himself back on his feet.

She sat on the sofa next to him. She couldn't begin to imagine what he must have been through over the past few days. She picked up his hand, and kissed the back of his fingers gently, one by one. He opened his eyes. She stopped, feeling incredibly foolish. He gave her a small, sleepy smile. She held his gaze, then bent her head to kiss the last finger. His smile widened, and he gave her hand the tiniest squeeze in return. Then his eyes closed, as if his lashes were unbearably heavy, and he fell back to sleep.

She sat, holding his hand, happy just to watch him until he woke again.